MW00718864

For: Barry

Just having fun!

HAUNTED SECRETS

SANDRA LaBRUCE

Sandra LaBruce

March 25, 2012

RSE Publishing
Laurens, South Carolina

© 2009 Sandra LaBruce. All rights reserved.

Edited by Amanda Capps

ISBN: 9780983710332

Printed in the United States of America

This book is printed on acid-free paper.

PUBLISHER'S NOTE

This manuscript is dedicated to my mom:

Thank you for being there through the struggles of my life. You are the most honest, strong-willed woman I know, and I admire you with all my heart. Watching you triumph through extremely difficult hardships taught me perseverance, gave me courage, and instilled a strength and honesty in me, even when you didn't know it.

As a child, we don't always sow the seeds we are given, but as adults, we value even the smallest. I believe as long as the parent takes the time to nurture and guide, those seeds of wisdom and love will sprout sooner or later.

Thank you for that. I love you.

A special thanks to the following for all the help you gave so freely:

Jim - thank you for being my husband, lending me your support, love and understanding
Belinda - thank you for your honesty, wisdom, and long hours
Diane - thank you for your optimism, long hours, and acting skills
Terri - thank you for your feedback and all your help
Linda - thank you for your thoroughness and feedback
Lisa - thank you for your research
Debbie - thank you for being my friend
Debbie - thank you for being my big sister and giving me your opinion
Sara - thank you for being my little sister and giving me support
Susan - thank you for being my sister and making it fun
Michael - thank you for being my brother and helping me relax
Lydia - thank you for trying to understand the way of the South
A special thanks to Herika Raymer

And to all my family and friends, thank you!

This book contains Gullah language.

Gullah is an old language that Africans used to communicate with people from other tribes. The slaves carried it to the Lowcountry region of South Carolina and parts of Georgia during the Colonial Period, where it continues to be spoken and used to this day.

The Gullah people are known for preserving more of their African linguistic and cultural heritage than any other African American community in the United States. The Gullah language uses words and phrases borrowed from their African ancestors. This combination of English, African, and slang languages creates its own unique sound and rhythm in grammar, sentence structure, and spelling; its pronunciation and spelling are as they look and sound. The Gullah language is related to Jamaican Creole, Bahamian Dialect, and the Krio language of Sierra Leone in West Africa.

While most of us associate slavery with 18th and 19th century America, the truth is that the African slave trade started long before America became involved. It is still alive today in certain parts of the African continent.

The African slave trade inside Africa itself was common in Ghana and Nigeria in the 18th century, where the countries' economies depended largely on the selling of hand labor to neighboring estates. Slavery inside Africa was often not for life. Slaves had the option of buying their liberty and were normally paid enough to do so after a certain number of years.

In the rest of the world, the African slave trade became common in Europe first, starting with the Portuguese, who took slaves to Brazil to mine the mountains. The Caribbean soon followed, and then other countries of South and Central America.

The earliest records of the African slave trade in America date back to the beginning of the 17th century, when racial slavery was a punishment for servants who broke the law. In the 18th century, slaves were mostly used in the South to work on plantations and farms. Typically, they worked for rich landowners who could afford the extra expense in order to maximize their profits. By the start of the Civil War in 1860, there were approximately four million slaves of African origin in the U.S.

The African slave trade was abolished around the world at different times. Britain stopped slavery in 1807, although slaves were not officially declared free until 1833, when the Slavery Abolition Act was passed. The rest of Europe followed close behind, with certain African countries forbidding slavery early in the 20th century. The African slave trade remains alive in certain parts of Africa. Nigeria is notable for selling sex slaves to certain European countries and for trafficking children inside African boundaries.

This information obtained from Wise Geek.

CHAPTER 1

T H E   E V I L   T H I N G

1976
Dogwood Plantation
John's Island, South Carolina

The old man crouched out of sight, watching the new residents carry boxes into the Godforsaken plantation house. His snow-white hair was a sharp contrast to his weathered ebony skin, but he was hidden in the dense woods about 15 yards from their chatter and laughter. He rubbed his aching, stooped shoulders with gnarled fingers deformed by arthritis. His physique was frail and withered with age, but his mind was still strong and sharp – filled with wisdom and raw determination. His soul revived both his spirit and body enough to carry out his necessary duties. At eighty years old, pain was a daily part of his life. However, there was no way a little discomfort was going to sway him from his quest. The strength of his mind, coupled with his fear for anyone living in the long-abandoned mansion, provided enough incentive to withstand whatever necessary to see this through to the end.

He had studied each member of the white family as they stepped out of their car: a man, a woman, and two children. They seemed excited as they toted their personal possessions into the house – the house that had instilled dread and horror in him since childhood.

Hidden amongst the branches of the pines, he patiently observed and listened, waiting for the high-pitched screams and thunderous banging on the walls. He waited for the spirits of the house to come alive, but nothing happened. All was quiet. "Today is a peaceful day," he thought. "The spirits are calm." Although he worried about the unsuspecting, naïve white folk, he dared not intrude. Even if they were to welcome him, he would reject their invitation. He knew the haunted secret. He knew all the forbidden secrets that were too dangerous to be unleashed.

He was old, but not stupid. He was the watcher, the protector, the only one left, and because of that, he carried the deep-rooted burden of his ancestors.

As daylight slid silently into night, it was time to leave his post. His fatigued form quietly disappeared into the darkness.

Before sunrise, the old man returned, lingering at the edge of the forest, watching for signs of life from inside the house. He paced back and forth, kicking his feet in the dust. From the windblown tree, he picked pine needles and nervously pulled them back and forth through his fingertips. Exhausted from his walk, he hunkered down on the damp ground, and leaned against the trunk of a tree, waiting. Waiting for what, he did not know; maybe nothing, but then again, maybe everything.

Hours had passed; the sun rose high in the sky. The house looked almost tranquil in the silence and the darkness. Distressed by the silence, the man allowed anxiety to pry its way into his mind. Once that happened, his grim thoughts quickly escalated to disaster.

"Where's ev'rybody? Why ain't da lights be on, or da curtains be open? Why ain't dere no movement? Maybe I shoulda told 'em. Maybe I shoulda warn 'em. If anyting hap'n to 'em, it be my fault. It be all my fault jest like afore. I shoulda went inside and warn 'em. I knew some'em bad would hap'n, I jest knew it. I knew it and I ain't say nottin.' God, forgive me for keepin' my mouf shut, and please let'em be ahright, please. I gotta get a closer look. I gotta make sure deys be ahright."

He held on to the trunk of the pine tree and pulled his trembling body upward. Peering through the thick woods, he took a step towards the dilapidated house. Leaving the security and shelter of the woods, he crept along the oak-lined driveway scurrying from tree to tree, taking care to stay out of sight.

He cautiously hobbled up to the house. Sneaking to the back, he nervously looked over both shoulders. He hesitantly reached out and touched the splintered boards; peeling white paint crumbled beneath his crooked fingers.

"If only I could change what hap'n," he muttered in a faint, despondent voice.

A loud, mournful wail penetrated the walls; he could feel the walls of the house vibrating. He jerked his hand away and lurched backwards.

"Da house 'members me!" he cried, eyes wide with terror.

Unable to move, he took a deep breath, exhaled slowly, and scolded himself, "Jesse, calm down, ya ole fool. Dat jest be crazy tinkin,' jest crazy. Da house don't 'member ya. It jest be da wind howlin' down da chimney, dat's all. It jest be da wind. Stop actin' like a child!"

Collecting his courage, he stretched upward on his tiptoes and reached for the ominous, dark windowpanes. The glass released an unnatural, icy breeze, which created a burning sensation in his eyes.

"Aaah!" he screamed.

He reeled backwards, momentarily blinded by the pain. Hoping to regain his sight, he vigorously rubbed his stinging eyes. After a few seconds, his vision returned. With determination, he gritted his teeth and returned to his former position. Cupping his shaking hands around his eyes, he shielded them from the glare and peered inside.

Stacks of cardboard boxes littered the room and blocked his view. He moved to the left, squinting, pressing his forehead into the frigid glass and straining to see. He saw nothing at first, but then something caught his eye. There in that sunless corner, something stirred, some evil thing, a profound, immoral thing from his boyhood.

"No, no . . . it jest be my 'magination," he whispered trying to muster the courage necessary to continue. "Nothin's dere, I only saw boxes, jest boxes, dat be it, jest boxes."

He had not ventured into the plantation house since that terrible morning so many years ago. Painful memories of the tragedy and his involvement in it tortured him day after day, decade after decade; he had experienced relentless suffering for a span of over seventy years. No matter how hard he tried to forget, his lifeless leg was a constant reminder. "No, I ain't 'maginin' it! I know I ain't! And dere ain't no foolin' myself 'bout it. Dat ting's still in dere. It always been dere; restless, hateful, and lookin' for some'em, lookin' fo' me. No, not me, I dunno what it be lookin' fo', but, I know what it need . . . peace, it be needin' peace. Dats what it be needin.' God knows dat be what I need too. Maybe dis be my chance, maybe my last chance. I ain't goin' ta my grave wid dis. And dose little kids dat jest moved in, dey be next. It be takin' dem next. I ain't lettin' dat hap'n agin, not dis time. Dis time I be goin' in. I be goin' in to fight."

Carefully dragging his left leg, he made his way up the steps to the back door. He stood motionless, staring at the aged brass knob, contemplating what might lie in wait for him. Forcing himself to move, he raised his hand toward the door, and just as his jittery fingers brushed the doorknob, it turned by itself. The rusty hinges creaked as the door slightly opened. The old man stepped back.

He reached for the door a second time; it swung open, slamming against the inside wall, then swinging back, stopping half open. Feeble and weak, he stumbled backwards; then with a rigid spine and unblinking eyes, he leaned in, and scanned the dark entrance. The huge oak door abruptly swung open wider. He was petrified and wanted to run, but he was tired of running from this thing. It had plagued him since he was a child, and he had to continue this quest.

Bracing himself on the door casing, he bent forward and craned his neck to get a better look. From the corner of his eye, he saw a shadow looming above his left shoulder. Jesse turned around; an icy gray cloud blanketed his head. Panic set in as he realized he was being suffocated. He began wildly pulling at his translucent attacker as he gasped for air; a coarse, inhuman voice whispered, "Jes–seee, Jes–seee." The phantom quickly released him, rose to the ceiling, and hovered menacingly while preparing for a second attack. As the evil entity began its descent, terror gripped Jesse's entire body.

Bitter-tasting bile rose in his throat as his stomach violently contracted. His heart pounded erratically in his chest. Legs, strangely weak and wobbly, threatened to give way. Fear clawed at the fringes of his brain like some ferocious wild animal determined to tear its way in. The urge to flee welled up inside him. Uncontrolled, spasmodic breathing took over. Then, with a tremendous burst of energy, Jesse turned and hobbled down the steps. He knew his escape would only be short-lived, but even that was cut short when he caught his lame foot at the bottom and tumbled face-first to the ground. Frantically, he grabbed at the grass, trying to scramble to his knees. His unsuccessful attempts resulted in pains shooting down his spine. He heard the entity behind him, still in the house, banging on the walls.

"It be watchin' me. I feels it," he whispered. "It tinks it won agin, but it ain't gonna win dis time."

Struggling to his feet he wheeled around, and faced the house.

"I ain't leavin.' Not dis time. Ya hear me! I ain't leavin'!" he shouted.

The banging ceased, and the house grew eerily silent. Confused, Jesse stood, shook his head, and heaved a sigh of relief. He clasped his hands and looked to the heavens.

"Lawd, I needs ya ta help me. Help me beat dis evil ting. My legs be weak, make me strong. I needs ya help, please help me, Lawd. Tank ya, Jesus."

Again, he willed himself to ascend the weathered treads of the stairs to the open back door. Pausing for a moment, leaning forward, he cautiously surveyed the entryway once more looking to the left and then to the right. He did not see the vile thing, but he knew it lingered nearby. Reluctantly and against his better judgment, Jesse slipped inside.

Pressing his back against the wall, the elderly man cringed as he scanned the room looking for the ghastly phantom. The thought of another encounter with that thing sent shivers down his frail spine. Jesse listened intently for any warning of the unearthly being, but heard nothing. He inched his way toward a long, black hallway, his hands flat against the wall as he moved further away from the filtered sunlight that shone through the dirty windows. The darkness followed closely and crept slowly behind him. Feeling his way down the black corridor, he was terrified of what might lie ahead; his mind constantly replayed the brutal attack. He felt his courage gradually diminishing. Should he retreat or forge ahead? Did he really need to confront his enemy?

Perspiration dripped from his brow, his hands felt cold and clammy, and his chest tightened just enough to restrict his breathing. He grew light-headed and slumped against the wall for assistance.

"Help me, Jesus," he whispered.

He stood erect, took a deep breath, and tried to move forward. His breath was rapid, but shallow. He focused on what he could not see; he shuddered in anguish, thinking of the bleak fate ahead of him.

"Jes…seee, Jes…seee," a ghostly voice hissed. He staggered and fought pugnaciously while the thing folded itself around his head.

"Nooooo! Get off me! Oh Lawd, get dis ting off me!" he begged.

Jesse fought the invisible foe; with arms flailing wildly, he tripped and fell to the floor. Instinctively he rolled onto his back to defend himself. Clawing at his face, his fingers became entangled in a sticky substance. It was stuck over his eye, restricting his vision. He frantically pulled it away, but the sticky substance clung to his hands. In a crazed state, he pulled at his fingers and realized it was not the phantom. It was no more than a huge mass of spider webs.

Gales of laughter roared throughout the mansion. The old man froze with fear. His body shook. The laughter grew louder, ricocheting off the walls like a bouncing ball.

Still in darkness, he felt the eight-legged insects skitter down his arms. Panic set in; he slapped at the unseen creatures. The spiders scurried away to safety. Jesse pushed himself to his feet.

"I gotta get outa here! I–I–I jest can't do dis!" he exclaimed.

He stumbled back down the hall wobbling on his feet. The dim sunlight flickered in the distance leading him toward safety.

"Jest a few mo' feet and I be outa here," he said. "Jest a few mo' feet."

A dark shadow appeared in the doorway. Jesse stopped abruptly. Hovering in the air, blocking his path, the monstrous phantom was floating toward him. It let out a high-pitched screech. Jesse turned and retreated toward the open door at the other end of the dark hallway. It slammed shut, capturing him, preventing any escape. The shrill screech followed closely behind him. He ripped at the knob and rammed his shoulder into the heavy wood. He pounded frantically with both fists. Everything grew eerily quiet; Jesse was immobile.

Suddenly, he heard a sharp noise on the other side of the door. He leaned forward and pressed his ear to the cypress structure; it was quiet.

Then the door creaked and slowly began to open on its own. It was waiting for him; he could feel it. He peered around the door expecting to see the monster, but the room was empty. Cautiously stepping into the enormous foyer, a black mist sailed in front of his face almost hitting him. Jesse quickly jerked away and dodged the assailant.

An eerie chuckle reverberated throughout the house. The room began to shake sadistically. Jesse grabbed the stair railing to steady himself. Again, the wicked sounds echoed through the air; the laughter was somewhat hollow, but it was recognizable just the same.

Was all of this his imagination? He could not think clearly enough to discern whether the shadows and screams were real or not. They seemed to be real, but he wondered if that were possible. Fear followed the path of the blood trickling through his veins. Terror crawled down his nerve endings to the tips of his fingers. His hands throbbed as he stood clenching them too tightly.

The old man followed the familiar mirth into an adjoining room, hoping to confront his fears. He wanted nothing more than to put the thing to rest once and for all. The laughter faded away into the darkness, only to be replaced by a shallow, raspy breathing that deliberately crawled up the back of his neck. Jesse staggered around to protect himself and saw the phantom dart away again. He could hear strange, heavy breathing coming from the opposite side of the room. His tenacious plan was to confront the entity; Jesse persisted and followed the horrible sounds. Passing from room to room, the ghostlike shadow always eluded him.

The old man surveyed his surroundings every inch of the way. Moving faster and faster, the phantom lured Jesse around and around in circles. Adrenaline pushed his mind beyond its limits: every step was punishing. His old body struggled to keep up. Exerting himself, he clutched his chest, as excruciating pain shot down his left arm. There was a vague hope that he would survive, but he could go no further.

The thing taunted him into draining the last of his energy. He had to stop before his heart gave out. Jesse did not want to die here. He was afraid his soul might get trapped with the evil entity forever. Knowing that he was vulnerable, he had to stop to regain his strength.

The old man forced one foot in front of the other and eventually found himself in the foyer once more. He sat down on the bottom step of the staircase to compose himself. Head cupped in his hands, he moaned softly, rocking back and forth while massaging his left arm. A tear seeped from the corner of his eye and slid down his dry, wrinkled cheek.

Slowly raising his head, Jesse whispered, "Ya ain't gonna win." Then he shouted, "Ya ain't gonna beat me. Ya be a coward. Ya hear me?" Regaining his strength, he shouted one more time, "I say youes a coward!"

A thundering noise shook the house. The panes of the windows rattled feverishly, and the shutters slapped wildly.

"I ain't be 'fraid of you," he shouted. "Sho' yo'sef!"

The apparition flew past him. Startled, the old man jumped to his feet but lost his balance and fell to the floor. He watched as the apparition began to take form. He stared in disbelief, eyes wide and bulging from the sockets.

"Oh, Lawdy," he cried.

The sounds of footsteps pounded on the steps in front of him. He waited for a monster to appear, but a small foot started to take shape instead. Then a leg began to materialize, followed by the rest of a little boy's body. Slowly the child floated up the staircase. The figure stopped on the fourth step, turning menacingly toward Jesse. The old man's crippled fingers dug into the hardwood floor as he pushed himself away. He threw his hand into the air, bowed his head, and closed his eyes.

"Youes be dead! I knows youes be dead! I sees ya die! Youes can't be real!" he yelled to affirm himself.

Hoping it was just a hallucination, he cracked one eye open to get a glimpse. "Oh no!" he shouted. "Ya still be dere! Go 'way! Pleeease go 'way!"

The ghostly child skipped up a step, stopped, smirked at Jesse, and continued up the stairs.

"Please don't go up dere; please don't go," he begged. "Ya knows what hap'ns up dere."

He held his shaking hand up, wanting the boy to stop, but the small spirit continued to climb the stairs. The man watched his childhood horror become reality again. A disaster destroyed a family, and it had left a little boy bitter and guilt-ridden. A story buried deep in the past brought haunted secrets into the present.

The front door banged open.

"Watch your little brother, Jesse!" a voice called from the yard. The old man forgot all about his pain and quickly jerked his body around to peer out the door. The familiar voice he knew too well was that of his dead mother.

"Momma!" he cried. She did not acknowledge his cry, nor did she see the wave of his hand. "Momma! It's me, Jesse," he cried again.

"Why ya do dis ta me!" Jesse screamed as he looked up the staircase where the little boy once stood; the ghostly figure had quietly disappeared.

Rage filled his face, and his body heated up like a boiling inferno. He sat with his fists balled tightly, blood pressure rising, heart pounding, as his body trembled with fury. Then laughter vibrated from the yard. He scooted his body closer to the door to see, not really wanting to, but unable to resist. He saw himself as a young child again, running across the yard.

"We'z gotta clean up dis here yard, boys," their mother said.

"Yes, ma'am," Jesse answered.

The two young boys played under the droopy willow tree next to the big house. They watched their mother and other family members work their way around to the backyard.

"Don't y'all go near dat house. Ya know dose spirits don't rest dere! Ya knows dat y'all ain't allowed in dere, ya ain't never been in dere afore, and ya ain't goin' in dere now!" his mother called out to them, but the boys' curiosity got the best of them.

For years, they had listened to stories about the restless spirits that wandered the halls of Dogwood Plantation. They did not really believe the rumors, but they had always wanted to check it out for themselves. Moses being the youngest and most mischievous just had to take a peek into the window, but he was too short to see. He ran up the huge front steps, took a quick look around to make sure no one was watching, and continued. The massive door was slightly ajar and enticed the youngster to enter.

"No, Moses!" the older Jesse said sternly, grabbing hold of his younger brother's shirt. Moses jerked loose and ran inside. The old man, still crouched on the floor, leaned aside as the little spirit hurried passed.

"Moses, Momma's gonna tan yo' hide," brother Jesse whispered from the front porch.

"C'mon, Jesse, she won't be knowin'," Moses whispered back.

Jesse had always wanted to see the inside of that old mansion, so he followed his determined little brother. He glanced back, making sure he was unnoticed. Quietly, the boys tippytoed through each room, opening and closing doors, in search of the unknown. The small intruders stared into the darkness of the unlit rooms. Nothing moved; nothing stirred. There was no screaming, howling, or beating on the walls - just the sound of the two curious brothers' tiny footsteps.

"Dere's nuttin' wrong in dis house, is it Jesse?" Moses asked.

"I dunno, Moses, Momma says it is. We needs ta go afore we gets caught in heah," Jesse replied.

"No! I'm goin' up da stairs." Moses ran up the massive staircase.

Jesse called out to Moses in a low voice, not wanting his mother to hear. Moses did not stop; Jesse chased his brother up the stairs.

The old man cried out, "Please don't," and his eyes filled with tears as his memory re-enacted the nightmarish incident.

"Are ya scared of haints, Jesse?" Moses taunted.

"No, ain't scared of no haint, but Momma is gonna whoop us," Jesse replied. Moses laughed, then ran into a room and disappeared.

Jesse called out, "Moses, dis ain't funny!" Moses did not answer.

Jesse realized that Moses was playing hide-and-seek. He wanted Jesse to find him, but big brother Jesse had a better idea. He snuck into another room to lure Moses out.

"Moses! Moses, help me! Pleeease!" Jesse called softly.

Moses peeked out from inside a closet doorway, sticking his head out slightly, but was unable to see Jesse. He shoved his head out a little further, but still could not see his brother. He crept across the room and looked toward the hallway. The corridor was empty. Jesse's plan worked; it had lured Moses from his hiding spot. In a tiny, unsure voice, Moses called out, "Where's ya at, Jesse?"

"In heah," Jesse chuckled.

Moses tiptoed across the hallway following his brother's voice. "I know youes be in heah," he said.

With a grin from ear to ear, Moses quietly stepped up to the door and jerked it open. He saw nothing; it was as black as coal. He checked a small dressing room, still nothing.

"Jesseeee," he whispered into the dark empty space. "Jesseeee," he said again in a soft voice, while feeling around in the dark. "C'mon Jesse, where's ya at? Jesseee!" he called out louder.

"Boooo!" Jesse shouted in a deep throaty voice while grabbing Moses from behind.

"Aaaaaah!" Moses screamed and darted from the room.

"Moses, stop! Quit runnin', it been me!" Jesse yelled.

Moses could not hear Jesse's voice over his own cries. He thought the spirits of the haunted mansion were trying to get him. He kicked, pushed and bit until he broke free. He bolted from the room and ran as fast as his little legs would carry him. His high-pitched screams echoed throughout the house. Jesse trailed close on his heels, grabbing at his shirt, trying to stop him. His fingers could not get a good grip on the slick fabric. Moses screamed louder with each touch of Jesse's hand; he weaved in and out of each doorway, escaping his brother's grasp.

"Mommaaaa!" Moses yelled, as Jesse's hands slid down his back.

"It gonna get me! Help! Mommaaaa!"

Family members heard the screams and ran toward the house. Jesse reached out one last time. He tripped, his hand hit Moses on the back, causing the smaller boy to stumble toward the staircase. Moses's heart pounded and the adrenaline rushed through his body as he tried to escape. His screams echoed off the walls, ceilings, and floors of the empty rooms. Tears streamed down his face and clouded his vision. He slid around the top baluster. Off balance from his brother's push, he missed the first step.

With a slight turn of his head, he caught a glimpse of Jesse's, outstretched hand. Moses's arms swirled into the air, and his body rocked back and forth. He tried to grab hold of something — anything to stop his fall; there was nothing . . . nothing within his reach.

Jesse lunged forward, trying to snatch Moses from the edge of the staircase, but he missed. Jesse's leg slipped between the handrail and the newel post. His body twisted, and his knee snapped backwards. Jesse screamed in pain and watched in horror as Moses stumbled defenselessly down the stairs, step after step. Blood splattered and sprayed across the white walls, dripping down the wooden rails. Moses's small body twisted bizarrely in the air. Bones cracked and protruded through his flesh. Piercing screams quickly faded into low whimpering sobs as he landed at the bottom with a sickening dull thud. His mangled, limp body slid slowly into a bloody heap at the old man's feet.

The spirit of young Jesse looked down at his lifeless little brother and gave a loud, heart-wrenching wail as it faded into yesterday. The seventy-year-old tragedy replayed as clearly as if it had just occurred. Old man Jesse cried, reaching out to Moses. He wanted to turn back the hands of time - to hold his brother, to heal him, to take him home.

"I wish I be dreamin,' I wish dis be a nightmare dat I wake up from, I jest can't wake up. It jest won't go 'way. Oh Lawd, why ya take my bruddah? It been real, it did hap'n," he cried.

Scared, trembling and confused, he asked, "Why ya run, Moses? Why? Ya shouldn'ta run. I was jest playin' wid ya. I didn't mean ta scare ya so. I was jest havin' fun, I'm so sorry. Can ya please forgive me, my bruddah?"

Moses's eyes opened, and he glared up at Jesse with pure hatred. Inhuman rage filled his face. "Ya pushed me! Ya pushed me down dose steps!" he yelled. "I been feel yo' hand shove me on my back. Ya kilt me. Ya kilt yo own bruddah."

Old Jesse scampered to his feet and started backing up towards the door, trying desperately to explain to Moses. "Noooo! Noooo! It weren't me! I didn't do it! It been an accident!"

"Ain't been no accident!" Moses shouted pulling his contorted body to its feet and swirling it through the air. Blood appeared to squirt from the apparition like lava spewing from a volcano. Jesse threw his shaking arms up, shielding his face. The vengeful apparition howled, "Ya murderer! I gonna haunt ya 'til da day ya die. I gonna get ya, even if I gotta pull ya from yo' grave!"

Horrified, Jesse fumbled for the doorknob behind him. Grasping it firmly, he jerked the door open and quickly hobbled down the steps to freedom, yelling as he descended, "It weren't me, I didn't do it!"

The shrill cries carried throughout the house and out into the fields. The front door slammed shut. Birds scattered from the trees. All Jesse could do was cover his ears with his hands and wish that he too could fly away. Dragging his lame leg, he ran for the security of the woods.

Halfway there, a bright light struck Jesse's eyes, temporarily blinding him; he threw his hand up for protection and squinted. He wondered if the spirit had followed him. Paralyzed by fear, Jesse stood motionless. The light shimmered and then disappeared. He took a few steps and it reappeared. He held his hand up once more and realized a car was coming up the drive; the light was actually nothing more than the sun's reflection off its bumper. The vehicle sped up the dirt drive leaving a trail of dust behind it. It stopped in front of the house as the old man neared the woods.

The homeowner, a tall, well-dressed man, stepped out and called to Jesse. "Can I help you with something, Sir?" Jesse did not reply. "Hey! Who are you and what are you doing here?" the man shouted.

Jesse turned slightly and looked over his shoulder, without missing a stroke, he limped into the brush and disappeared. He was glad to see the homeowners were safe. They stayed all night and nothing had happened to them. Jesse was relieved, but did not understand why the evil thing did not torture them.

Was his brother the only restless spirit in the mansion? What, if anything, could he do? How could he make his brother see that the accident was not his fault? Was this his battle alone? How could he defeat his brother's spirit and lay it to rest? He slowed his pace to a solemn walk, with head down and shoulders slumped. Completely exhausted, Jesse exhaled a deep sigh of relief and headed for home.

The perplexed homeowner was left standing next to his automobile scratching his head, wondering who the elderly man was and what he was doing there.

CHAPTER 2

THE RENOVATIONS

2005
Dogwood Plantation
John's Island, South Carolina

She pulled her old Buick into the driveway and parked. Getting out of the car, she heard her grandson's voice, "Grandma, Grandma!" She turned a little and smiled as Jackson galloped toward her.

"What's in the bag?" he asked, jumping up and down.

"Don't be so impatient," she replied. "There might be something in Grandma's bag for you. Let me see." She smiled as she watched his large blue eyes light up. Six-year-old Jackson adored his grandma; she always tried to bring something special back from town. Whether the gift was large or small, Jackson eagerly accepted and appreciated it.

Reaching into the large plastic bag, she removed a small paper sack filled with candies. The package bulged with hard and soft confections: lollipops, butterscotch, mints, pink and green taffy, and lots of caramel.

"In my day we called it *penny* candy, however, I really can't call it *penny* candy anymore. Now it's more like *dollar* candy!" she thought to herself.

Eyes wide with excitement, Jackson peered into the miniature bag. "Thanks, Grandma," he said. He pulled a red lollipop out and bounded up the stairs to the porch swing.

The silver-haired grandmother smiled, knowing she had made him happy. Then, she noticed something odd. "Jackson?" she said.

"Yes, Grandma," he replied.

"Do you have your shoes on the wrong feet?" she asked.

"Huh? What do you mean, Grandma?"

"Your shoes, they're on the wrong feet," she informed him.

Jackson looked up with a bewildered expression. He shrugged his shoulders and said, "But Grandma, I don't have any other feet."

"Oh my! I guess you're right, child!" she laughed.

She plucked her curved, handmade mahogany cane from the back seat of the car and strolled toward the front of the house. Her swollen, arthritic knees could barely carry her. "How did I get so old and unsteady on my feet, and so quickly too? Oh well, as long as I have a good heart and a sound mind, I'm thankful for that."

Reaching the huge cement steps, she gripped the rail tightly and slowly struggled up. Relieved to reach the top, she opened the screeching screen door and tottered inside.

Jackson yelled from the old white swing, "Grandma, don't slam the screen door! That's what you always tell me!" He giggled loudly. "Daddy says that slamming doors is one of your pet pees!"

"One of my what?" she questioned him.

"One of your pet pees!" he repeated.

She grinned, rolled her eyes and explained, "That's pet *peeves*, not pees!" Laughing, she eased the door shut and asked, "How's that, Jackson? Quiet enough for you?"

"That's pretty good, Grandma!" he shouted, waving his half-eaten lollipop. She made her way through the house with her cane in one hand and her plastic sack in the other.

"Two long weeks since I placed the order, and now, at last, I have it in my hands," she said moseying through the house.

Entering the kitchen, she placed the bag on the counter and smiled. Her eyes reflected a youthful enthusiasm as she withdrew the leather seafoam green writing journal and held it to her chest. Her long, wrinkled fingers stroked the cover. Custom-embossed with beautiful gold lettering, the inscription read, "Dogwood Plantation."

She gently laid her book on the old oak table and seated herself in one of the high-backed chairs, happy to be off her feet. "What a treasure," she thought opening the book to its first page. She removed the acid-free, blue pen from the slot inside the journal. Closing her eyes, her imagination transported her back to another time. Her memories flowed like a raging river, waiting to escape her zealous mind. Opening her eyes, shifting, getting settled in her chair, she began to write.

My name is Vivian Godfree. I am the young age of sixty-seven years. I enjoy my life to its fullest and wish to share my memories with my descendants while I am still of sound mind.

This is my legacy, the greatest and most important gift that I could possibly leave to my family. May my children, grandchildren, and great grandchildren value and preserve this journal. My fervent desire is for our heritage to live forever. I am the keeper of the legacy, and now I pass it to you. I would like to reveal the haunted secrets of the past, put the tortured spirits to rest, and bring peace into our family's' future.

This is the story of my life and the lives of those who preceded me. I feel that it is important to tell the *entire,* uncensored story. In doing so, I can spare nothing or no one. I must expose the agony, terror, and the scandal. You may find the details of betrayal, tragic deaths, the horrors of slavery, and forbidden love shocking to your senses. It is the saga of our Southern roots, and I cannot withhold the startling facts that brought us to where we are today. My mental faculties are still intact, and I write this to the best of my recollection. In my mind's eye, this is what I remember:

It was an extraordinary time, a time when the tortured souls of Dogwood Plantation, desperately wanting to reveal their haunted secrets, rose up and gripped the living. These spirits had been silenced and shackled by unpardonable sins. A skulking, monstrous evil, frantically sought to escape through those who unwittingly entered the shadowy halls of the abandoned plantation.

It all began thirty years ago in 1976, with the inheritance of a deserted mansion on a tiny rural island near Charleston, South Carolina. The move from the bustling city to the quiet, secluded, Lowcountry was a difficult adjustment for my family, but not for me. I was coming home to the island. It was hard to believe that my mother's family owned this plantation and she never once mentioned it to me. I could not understand why they would keep it a secret. Why leave it to me in a will and never reveal its existence or its heritage — *our* heritage?

I had just arrived from Chicago. The drive from downtown Charleston to John's Island required crossing a number of bridges that connected one island to the next. The bridges had not always existed. In the old days, a ferry shuttled people and goods back and forth across the black, murky river. The old ferry served faithfully for many years, and as the population grew, a more efficient, long, wooden bridge took its place. The wooden planks clattered as the old cars rolled across. Years passed, and as it is with all things, time and nature ravaged it, drying and splintering the old timber. The combination of sun and salt water blistered, baked, and warped the old wood, causing irreparable deterioration. Inevitably, even the tiny islands could not escape modern technology; sadly, contractors had destroyed the charming cypress bridge and replaced it with sturdy cement.

Cruising over the last bridge from James Island to John's Island, I lowered the window. A warm, moist breeze blew across the dark waters, carrying the familiar scent of salt air and plough mud. Although the marsh mud smelled vaguely of sulfur, it was not an unpleasant scent to me. It raised delightful memories of outings with my mother and father: visits to the harbor, boat rides down the river, and shopping at the old slave market. My memories included dusty wagon rides over bumpy dirt roads that have since been resurfaced with asphalt. Forever etched in my mind are those long ago days, and I derive great pleasure from recapturing them.

The scenic drive down River Road brought feelings of awe and peace. Great twisted oaks skirted both the north and south sides of the road. Rafts of gray Spanish moss draped gigantic oak limbs and resembled an old man's scruffy beard. Driving deeper into the wooded island, the number of houses dwindled, and the sinuous road narrowed. For many miles, swamps and trees dominated the landscape. Nearing the estate, several small homes housed the only other residents for miles.

Rounding the next bend, the plantation's ornate and rustic iron gates invited me to enter. Turning onto the long, tree-lined driveway, I felt the Southern mansion welcome me; I felt as though it was waiting — just for me. Admiring its beauty from the distance, I knew immediately that I belonged there. A feeling of serenity and contentment washed over me, but my heart pounded with excitement. There was no greater place in the world, and I thought how lucky a person I was to have such a magnificent place.

Seeing this house for the first time astounded me. Learning that the mansion had been built by my great grandfather, Johnny Simmons, more than one hundred years ago, thrilled me. For some strange reason, my mother saw fit to leave it to me in her will. I had no living relatives who could answer any of my questions. Therefore, I was on a lone journey of discovery into the unknown. This house with its many secrets was an intriguing mystery waiting to be unveiled. It was a dream my great grandfather built, a dream I wanted to rebuild in his memory.

I was glad my husband, Jim, could not come with me on my first visit. The house was a mess with boarded windows and paint crumbling at the touch of a finger. Colonies of spiders had taken up residence on the front porch, and believe me, there were many. Jim was terrified of spiders.

Standing on the veranda, I heard an approaching car. I scanned the driveway; I knew it had to be the attorney I was waiting for, the one my mother had hired in years past.

Stepping out of his fancy new Cadillac, he reached into the pocket of his expensive-looking blue suit and retrieved a small yellow envelope. Fumbling with the sticky flap and unable to catch the edge, he gritted his teeth and ripped it into two pieces. A shiny silver key dropped to the ground and lay at his feet. He sucked his teeth and rolled his eyes, making me feel uncomfortable. The look of annoyance clearly depicted he did not want to be there, but I welcomed him to Dogwood Plantation anyway.

He responded, "Did you bring your garlic and Bible?" I knew he was trying to scare me, but it was not going to work. I stood firm and waited patiently. I had traveled too far to let an overpaid attorney discourage me.

He bent over and retrieved the dirt-covered key from the ground. He blew the soil from the key, snarled, and walked toward the front door. He released another gulp of air over dropping the key before inserting it into the lock. He jiggled it back and forth until the lock clicked.

"Finally!" he snorted.

Pushing the large cypress door open, he asked, "Do you know evil spirits roam about this plantation?"

"Really," I answered inquisitively. "Have you seen them?"

"No, but, everyone knows it's true."

"I think I'll take my chances."

He then bowed at the waist, tipped his black-rimmed hat and sarcastically said, "Enter if you dare!"

I did.

From the doorway, he proceeded to fill me in on every detail that he had heard. I really was not listening. The only concern I had was taking the opportunity to explore the house.

"You go ahead. I'll wait outside," he said.

The first visit inside the mansion was not a very pleasant one. The welcoming committee consisted of a horde of huge brown spiders that were gathered silently in the corners of the ceiling. When I entered, they quickly scattered, disappearing into the cracks of the plaster.

Their translucent webs filled every crevice. The white, cottony strings stretched in every direction to block all openings and trespassers. A beautiful display of spiral art held the carcasses of the spiders' unfortunate victims.

Finding a stick about the size of a walking cane, I patted it on the palm of my hand to check for sturdiness; it was a good tool for knocking the webs down. I retrieved a flashlight from my purse and held it in one hand and my stick weapon in the other. Passing through the doorway, I swatted at the thick mass of cobwebs. I was sure the eight-legged, bulgy-eyed creatures were watching me from their safe havens. At any time, I thought they might attack. Visions of the creepy pests leaping on me and crawling down my back made me shiver.

The crude lawyer yelled out, "Hey, are you still alive in there? I really have to go; I have work to do!"

Returning to the front door, I informed him that he could not leave. I was still in the process of making a list of necessary repairs that he would need to take back to the office.

"Hell, if I had known that's what you needed, I wouldn't have wasted my time out here. I have a list in the car that your mother left."

He reached through the car window and pulled a folder from the front seat. Shoving the folder and the house keys in my face, he said, "Everything I have on this Godforsaken place is in here! If you need anything else, don't call me! I was paid to bring you this folder and the keys, which I have done." He turned arrogantly on his heels, climbed into his shiny black car and drove away.

The file contained a letter from my mother that described her plans for the renovation and sale of the house. The attorney had scribbled a note on the bottom, "Renovation not completed."

Because of the mansion's state of deterioration, most people would not have found it impressive, but I could see the hidden beauty. I belonged in this house.

According to the attorney, most of my ancestors were afraid of the violent spirits that allegedly wandered the grounds. My mission was to uncover the haunting secrets and lay the spirits to rest. I would search for them — the grounds, the house, or wherever they might be. The search would begin for my great grandfather's cold, dark, lonely grave.

With the money from my mother's insurance policies, I planned to restore my great grandfather's dream home. Remodeling was going to be a challenge, but I loved challenges. My mother's list seemed to be incomplete, so I began making my own list of much needed repairs. It was very long, and I did not have much time to get it done.

I returned to the hotel and phoned the attorney. I requested his presence at Dogwood Plantation for a meeting the next morning. In my mother's final days, she had paid his firm to assist me in hiring a contractor to renovate, if I so desired; convenient for him or not, I desired the paid-for assistance.

He arrived late, still wearing that sour scowl on his handsome face. His arrogance definitely took away from his attractiveness. "His good looks were surely a waste of God's precious time," I thought as his rude display of impatience continued to offend me.

Sitting on the steps and adding to my list of improvements, I motioned for him to wait a moment. My list consisted of work for exterminators, housekeepers, electricians, and plumbers. The painting could wait until we moved in. I wanted whatever was needed to make this house livable; it was the attorney's job to see that it was done.

I occasionally glanced his way and witnessed his childish, unprofessional behavior. He kicked at the dirt and swore under his breath. I wondered if my mother had ever met this obnoxious, cold-hearted lawyer. Surely if her only contact had been with this particular man, she would not have hired his firm. Obviously, the other attorneys had realized that he was incapable of handling anything important, so they passed the petty and mundane cases on to him.

He was paid to find a contractor and with his distasteful disposition, I was sure it would be a complicated task for him. For a self-important, high-dollar lawyer of his magnitude, getting estimates from contractors would be a menial task, but that is what my mother paid him to do. It would be worth every penny just to see this jackass earn his money.

I handed the list to him. When he read it, I thought his eyes would pop out of his head. His face reddened, his nose flared, and his breath grew short. He looked at it, then at me. Again, he glanced at the paper. Then he glared at me as if he thought I was crazy.

"You're kidding me, right?" he asked, trying to hand the list back to me.

"No, not at all," I replied withdrawing my hand. "From what I understand, my mother paid dearly for your assistance in renovating this house. I'm not familiar with the local contractors. However, you are, and I'm sure you will able to locate one for me."

"Come on lady, take a good look around. There is nothing holding this place together. Why, if a strong gust of wind came along, the entire house would collapse. You can't be serious about spending money on this rotten old place."

"I am dead serious," I replied.

He removed his hat, gave a half-cocked glance at me, bit his lip, and crammed the list into his suit trousers. Jerking his car door open, he plopped down and slid his rump across the leather seat, which made a loud squeaking sound. His hands gripped the steering wheel tightly; his knuckles rolled back and forth with frustration. Angrily, he started the engine, slammed the gearshift down and stomped on the accelerator.

The Cadillac fishtailed across the grass and plowed through a bed of red tea roses. Halfway down the driveway, the irresponsible idiot lost control of the vehicle and sideswiped a huge oak tree. Furious, he got out of his car to assess the damage; he stomped his feet and kicked the door panel repeatedly. After his juvenile display, he got back into his car and exited the property in a more responsible manner. I had to laugh at him as he drove away.

Slowly putting one foot into my car, I felt a force pulling me back. I stood holding the car door opened looking about the house. "I'm coming back, I am coming back to you," I whispered.

CHAPTER 3

FOUR MONTHS LATER

Tina

Driving down the long dirt road to Dogwood Plantation, my excitement was overwhelming. I could hardly wait to see the improvements. I know my family felt the same way. They had suffered through the endless recounted details my mind envisioned from the plantation. Of course, they were tired of hearing the same old lore, but they still pretended to listen to my every word.

Unfortunately, when we arrived, things were not as expected. Four months had gone by, and I expected the condition of the house to be better. However, the new wiring and plumbing did not work properly. Spiders and other insects crawled about the house, but judging from the foul odor, the exterminator had just treated the property. Jim was not happy.

I met with the contractor responsible for supervising the renovations. He assured me these issues would be resolved in a matter of weeks. In the mean time, we stayed at a local hotel, which was a half hour away.

Even though the Bekins movers packed most of our things and brought them for us, the move was exhausting. Thank God for Jim's job or we would never have been able to afford it. Unpacking the boxes and finding the perfect place for our belongings was mindboggling. We worked from sunrise until sundown. Traveling to and from the hotel did not help matters. Finally, to be moving in was pure joy for all of us.

I stood in front of my century-old home and stared with astonishment. I wondered what story this old place had to tell. The presence of something or someone lingered around me. I could feel eyes watching my every movement. Taking a quick account of my surroundings, I saw nothing.

Sometimes I would catch a shadow from the corner of my eye, but it always seemed to disappear with the slightest movement of my head. Could it be my great grandfather? Was he happy I was here? Did he want me to stay? I wondered.

The house had been empty for many years — alone, vacant, and surviving on its own. There was no one to care for it or the beauty that was hidden deep beneath the crusty exterior. The stature of the monumental columns seemed to assure the sturdiness of the house. Yet, the distress cracks resembled a road map from top to bottom. The horrific storms and hurricanes that had passed through there over the years had taken their toll on the old gigantic timbers.

The interior was cold, damp, and lonely; we moved in hoping to bring warmth, laughter and love with us — enough to fill it the way I was sure it had been in the past. I could envision the grand parties, the laughter and joy filling the rooms.

Although the structure was dilapidated, I noticed something strange: it looked like there was still a caretaker of the grounds, and whoever it was did a beautiful job. I was clueless as to who would keep this place up and why.

I gazed around the flowerbed and looked up at the four huge columns that stood so boldly. Each column stood parallel with the other. They gave my home a sense of strength and beauty.

Midway up the front of the house were balconies on each side of the columns. The balconies had white pickets that were short in size, but thick and rounded. They encircled a private sitting area where residents could view the beauty of the land. There was green ivy intertwined around these small pickets. It grew wild and rampant, and I was sure it was the only thing holding the wood together. It disguised the rotted timber that lay hidden beneath. Below the sitting area, there was a group of small columns with more pickets. All this ran perpendicular to the handrail that led to larger columns, concealing a wrap-around porch. The focal point on the ground level was a huge, open entryway that invited whomever would venture in.

A diamond shaped stained glass window was in the center between the columns on the second level. It seemed to have no purpose beyond its own uniqueness. I felt it brought a personal and pleasing atmosphere to my home.

At the edge of the big columns, two large weeping willow trees swayed in the breeze. The long leaf branches drooped as one would expect, but they hung proudly on the trees and seemed to come alive with the soothing breath of the blowing wind. The thin limbs were like arms stretching and reaching out to the colorful stained glass. The tiny leaves displayed lifelike fingers, spreading wide and gently touching, stroking the unusual window, brushing ever so softly across the glass.

The paint on the exterior was old and brittle; each crack exposing the nakedness of the house. The dry rotted shutters, barely able to hang on, clutched to their rusty hinges. The home was losing its battle against time and weather, and we both were unaware that the war was just beginning. The fight of restoration was going to take a miracle, and I promised to prevail against all odds.

There were huge live oak trees lining the driveway up to a circle. The trees had long, gray Spanish moss hanging in them, like an old man's beard mimicking the River Road oak trees. Between each tree, the beauty of wisteria vines mesmerized us with the full bloom of their purple flowers. The fragrance attracted the passion of the bumblebees, which buzzed fervently around each and every flower. All of the branches were neatly trimmed. They displayed the shape of a fountain, a beautiful cascade of purple tears, hanging in limbo.

Looking around this property, I wondered what made me feel this loneliness. What brought me here and made me want to stay? Why was I so determined to uncover the secrets that had remained hidden for decades? Staring down my long dirt driveway, I did not understand this sadness. Where was it coming from? Why was it inside me? What secrets were hidden here? There were so many unanswered questions. Why did my family abandon this beautiful mansion? I had to know. I had to find out.

"BOO!" said someone behind me.

"Aaaah!" I jumped, screamed and spun around. "You scared me to death, Jim!"

"Sorry Babe. What are you doing out here?" Jim asked.

"Just thinking," I answered, as he wrapped his arms around me.

Jim was my husband. He was 45 years old with brown hair, hazel eyes, and a dark tan; he stood six feet, three inches tall, and was built very well — almost too good to be true. There was only one small problem: Jim had no time for anything except the four-letter word … *work*. When he was home, he was great, but that was very seldom. Our marriage was great; we didn't see each other enough to get tired of one another. When we were together, the excitement we shared was overwhelming. Little did I know, all that was about to change.

"What are you thinking about?" Jim asked. "Wait, don't answer that. Let me." He held his fingers to his temples, as a psychic would do.

"Hmmm," he hummed. "I bet you are thinking that maybe we have made a mistake. Hmmm, maybe we should move back to the city and get away from the bugs, snakes, and all these critters out here. Maybe this place is too old, creepy and musky for us."

"Wrong, you lose," I retorted. "I was just thinking about the stories this place must hold. Can you imagine the things that might have gone on here or the events that occurred in this big place? I bet our new house has stories that would send chills down your spine."

Jim laughed. "New house, huh? Babe, you need to look again. It's far from new, but halfway right you are; it does send chills down my spine. Not from the stories, the appearance alone makes me shiver."

"Smart ass, you're so funny, city boy," I said. "It's going to look beautiful when I'm finished with it. You wait and see. You won't believe what a little paint could do. Sand off all that loose, crumbling paint, caulk, and reglaze the windows, replace a couple of boards, slap on a little paint, and we have a beautiful mansion. We can repaint it white and maybe have a dark green accent color, like Charleston green to match some new shutters of course, and …"

"Wait a minute," Jim interrupted. "You are babbling. I think you're going way too far. You need to slow down and get a grip. We should sit down tonight and discuss what we can do. Take one step at a time, Honey. One baby step at a time," Jim said as he walked away.

"Where are you going?" I asked.

"I have to hide my money from you, of course. We are going to have to file bankruptcy just to paint this damned place," he replied.

"Ha! Ha! Ha!" I laughed. "You are so funny — such a smart ass. You had better hide it well! After that remark, I might just spend it all if I find it."

Jim threw his hand up and quickly disappeared into the house. I stayed outside and started to plant some flowers, something I loved to do. I smiled, piddling, pushing my fingers deep into the black dirt. The soil was warm and had a calming effect. I was thinking how lucky I was to have such a loving, understanding husband. He had given up a lot to move out here in the woods to my country estate.

My smile quickly left as I caught a glimpse of a black shadow from the corner of my eye. I had that eerie sensation again: the feeling I was being watched. This time the dark silhouette stayed a few seconds longer and somewhat resembled a human being. I knew my every movement was being observed, scrutinized by someone or something.

Gazing around, trying to be inconspicuous, uneasiness settled over me. It was a hair raising, breathing down your neck, frightening kind of feeling. I quickly stood up and hurried to the house.

As I walked across the yard, I stole a quick glance behind me, praying not to see anyone. I hastened my step and increased my pace as I neared the house. It was a crazy feeling, but for some reason I could not wait to get inside.

A strong wind came out of nowhere and unbalanced my step. I put my head down and continued to climb the stairs. As I neared the front door, the speed of the wind increased.

The willow branches swung all around me and stretched across the entryway blocking my path. They surrounded me like a cage for an animal. The thin branches appeared to come alive and united tightly around my legs like thin ropes binding me. It was like an octopus swinging its many arms and trying to capture me. They popped and snapped like lashing whips, stinging my entire body. Each strike was excruciating as it cut through my skin. The blood poured from my back, arms and legs.

The black clouds swallowed the sun and cast an unnatural shadow beneath the tree. I stood deprived of movement in the depths of the darkness, knowing the perils of hell, with Satan scratching and pawing my body.

I screamed for Jim as I struggled to get free, but he did not answer. I screamed again, louder and louder, but no one came. The two trees rocked back and forth, straining and reaching out with their finger-like branches to grab me. They resembled two giants hovering over my head. The branches whirled through the air and crawled along the ground, scratching up my legs. I pulled the tightly wrapped branches with both hands and tried to free myself. I cried and begged for help.

A funnel of sand spun up and danced around me, I could barely see. I was in the cone of a mini tornado all alone. I shielded my eyes and squealed with fright. The funnel whirled around me until there was nothing but a wall of sand. It slammed against my body, knocking me from my feet. I was aching, burning, and covered with blood. Struggling to stand, the severity of the pain made me weak and frail. I screamed and cried louder; still, no one came.

My strength was gone. The battle with Mother Nature was over, and I had lost. The pain was excruciating. I curled into a fetal position trembling, and quivering with fear, I awaited my fate.

And just like that, as quickly as the storm had begun, it stopped and everything grew still and quiet. The whipping arms fell open, and I was released. I brushed the hair from my face and gawked with disbelief. The tiny branches drooped back into their natural setting. The wind was calm again — nothing out of the ordinary and nothing disturbed.

I quickly struggled to my feet and ran to the door. It was locked, of course. Frenzied, I beat on it with both hands while screaming for Jim. I pounded and pounded as hard as I could. My heart raced, palpitating uncontrollably in my chest. Frantically, I kept jolting the doorknob, hoping it would open, jumping up and down, screaming at the top of my lungs.

"Hey," a voice came from behind me.

I froze and plastered myself against the door. I was scared to death, scared to move, scared to breathe, and scared to look. I took a deep breath and held it; I closed my eyes and clutched my fists tightly. I was terrified to look.

"Are you all right?" I heard the voice ask.

I slightly peeked with one eye, my mouth dropped open, and my eyes quickly widened, paralyzed in disbelief. I saw a strange looking woman standing at the bottom of my steps.

"I'm sorry, I didn't mean to scare you," she said. "My name is Tina, Tina Bailer. I saw y'all pass by my house with the moving trucks, and I wanted to welcome you. I live just through the woods on the other side of the hill, right over there," she said as she pointed to the woods.

I settled into a fixed trance, focused on the short, chubby, middle-aged woman with bleached blond hair. Her eyes were blue, and at each corner, traced with thick black eyeliner. Red rouge encircled each cheek with glowing red lipstick to match. She wore a homemade dress, which she had altered to fit her taste; the neckline dropped, pulled tight, and exposed too much of her oversized breasts. Her shoes were pointy, bright red, and matched her face and dress color. She looked as if she had been painted by a crazed artist from head to toe. I stared at her, wondering if she was real, or if I was dreaming, but then she spoke a second time.

"Is anything wrong? Are you all right? I heard you yelling. I don't want to seem nosy or anything, but I thought something might be wrong."

I stood quiet, dumbfounded, not saying a word, and just staring down at this strange looking woman. Then I thought about all the cuts on my legs and arms. I knew she must have wondered what had happened to me. I looked, and there was not a mark on me. All the pain was gone. I searched up and down, checked both the front and back of my legs and arms. I was squirming around in a circle trying to understand. Confused, I stared at my unscarred body, trying to make sense of what had just happened. Had my imagination gone wild? Was I hallucinating?

I looked back at the strange person; her expression was unmistakably one of her wanting to get the hell out of my yard.

"Forgive me, I'm sorry." I shook my head to get out of my puzzled state. "My name is Vivian, and no, there's nothing wrong. I tripped over my own two feet and yelled out. I'm surprised you even heard me; no one else seemed to. My husband must have locked the door by mistake."

I ran my fingers through my hair, shaking out the leaves and brushing my legs as I spoke.

"My husband had to have locked the door. I can't get into the house. I got tangled in those willow branches when that strong gust of wind blew, and I couldn't move. When I got free, I couldn't get into the house. I think the door is locked. My husband must have locked it by mistake. He does that sometimes when he's not paying attention to what he's doing. I said that already, didn't I?" I repeated myself, rambling, still leaning against the door.

"Are you sure you're all right?" Tina asked.

"Yes, I'm fine," I assured her. "I know I don't sound like it because I'm rambling on, but really, I'm fine. Thank you," I snickered a little.

"Well, I'm not sure what happened to you, but the wind wasn't blowing, not hard enough to speak about. Not that I've noticed, anyway," Tina said, looking at me as if I were crazy.

Before I could answer, Jim opened the door and I fell in. He caught me by my arm and helped me to my feet.

"What's," he paused, staring at Tina, "wrong?" he continued with a bewildered look on his face.

"You had the door locked. I couldn't get in," I explained.

"No I didn't," he said softly, never taking his eyes off Tina.

"Well, it must have been stuck, because I couldn't get in," I angrily responded.

"Yes, it must have been," he said, still staring.

"Hi!" Tina said, as she reached out to shake his hand. "I'm Tina."

Jim just stared. I nudged him with my elbow.

"Tina," he blurted. "Well, it is nice to meet you, Tina; my name is Jim."

"She's our neighbor, Jim. She lives over the hill," I said trying to get him to quit staring.

"Lucky us," he replied.

"Huh?" Tina said putting her hands of her hips.

"I mean, we're so lucky to have neighbors," Jim quickly answered. "I thought we were all alone out here."

I gave him one of those looks, and he knew he had better think of something quickly.

"Jim's a city boy and used to having neighbors within arm's length," I replied.

"I can't believe someone finally moved into this old place," Tina said, standing on her tiptoes, stretching her neck to view the inside.

"Why is that?" Jim asked.

"Oh you know, people allege things … things that might have happened. All the rumors that float around regarding this old place … everyone is scared to death of it."

"Scared, why would they be scared? What kind of rumors?" I quickly stepped up to ask. "Please, where are my manners? Would you like to come in?"

Jim shot me a look as I invited the weird looking woman into our home, but I was curious about what she might know.

"Sure, I'd love a glass of tea if you have some made. I don't want to put you out, though. You do drink sweet tea, don't you?"

"Sure do, and I just made a fresh pitcher. Come on in, and we can sit and talk. I would love to know more about these rumors."

Jim sucked in his stomach and watched us go by. I just shrugged my shoulders, smiled, and kept on talking.

Walking into the house, Tina glanced into each room we passed. The inside was so beautiful, it would be hard for anyone not to look. That is, after we finally destroyed the habitat for the eight-legged creatures and after we had cleaned every inch, from ceilings to floors — the unveiling of the interior was beautiful.

The entryway presentation alone was stunning: a huge foyer with a stairwell that stretched and curved up the wall. Two beautiful handrails led the way to the top. The lowest post displayed a huge claw foot, like that of a lion. It was a most magnificent, unique piece of hand carved wood. There were four claw foot posts altogether: one at the bottom, one midway, and two mounted at the top step, opposite from one another. On each side of the foyer were two large rooms. The living room was to the left and the dining area to the right; through the dining area was the kitchen. The floors were hardwood with a cherry stain finish. The floorboards did not run in a horizontal or vertical direction. They started in a circle and wound their way to a diamond shaped center. The ceilings were tongue and groove, the same shape as the design on the floor. Antique light fixtures hung with dignity to enlighten the rooms; each had been designed with its own unique fashion and color.

The old gas lanterns were still mounted and were in working condition in several rooms.

The walls were plaster and in dire need of some tender loving care. The stress cracks could almost be read like the lines in the palm of one's hand, however, instead of reading the future, I saw flashbacks to the past. Cracks in the plaster throughout the rooms were in desperate need of repair and paint, yet each had a character all its own; each sheltered a secret tale. The large, eight-paneled doors stood ten feet in height and were accented with crystal clear doorknobs. Those doors kept the business and affairs conducted behind them private and mysterious.

My furniture was modern, not appropriate for such a house, and it clashed horribly. The house was my main concern; the furniture would be replaced at a later date.

"Well, you ladies have fun. I have to get some rest before I leave," Jim said, walking up the stairs.

"Leave. Are you leaving already?" Tina shouted out to him, as he quickly disappeared without answering.

"Jim's an airline pilot. He has to leave tonight," I explained.

"So where will you be staying while your husband is gone?" Tina asked on our way to the kitchen, checking out everything as she went.

"Right here, the kids and I are used to it. We stay by ourselves all the time," I replied.

"Used to what?" Tina asked.

"Used to staying by ourselves."

"Right here, in this house! By yourselves?" she asked worriedly.

"Yep, right here by ourselves."

"You have more guts than I do. I would never stay in this place alone. You couldn't pay me to stay one night here, even if I weren't alone." When those words rolled from her lips, the back door slammed, shaking the windowpanes.

"Damn!" Tina screamed. "That scared the piss out of me. Things like that are why I would not stay here."

"Oh, that happens all the time," I assured her calmly. "When I first moved in, I was the same way. I was constantly screaming because doors were slamming behind me. Windows fly open, and the television even comes on by itself sometimes. I've been here a couple of weeks, and I'm just now getting used to it."

"Used to it? Damn girl! I'd be moving." Tina stood up and started opening all the doors in my kitchen. She looked inside my pantry, my cabinets, the closet, and then the cellar.

"Boohoo," she called out looking down the dark cellar stairwell. "That looks spooky down there," she shivered and closed the door.

Then, all of a sudden, she screamed. She rushed toward the back door, jerked it open and ran out. Tripping over a pair of shoes, she stumbled, gathered herself up and scurried across the back deck.

"What's the matter?" I called out, running behind her. "Did you see something?"

"No, look on the hill," she screamed back.

"Oh my God! Jim! Jim! Come quick!" I screamed, as I too ran behind her.

Angel, my little girl, was sitting in the top of a tree on the hill. There was a pond at the bottom, and all I could think about was her falling and rolling down into the water.

The grass was thick and knee high, so just walking was treacherous. Tina was gasping for air as I passed her. My stride was long, my gait steady, and my adrenaline was pumping. My baby was up there, and nothing was going to slow me down. When I finally reached the top, I slipped head first into a mud hole. I stood up and tried to sling the nasty goo from my fingers. It was black and slimy, and it stuck to my hands and dripped off my face. I used my arms, rubbing, trying to remove the muck from my eyes.

"Angel, how did you get up there? And what in the world are you doing?" I shouted, still trying to remove the magnetic mud.

She started to come down.

"No, you be real still. Daddy is on his way, and he'll help you down."

Angel began to laugh. "Mommy you look funny. Your face has mud all over it."

"Well, you just sit tight young lady. I'm not very amused right now, and I don't care how funny I look. I am very upset with you. You should know better than to come up here by yourself."

Angel's long blond hair blew in the wind, and her big brown eyes filled with excitement as she sat on the branch swinging her legs. "But

Mom, I didn't come up here by myself …"

Jim reached the top of the hill and interrupted. "Angel, what in the world are you doing this far away from the house?"

"But Dad," Angel whined.

"Don't 'Dad' me. Come on, and let me help you down." He quickly climbed up one branch at a time and helped Angel get out of the tree. Slowly, he handed her to me. He turned around and looked back.

"Vivian, look how beautiful this tree is. I don't remember any blooms on it," Jim said.

I looked up. He was right. It was awesome. A dogwood tree covered with gorgeous white flowers. Each limb had a snow-white blossoms with unique yellow centers.

"I don't recall its blooming, either," I said with a puzzled look.

"It wasn't," Tina said, leaning over with her hands on her knees, trying to catch her breath. "I've been here all my life, and this tree hasn't ever bloomed."

"It had to be blooming," Jim said sarcastically. "There is no way that all of these blossoms came in overnight."

"I'm telling you I just came up this way, and the damned tree wasn't blooming," Tina argued as she tried to stand up straight, gasping for air.

"Mr. Issy made it bloom," Angel's tiny voice replied. She was smiling from ear to ear. "He's a magic man, and he knows how to do all kind of tricks. He's the one that makes that purple flower bloom too."

"What!" Jim snapped.

"Mr. Issy, he brought me up here," Angel explained.

"What?" I snapped angrily. "Someone brought you up here and left you?"

"No Mom, he didn't really bring me, I came by myself. He called for me to come and play. So I did. He's very nice, Mom."

"Honey, you know that you don't talk to strangers. We have told you that before. Not all people are good; you know that."

"Mom, Mr. Issy is very nice."

"Well, where is this Mr. Issy?" Tina asked. "I've never heard of anyone named Issy, around here."

"He's gone. You scared him away," Angel replied.

"Scared him away! Why would he be scared?" Jim asked.

"I don't know, Daddy. He just don't like strangers."

"Well, I don't like strangers with my little girl. If you see him again, you come and get Daddy," Jim said as he took her from my arms. "Do you understand me, young lady?"

"Yes sir," Angel answered in her tiny little voice as Jim lowered her to the ground.

The beautiful tree with the white flowers was remarkable. Every tiny little branch had a bloom. They clustered together, offering a shower of life to the early spring season. A couple of birds accepted the gift and started building their nest to bring in new life of their own.

Observing the tree, I noticed one branch about seven feet high, which appeared to be dead. It was without leaves or flowers, just a raw, naked branch that had been stripped bare, showing just a small glimmer of life beneath the bark. The limb was alive, however it was completely without new growth.

"Look at this branch," I said reaching up to it. "Doesn't it look weird? It seems strange that it doesn't have flowers on it. All of the other branches are covered." Before anyone could answer, I felt something brush against me.

"What was that?" I turned around searching, but I found nothing.

"What was what?" Jim asked.

"I felt something touch my backside just as I reached for that limb."

"Mommy, who is that lady?" Angel interrupted, pointing to Tina.

"This is our neighbor, Ms. Tina."

Tina squatted down and held both of Angel's hands. "You sure are a pretty little girl. I'd l like to take you home with me. You are so adorable, but you need to listen to your mom and dad, and be very careful not to talk to strangers. Someone really might take you away, you know. I know I would love to have you."

Out of nowhere, a gust of wind blew, unbalancing Tina and causing her to fall forward to her knees. Angel laughed as she reached back for me. Tina looked at Jim and shouted, "If you knew what was good for your family, you would move!"

She rocketed down the steep, slippery hill. The wind seemed to gain strength and push against her back. The tall brown broom straw separated and laid a path for her to descend. Her exposed bulge wavered as she flapped her arms to stabilize her posture. Her short chubby legs folded, tumbling her to a spiral decline.

"Ahhhh ..." she exclaimed.

Never looking back, she leaped to her feet and ran, disappearing into the woods and leaving us in pain from laughter at her comical departure.

Jim turned to me, still laughing, and said, "Babe, if you think Tina looked funny, you should see your face. You have mud all over it, in your ears, up your nose, and all in your hair. You look a little bit like one of those Southern raccoons that live around here. You know the ones that have that black mask."

Jim and Angel chuckled while he tried to brush the mud off me.

"You know, I do have to agree with Tina," Jim said as he picked Angel up and started down the hill. "This place does seem a little weird. I mean, it just has an eerie feeling about it."

Angel snickered, peering behind us as we descended the hill. I turned to look. The blooms were falling from the tree and dropping to the ground. They were floating in the soft breeze, following behind us, creeping down our trail.

Jim looked over his shoulder, ignoring what he saw. Instead, he said, "I'll race you."

To me, he was saying, "Let's get the hell out of here." Of course, being a man, he would not admit he was scared.

Reaching the bottom of the hill, he put Angel down and started racing her to the house. We approached the back yard; Gary was calling out to us. "Mom, Dad, where are you?"

"We're out here, Gary," I yelled.

Gary was our 14-year-old son; he took after his dad. He had Jim's dark, olive complexion and brown hair, but his big brown eyes were like mine.

"Groovy!" He said coming around the house.

"What's groovy, Gary?" Jim asked.

Gary pointed to the hill.

We both turned, astonished by what we were witnessing. The tree was in full bloom again. The flowers that had fallen off seemed to have reappeared.

"That tree, it's really awesome. I haven't noticed it before," said Gary.

"That's cause Mr. Issy did it," Angel said shrugging her shoulders and shaking her head in a knowing fashion.

"Did what?" Gary asked in a bold voice.

"Made the tree bloom, stupid," Angel replied.

"Angel, I've told you before, do not call your brother that again. Do you understand me?" I said sternly.

"Yes ma'am, but he always calls me that."

"Well neither one of you had better say it anymore," Jim said walking up the steps.

"Who's Mr. Issy?" Gary asked.

"He's Angel's imaginary friend," I answered.

"Who's calling who stupid," Gary said laughing at Angel.

"He's not imashin'ary, he's real," Angel angrily yelled out.

"Ha, ha, ha," Gary snickered.

"Gary, that's enough. You leave your sister alone."

"Sure Mom, no problem." Gary walked away teetering behind Jim into the house, and Angel put her hands on her hips and stuck her tongue out at him.

"Mommy, Mr. Issy is real. He said he was all alone until we moved here. He's glad we came," Angel insisted.

I stared at Angel as she talked. She really believed she had talked to someone. I was beginning to believe her; maybe he was real.

"Angel, do you know where this man lives?" I asked.

"No, I don't know," she answered, as she sat down and started playing in the sand.

"Well, what does he look like?"

"A man," her response now unconcerned and her attention was no longer with me. I sat on the ground beside her and watched her play. My interest remained on the hill with the mysterious tree. The flowers were breath taking. It was so strange for none of us to have noticed them before. It wasn't possible for this tree to bloom overnight, or was it?

I began to think about all the unexplainable little things that had happened since our arrival. I fell into a trance-like state, one of deep concentration. I was oblivious to my immediate surroundings, and all I could think about was the mysterious history of the place.

Was this plantation haunted? Is that why my mother never told me about it? If by chance it really were haunted – by what, or whom? Did my mom even know? I wondered what secrets my family might have been hiding here. Could they possibly have murdered someone?

"Vivian. Vivian. Vivian!" Jim shouted.

"What!" I shouted back.

"Did you not hear me? I called you several times."

"I'm sorry. No, I didn't hear you, I was just thinking," I said.

"I know. You were thinking about this damn place, again," Jim interrupted. "You're always thinking about this place."

"I'm sorry Babe. What do you need?"

It's time for me to go. Do you think maybe you and my precious little Angel could think about kissing me goodbye?"

"Why of course we can," I said smiling.

"I won't be back until next week. I hope you'll be all right by yourself. I hate not having a man close around. There seem to be a lot of strange things happening around here," Jim said.

"Don't worry Daddy, Mr. Issy will watch out for us. And he's a man too," Angel reassured him.

Jim's lower jaw dropped. He eyeballed Angel, opened his mouth to reply, paused, then leaned toward me and whispered, "Things like that are what I'm worried about."

He tilted his head in Angel's direction, as to point at her with it; I couldn't help but to laugh.

"We'll be just fine, don't worry. I just wish you didn't have to leave so soon, Jim. There's so much to do here," I pleaded.

"I know, but don't you recollect that little discussion we had before our move? I told you it was going to take a lot of hard work to fix this place up, and I wouldn't be here a lot of the time to do it, remember?"

"I know, you're right. I'll just take it one day at a time. Maybe Tina would be interested in helping me."

"See, there you go. It didn't take you long to come up with some help. I'm sure she would love to help you — that is if you can keep her nose out of everything."

"You're not being very nice, Jim. She may be a really good person," I scolded.

"I'm sure she is — didn't say she wasn't, but I have got to run. You'll have to find the answer to that all by yourself," he said.

Jim gave us a kiss and a hug. We stood on the front porch and watched until he disappeared down the long dirt drive. I missed him already.

CHAPTER 4

T H E   B O A T

As the night slowly crept in, I was very tired from the long, hot day. After getting out of the shower, I moseyed through my bedroom to the balcony; I needed a breath of fresh air. The crickets were chirping, the frogs singing for rain, and a bark in the distance from a neighboring dog was all I could hear. The sounds were serene without sirens, honking horns, and screams from the wild violence that we left behind. The calm was unbelievably peaceful.

I leaned against the railing and looked up toward the hill. The moonlight danced off the petals of the beautiful dogwood blossoms. The flowers reflected like hundreds of tiny white candles flickering in the wind, lambent in the moonlight.

As the breeze blew softly, the clouds drifted across the moon. One by one, the tiny white candles began to disappear. The fog swiftly approached from the side of the house. The smoke-like mist drifted up the hill, accumulating, as if that were the only direction it knew. Within a matter of minutes, the haze completely covered the mound.

The moon was obscured by the heavy dense clouds. The last glimmer of light abandoned me, leaving total darkness. The wind blew with a sudden gust, slamming the bedroom door, jetting fear throughout my body.

Alone in the blackness, I leaned on the rails of the balcony and stared out into the dark. Unable to see, I closed my eyes, visualizing every detail in my mind's eye as I remembered it. I was blind, however the vision was still there, and I could have described every inch of that hill. I embraced the rumination of my mind.

I heard the tiny branches of the willow tree blow over the monstrous columns and scratch the fake center window furiously. I was sure it would break at any time.

The ivy plants that twisted along the balcony shook wildly in the wind. I had a horrible sensational feeling of tiny snakes, crawling, inching around my hands, then lashing around me like ropes, tying me to the rail. I tried to lift my hands, but I was unable to pull free; the small vines were conjoined and unbreakable.

Desperately, I continued to jerk backward thinking the weight of my body would set me free, but the tight restraint controlled my freedom of movement.

The crickets and frogs raised their voices and drowned out the shrill sounds of the wind blowing through the trees. The fog dispersed as quickly as it came and shuffled back to the front of the house. The high-pitched screeches and screams of the animals and insects filled the air. Amid all of it, I stood silent. I could not cry, scream, or even give a whimper. I was hypnotized into a blank trance, left only to stare at the beauty of the dogwood tree on top of that hill. That was the only thing revealed to me. The only thing that was visible was a glimmer of light. Its dimness dismissed little of the darkness, but it draped a familiar, mysterious shadow.

I was tense, staring into the night, as the clouds swirled and danced past the moon. The pale moonlight occasionally peeped out and shined its rays, allowing me to see one tiny flower glowing in the light. I strained my eyes to see more, and then I noticed it wasn't a flower at all.

It appeared to be a man standing under the tree holding a candle. I blinked and squinted repeatedly through the darkness. I pulled with all my might against the ivy branches that had entangled my hands.

All of a sudden, the branches popped off, and I fell to the balcony floor. I jumped to my feet only to find the wind calm, the willow branches hanging in place, and the moon in full light upon the tree. Just like before, there was no one in sight, only that beautiful tree.

I stared up at the hill for a while trying to make some sense of what I saw, or what I thought I saw. Yet, there was no explanation. I watched for movement, but there was none. There was only a soothing breeze that carried the country sounds across the land. After hours of anticipation of waiting, watching, and pacing, I gave up and went to bed.

"It's 6 a.m., sleepyheads. Time to rise and shine!"

I jumped straight up, scared to death as the strange voice entered my room. Focusing on my surroundings, I realized it was only the radio alarm. I smacked it off and sat on the edge of bed. Rubbing my temples, I was trying to remember what had happened the night before. Had I really been sitting on the balcony, or was it just a dream?

Stepping through the French doors, I looked out to the hill. Scoping the area, I saw nothing out of the ordinary, just that beautiful tree.

Sighing with disappointment, I lowered my head. As I turned to re-enter my room, something caught my eye. A small piece of ivy was laying on the floor. I followed the trail to the balcony pickets where many more pieces laid.

"So, I was out here last night; it wasn't a dream." Snapping my head back toward the mysterious mound, I shivered when a cold shadow darted across me.

"What is it that you want? What is it?" I shouted. Of course, there was no answer.

My imagination seemed to be working overtime. "I must be losing my mind. Maybe I'm trying to make something out of nothing. It was probably some kind of gases reflecting off the fog," I told myself.

I looked around hoping for an explanation, but there were none. Did the answers lie with the living or the dead? What a hell of a question for someone to think about.

I returned to my room, closing the doors behind me. I quickly dressed and called for Gary to get out of bed.

"Hurry, you're going to be late for school. Make sure you wake your sister too," I yelled as I headed to the kitchen. There was too much time wasted up stairs; I had to make it up.

I went to the refrigerator and got the bacon and eggs out. I filled the frying pan with bacon and scrambled the eggs in a bowl. Crack! Pop! And a screech that sounded human. I jumped and knocked the bowl of eggs off the counter. I ran to the back door to see who was yelling. The sound came again.

Crack! Pop! Screeeeech. A distinctive sound echoed through the house.

I ran into the yard calling, "Who's out here? Where are you? Do you need help? Please answer me! Are you hurt?"

"Mom."

I turned to see Gary staring at me with his eyebrows raised.

"Are you losing it out here? Who are you talking to?"

"I heard a weird noise and a piercing scream. Someone was crying out. You didn't hear it?"

"All I heard was the smoke alarm."

"Oh no: breakfast!"

I ran into the house to find the kitchen full of smoke. Gary had already taken the frying pan from the stove. The bacon had burned to a black crisp, and the bowl of eggs was splattered across the floor. I just stood there in disbelief.

"Well Mom, are you just going to stare at your mess, or are you going to clean it up? I'll get the cereal for me and Angel."

"Okay boy, I wouldn't get too smart-mouthed if I were you. I'm not in the mood."

"Yeah, I can tell. So what's up with you? Are you hearing things again?" Gary asked pouring his bowl of cereal.

"No. I'm not hearing things. It was probably a dog, or a stray cat. It just sounded like something … else."

"What else?" Gary asked.

"I don't know," I snapped back. "Just eat your cereal."

"Angel," I called.

"I'm right here, Mom," Angel said coming through the back door.

"What were you doing outside by yourself?" I screamed at her.

Angel started to cry. "I thought I heard someone crying out there," she sobbed.

"Oh no, not you too," Gary replied.

"Gary, that's quite enough! Honey, I'm sorry for yelling at you, but you shouldn't be wandering outside by yourself. The next time you think you hear something, you come and get Mommy, okay?"

"Okay," Angel sniffled, wiping her tears away.

"Now hurry and eat. We need to get Gary to school."

"Maybe it was your imaginary friend. Better yet, I bet this place is haunted. That's what all the kids at school say. They say the house is full of ghosts."

"What does 'haunted' mean?" Angel asked.

"Ghosts!" Gary shouted, wiggling his fingers in her face.

"We don't have ghosts, do we, Mom?"

"Gary, don't put stuff like that in your sister's head. You'll make her have bad dreams. Come on you two — just hurry so we can go."

I weaseled my way out of that, but I really had to agree with Gary. I really did believe we had ghosts. There were too many weird unexplained things that happened here.

On the way to the school, my mind was preoccupied with the unnatural happenings that had just occurred. I tuned out my bickering children and thought about my strange house. There seemed to be many things going on in our house, and I needed to find out what and why.

Arriving at the school, Gary quickly gathered his books, and out the car he went. A group of boys called to him. He threw his hand up and ran toward them. It was nice to know he had made friends so quickly.

Pulling out of the parking lot, Angel stuck her tongue out at him until we got out of sight; this seemed to be one of her favorite things to do.

Talk about hidden secrets — the love between those two was a hidden secret all its own. They could fight all day, but if we scolded Angel for something, Gary would be right there to smooth it over. Sometimes Gary sat and read to Angel, and she loved that. I even witnessed them snuggled up together in front of the television eating popcorn a few times. I remember thinking, "I really need to take a picture of that, because it is happening less and less frequently."

"I guess my boy is growing up; one day both of them will marry, go off on their own, and have their own children. That's a scary thought. I need to get back to concentrating on the scary things in my house and how that might affect my children."

Driving up that long beautiful driveway, I could not imagine why my family had stayed away for so long. The beautiful oaks and wisteria were landscaped so perfectly; it was stunning. Someone had taken a lot of care with the yard. I couldn't wait to find more information on it.

My mind drifted to yesterday; I found myself imagining walks down this beautiful road, holding hands with a loved one, stopping to pick a flower, or sitting under one of the big oaks just to talk. How romantic the place must have been. Daydreaming about its past and its future gave me goosebumps.

Before entering into the house, I stood in front, closed my eyes, and wondered what had happened here. It seemed so hard to believe that my family could just board this house up and leave it. There had to be an answer, and I was determined to find it.

I looked around for Angel. She was sitting on the ground playing.

"Angel, Mommy is going in the house now. Are you coming with me?"

"No Mommy, I want to stay outside and play."

"Okay, but don't you leave this front yard."

"I won't."

I went straight to the kitchen to finish cleaning up the mess I had made. My mind was cluttered with the events of the previous night. I would catch myself standing still, fixated on the mysteries instead of doing my daily chores. I had to shake my head occasionally to get focused on my work.

Now and then, I would go to the window and check on Angel. Every time I did, she would be talking to her imaginary friend, laughing, singing, and having a good time. I stood at the window seriously paying attention to her. She appeared really to be talking to someone. I leaned out as far as I could, but nevertheless, saw no one. I walked to the front door, eased it open, and listened. I did not hear anyone, and she seemed fine, so I continued my work.

I rushed through the rooms making beds. I swept the kitchen, vacuumed, and cleaned the bathrooms. I gathered up the dirty laundry and put a load in the washer. It was a tremendous job, though now it was finished.

I walked outside and called for Angel. There was no answer.

"Angel," I called again, no answer. "Are you hiding from me?" I peeped into the bushes. I did not see her anywhere. "Okay Angel, this is not funny. Come on out, right now!" There was still no answer.

"The hill!" I shouted aloud. I ran around back scared to death of what I might find.

"Angel," I cried out.

"What Mommy?" she answered from her sand pile. "Is something wrong?"

"I couldn't find you, Honey. I was scared you went up to the hill again."

"No. I told Mr. Issy I couldn't go. I told him I would be in big trouble if I did."

"Good girl," I said, hugging her with relief. "You know Mommy told you to stay in the front yard."

"I forgot."

"That's okay, I'm just glad you're all right. How would you like to walk over to Miss Tina's house?"

"Miss Tina," she said curling up her nose.

"Don't you remember, you met her yesterday?"

"That funny looking lady?"

"Yes, you could say she's funny looking, but let's not tell her that, okay?"

"Okay. Where does she live?"

"I'm not sure. She said on the other side of the hill. You want to take a walk through the woods and see if we can find her house?"

"Yeah," she said jumping up with excitement.

She brushed the sand from her hands and reached for mine. We skipped away holding hands and talking about all the beautiful things on our land. I was pointing out the different types of birds and trees, teaching her the proper names of those that I knew. Angel was very interested, and asked me to name the birds every time she saw one fly over.

"If you want to be a country girl, you need to know these kinds of things," I said as we walked through the woods.

"Are you a country girl, Mommy?"

"I sure am, Honey."

"Well, I want to be a country girl too. I want to be just like you."

"All right, then a country girl you will be."

"Look over there, Angel," I said pointing to the pond. "There's a row boat. Let's get in and row to the other side." Angel laughed and took off running toward the boat.

"I'll beat you, Mommy."

"Oh my goodness. You run so fast. Oh, no, I think you are going to win. Mommy can't keep up." Angel laughed so hard she could barely run. Then all of a sudden, she stopped dead in her tracks. It was as if she were frozen, staring into the black water.

"What's wrong, Honey?" I asked.

"I don't like this water," Angel said backing away.

"Oh it's all right. It'll be fun. All you have to do is sit and be pretty. I'll do the rest."

"No Mommy, I don't want to."

"Come on, it will be fun," I said tugging on her hand. "I won't let anything happen to you, I promise."

Angel reluctantly got in. I pushed the boat off the bank, and it rocked back and forth as I jumped in. Angel grabbed the sides and screamed.

"It's all right," I said again reassuring her.

I didn't know how deep it was, so I paddled us along the side. I didn't want to go out too far, because Angel didn't have on a life vest.

We took it slow and easy. I started singing, "Row, row, row your boat."

"Come on Angel, sing with Mommy."

The rocking of the boat frightened Angel, but it didn't take long for her to relax and start singing with me. I dipped the paddle and splashed water toward her. Giggling, she cautiously reached over the side and scooped up a handful of water to throw on me. We played back and forth, getting each other wet and singing as we went. It was nice to see Angel enjoying the water and conquering her fear.

We were halfway across the pond when a cold burst of air came across us. The water began to ripple as the wind surged across the top. The boat swayed violently over the uneven water, jarring us up and down like a bumpy road maneuvers a little car. The gusts got stronger, causing us to tip from side to side — right to the edge of the black water.

I lifted the wooden paddle and struggled to get us back to the bank, but the wind was too strong. Angel screamed with fright. I tried to calm her, though I too was frightened. I wanted to go to her, but feared the boat would tip over. I called for her to hold on tight.

A funnel surrounded us, and we began to spin like a top in a whirlpool. A waterspout held us captive in a spiral of terror.

"Hang on, Baby!" I screamed.

The water whirled around us like a tornado; our bodies lifted from side to side, but the force of gravity held us in our seat.

"Hold on tight, Angel."

"Make it stop, Mommy!" Angel cried.

"It will stop in a minute, Honey, just hang on."

The boat spun us to the center of the pond, rocking us in every position possible. Then as quickly as the wind came up, it stopped. The waterspout descended into the murky pond. The wind brushed across our faces, blowing over the top of the water, and vanished throughout the trees. The water was calm, but Angel was crying hysterically.

"Don't move. Just be real still. Mommy is going to paddle us to the bank."

I paddled just as fast as I could, never missing a stroke, but we stayed stationary. I looked all around me. There was nothing noticeable preventing our movement, yet, the boat would not budge. I tried paddling again, only to remain immobile.

"I'm scared," Angel said, wiping the tears from her eyes.

"I know you are, it will be all right. Reach out and grab my hand."

"No. I'm scared."

"Come on, Angel. Come sit down here with me. Just grab my hand."

Angel reluctantly eased her hand toward mine. Then she jerked it back.

"No, I can't," she cried, quickly grabbing the sides of the boat.

"Angel, listen to Mommy. The water is calm now. I want you to reach for me slowly. You need to come down here so I can hold on to you. Come on Honey. You can do it."

Angel aversely reached out for me. With lips quivering and tears running down her cheeks, she shifted her tiny little body.

"That's right, Baby," I said, holding my hand out to her.

She grabbed my fingertips and leaped into my arms.

"I've got you, Baby," I said as I slowly pulled her close to me. "It will be all right. I'll just paddle us right back to the bank."

I don't know if I was trying to convince her or myself. Again, I started stroking deep into the water, turning the front of the boat and pointing it toward the bank. The boat quickly spun back around and stopped. I paddled harder. Again, it spun back and stopped. I tried time after time, however, I could not make it turn.

"What's wrong, Mommy? How come you aren't paddling?"

"I'm trying, Angel. It's okay. Just give me a minute."

I looked all around for some help. There was no one in sight. I was hoping Tina would come by, but it didn't happen.

I thought since I could not go forward, maybe I could go backward. I tried it, and finally, the boat started to move.

"Thank you, Jesus," I said out loud.

All of a sudden, the boat started to rock again. Angel screamed and wrapped her arms around my neck.

The boat began to rock harder and harder until highest points on its sides touched the water. With each rock, water dribbled over the rim. Angel was hysterical, and I did not know what to do. I just held her tightly.

I looked around again for someone to help, but still, no one was visible. Then I heard a crackling noise like someone walking on leaves or rattling a paper bag. Not sure of what it was and unable to pinpoint where the sound was coming from because of the wind, I kept turning my head from side to side. Angel pointed to the hill; the dogwood tree was bending and shaking. I stared in disbelief.

The inexplicable wind had surrounded the tree and was ripping at its limbs. The flowers were falling off the branches and dropping to the ground. The petals blew through the air like snowflakes and landed in perfect alignment on top of the water. They appeared to be crawling across the water's surface — straight toward us.

I was so scared; I covered Angel's eyes with my hand. I did not know what to expect. The white blossoms surrounded the boat, and slowly, it proceeded to turn. Angel sat up straight, removed my hand, and looked at me.

"Just hold on," I said.

We held tightly flowers pulled us to the bank. They encircled the boat and carried us all the way. Reaching the bank, the blooms separated and scattered across the water. I quickly grabbed Angel's hand and jumped out to the land, pulling her with me.

"That's a bad pond, Mommy," Angel said, backing away from it.

"Yes, Honey, it is, I'm sorry it scared you." I knew I needed to get her mind off of the incident.

"Let's hurry to Tina's. I bet this trail leads straight to her house. I'll race you," I said running toward the woods. The quicker we got away, the better.

Angel ran past me. "I'm going to win," she said looking back at me and laughing.

"No, you're not." I followed close behind her. "You better run faster." Angel ran, laughing as if nothing had ever happened.

It is funny how quickly kids can forget about something that scares them. I tried to keep her laughing. I didn't want her to ask about what had happened, for I had no explanation to give her. We continued to run and laugh through the woods until I spotted a rooftop.

"Look over there, Angel," I said pointing through the woods. "I think I see a house. I bet that's Miss Tina's house."

"Which way do we go, Mommy?" Angel stopped.

The trail split like a "Y." One way led to what I believed to be Tina's house, and the other way continued toward the unknown.

"Let's go this way. It may lead us over to that house, and it may be Miss Tina's house. Hold my hand, and we'll stroll up there together."

Hand in hand, we wandered on. Stepping from the shadow of the trees, we could see that the sun was projecting our image upon the ground. A dog approached us from the corner of a small wood-framed house. It was a huge longhaired black shepherd, baring teeth and barking with every breath.

I grabbed Angel and pushed her behind me. "Be real still Angel. Don't move."

The front door quickly opened.

"Sergeant," the voice yelled out. "It's all right. He won't bite you. He's harmless. He just lets me know when something is in my yard."

The voice belonged to Tina, who was very surprised to see us.

"Angel and I thought we would take a walk through the woods, so we decided to come on over. I hope you don't mind."

"Mind . . . of course not. Come on in. I don't get too much company out here."

"Everyone is probably too scared of the dog," I replied.

They could have been afraid of Tina herself. That day, she was wearing a tight baby blue imitation leather jumpsuit. I wondered if she was trying to start a new trend. God, I hoped not. Nevertheless, she was different: friendly, just definitely different.

"Pick up a stick and throw it, Angel. He'll play fetch with you all day long . . . Damn girl," Tina said as she turned back to me. "You look like you've been through hell."

I took a quick glance at Angel to affirm she was not listening to my reply.

"I think we have," I said in a joking way. Deep down, I really wasn't joking at all. "I hope you really don't mind the drop-in, I didn't have your phone number."

"No not at all. It's nice to have company. Like I said, living way out here, no one ever visits. It's too far in the boonies for most folk. So tell me, what happened to you? You fall in the pond?"

"No, I didn't fall into the pond, though you are not going to believe what did happen. Angel and I saw a boat on the bank, and we decided to get in. We were paddling the boat around . . ." I went on and told the story of what had happened. Tina just raised her eyebrows and listened, never saying a word. "It was the strangest thing. It was almost as if the flowers were protecting us. Strange, huh? You probably think I'm crazy."

"Well, I think you are crazy for just living over there, so that's not the point. As far as weird, on that plantation, everything is weird. Nothing that happens over there could ever surprise me."

"Why do you say that?"

"The place is haunted," Tina said in a loud voice. "Come on, you have to know that by now."

"I know there are a lot of unexplained happenings, but the weird thing is I'm not really scared. Well, I wasn't until the pond incident. If the plantation is haunted, it seems like someone is watching over us. There is a profound sadness I feel in the house, although the dogwood tree . . . well, that place is kind of hard to explain."

"Go ahead, I'm listening."

"Well," I turned and looked at Angel, who was still playing with the dog.

"Never mind. Just forget it."

"Forget it? No way. You started this; now spit it out."

"It's embarrassing."

"Hey, it won't be the first time I've been told about some embarrassing moment. Obviously it's something that is bothering you."

"It is – just don't laugh."

"I'm not going to laugh. Come on, let's hear it."

"It's up on top of the hill. I went there a couple times by myself. Something happens to me up there."

"What?" Tina asked excitedly.

"Well, actually, it's like someone takes over my body. I mean, I feel like I'm someone else. When I go near the tree, it seems that someone starts loving me all over. The passion I feel there is unbelievable."

Tina looked at me as if I were crazy.

"Really, Tina, I think I have a friendly ghost on the hill. I can't resist it. It's like I'm someone else, or it thinks I'm someone else."

"Boo hoo. I'm jealous. Maybe I need to go to that hill. I surely could use some loving," she said, laughing. "It's been awhile. You know what I mean? Do you wanna share?"

"See, I knew you would laugh."

"I'm sorry, go ahead and finish. What does it do?"

"I'm not sure. It so weird. I haven't stayed up there very long at a time. When I stroll on the hill, I get the sensation like someone is touching me . . . caressing me. I couldn't resist going."

"Damn girl! I call that heaven. Resist? I would probably move to the top of the hill. Hell, I may go there as soon as you leave. And to think I have lived here all my life, and not one time have I dared to venture there. Look what I missed out on."

"Last night I was out on the balcony ..." I continued to tell her about my mysterious night. "When I'm outside, I sense he is watching me."

"He, why do you say it's a he?"

"I don't know. It just seems like a man. I don't think a woman could make me feel like that. I feel so, so . . . "

"Yeah, so, so . . . what?"

"Soooo passionate," I answered, turning away. "I know how it sounds, but I swear it's true."

"Hey, I told you. There is nothing that I would not believe about that old house. What about inside?" Tina asked. "Is he not in the house?"

"No, he's not. I don't think so. There's no passion inside. The air has a wretchedness about. It seems to come from the spirit of a woman. She whispers, but I can't understand her. I'm not sure what or who is there, but it is definitely a female. I know it sounds like I've lost my mind. I can't say that enough, but it's all true. I just need to locate someone that knows the history of this plantation."

"If I didn't know about the rumors of that old place, I would agree with you. I've lived here a long time. So has my family, and everyone knows that place is haunted."

"How?"

"How what?"

"How would anyone know that the house is haunted if it hasn't been lived in for years?"

"Just because it's empty, that doesn't mean people haven't been in it. When I was a kid, the biggest dare around town was for someone to stay all night. I can't think of even one person who ever did. Then you came along, and we started taking bets if you could last a night. Now y'all are the biggest talk around town."

"We are? Why?"

"Lady, you are like news. Like I said, ain't nobody ever even spent a night in there before. Now you have come here and stayed a few weeks. When everyone heard you were moving in, we could not wait to see what you looked like. Every time I went to the store, someone would ask had I met you, especially the older people. The younger ones don't give it much thought. Although us older ones, we all thought you would look like a witch, or something. When we heard you were relatives of the late Mr. Simmons, we were shocked."

"Mr. Simmons was my great grandfather. He's the one who built the plantation mansion, I think."

"Oh yeah!" she said. "No one knew he had any relatives alive."

"I didn't know anything about this place until my mother passed away, and I inherited it. I was very surprised myself."

"Lucky you," Tina said nodding her head.

"What rumors have you heard?"

"I don't know how true the story is because it's been circulated through generations. You know how things get added and deleted. It seems Mr. Simmons's wife died during childbirth, I think."

Tina continued, "Mr. Simmons became a very bitter and hateful man after his wife died. The people in town hated him. Rumor has it, the slaves raised his daughter. He was an important man in the army, or the government, so he couldn't spend much time at home. This is how the story has been told."

"One hot summer, he came home unexpectedly. There was a terrible storm that lasted for days. Maybe it was a hurricane or just a severe summer storm of some kind. The roads were flooded, and trees blocked any passage – in or out. People were barricaded in their houses for days or weeks. It took awhile before everyone could be accounted for. No one ventured out to the Dogwood Plantation, because they didn't like Mr. Simmons; actually, they hated him. They figured that he and the slaves made out just fine. No one ever saw Mr. Simmons again."

"That's kind of hard to believe. What does everyone think happened to him?"

"Speculation is that Mr. Simmons came home to find the slaves had taken over. They had been running the plantation by themselves for a long time. They had pretty much been free. When Mr. Simmons tried to tell them what to do, they wouldn't hear of it. They killed Mr. Simmons and his daughter. They knew people would start asking questions, so the slaves got scared and fled."

"That's crazy," I said. "If that was so, where did my father come from? How did I get the plantation?"

"I can't answer that. You have to figure that one out. Nevertheless, that has been the Dogwood Plantation gossip for years and years. The two, Mr. Simmons and his daughter, haunt the house in search of one another."

"How could everyone have disappeared? And if the slaves had raised this child, how could they have killed her?"

"I don't know. That's just the tale as I know it. No one knows for sure what happened."

"I just don't believe that."

"So be it, you don't have to."

"I wonder why it's called 'Dogwood Plantation.' I have seen only one dogwood tree on the entire place: the one up on the hill."

"At one time, there were a lot of those trees, or so people say. They say the hill all around the pond was lined with beautiful trees. They all died except the one on the hill. I guess the storm might have destroyed them."

"That seems bizarre. You know, speaking of the hill, I would like to get all that tall grass cut. I'm worried about snakes making beds. Do you know anyone with a tractor that might be interested in the job?"

"Yep, I believe I do. I'll give you some phone numbers to call, although, I doubt you'll get anyone out here. If you do, it will cost you a pretty penny."

"A pretty penny, huh? I haven't heard that expression in a long time, but if it costs a pretty penny, then that is what I'll pay. So, if you give me some numbers, we'll be on our way. I have a lot of things to take care of today."

Tina went into the house to get a pen and paper and returned with four numbers. She also put her phone number on a scrap of paper and asked for mine.

"You never know when you or I might need each other," she said as she wrote down my number. I think she really meant when I might need her.

Angel and I said goodbye to Tina, and off through the woods we went. I started thinking about the path. If no one ever came to my house, why was it there? It was a very beaten down trail, and it looked to have been used often. I was going to make a point of asking Tina about it later.

Angel and I sang and laughed as we continued our walk. We stopped and watched two squirrels playing chase around a tree. While we were standing still, we saw a doe and her small fawn creep silently through the woods. I whispered to Angel to be real quiet. She smiled, and her eyes gleamed with excitement. We observed the protective mother cautiously leading her baby through the forest, occasionally stopping and nibbling along the way.

Observing this natural beauty on my own property was fulfilling. I wondered how I could have ever lived anywhere else. Watching Angel's eyes light up was priceless. As we strolled along, she was very quiet, as she hoped to see more animals. She didn't miss a thing; she was taking in every creature we came upon.

Coming to the clearing, we could see the pond, but the peacefulness had disappeared. An eerie feeling came over me as we stared at the boat. Angel and I kept our distance. She was huddled against me, clinging to my leg as I tried to walk. I have to admit, I was scared too. The feeling was very uneasy.

"Let's race again, Angel. You want to?"

"Yeah," Angel said, taking off running.

I was right behind her. We did not stop until we had reached our backyard.

"Look, look Mommy!" Angel shouted, pointing to the pond.

I turned around and could not believe my eyes. The boat was in the center of the pond going round and round. It looked like a whirlpool or a vortex of water draining from a sink. The wind was calm, and the water looked as slick as glass – everywhere except the middle of the pond. I looked to the top of the hill at the dogwood tree. It stood strong and beautiful, nothing out of place. I couldn't explain it, I'd never seen anything like that in my life.

"It's only the current in the water, Baby. Let's go in the house. I bet we can find some good cartoons for you. You can watch television while I make some phone calls."

"Okay Mommy," she said looking, back over her shoulder as we walked into the house.

Angel sat down in front of the television, and I went to the kitchen to use the phone. I called three of the four numbers Tina had given me.

As soon as they asked where I lived, they would say, "No thanks." They weren't interested.

I was getting so frustrated. I sat at the table tapping my finger, wondering if I should even bother calling the last number. I stared at the list for a few minutes. The fourth number belonged to a Mr. Jones. I picked up the phone.

"What the heck?" I said out loud. "He will either say 'yes' or 'no.'" So I dialed the number.

"The old Simmons house, huh," he said, as I explained what I wanted.

I was ready to hang up the phone. Removing it from my ear, I heard a loud voice reply . . .

"Sure, I can do it. It'll cost you two hundred dollars."

"Two hundred dollars!" I shouted. "It's only an acre, maybe less."

"Yeah, maybe more too. Two hundred dollars – you want it cut or not?"

"All right, when can you do it?" I asked.

"Noon, I'll see you today at noon."

I was shocked it was going to cost me two hundred dollars just to get a little grass cut. I hung up the phone and glanced out the back window. Startled, I jumped from my chair and ran out the back door. I was stunned: the boat had returned to the bank where Angel and I had first discovered it. I walked out to the porch and stared at it. How could it be possible? Was I losing my mind? Standing there dumbfounded, I heard Angel call out for me. I shook my head and sauntered into the house.

"What do you want, Angel?"

"Nothing," she answered, never looking my way.

"Why did you call me?"

"I didn't," she replied again, never looking up.

"What do you mean, you didn't? I heard you."

"Not me, Mom; it must have been Gary," she said, giggling at the cartoons.

"Gary's at school."

"Oh yeah, I don't know. I didn't hear them."

"I must have been hearing things."

"I guess so, Mom."

"Angel, who wrote that?" I shouted, pointing to the aquarium.

"Wrote what?" Angel slid around and looked. "I don't know," she shrugged her shoulders. "It was probably Gary."

"Why would Gary write something like that, Angel?"

"What does it say?"

"It's nothing for you to worry about, Honey. You just watch cartoons. I'll deal with Gary when he gets home. There is no sense in him doing stuff like that. I'm going to finish cleaning, and then we can have some lunch."

I walked over to the aquarium and stared at the words written in the moisture: "Help Me Please." I was so upset with Gary. Why would he write such a thing? Was he just taunting me? He would surely hear about it when he got home from school.

I began going on about my usual day, still unpacking the boxes, and engaging in the everyday ritual of finding the perfect place to put things. The time seemed to fly by. I got lost in my thoughts, constantly finding myself just sitting and daydreaming. I could not keep my mind from the haunted secrets that were bound in these walls.

Upon finding a box labeled "kitchen items," I picked it up with the intention of placing the much-needed items on the counter. Instantaneously, the clocked chimed 12:30 p.m. Startled by the unexpected sound, I dropped the box, and all my things scattered across the floor. Thank God, there were many towels protecting my breakables.

I then realized we had not eaten. I opened the fridge, grabbed some cold cuts, and quickly made some sandwiches. I called out to Angel to come sit at the table with me. We made small talk as we ate. She told me all about a cartoon she had just finished watching.

She was a lot like me. She would get caught up in the TV and drown out anything else. I smiled and listened to her every word. I loved to watch her expressions as she talked.

As soon as we finished lunch, we both went upstairs. It was time for her to take a nap. When we reached her room, the doorbell rang. I kissed her on the forehead, asked her to go to sleep, and told her I would wake her in an hour so we could go outside to play.

The doorbell rang over and over. I rushed down the steps, hitting my shin on a box at the bottom. I hobbled to the door, rubbing my leg as I went. When I opened it, I was at a loss for words; I forgot all about my pain. There stood a man with long black greasy hair that was plastered to his head. His T-shirt was two sizes too small; his fat belly was hanging over his raunchy, dirty pants. Judging from his odor, he had not bathed in days. His jaw was stuffed full of tobacco. He looked at me and smiled, exposing a hollowness that was missing his front teeth. The other teeth that were visible had brownish slimy tobacco juice stuck to them.

He spit on my front porch and said, "I'm Ray Jones, ma'am. I've come to cut your grass."

The bile rose in my throat; I swallowed hard and nodded my head.

"How are you doing, Ray? It's nice to meet you."

Before he could say another word, I quickly pointed to the hill, avoiding the customary handshake.

"That's what I want you to cut. Also, there's a hole under the edge of the tree up there. I see you have a blade on the front of your tractor; would you mind pushing some dirt in it for me?"

"No ma'am. I wouldn't mind," he said, spitting again and smiling.

"Thanks a lot, and I don't mean to be rude, but I am trying to get my daughter to take a nap. The doorbell rang just as soon as I got her to her bed. I really need to get back upstairs with her."

"So you have a little one living here, too?" he said, looking over my head inside the house.

"Yes I do. If you don't mind, go ahead and get started. I'll come out when she falls asleep."

"Don't mind a bit ma'am."

The repulsiveness of this man made me gag. I closed the door and covered my mouth to keep from getting sick.

I ventured back upstairs to check on Angel. She had already drifted off to sleep. Easing her door shut and creeping back downstairs, I anxiously went to the phone and dialed Tina's number.

"Hello Tina, this is Vivian. I called to thank you for the numbers you gave me."

"Well, did any of them work out for you?"

"Just one; I called all four, and only one would come."

"Don't tell me. Let me guess. I bet it was Ray, Ray Jones."

"You guessed right. When I opened the door, I could not believe what I was seeing. He's so, so, so . . . "

"I can finish that sentence for you. I know the word you're looking for: disgusting, gross, and stinky. Does that sum it up for you?"

"Yep, that about sums it up," I said laughing. "Why don't you come over for some tea? There are questions about this place that you may be able to help answer."

"I don't know about helping you find the right answer on that old place, although I will surely give you an honest one, right or wrong. I'll be over shortly. I have a few chores to do first."

I sat down at the kitchen table, watching Ray as his fat belly bounced over his pants. He rode back and forth, up and down, until all the grass was neatly cut and shaped. He ascended the hill and began pushing dirt in the hole. I watched until the last load of soil was released and packed tightly. I rushed upstairs to get my purse so I could pay him. Returning to the kitchen, I opened the back door to a surprising sight. There was smoke coming from beneath Ray's tractor. I did not know if it was on fire or what.

I ran toward the hill; the tractor was making a squealing high-pitched sound. The brake seemed to be stuck. The tires were not moving, however, it was sliding, descending straight toward the pond. Smoke was barreling from the back, from the sides; it was coming out from everywhere.

Ray was cussing and stomping on the brake. He reached down with his hand and tried to pull the pedal. It came to a sliding stop, turning itself around. He started driving back up the hill. All of a sudden, it stopped for a second time. The tires locked in place. They were spinning, although the machine was not moving. The tractor started to slide down the hill once more. Ray was pushing and pulling all kinds of gadgets, but it was not stopping that time. He began cursing, screaming and stomping his feet again. He was turning it off and back on, but nothing worked; it just kept plunging down the hill. Ray was looking over his shoulder as the heavy equipment raced toward the pond; it hit the water with a splash. Ray jumped off and landed in knee-deep water. The tractor kept going; it puttered a couple of times and then sank out of sight.

I ran over to him with great concern.

"What happened? Are you all right?" I asked.

He was huffing and puffing.

"Hell no, I am not all right. Do I look like I'm all right? Look what the hell happened. Does it look all right to you? I should have known better than to come to this Godforsaken place. I sure hope you have good insurance, cause you're going to need it, Lady. This hellhole is cursed with demons."

Ray walked around mumbling and kicking at the dirt. He spit out a mouth full of tobacco and turned to me. He took the back side of his hand and wiped his mouth. His nostrils flared; he was sucking and blowing the air. Then he spoke, "You have to be crazy as hell to live in this evil place. What's wrong with you? Are you possessed or something? I bet you called other people, and they wouldn't come. I should have known better myself. Everybody knows this place is haunted!"

In that moment, a squall of air blew the dirt right out of the hole from beneath dogwood tree, and the coarse granules rolled down the hill like tumbleweed. It slapped against Mr. Jones's backside like a raging bull. The gust of wind swirled around, encasing his body, stinging him from head to toe. I shifted away, although there was nothing touching me.

Ray started to run to his truck, stumbling and falling like someone was pushing him. I called to him. He had forgotten his money, but the only thing he was worried about was escaping from the invisible foe. He jumped into his truck, spun his wheels, and out of my driveway he went — never looking back. The flatbed trailer fishtailed, almost flipping over, as he sped away.

"Was that Ray?"

I turned around. It was Tina.

"Yes it was," I answered. "I guess my ghost didn't like him. Did you see what happened?"

"Yeah," she said laughing. "I didn't know that fat thing could even walk fast, let alone run. This will be the talk of the town for sure now. When Ray finishes telling this story, people are going to be scared to death of you. They'll whisper as you walk by, 'That's the witch lady.'"

"If they are going to talk, we might as well give them something to talk about. And this was surely something to talk about."

"By the looks of things, I would guess you to be right. Your ghost did not like him," Tina said, looking down at the tractor that was covered by water.

"I don't know how he is going to get it out of there."

"Get it out! Girl that man ain't coming back here. That tractor is here to stay. It's your property now. You'll get your bill in the mail.

Believe me, he will bill your insurance."

"Well, I guess that's why we have it. Come on in the house. I'll fix you a glass of tea and we can talk. I have some things I want to ask you."

Tina followed me into the kitchen, pulled a chair out and sat down at the table.

"So what's up? What kind of things do you want to ask me?"

"To begin with, why does the path between your house and mine look like it's been used frequently? You said no one ever came here. Someone had to be using that path in the woods."

"Oh, old man Jesse did. He walked this way two or three times a week. He made sure everything was kept real neat."

"Who is old man Jesse?" I asked.

"He was the caretaker. You really don't know anything about this place, do you?"

"I told you I didn't. I was told a black man took care of it, although I didn't know why or who he was. Where does he live, and why did he keep it up?"

"The slaves that lived here were his ancestors. From what I was told, a member of his family has always taken care of this place."

"Why? And I thought you said everyone had disappeared including the slaves?"

"I'm not really sure just who his ancestors were. I asked him one time why he always came out here and worked. He answered by saying, 'So the spirits won't get lost.'"

"So the spirits won't get lost; what does that mean?" I asked.

"I'm the wrong person to be asking. I always thought he was crazy as hell."

"Do you know where he lives?"

"Yeah, about a mile on the other side of me."

"Can we go there? Would you mind taking me to talk to him?"

"I don't mind. Just tell me when."

"Now! I'd like to go now," I said excitedly. "Let me wake Angel and we can go. I mean, if that's all right with you."

"I have nothing else to do. Go get Angel up and let's go."

"Do you think Mr. Jesse would mind? What kind of person is he? Is he friendly?"

"Jesse? He's a nice old man. He's quiet, polite and strange. He must be 80 years old, and sometimes I think he's a little senile."

I was all excited. I ran upstairs to wake Angel. When I walked into her room, she was sitting on the edge of her bed.

"Did you have a nice nap, Honey?" I asked.

Angel sat rubbing her eyes not answering me.

"Come on, Angel, Miss Tina is downstairs. She's going to take us to see a friend of hers."

"Why was she crying, Mommy?"

"Crying? No one was crying."

"I heard a lady crying, but I couldn't see her. I don't know where she was. It sounded like she was in my room, I looked, but she wasn't there."

"It was probably the television, Honey. It was turned up very loud. Come on, let's hurry. Gary will be home soon."

I rushed Angel downstairs. I was anxious to meet the stranger who might have some family history here. Perhaps he would know what had happen so many years ago.

Driving down the road, I was thinking of all the things I wanted to know. I was trying to get them in order in my mind. There was so much I didn't know, and there were so many secrets. I couldn't wait to get there.

"This is it," Tina said, turning into a driveway.

"Oh, I'm so excited," I said, unbuckling my seat belt.

Mr. Jesse lived in a small old wooden framed house. The wood was bare, unleveled, and seemed to have shifted on its foundation. It looked primitive, but very neat and clean. There was a huge oak tree that shaded the entire house, several cats, a couple of dogs, a mule tied to a tree, and an old man sitting in a rocker on the wooden porch.

"How ya doing, Mr. Jesse?" Tina yelled out. She turned to me and whispered, "He's a little hard of hearing."

He rose from his chair like a gentleman and nodded his head.

"I doin' jest fine, Miss Tina. Real hot t'day, dough."

Mr. Jesse had a strong Southern drawl, but it was kind of neat to listen to it.

"Mr. Jesse, this is Vivian and her daughter, Angel."

He reached his hand out. "Nice meetin' ya, ma'am, an' da lil' one."

He looked down at Angel and smiled.

"Mr. Jesse, I hate to bother you, but I was wondering if you could answer some questions for me."

"No botta, I ain't doin' nuttin' but sittin.' C'mon up on da porch, and pull up a chair. Deese old legs won't let me stand too long. What kinda questions ya got? Questions bout what?" he asked sitting back to his rocker.

"I just moved into the old house at Dogwood Plantation. It seems I know very little about that place, and Tina tells me you have always taken care of it. I was wondering if you could tell me why."

"Cause my fam'ly lived dare long time ago. I promise my motter I'd keep an eye out fo' it, and I'd take care of it, my fatter promised hims motter 'fore me. We do dat fo' da mem'ry of our loved ones dare. I gots too old ta do it lately, so my churen do it now."

"My ancestors built the plantation, and I know nothing about them or what happened to everyone. I was hoping you could tell me."

He gave me an intense look, not saying a word. His head shook, his eyes filled with anger, and his wobbling legs brought him to a stance.

Leaning close to my face, a crackling voice shouted, "Get out! I wan' ya off my prop'ty now, no Simmons ever step foots heah. Dis be my land, leave, I trow ya off if ya don't."

Startled by his demeanor, I started backing off the porch.

"Excuse me, what did I say?"

"Cuse ya? Ain't no cus'n yo' kind. Get out a heah!"

"Mr. Jesse, what's wrong?" Tina asked.

"How dares ya bring her kind ta dis heah house," the raging voice shouted. "Don't come back, ya hears me," shaking his finger and yelling at us.

I grabbed Angel's hand and started toward the car.

"Missy," he called out. "Don't let da churen ta da pond. Ya keep 'ems from dat deres pond. Ya hears me?"

"Yes sir, can you tell me why?" There was no reply. He just turned, walked into the house, and closed the door behind him.

"I thought you said he was a nice old man, Tina."

"I've never seen him talk to anyone like that before. You really pissed him off."

"What did I say wrong?"

"It had to have been your relatives. Evidently, he doesn't like them."

"Evidently," I said, as we headed back home. "I wonder what he could be so angry about."

"I don't know, and I don't think you're going to find out either. If you do, it won't be from him."

"I will find out somehow, but I think you're right: it won't be from him."

Tina dropped us off at our house. I went in and started preparing dinner, not understanding what I said that made Jesse so mad. "There must be someone else who would know what happened here, but who? I am more curious now than I was before," I said out loud.

"Mr. Issy does," Angel said as she was setting the table.

"What?" I asked.

"Mr. Issy. He lived here a long time ago."

"Angel, Mommy already told you, Mr. Issy isn't real."

"He is real, Mommy," Angel said in a demanding voice.

"What's real?" asked Gary, walking into the kitchen, just getting home from school.

"Mr. Issy," answered Angel.

"Oh, we're talking about your imaginary friend, again. If he's real, how come no one else can see him?" asked Gary in a sarcastic manner.

"Cause, he don't want you to, that's why," Angel said, sticking her tongue out at Gary.

"Okay you two, that's quite enough. Let's try to have a peaceful evening together. I've had a very rough day, and I don't feel like hearing all this bickering. Now both of you go wash up, and let's have dinner."

"Wait a minute, Gary," I called out. "I have something to show you."

"I didn't do anything, Mom."

"Come into the library, I want to know why you wrote that." I pointed to the aquarium. Gary looked around and then back at me.

"What are you talking about, Mom? Wrote what?"

I turned and looked. I walked over to the aquarium, and there wasn't anything on it.

"It had some words on it this morning. Angel must have wiped them off. Did you write them?"

"No," Gary said sternly. "Why would I write on the aquarium? What did it say?"

"It said, 'Help me please.' I know you had to have written it, because Angel doesn't know how to write. There is no one else here but me, and I know I didn't do it."

"So maybe it was your ghosts," Gary replied.

"Don't get smart with me, Gary. Just don't do it again."

"Mom, I swear I didn't do it; maybe it was Angel's Mr. Issy."

"No it wasn't. Mr. Issy can't come into the house," Angel said as she walked through the door.

"He can't come into the house? That's dumb. How come he can't come into the house?" Gary asked.

"I don't know. Sometimes he comes into the yard, but most of the time, he stays on the hill. He says he can't come down here for very long."

"That's really stupid, Angel. I told you he wasn't real. No one could stay in one place all the time. If he were real, he could go anywhere he wanted," Gary laughed.

"He is real!" Angel shouted. "Mom, tell Gary Mr. Issy is real."

"I think he is real to you, Honey, but if no one else can see him, I must agree with Gary."

"I told you," Gary said, slapping Angel on the back of her head as he walked by.

Angel cried out. "Owee!"

"Gary, I will not have you hitting your sister. You tell her you're sorry, and I don't want you to ever hit her again."

"I barely tapped her."

"It doesn't matter; you should not have put your hands on her at all. Tell her you are sorry."

"I'm sorry," he said abruptly.

Angel crinkled her nose up at him and laughed.

"You know what? I think after dinner you two can spend the evening together – just the two of you. I don't care if you watch television, play a game, or just sit looking at each other. You will get along with each other, or you'll go straight to bed. If I even hear one more unkind word, both of you will go to bed without dinner. Is that understood?"

"But Mom, I wanted ..."

"It doesn't matter what you wanted, Gary; I want you and Angel to get along. If you can do that tonight, then you can do what you want tomorrow. If you don't get along, you will spend every night playing together. Now go wash up. Both of you can start your togetherness at dinner. If one more word is said, you will wash dishes too."

Gary stood there for a minute staring at me, but he knew I was serious. I had a lot on my mind, and I had had enough bickering. After washing up, they served their plates and sat down to eat. Everyone was quiet for a change at the dinner table.

After dinner, I went into the library to sit and relax. I couldn't get Mr. Jesse off my mind. He was so angry with me, and I just couldn't understand why. He had to know something about the house. I thought something terrible must have happened here, but what? The rumors have to be wrong because we both are descendants. If everyone had vanished as they say, where did we come from? I settled back on the sofa and watched the fish swim around the aquarium. I was very tired and getting sleepy. I could feel my head bobbing and my body relaxing, as I kept drifting in and out of sleep. My eyes were fighting to stay open; it was a lost battle. So I lay my head back and gave in. As my eyes closed, I could feel myself slipping away into a deep sleep. Everything was quiet as I entered my dream world. Soon, I could hear someone talking to me, so I answered.

"What do you mean you're lost? I don't know where you are. Okay, I'm looking for you, and I don't see you, this is not funny ... Why are you crying? You're lost, lost where? How can I help you? I have already told you, I don't know where to find you. Where do you think you are? No, I cannot see you. I'm looking. I can hardly hear you. Wait! Your voice is too low; I can't hear you anymore. Don't go! Tell me where you are, please, don't go!"

"Mom, Mom! Wake up!"

I opened my eyes to see Gary and Angel standing over me. I jumped off the sofa.

"Where is she?" I screamed. "Did you see her?"

"Did we see who, Mom?" Gary asked.

"The lady was whispering that she was lost. She wanted me to find her," I said, walking around the living room.

"Mom, you were asleep; you were dreaming. Angel and I heard you talking. That's why we came in here — to see who you were talking to. When we walked in, you were talking in your sleep. There was no one else here."

"I was not asleep," I snapped.

"Whatever you say, Mom, but we're finished with the kitchen. What would you like us to do now?"

"Nothing," I looked around the living room. I could not believe what he was saying. It seemed so real, but the kids were staring at me like I was crazy.

"Okay, maybe it was a dream, and I'm sorry for snapping at you. It just felt as though I was awake. If you'd like to watch television or play a game, you may. I'm going upstairs to turn in early tonight; I'm very tired. Make sure you turn the lights off before you come up."

"Yes ma'am," they both replied.

I staggered up the stairs and sluggishly retired to my room.

Closing the door behind me, I leaned against it and closed my eyes. I felt insane — like I was really losing it.

Drowsy and half-eyed, I made my way out to the balcony, staring at the tree with the assumption that it held all the answers. What was it trying to divulge to me? Could I have been dreaming when I was lying on the sofa? Was anyone crying for help? I was so confused and exhausted from trying to make sense of it all. Maybe I just needed a good night's sleep. The house had so many strange occurrences, I knew something was not right, but what? I asked myself if this place really could have spirits hovering about. I wasn't sure.

I was lying across my bed wondering if someone was lost in the house, trapped between worlds, and if so — why and who could it be? I wished my mother or father had told me something about the plantation. I knew the townspeople were somewhat right: the place was haunted by something or someone. I really didn't feel like we were in any danger. It was more like someone was watching over us.

Often there was a sad feeling, a feeling of loneliness and emptiness. Some rooms felt cold when I entered them. Sometimes I could catch a glimpse of someone standing behind me, but when I turned my head, no one was there. Lights turned off and on by themselves, the alarm clock went off in the middle of the night, and then there were the voices, those strange, spine-chilling voices.

There were just too many inexplicable events. The only time I felt real happiness was on the hill; sitting under that beautiful tree was so peaceful. When I was feeling sad, I could go there and feel better. When I missed Jim, I would go sit on the hill, and it would seem like he was right there beside me, loving all over me. It was magical. I felt as if a spirit had possessed me.

I closed my eyes, smiled, and drifted away …

Startled by the alarm clock, I was surprised that it was 5 a.m. Despite all that was on my mind, I had slept very peacefully all night. No one or nothing strange had disturbed me. The last thing I remembered was trying to determine what was real and what wasn't. What if my uneasiness was detected and all the spirits left? Maybe they were my ancestors and they did not want to upset me. Maybe they thought I'd move.

"What if they've gone for good?" I said aloud, suddenly sitting straight up. "What if I never find out? I have to know. They can't leave me now. This is crazy, I'm crazy, and what am I thinking? Get a grip," I said to myself.

My eyes wandered around my room for a few minutes. I stretched and got out of bed. My morning chores were starting over. I had my shower, cooked breakfast, and drove the kids to school. Gary's teacher had recommended a daycare program for Angel, and fortunately, there was an opening. Angel was excited to be going to her own school. Leaving her there was very hard, harder than I had anticipated. She was my baby, and I knew even though she would be gone for just a few hours, I was going to miss her.

I walked her in and introduced myself to her teacher. Surprisingly, there were no remarks about who we were or where we lived. Of course, the teacher fell in love with Angel immediately, and that made it a little easier to leave.

Getting back home, I did the same old same daily house chores. I thought about Angel frequently as I watched the clock tick away. I hope she was enjoying her new school and making new friends.

It was the middle of the day, the kids were in school, and I had the whole house to myself. I decided to take a walk around the property to enjoy the peace and beauty that it offered.

I strolled through the garden, picked a few flowers, and worked my way to the hill. Feeling drawn to the natural beauty of the tree, I knew it needed me as much as I needed it. Visions of my unknown ancestors clouded my mind. Wandering around the pond, smelling my flowers, I noticed something at the edge of the water. Eager to find out what it was, I tried to evaluate it from the bank. At first, I was hesitant to get too close. I remembered Mr. Jesse's warning, but I had to see what it was.

Slowly easing myself down the embankment, I slipped off my shoes and stuck one foot into the murky water. Feeling around the bottom with my toes, I felt sand, so I stuck my other foot in. Sliding myself to the object and stretching my leg out, I touched it with my toe. As I stood in ankle deep water, this thing, whatever it was, was still about knee deep. I glanced around for a stick or something long that I could use pull it out, but nothing was in sight. Carefully, I started toward it, easing ever so slowly into deeper waters. Cautiously, I reached my hand down and quickly plucked it out. It was a teddy bear, a very old teddy bear. I tossed it to the bank.

Not taking the time to examine the saturated toy, I scurried to get out. Reaching the edge of the bank, there was a tug at my feet. Something was pulling me back in. The sandy bottom had turned into a muddy nightmare. It had a hold on my feet and I couldn't get loose; I began to sink. I tried desperately to pick up my feet, but I was unsuccessful. I screamed, but no one came. As I struggled to get free, I just kept sinking deeper; it was like quicksand. The more I fought, the further I sunk. My eyes were frantically searching, but no one was there; I began to cry.

All of a sudden, a gust of wind exploded across my face. I quickly turned my head. When I did, I could not believe what I saw. The dogwood tree was shaking furiously; the white blossoms were coming to my rescue again. Crazy, that was what I was thinking, but no matter how crazy it sounds, it was what I thought. I felt relief as the flowers encircled me.

The water was up to my chest, and I was still sinking. "Help me," I cried looking toward the tree. The tree shook, and as the water got deeper, I screamed louder. I called for Tina, Mr. Jesse, anyone who might hear me, but no one came. Thrashing my arms wildly only caused me to sink deeper; the water had reached my chin. I knew I was going to drown.

My thoughts turned to my children – how much I loved them and the fact that I would never see them again. Tears rolled from my eyes and fell into the dark water. I tilted my head back and gave one last cry for help. My body sank another inch, completely submerging into the mud and the black water.

I began to wonder if I would ever be found. If it was quicksand, how deep would I go? Would I just disappear out of sight? Then I thought about the plantation people. *Could this be what had happened to them? Was this why they were never found?* I was totally hysterical to know my fate would be the same. I would join my ancestors in the depths of darkness, never to be found or heard from again.

As the water completely covered my face, I could see in the distance a man and a little girl in a boat. Holding my arm in the air, I tried to motion for them by waving it back and forth. They mysteriously vanished before my eyes. I saw two black men holding up what appeared to have been a white man, but they too vanished. I could see a man standing in the distance under the dogwood tree – just standing, watching me sink deeper. Why would he not help me? Is this the person I've been seeing and feeling? Is he some spirit that wants me to join him?

I felt a quick jerk at my feet; my eyes wide open, filled with fear, I quickly sank. I knew no one could see me. My fingertips were barely visible as I held my arm up as high as it would go. I held my breath until my lungs felt like they would explode. I was hoping the people in the boat, the two men in the water, the spirits, or whatever they were would come save me. Of course, they did not.

Then slowly, one breath at a time, one bubble after another, all the air escaped from my body. I closed my eyes and prepared for my fate; a peace came over me as I felt myself go limp.

CHAPTER 5

A SHRINK

Coughing, gagging, and choking, I awoke lying face down on the bank of the pond, covered in mud and slime from the murky water. I rolled over, brushed my hair from my face, and sat up. Still coughing and trying to catch my breath, I looked for the person who had pulled me to safety. I did not see anyone.

"Help me," I hoarsely cried, vomiting water and mud from my lungs. I was hoping my rescuer would hear me and return.

No one came. I sat alone and scared, trying to recover from my near-death experience. My teeth filled with grit; I ran my tongue around them and spit the nasty taste from my mouth. I reached for my shoes and staggered to my feet. As I stumbled in the direction of my house, I kept looking around, searching for my savior. There were no signs of anyone — no footprints or anything. I just could not understand how or why they would save me and just leave me alone.

I walked back to the house dazed and confused. Dragging myself up the stairs, I made my way in for a long hot shower. Closing my eyes, I tried to focus on the face of the man in the boat, but it remained blurred. Who could have saved me?

I needed to talk to someone, so after my shower, I hurried downstairs to call Tina. When she answered the phone, I burst into tears.

"Tina," I cried. "Can you please come over?"

"What's wrong? Are you all right?"

"Yes, but I'm shaken and very upset. I need a sympathetic friend. Can you just come over?"

"I'm on my way."

That was all she said. There was not a goodbye or anything; she just hung up the phone. I rinsed my mouth and spit the remainder of grime from my throat. There appeared to be an endless supply in my mouth.

Sitting down at the table, head in hands, I waited for Tina to arrive. Even though she could not do anything, I thought just having someone with me would help. Although it was only minutes, it seemed like forever before she approached my back door.

"Damn! What happened to you?"

I sat there shaking, tears streaming down my cheek as I looked up at her. "I'm still a little shaken up, but I think I'll be fine."

"Damn girl, you look more than shook up, you look like you've been scared to death. What the hell happened to you?"

"I'm not sure, I was at the pond."

"That damn pond again, huh? Didn't Mr. Jesse tell you to stay away from the pond?"

"Yeah, you're right, he did," I said, surprised. "I had forgotten all about that."

"Not only him, what about the incident with Angel in the boat?"

"I just wasn't thinking."

"I'll say, what happened this time?" Tina asked as she pulled out a kitchen chair.

"I saw something submerged at the edge of the water, and I went in to get it. The next thing I knew, I was being sucked in."

"Sucked in? What do you mean sucked in?"

"I don't know, it was like quicksand. It had such powerful suction, I couldn't get loose. Even though I was screaming for help from the top of my lungs, no one came."

"Well, that's not surprising out here. Who in the hell did you think was going to hear you?"

"Evidently someone did."

"What? Someone heard you? Who?"

"I don't know. The last thing I remember was seeing a boat with an old man and a little girl in it, and I saw two black men carrying a white man. I sank completely out of sight, actually I had drowned, and my body went limp. The next thing I recall, I was on the bank of the pond all alone, choking and vomiting."

"You mean someone just pulled you out and left? Who were the people in the boat, and what were they doing? Did you give anyone permission to go fishing?"

"No I didn't. I haven't got a clue who they were. They never acknowledged that I was even there. I'm not even sure they were real," I said in a very soft voice.

"What do you mean, they weren't real?"

I put my elbows on the table and my head back into my hands. "They didn't help me. If they were real, wouldn't they have helped me? I'm beginning to think I'm losing my mind."

"Well, someone helped you. It had to be them, but I can't believe they just left you there."

"I know, but they did. A real person would have stayed with me, don't you think?"

"Maybe they were trespassing and didn't want you to catch them. At least they got you out. That's all that matters. It would be nice to know who they were, huh?"

"It would be very nice."

"Perhaps Mr. Jesse came back by," Tina said. "He surely would not want you to catch him here after the way he acted."

"I doubt it was Mr. Jesse. He's very old and weak, and definitely not strong enough to pull me out. I'm telling you it was like quicksand. There was suction on my feet. I could not move. There is no way Mr. Jesse could have pulled me free."

"Well, who do you think it was, your ghost?" Tina said laughing.

I turned and stared at her, hesitating for a moment.

"Yes," I answered. "Yes, I do. I know you think I'm insane, and I'm not sure you're wrong. I think whoever has been watching me from the hill saved me."

"Watching you from the hill. Someone has been watching you from the hill?"

"Yes, I see him at night from my balcony. I told you about him."

"I didn't know you had seen it, him, whatever, more than one time. How often do you see him?"

"Just now and then – things seem so strange around here, it's hard to determine what is real and what isn't. I know there is something not right in this house, but I'm not sure what."

I turned and stared out at the woods through the windowpane.

"Do you think? I mean . . . is it possible . . . could this place really have spirits floating about? I know it sounds crazy, I'm beginning to believe it holds many haunted secrets, but whose secrets?"

"Probably your ancestors."

"I don't feel like we're in any danger. Like I told you before, sitting under that beautiful tree is so very peaceful. When I miss Jim, I go sit on the hill, and it seems like he is right there beside me, loving all over me. I can feel Jim's hands, as they slowly move over me . . . and his lips kissing my neck, his hot breath moving slowly down . . . "

"Oh, I think I get the picture," Tina interrupted. My face reddened with embarrassment as I was describing my experience to Tina. I had gotten lost in my own little world, not realizing what I was saying until she interrupted me.

"It sounds more to me like you need a man, or either you are pursued by a horny male ghost. I tell you what, if a ghost made me feel like you said he does you, I'd never leave the damn hill. I would lay up there all day long, night too, if he kept me warm enough," Tina said laughing. "If you get tired of him bring him to my house. I could use some of that loving."

"Yeah, right."

"Look here, all kidding aside, you better be careful going up there, especially all alone."

"I'll be fine."

"I don't want to be stepping out of line because I don't really know you that well, but you might need to see someone for help."

"What kind of help – you mean like an exorcist? You think someone would come to my house and do that? I mean, do they really perform exorcisms?"

Tina raised her eyebrows and just stared at me for a minute. "No Honey, I wasn't thinking exorcist. I was thinking more like . . . a shrink. I don't mean to imply anything, but things are getting out of hand here. You need to get a grip on reality. You said yourself you are not sure what's real and what isn't."

I just looked away. I was embarrassed and furious, but I did not want her to know it.

"Maybe you're right, it gives me something to consider anyway.

This could just be all in my head."

"Well, I've got to go. I have some chores I have to do. If you need me, you call. You'll be all right, won't you?"

"I will. Thanks, Tina."

I stood at the door and watched Tina walk around the pond. She went quickly, not loitering at all, and never taking her eyes off the water. She must have believed some of what I was saying or she would not have been so cautious. She knew something strange was happening there. I observed her stride get faster as she hurried along and quickly disappeared into the dense pine forest.

I sat at the table sipping on a glass of ice tea, mind-boggled about what had happened to me. I kept trying to recall how I got out of the mud, but my mind drew a blank. I could only remember being in the water. There was no recollection of how I got out.

Maybe Tina was right; I might need some professional help. I thought perhaps someone could put me under hypnosis, and then I could find out what was going on.

"What about Jim? I haven't told him any of this. What if he thought I was going off the deep end? I have got to get a grip and stay focused. Maybe I just need some time away from this house," I determined. I picked up my car keys and went for a drive.

My eyes were on the winding road, but the bizarre events dominated my thoughts as they replayed in my mind. I thought going shopping might help release some tension; it normally made me feel better. Little did I know, it was about to get worse.

I walked around the small supermarket and felt like I was some kind of exhibit. People pointed and whispered as I passed by. Although I was a stranger to the town, everyone sure seemed to know who I was.

I guessed it was true what I had heard about living in a small town – everyone knows everyone – except the newcomers who could be considered such for decades. I must have stood out like a sore thumb, as I became the center of attention. Men and women drew their bodies inward and seemed to hug the walls as I approached. I was beginning to wonder if I was imagining this too.

I finally had enough of the snarled mouths and raised eyebrows, so, being the person that I am, the person I have to be, I gave the town something to talk about. No one really knew me there, but they were surely going to get a revelation and a lasting memory. I have never been one to keep my mouth shut, and I was too old to start then. They did not really know me when I got here, but they would damn sure not forget me when I left.

Standing in line at the soda fountain, I heard someone whisper, "That's her; she's a witch. She's possessed by the ghosts of Dogwood Plantation. I heard she talks to the dead."

I stood still and glared at the lady for a moment. Then I couldn't resist. I couldn't take any more; the devil made me do it. I politely turned around, walked over to where she was standing, and leaped onto the counter. I threw my arms in the air and shouted, "You're right; you all are right. Many ghosts who live in my house possess me. I walk with them, sleep with them, and eat with them. I must add that they are much better company than I have seen here. They are kind and have a great sense of humor, much more than I can say about any of you. They also entertain me all day, and, if I may also add, they have taught me well. If y'all keep irritating me, I will cast a demonic spell upon you too."

I heard a lady laugh behind me. I jumped down from the counter and strutted over to her. I stretched my big brown eyes as wide as they would go and stared into her face. She leaned her head back away from me. I could see the fright in her eyes. I slowly reached up and grabbed her head, and I pulled her toward me. She was pushing on my shoulders trying to get free. I just held on tight, pulled her to me and kissed her. I couldn't think of anything else to do. I just kissed her. I wiped my lips, smiled, and then slowly, I turned and left the store.

Everyone watched. No one said a word. Chins dropped, leaving mouths wide open as I sauntered past and closed the door behind me.

I chuckled under my breath getting into my car. Driving down the road, I beat on the steering wheel, and laughed aloud about what I had just done. I could not believe I kissed that woman.

"Talk about giving the town something to talk about," I said aloud.

I could not quit laughing, and I felt so much better. All my tension was gone. I drove on to Angel's daycare and picked her up. Then I went to Gary's school and signed him out a little early.

"What's going on Mom? How come you picked me up early?" Gary asked.

"I thought we would spend some time together, just the three of us."

"So where are we going?" Angel asked.

"Oh, I don't know. How about the beach?" I said reaching over and tickling her.

"The beach!" Gary exclaimed.

"Yes, the beach. Let's go look for some seashells by the sea shore. Let's watch the beautiful sun set upon the water. Let's listen to the waves. Let's . . . "

"All right, already," Gary interrupted. "We get the picture. Are you okay, Mom?" Gary asked.

"Yes Gary, I am fine. Actually, I have not felt this good in a long time. I think we all need a relaxing break, and what better place to relax than the beach?"

"Can we go swimming?" Angel asked.

"Not today, Honey. We don't have bathing suits, and it's still a little cool to go into the water. Let's grab a bucket of chicken and have a picnic."

"Yeah," Angel shouted.

"Yeah," I said, softly agreeing with her.

The kids and I sat on the shore and watched the waves come crashing down. I loved watching a surge of water pushing the sand beneath, tumbling it over and over. Then, like a huge vacuum, the ocean would suck it back, grasping hold, reclaiming its belongings, and pulling them back to sea.

The warm soft breeze surrounded us with a salty scent of the ocean. We all three lay silently together on a blanket. We watched the sea gulls soar above us within arm's reach. They screeched, calling to one another in their own secret language, darting down occasionally to grab a crumb.

After relaxing and enjoying the peaceful atmosphere, I joined the children the in the sand. For hours, we played together. We built a tremendous sand castle and played make-believe. It was a place that we became the kings and queens.

As the tide came in and swallowed up our make-believe home, we took a long stroll on the quiet beach to pick up shells. We played, kicking the cold water on one another, running back and forth, splashing up and down. The water was so cold, I had not planned to get wet — but sometimes these things are irresistible.

We ran back to our blanket. The sand dunes seemed to have an endless supply of the coarse particles and didn't mind sharing them a bit. We picked up the corner of the blanket and shook it furiously. Quickly, we laid it back in place, spreading it out, and simultaneously we jumped on and huddled closely. The sun felt so good beaming down on our wet bodies. Enjoying the warmth, listening to the waves crashing on top of the water, it was not long before Angel drifted to sleep.

Gary and I talked about school and the move to the little town. He was finally starting to fit in. Our conversation faded with the sun as the it slid behind the sea. Sitting quietly, we watched as the big orange ball mirrored across the ocean, making the blue surface a product of its own imagination and then hiding behind the blanket of water.

I lifted Angel into my arms while Gary collected our things. I was hesitant to leave, but I had to acknowledge that it was time for us to go home. I did so knowing we had found a place where tranquility was ours, and we were always welcome. We left that day with total peace and contentment.

CHAPTER 6

THE HIDDEN ROOMS

I tried to keep focused and busy. There was a lot of work to do in that big house, and I was determined to get it done. I finally had painters scheduled for the following week. Jim was right; it was going to cost a fortune to fix it up. The price always doubled when they found out it was Dogwood Plantation. It seemed the whole town thought our house was haunted. People said it had a curse on it, and no one wanted to come near us. I did believe it was haunted with a restless spirit. I was not sure whose it was, but I was sure it was someone from the past who had not crossed over.

Several times throughout the week, the lights turned on and off, the TV channel changed by itself and the stove turned off while I was in the middle of cooking. I tried to convince myself it was an electrical problem; even the alarm clock would go off in the middle of the night, and it was battery operated. I still tried to make excuses.

Sitting on my bed, unpacking boxes, I missed my husband terribly. I could hardly wait to see him; he was expected at any moment. It felt like he had been gone for months instead of a week. I wanted to tell him about the strange sequence of events that had taken place – things I was sure he wasn't going to believe.

Out of everything that had happened, the incident with Mr. Jesse bothered me the most. Why did he dislike my family so much? How could he hate me, especially for something I knew nothing about? Whatever my family did, it had nothing to do with me. It had to have been at least a hundred years ago. I wondered how he seemed to know so much about them. Did he really know anything, or was it just gossip too? What could possibly be bad enough to inspire such animosity for so many years? I was determined to find a way to get him to tell me. I had to win him over. I needed to think of plan.

I thought about the library in the town. It would have old newspapers and records of different places and events that had occurred over the years. Downtown Charleston had plenty of history; there had to be some answers there.

"Old records, that's it! I can't believe I didn't think of this before now." I got excited for a minute, but that was quickly interrupted. I heard Gary calling for me.

"Mom!" Gary shouted. "Mom!"

"I'm coming, Gary. What's wrong?" I yelled back.

"Dad's home."

I ran down the stairs and out of the front door. I felt like a teenager waiting for my first date; I was all excited and giggly. We all ran out to his car to greet him. When he stepped out, the kids and I were all over him.

"Whoa! What did I do to deserve this kind of welcome?"

"We missed you, Daddy," Angel said holding on to his pant leg.

"Yeah Dad, we missed you. So what did you bring us?" Gary asked, walking in front of us carrying Jim's suitcase.

"Bring you? So that is what this welcome is all about?"

"Yeah Daddy, what did you bring us?" Angel asked looking up at Jim.

"I may have a little something for you, go look. It's in my suitcase in a bag."

The kids ran ahead to get their surprise.

"What about you, my little lady? Do you just want to know what I brought you too?"

"No, I have what I want right here: my wonderful, big strong husband. I have missed you so much; it's just great that you're home," I said, kissing him all over his face.

"So living out here in the woods does this to you?"

"Baby, you just don't know what living out here does to me."

"What's that supposed to mean?"

"I'll tell you later."

"I can't wait!"

We went inside to find the kids with their surprises. Jim had brought

Angel a new doll from Spain and Gary, a real sword. They examined them from top to bottom. They wanted to know everything about his trip, so we all sat down and started exchanging stories.

Gary talked about a couple of so-called tough boys that he had made friends with at school. He said he was very surprised to find out how tough these kids were in the country, but a few boys were all right.

Angel talked about all the animals she had learned. She started going into detail about the different kinds of birds we had living in the trees. I was glad to know she really was paying attention and remembered what I had told her. She also told Jim about her new school.

I snuck off to take my shower while Jim talked with the children. They filled him in on what he had missed. And, of course Gary had to let him know Angel still had her imaginary friend. Then of course, that started another argument. I could hear them bickering back and forth. Jim finally had heard enough.

"Okay, I think it's time for you to go to bed," he said. "We can discuss everything else in the morning. Come on, upstairs. Let's go."

Jim tucked Angel into bed. He told Gary since it was Friday night, he could stay up for a while, just not too late. Everyone had a lot to do in the morning. He closed Angel's door and came to our room.

"Oooh, la, la," Jim said.

I lay stretched across our bed in my white sheer negligee, showing off the shapely figure I tried so desperately to keep. My long brown hair was perfectly arranged all around me. The balcony doors were open; a soft warm breeze carried the aroma of my perfume. The flames of the candles danced, flickering in the dark.

"Is all this for me?"

"All this and more," I answered, pulling him to me.

Jim eased himself down on me, kissing every inch as he went. I devoured every breath, every touch that swept across my body. He stood back up and started removing his clothes. His muscular body looked so strong and hard. He slowly lifted my gown, dragging his tongue up my body as he went. I quivered with excitement. He lay down slowly on top of me. My hands caressed him tightly as he went. I wanted to feel his flesh – to dig my fingers deep into him. I had to know he was really there – that it was not my imagination.

The tighter I gripped, the more excited he got. I rolled over and got on top of him. Slowly, I sat up and started to ride, slow and easy, up and down. I wanted to see his face, to look into his eyes, hear every moan of pleasure he had to release. I did not want to miss anything — his voice, his touch, and most of all, his face.

I watched as the ecstasy rose in his body. His muscles bulged and twitched with pleasure. Perspiration covered our bodies as our passion escalated. We could not get enough of each other. We made love for hours that night. It was like the very first time. Every touch, every kiss, and every moan was filled with passion. Nothing missed, nothing taken for granted. Jim knew every secret button of my body, and he pushed them all. It was great having him home. I wanted to know he was there. And I did.

We filled each other with love, lust and ecstasy all night. I had not felt so satisfied, so complete, in weeks. I slept like a baby.

The next morning, waking up in Jim's arms was wonderful. I gently kissed his lips to wake him up.

"Good morning," he said smiling.

"Good morning," I replied with a smile.

"Whatever happened while I was gone this time, I hope it happens again."

"What do you mean?" I asked.

"What do I mean? Last night, Babe, you were great! You haven't made love to me like that in, in, well really, I don't think you ever made love to me like that. Are you sure you were making love to me, and not pretending it was someone else?"

"What is that supposed to mean?" I asked angrily.

"Hey, I was kidding. Why are you so snappy?"

"I'm sorry, Jim, there have been a lot of things happening here lately, things that can't be explained. I'm just tense, and I've missed you so much," I said kissing him again.

"I can tell," he said, returning my kiss. "I might leave again tomorrow if I can get another welcome like that one last night."

"Not a chance. You are not going anywhere."

"So the old man hasn't lost his touch, huh?"

"I don't see an old man. If you are talking about you, not at all, Baby, not at all."

I wanted to tell Jim about my ghost, but I was not sure how. I did not want him to laugh at me, or think I was crazy, but I had to tell him.

"Jim, I have to tell you something. There has been a lot of stuff going on around here since you've been gone," I said as I rolled out of bed.

"Stuff, define stuff."

"Well, I've been hearing things and seeing things." I proceeded to tell Jim about all of the weird events that had been taking place.

"So let me get this right, instead of mice, we have ghosts," he laughed, making a joke of it.

"I don't find it very funny at all; I'm serious Jim. This house has a spirit in it."

"Just one," he laughed some more.

"I swear, Jim," I said throwing the blankets up to make the bed. "There's something not right in this house; the lights, the stove, the radio — they come on and turn off all by themselves. The pond, there is something in it, and the hill, someone, or something is up there."

I stared at Jim waiting on his response; he just laughed. He told me I was imagining things. I stomped out of the room and went down to the kitchen. I began slamming cabinet doors and banging pots as I cooked breakfast. I could not believe Jim made a joke out of such a serious matter.

I stopped for a moment and stood there. I thought about what I had just said to myself. Such a serious matter, was it? Was it really a serious matter? I hoped not. I was the only one who seemed to think so. "How could I be mad at such a dumb thing? I have to go apologize to Jim," I thought.

"I'm sorry, Baby," Jim said, walking into the kitchen. "I didn't mean to upset you. It just sounded odd that you were being so serious about a ghost."

I turned and looked up at him. I wanted to say I was sorry too, but the words would not come out. They were right there, but they could not find an exit; they just couldn't seem to roll from my lips. Anyway, he had apologized to me, so I decided maybe it was not all my fault. I guessed I should take some of the blame though; all that had to sound really crazy.

"It's all right, Jim; it's no big deal," I said, walking over to him. "We have plenty of time to talk about my ghost stories. How about calling the kids down for breakfast?"

"For it not to be an important thing, you sure got mad about it. But, if you are sure you don't want to talk about it, breakfast sounds great to me."

"Some other time," I replied. "Now go call the kids."

Jim walked over to me and kissed the back of my neck. "I'm sorry I made you mad; I will make it up to you tonight. That is, if you cook me a good breakfast, I will think about making it up to you."

"You better think hard, Baby," I yelled as he walked out of the room.

A few minutes later, the kids came running downstairs for breakfast. They still had many questions for Jim about his trip and more things they wanted to tell about their new school. I watched and listened as each one told a story. Everyone talked and laughed at what was said – everyone but me. I wanted to tell my stories, and I wanted someone to believe me. I did not want to be laughed at again, nor did I want anyone to think I was going crazy.

After eating, we all had chores to start on. Angel and I had the kitchen, and Jim and Gary had the library. Then there was the big job of unpacking and finding the right spot for everything. Angel and I eventually made it to her room. She did not have as much stuff as everyone else, so we thought it should be the fastest. Gary came in to help hang her pictures.

Angel would say where she wanted it, and Gary would place it.

He hung a picture on the far wall, opposite from the bed, as Angel had directed. Every time he hit the wall, a sound would come back, like an echo. We laughed and laughed. When Jim came into the room to listen, he did not think it was funny at all.

"There's no way there is an echo in your bedroom. It's coming from somewhere else," Jim said. "It's not an echo, it's like . . . it's like someone's knocking back. Listen to it. Gary, knock again."

"Maybe it's a ghost!" I said laughing. But really and truly, I was not kidding.

"It's not a ghost," Jim replied, rolling his eyes. "It's probably a rat."

"It must be a pretty intelligent rat," I smarted back. "I've never known one to knock before entering."

"Listen," Gary said. "It's not in my room; it's coming from the ceiling."

Gary hit the wall and we all listened. Sure enough, it was coming from up above.

"It must be something in the attic, wherever that may be. I'll go see if I can find it. You keep knocking," Jim said, leaving the room.

"I'm coming too," I shouted, following behind him. It was exciting to me, like an adventure. I could not wait to see what it was.

"I'm not sure how to get into the attic, Jim. Do you know? I looked before, and I couldn't find an access. I found a little door that probably leads there, but it won't open," I replied.

"What do you mean, it wouldn't open?"

"I mean what I said, it would not open."

"Where is it? Sometimes you have to have a little muscle to open things," Jim smarted back.

"I would not get too cocky if I were you; you are not off my shit list, Buddy. But I'll be glad to let your muscles go to work; follow me. What do you think it is?"

"I don't know, Babe." Jim stopped and appeared to be listening for something. Then he shouted, wiggling his fingers in the air, "MAYBE YOUR GHOST!"

"Ha, ha, ha. You are so funny."

Jim laughed. "I really am clueless. Maybe there's a wild animal making a nest up there."

Jim followed me to the upstairs hall that led to the little wooden door. It was about two feet wide and about six feet high. It camouflaged itself with perfect wood that blended with the wall. The door was made from tongue and groove cypress lumber with a small, rustic looking wooden doorknob on it. It was very precise and distinctive.

Jim tugged on the door, but it would not budge. He jerked on it; it was rusted shut. I rolled my eyes and smiled. His muscles were evidently not working. He put his foot on the wall and pulled with all his might. The door screeched as the rusty hinges started to give. Jim strained a little harder, and the door gradually started to give. Then he looked at me and gave a grin.

"You just have to have the touch," he said.

The door continued to creak and pop as Jim eased it open. Rust broke loose, crumbling and dropping to the floor. A cold breeze jetted out as he opened the door wider. It made the hair stand up on the back of my neck.

"Did you feel that?"

"Sure I did. It's probably a hole up there, or did you think that was your friendly ghost?" he said laughing.

"Well, if it was, we just freed it."

He stuck his head around the door. It was dark. I was hanging onto the back of his shirt, looking over his shoulder. Through the darkness, I could see a long, spooky set of stairs. The flight of stairs was steep and narrow, leading up – I assumed – to the attic. The walls were solid on each side – not over three feet wide. It was like looking into a dark cold cave, going deep into a mountain.

We both stood there and peered inside.

"Wow, it is dark in there," Jim said.

"Can you see anything?"

"I think I see a light up there," Jim answered.

He ran his hand along the wall until he found a light switch; he flipped it on.

"That's odd."

"What's that?" I asked.

"Why would the light bulb still be working after all these years?" Jim asked in a low voice.

"Yeah, I guess it is odd. Maybe they rewired the attic when they rewired the main part of the house."

"If they had rewired the attic, they surely didn't get in through this rusty old entrance. Have you been up here since I've been gone?"

"Are you kidding? There's no way I would come up here by myself. I couldn't get the door open anyway, remember?" I whispered holding onto Jim's shirt tightly.

"Oh yeah, that's right. Look at the spider webs up there. You know

I hate spiders."

"Well, you're the man," I whispered. "Don't let a little thing like a spider get in your way."

"Don't worry, I'm not," he said brushing at the webs. "Hey Babe," Jim whispered.

"Yeah," I whispered back.

"GET OFF ME!" he shouted. "I feel like you're trying to catch a ride on my back, and why are you whispering? Are you scared or something?" he said laughing.

"Like you're not, Mr. Macho Man," I replied.

"Of course I'm not," he said sternly. "I would like to get up this stairwell, and I cannot if you are going to stay on top of me."

"Okay, go ahead. I'll try to stay back away from you . . . just a little." Believe me, a little it was.

We started walking up the steps, and I was not about to let go of him. We walked one step at a time, slowly and carefully. The old boards creaked and cracked as we stepped on them. I thought at any time, they may break, and we would fall into a dungeon like in an old scary movie. We continued toward the top, then Jim stopped abruptly.

"What are you stopping for?" I asked.

"We're out of steps; look at this. Why wouldn't they put steps all the way up? That doesn't make any sense. Why would they just go to here and stop?"

Jim studied the side of the wall and ran his hand across it. "Once upon a time there were steps here. See where the boards were?"

I observed where Jim was rubbing. He was right; I could see a faded area where boards had once been.

"Maybe they just needed replacing, and no one ever got around to it. You know, one of those man things. One of those, 'I'll do it later Babe,' statements. The honey-do list that honey don't do."

"Yeah, yeah," Jim said. "I think maybe they just needed replacing, and no one ever had time to do it — probably because the honey-do list was as long as yours. You know, one of those two-pagers. After all, these are your ancestors, and I'm sure there are some things you have inherited from them even though you didn't know them."

"You will never know, Baby."

"Look, I think I can pull myself up onto the attic floor. It sure looks dark in there."

He reached up to the ledge, burying his elbows into the dust that coated the planks. He kicked his feet, and with a small leap, he was able to pull himself to the top.

"It's really dark up here; I can barely see," he said.

"Can you make out anything up there?"

"No … wait, it looks like there's something on the other side."

"On the other side of what?"

"On the other side of the kitchen."

"On the other side of the kitchen? You can see the kitchen up there?"

"No … I was being a smartass. The other side of whatever this room is."

"It's a room; it's not an attic?"

"I'm not sure what it is, Vivian. I can't see. I don't hear Gary either. Why don't you go get a flashlight, and tell Gary to beat a little harder? I'll sit right here and wait on you, but hurry up. There's no telling what may be up here."

"Are you going to stay up here by yourself?"

"Well, I don't know. Do you know of anyone else who might be up here? I can call out to them and ask if they would like to join me."

"No, I just thought, I . . . never mind."

"Just hurry up," Jim said again.

"Okay," I answered. "I know you aren't scared or anything. You're just a little worried about what may be up here – like one of those wild raccoons – or even worse: I bet it's spiders!"

"You keep talking, and we won't find out what is up here because I'll be coming down."

I slowly eased myself back down the steep, peculiar smelling stairwell. I hurried to Angel's room. I could hear Gary knocking as I came down the hallway.

"Gary," I called out. "You need to knock louder. Daddy can't hear you."

"Gosh Mom, I'm knocking as loud as I can without putting a hole in the wall. My arm is getting tired too."

"Well, just try a little harder."

"All right, but if I knock a hole in it, it's not my fault."

Boom, bang, "Aaaahhhh."

We heard a scream and a loud thump; it came from the attic. All of us ran to the attic door, it slammed shut right before we reached it. I pulled, but it wouldn't budge. I tried to get a grip at the edge; it was impossible. We heard more screams and cries for help.

"Gary, run and get the flashlight and a hammer, hurry!"

Gary turned and ran down the hall. I beat on the door with both hands, calling out to Jim.

"Jim," I shouted. "Can you hear me? Are you all right?"

There was a terrible pounding sound that echoed through the house. I was scared someone had been hiding in the attic and attacked him.

"Hurry Gary!" I cried out. "Oh, hurry Gary! Hurry!"

"Mommy, I can open the door," Angel said, reaching for the door-knob.

"Angel, the door is stuck," I snapped back at her. "You are not strong enough to open it, now move back out of the way."

I shouted again, "Come on, Gary."

"I can open the door, Mommy," Angel said, reaching for the door-knob again.

"Angel, you cannot," I snapped again and pushed her back. I ran to the top of the main stairway and shouted to Gary again. When I turned to go back, I could not believe my eyes. Angel was pulling on the door, and to my surprise, it was opening. I heard it screech a little.

I ran back to her and watched with amazement. The door slowly submitted to her gentle touch. I looked down at Angel and shook my head. I did not take time to say a word. I rushed up the creaky wooden steps.

"Jim, are you all right?" There was silence, nothing stirring at all.

"Jim," I shouted louder.

Still there was no answer.

I called down to Angel, "Don't come up here." I was afraid that something bad had happened.

I leaped up, digging with my elbows, squirming, and struggling to pull the weight of my body behind me. Kicking my feet, I finally pulled myself to the edge of the attic floor. I looked around and saw nothing.

Scared and impatient, I could only wait for Gary. It was just so dark in that creepy musty place.

"Jim," I called softly.

Everything was quiet.

"Jim," I called again, but a little louder.

I waited for a response. There was no noise at all except Gary, who came running up the steep stairs shining a flashlight.

"Here Mom," he called out. "Is Dad all right?"

I reached for the light.

"Aaahhhh," I screamed. Before I could get a good grip on the light, someone grabbed me from behind and dragged me away. I scratched, pawed and beat the unforeseen attacker; I could not get free.

"Run, Gary!" I shouted.

I could hear Gary running back down the steps. I was kicking and fighting with all of my might, not able to see my assailant.

There was something around my eyes, and I was being hauled across a rough floor. I screamed, scratched, and slapped like a wild cat. Turning my head, I buried my teeth like a vicious dog.

"Owey, calm down," a voice grunted in the darkness. "You're going to get hurt or hurt me. I was just trying to surprise you."

It was Jim; he had a shirt wrapped around my eyes.

"Surprise me! You scared the hell out of me. Are you crazy? You could have given me a heart attack. Have you lost your mind? And where the hell were you? Why didn't you answer me? What were all the pounding and screaming sounds about?" My voice was cracking, trying to hold back my tears.

"Pounding sounds? I didn't hear any pounding sounds or any screaming. I was crawling around up here, but I wasn't making any noise. I'm sorry I didn't answer you; I didn't hear you. I apologize for scaring you, just wait till you see what I found. And by the way, did I answer all your questions?"

"Yes," I snapped.

Jim was holding my hand tightly, leading me across the musky dirty attic.

"There's another room up here. You are not going to believe all the stuff that I found," he said boasting.

He hurried along, pulling me behind him in the dark. He opened another door, which led into a room with a light. When I walked in, Jim was right, I could not believe my eyes. Furniture was stacked on top of furniture, beautiful antiques in mint condition: sofas, chairs, tables, beds, lamps — everything I needed for each room was right there the entire time.

"I can't believe this. Look at all these beautiful things. Oh my God, it feels like Christmas."

"I told you. Is this awesome or what? So do you forgive me now?"

"Mom!" Gary shouted.

"The kids! I forgot about the kids. We're all right, Gary. Everything is fine," I yelled out.

"How come you didn't answer us? We thought something had happened to you." Gary walked into the room holding the flashlight in one hand and the hammer in the other.

"I'm sorry, Gary. I didn't hear you call for me."

"Call for you? We screamed for you," he said in an angry voice.

"Where is your sister?" I asked.

"She's at the bottom of the steps crying. I told her to wait for me to come back."

"I'll get her," Jim said, leaving the room.

"Look, Gary, at all this old stuff your dad found."

"Yeah, I see it."

I began taking the furniture down. I know I looked like a kid in a candy store, but I loved antiques. I was so excited, I rambled to myself over and over about how I could not believe what Jim had found. It was remarkable. I had a smile on my face so big, my jaws hurt.

Jim returned with Angel. Each one of us scurried around, digging in the boxes. We found a couple of old trunks trimmed out with tarnished brass locks. The first one we opened was filled with old toys, which kept Angel and Gary occupied. The second one had several old-timey dresses. Beautiful, but old, some were dry rotted, yet some were in perfect condition. The dresses appeared to be homemade, maybe from cloth potato bags. That is what my grandmother said they used to make them from in her day. The third trunk held letters and pictures, which definitely caught my attention.

I sat on the floor, going through one piece at a time. Jim walked around the room moving furniture; he thought there might be another door. The house had become a treasure hunt for him. He was almost as excited as I was.

"Jim, how are we going to get this furniture downstairs? I know it surely won't go down the steep stairwell that we came up on."

"We'll figure something out."

"I can't believe all this stuff has been left here for all these years."

"Hey," he called out. "Look at this."

We all turned around; there was another door hidden behind all the furniture.

"Everyone, come give me a hand. This door seems to be stuck too. What is it with these damn doors?"

We all tried pulling, except Angel; she never left the toy box.

"Do you want the hammer, Dad?" Gary asked.

"Yeah, that might help. I might can beat on these old hinges and loosen them up."

Gary ran and got the hammer from across the room. Jim tapped on each hinge. It did not work, so he hit them a little harder.

"Vivian, you and Gary pull on the door while I beat on the hinges some more."

"Okay," I replied.

Jim tapped and we pulled until it worked. I put my foot against the wall and pulled with all my might. I wanted in, and I was determined to get in. The door creaked, squeaked, and slowly it started to open. We kept working the door back and forth until it finally broke free and opened all the way. We barely stuck our heads inside; there was another dark hall.

"I can't see anything," Gary said.

"Go get the flashlight, Son," Jim said with excitement.

"Where do you think this goes?" I asked holding onto Jim's shirt again.

"I don't know, but get Angel and we'll find out," he said, reaching for the flashlight.

"Groovy!" Gary shouted. "This place is groovy," he said, bobbing his head up and down.

Angel did not want to leave her new toys.

"No Mommy, I want to stay here and play. I don't want to go in there; it's dark."

"Look Angel, Daddy has a flashlight. You can play when we get back. We want to see where this leads."

She still insisted she wanted to stay. I had to pick her up and carry her to the doorway. We all walked slowly, single file, down the dark aisle. Jim led the way, Gary next, then Angel, and I brought up the rear. Gary was hanging onto Jim, Angel to Gary, and then to me.

The hall was dirty and creepy. There was a pungent smell of musk and mold. Spider and cobwebs obscured our paths. The corridor was wide, but short in height. Jim was unable to straighten his tall stature; his shoulders slouched, and his neck extended forward. There were no windows or lights – and no other doorways to exit. We ran our hands along the walls, feeling every inch of the way. The muscles bulged from the calves of our legs; our feet burrowed to the floors that spiraled downward to our unknown destination.

The end seemed to be an eternity away as we navigated all the twist and turns, descending with each one. Angel was tired and had to be carried, so Jim and I took turns in doing so. I was just about to say, "Let's turn around," when abruptly, we came to a halt. Our grueling adventure ended at a solid brick wall.

My arms ached, and my legs were clammy, cold, and rubbery; I was not in as good a shape as I thought. I put Angel down, shook my arms out, and leaned over trying to catch my breath. Jim leaned against the wall; he too was gasping. He shined the flashlight along the wall, inspecting every crevice. The bricks were secured from the ceiling to the floor.

"Well, this doesn't make any sense," Jim said, exhausted.

"Maybe the whole wall turns. You know, like in the movies," Gary shouted, pushing along the wall. "All haunted houses have them."

"All haunted houses," replied Jim, looking at me.

"Angel, you stand right here while Mommy helps Gary."

"Look Honey, don't tell me you believe what Gary said. I know you think this place is haunted and all, but a turning wall, come on!"

"Okay, I won't tell you. You just hold the light for us."

Gary and I pushed and pulled on every brick that we could reach, but nothing moved. We beat along the walls while Jim leaned back and snickered. Then little Angel spoke up.

"I know how to open it," she said.

I was silent, reluctant to ask, but what the heck, I asked anyway. "How?"

"Right there, look Mommy, it's locked," Angel pointed to the floor.

Sure enough, there were locks on the floor. I slowly exhaled; it was a relief knowing it was just a lock. After observing her opening the attic door, I was apprehensive about how she would do this one.

Jim stooped down and proceeded to pull on the rusty metal. They too were rusted, jammed, and immoveable.

"Is every damn thing rusted in this place?"

"I think you already asked that question, Honey."

"Well, did you answer me?"

"Nope, sure didn't."

"Well, would you like to?"

"Nope, sure wouldn't. I'd rather wait."

"Wait! Wait for what?"

"Wait to find out if every damn thing is rusted in this place."

"Vivian, do you have to be such a smartass?"

I laughed and shrugged my shoulders.

He took the flashlight and began beating. Before I could say, "Don't do it," the light went out. No blink, no flash, no warning – just out, and it was dark. I mean damn dark, cave dark, night dark, black dark!

"Good going, Dad," Gary sarcastically said.

"Are you playing with us, Jim?"

"No, Vivian, the damn thing merely quit. Everyone just stay where you are. I'll have it working in a minute."

We could hear him pounding the light on the palm of his hand, but we could not see a thing. He cursed, swore, and was clearly aggravated.

"Well, you picked a good place to do such a stupid thing; we can't even see how to get back," I replied.

"You don't have to see, it's a straight shot. I don't think even you can get lost in a one-way hallway, can you?"

"Are you sure it's only one way?"

"Come on Vivian, think. Did you see any other openings when we came this way?"

"Hey, there could be another hidden door," Gary blurted.

"Man, what have you all been doing while I was gone? Do you really think this house was made for the movies or something? All we have to do is follow the walls."

"We can't see, Jim," I was quick to remind him.

"I guess you can't feel either. Think about it, Vivian. Everyone reach out and find a hand. We'll just single file it back."

"Angel, come grab Mommy's hand."

I held my hand out and wiggled my fingers in the air, but I felt nothing. I waved my arms all around, still nothing.

"Angel!" I called out again. "Hold your hand out so I can find you. Angel, where are you?"

"Angel this isn't funny, you answer your mother, now!" Jim demanded.

Everything was quiet. She did not answer.

"Oh my God, where is she?" I panicked. "What could have happened to her?" All kinds of things raced through my mind. I groped blindly through the darkness.

Jim spoke up. "Everyone be still. Vivian, where are you? Reach out until you find my hand, and Gary, you reach out too."

We reached through the air, until our hands touched. Then we gripped them together and held them tightly.

"Okay, now you and Gary sit down and stretch your arms out as far as they will go across the hall. I am going to crawl around the floor until I get back to you. I'll be able to find her if she's in here."

"What do you mean, 'if she's in here'?"

"I mean so I can find her; just stretch out. That way I'll know when I've searched the entire area."

"Hurry Jim, she might have hurt herself."

Gary and I sat on the floor and stretched out our arms as Jim instructed. We listened as he scurried around the room. It was so black, my hand was not visible in front of my face. I craned my neck from side to side listening for something, anything, but I did not hear a sound, nothing but the rustling noise of Jim's determination.

"Where could she have gone, Mom?" Gary asked.

"I don't know. She must have gone back to the attic room."

"By herself? No way," Gary replied. "I wouldn't even go by myself."

"Listen up, everyone grab a hand and let's go," Jim said in an agitated voice.

Gary and I felt for Jim, locked our hands, and set off blindly up the cavernous hall. Jim led the way. Our backs were to the wall, our free hands held out in front, swaying through the air. The blind was leading the blind into the darkness of uncertainty. Our bodies were consumed with only the emptiness that the corridor had provided. The wetness, the crawling creatures, and the invisible freedom of sight – none of that mattered. All I cared about was finding my baby, my precious little Angel.

"SHHH," Jim said, unexpectedly stopping.

Gary and I fell forward from the abrupt halt. There was a soft voice ricocheting through the impenetrable shadow of the hall. We listened intently, but were unable to understand. The voice was like a whisper, a whimper of despair.

"Everyone be really quiet," Jim said as we slowly crept through the black hall. A soft light glowed from the half-cracked door of the attic room. The unfamiliar, mimicking whispering continued to get louder as we neared the exit.

"Vivian," Jim said softly.

"Yeah," I answered.

"You and Gary stay in the dark until I can see what's going on."

"What if someone has Angel?" Gary whispered.

"No one has Angel," Jim quickly answered.

I was praying he was right, not as convinced as he evidently was, but just the same, I hoped he was right. Gary and I hid quietly in the dark. The dim light cast a silhouette of Jim's body as he paused at the door. We heard that familiar creaking sound as he slightly moved it.

He leaned through the doorway easing his head around the corner, and then abruptly, he swung it open.

"Angel Marie," he shouted. "What are you doing back in here? Why did you leave us? We were worried about you."

When we heard Jim shout, we walked out. I ran over to Angel, who was sitting on the floor playing with the toys in the box. My fear made me angry, but my love made me forgiving.

"Angel, why did you leave us, Honey? We were worried about you."

"The lady brought me here. I thought it was you, Mommy. She whispered in my ear when I was sitting in that room. She told me to come with her, so I did."

"What lady? What did she say?" Jim asked.

"The white pretty lady, she said for me to follow her. She held my hand and brought me back to my toys. I thought it was you, Mommy."

"So where's this lady at, Angel?" Gary asked.

"I don't know; I never saw her."

"Oh, so now you have a lady you can't see. I thought you said she was a white lady."

"She is white, but I couldn't see her face."

"Does she have a name?" Gary said laughing.

"I don't know. She didn't say."

"Angel, that is enough, young lady. You can't keep inventing imaginary people every time that you get into trouble."

"Daddy, they're real, I promise," Angel whimpered. "Why don't you believe me? Mommy you believe me, don't you?"

How could I say "no"? With her innocence shining through those big puppy dog eyes, I had to agree.

"Sure Baby, I think you really believe you see someone."

"Vivian," Jim snapped angrily.

I raised my eyebrows and just shrugged my shoulders.

"Did you get the door open, Mommy?" Angel asked.

"No, we have to get another light," I answered.

"Speaking of which, I think I will go get another one, now," Jim replied.

"Can I stay here and play? I don't want to go back in there."

"Sure you can. But you have to promise not to leave this room unless I come and get you. Better yet, I think I will just stay here with you. I'll let your dad and Gary return to that dungeon by themselves."

"Yeah, and don't follow anymore of your friends that you can't see. I don't like going through these dark halls," Gary mocked Angel.

Jim came back into the room. We all stood there staring with our chins dropped and mouths open.

"Well, don't just stare at me. Help."

Jim looked as if he were ready for combat. He decided to carry drop cords down the hall with a lamp, plus two flashlights, candles, two books of matches, two hammers, and oil to loosen the locks.

"Gosh Dad, you look like you're going camping. Do you think we may get lost? Did you bring any food?"

"Funny, Gary."

"So what's up with all this?" Gary asked.

Jim snapped back, "I just don't want to be left in the dark again, that's all."

"I didn't know you were scared of the dark, Dad."

"It's not the dark. It's all those damn spiders. They still feel like they're crawling on me. You know I hate those damn things. At least now I'll be able to see them."

Jim and Gary worked together unraveling the cords and stretching them down the passageway. I stayed in the room with Angel and intently started going through the old trunk. There were letters after letters, most being addressed to a Johnny Simmons, and there were a couple for Mary Beth Simmons. I was so fascinated with my find, I could hardly stand myself; I sat down beside the trunk and started to read. There were many letters expressing sympathy for the loss of Mr. Simmons's leg. One letter particularly stood out. It was from a lady in England.

Dear Mr. Simmons,

I am deeply sorry for your loss of Miss Carol. Her death is such a tragedy. Her beauty and kindness will be greatly missed. We pray the plague will be over soon. Please express our sympathy and love to little Mary Beth.
Sincerely,
Lady Ann

The trunk was filled with similar letters expressing grief. Then, there were those profound ones expressing sympathy for the loss of his leg. They gave the impression that Mr. Simmons's leg was lost during a war or for some noble cause, but the timeline didn't quite make sense.

"We got it open!" Gary yelled with excitement. "We got it open, Mom! Come look! You are not going to believe where it opens at. It is so cool. It's just like the movies. This place is so cool."

"I know," Angel replied sarcastically.

"You know what?" I asked.

"I know where it opens to."

"Oh yeah, smarty pants, where?" Gary asked.

"The living room," Angel said, making a face and shaking her head at Gary.

"The living room," I laughed.

"How did you know?" Gary asked.

"What! You mean it does?"

"Yeah Mom, it does. How did you know?" he asked again.

"Cause the lady told me, stupid."

"What lady?"

"The lady that brought me back here," Angel said as she continued to play.

"Whatever. You just made a lucky guess. It's so cool, Mom, the door slides into the wall right beside the fireplace. Come on, you gotta see it; Dad has it open."

Gary grabbed my hand and pulled me down the hall. Angel trotted behind, holding onto my shirt. The hall, brightly glowing from Jim's monstrous amount of lights, uncovered the grotesque havens of our eight-legged friends, which became clearly visible. Although Gary's eagerness to unveil his findings kept him from focusing on them, we were observant as we navigated our paths.

There were small bits of paper lying about on the floor, several cups and a spoon, too. I thought this to be very odd to be in the middle of a dark hallway. Gary did not give me any time to stop; he was on a mission.

The smell of such repulsive musk was nauseating. Many years of unattainable habitat were unmistakable. Angel gripped her free hand firmly over her nose and mouth, mumbling a muffled complaint about the stench. When we got to the end, Gary was right. The door slid and disappeared into the walls.

"Well, Babe, here is how you can bring out the furniture," Jim said with enthusiasm. "After lunch we can get started on it. If you want, we can move our furniture into the attic and put that old stuff down here. Just switch places with one another."

"What about the smell?" Gary quickly pointed out.

"Now would be a good time for your mom to use that $1000 vacuum she bought. You know Honey, the one that cleans furniture and everything. The one you never use, that old, but brand new one."

"You are such a smartass, Jim."

"Well, will it, or will it not clean the furniture?"

"I guess we will find out, huh. If you and Gary want to go ahead and get started moving the furniture, Angel and I will fix lunch, and then we can try it out."

"That sounds good to me. I'm starving," Gary said, rubbing his stomach.

"Come on Angel, you can help Mommy throw the salads together."

"Salads," Jim said. "I need food, real food."

"I'm going to fix you some real food. The salad is just to get started. You just do your thing, and let us women do ours."

"Yeah Daddy," Angel chuckled.

"Come on, little girl, let's go wash our hands and get this nasty smell off. We don't need any old, unwanted germs spreading around here."

"Okay Mommy."

After washing up, Angel and I went into the kitchen. I got everything out that she would need to get the salad started, along with what I needed for some hot sandwiches. I walked to the stove and turned the knob, but it didn't work. I switched it back and forth, but had no results. "Damn," I said aloud.

"What's wrong Mommy?" Angel asked.

"The stove won't come on, again. The breaker must have tripped. It probably happened when Daddy plugged in all those extension cords for the lights. I have to go down to the basement for a minute. You stay right here and finish making the salads like a big girl."

I crept down the dark dungeon steps, frantically feeling in the air for the pull string used to turn on the light. It was very spooky, just as

Tina had said when she looked in. Even with the lights on, it was still intimidating. I did not waste any time, I wanted to get to the box, flip that damn breaker, and get the hell back upstairs.

When I pulled the string, the light swayed back and forth, casting a shadow about the walls. I hurried around the dimly lit room to the metal box that was secure on the far wall. Of course, it was on the furthest wall.

I quickly opened the cold metal cover and identified each and every breaker until I discovered the one that was off. I flipped it on. Simultaneously, the lights went off; the basement was black. My tense body spun around. Frozen with fear, I stood vulnerable in total darkness once again. I squinted. I could barely see the light from the kitchen. I shuffled across the black room with my hands in front of me, sliding my feet as I went. Three tiny, trivial feet from the stairs, the door slammed shut, taking away all my discretion about what to do. I moved slightly, just a hair. Then I tripped over something and fell to the floor.

"Help me. Please, help me," a woman's voice whispered in the dark.

I lay vulnerable, not moving a muscle, scared to look, but too intrigued not to. My voice stuttered, and the vibration of fear welled up inside me. Overcoming my anxiety, I asked, "Who are you?"

I listened intently. Silence covered the room. I lay still for just a few seconds, and then I crawled along the floor until I found the steps again. I began to ascend carefully, but quickly. I paused at the door, hoping for something, but heard nothing. I turned the knob slowly, and it opened without any problem. I stepped inside the kitchen and closed the door behind me.

Angel, still at the table happily separating the lettuce, did not acknowledge my entrance. I looked at the stove. It was already on. I did not say a word. I went straight over and proceeded to prepare our lunch. When everything was ready, I sent Angel to get Jim and Gary.

As I watched her leave the room, I thought of the voice I had heard. Then I thought of Angel's mysterious lady who had taken her from the hall. I sprinted out of the room behind her.

"Angel, wait," I called. "Mommy will go with you."

I wasn't sure what was going on, but I knew it was not right. There was something strange and unsettling in the house: a mystifying lady, baffling sounds, and so many other inexplicable happenings. I did not want Angel to disappear again.

Jim and Gary had moved most of our furniture out, but they had transferred just a few antiques from the attic.

"That old furniture is really heavy, Vivian," Jim said. "We might have to hire someone to help us. On the other hand, maybe your friend Tina can get her husband over to give helping hand."

"She's not married; she's divorced."

"Well, that doesn't surprise me. Anyone that dresses like that, it would be a surprise to me if she did have a man, a normal one anyway. When you get to know her better, maybe you should take her shopping and help her dress herself."

"Jim. That lady is older than I am. I'm surely not going to tell her how to dress. Anyway, she is her own person. If she is comfortable with her attire, well, that's her business."

"I guess," Jim said. "So how are we going to get that heavy furniture in here? Now that Gary and I have moved most of ours out, we don't have anywhere to sit tonight."

The birth of an idea exploded in my head.

"Hey Jim, I have a plan," I blurted. "Gary, go get your two skateboards."

"My skateboards, why?" Gary asked.

"Just go get them," I answered.

Gary ran upstairs and returned momentarily with both of his boards. He handed them to me. Jim was puzzled, clueless of my ingenious idea.

"Honey," he said. "What are you doing with those?"

"You'll see," I answered. "First we're going to eat. Come into the kitchen; let's have lunch, and then I'll explain it to you."

"This I can't wait to hear, but did you say something about eating?"

"Yes, lunch is now being served in the kitchen. Those who care to join me may follow," I said leading the way.

We ambled our way through the living room and returned to the kitchen. Jim and Gary slid the wooden chairs from the table causing a screeching sound against the floor. I shivered as I lifted my chair and sat down.

They consumed their lunch in minutes, devouring every crumb. I replenished their plates with second helpings, and they continued to eat as if they were starving. Angel started snickering under her breath.

"What's so funny?" Gary asked with a mouth full of food.

She did not answer. She just kept on laughing and got louder and louder. We all started to chuckle with her, not having a clue what we were laughing at. We cackled like a flock of chickens, staring and waiting for an explanation. Then she slowly lifted one finger and pointed to Jim. Gary and I turned our attention to him and our laughter burst into uncontrollable snorts.

"What?" he said, looking down at his shirt. "Do I have something on me?" He took his hand and wiped his mouth. "Did I drop my food on my lap? What is it?"

Gary was rolling on the floor laughing, doubled over in pain.

Jim could not help but to laugh at Gary, yet he still did not have a clue. Then I pointed to his shoulder. He screamed like a girl and fell backward in his chair. He rolled over, and then quickly jumped to his feet.

Jim finally saw it. "Oh! Oh!" he yelled. "Get it off! Get it off!" he screamed, slapping at his neck.

"It's off!" I yelled back, trying to conceal my smile.

Gary and Angel were hysterical by then.

"What's the matter, Dad? You're not scared of a little lizard, are you?"

"Oh you all are so funny. I hope I have amused all of you very much, now that I think I've peed my pants," he said, looking down at his wet trousers.

Gary was beating the floor and yelling with stomach pain from laughing so hard. Jim did a little dance and left the room. I did not know if he really wet his pants or if he had spilled his drink when he fell.

Lizards were among those of God's creatures that terrorized him. With any kind of bug, snake, or crawly creature, he always reacted the same way: terrified! The kids loved pulling practical jokes with rubber creatures. Angel knew when she saw the lizard, Jim would freak out. And he reacted, just as always, like a maniac.

After everyone finally composed themselves, Angel and I cleared the table.

"Okay, let's get back to work," I called out to the guys. "Look, I need your help. I have to show you how this is done."

"I wouldn't miss this for the world," Jim said, re-entering the living room.

We strolled back up the long hall to the furniture, and on the way, I began to explain my plan. I stood in front of the antique sofa and said to Jim, "Okay, pick up one end so I can slide the skateboard under it."

"Do what?" he said.

"Lift one end of the sofa."

"Lift one end of the sofa, then what?"

"Just lift one end of the sofa, Jim."

"Oh, I see what you're doing," Gary quickly exclaimed. "Come on Dad, lift. I'll help you."

Jim glared at both Gary and me. "This is not going to work," he said.

"Don't be so negative. Just do it. If it won't work, it won't work. At least it's an idea."

"Okay Buddy, come help me," Jim said to Gary.

Jim and Gary lifted each end of the sofa, and I guided the skateboards under. The wheels slowly began to trundle as we pushed it down the forgotten passage. It was not perfectly balanced, but it was rolling and moving to its natural domain.

"Don't say a word," Jim sarcastically said. "Just don't say a damn word."

"I wouldn't dare," I replied with a snicker. "Words aren't required. It simply speaks for itself."

One by one, we moved the abandoned pieces of furniture. It was perfect; there was a place for each and every piece. Once lost, tucked away, and hidden from time – all of it had been trapped in another era containing haunting secrets for me to unveil.

My house was finally coming together. It was starting to take the form of what I was sure it was built to be. To have it decorated in its original century-old fashion was unbelievable. I was very pleased with our accomplishment. The downstairs was complete, but the upstairs was a different matter. I had yet to come up with a plan for getting the furniture up there, but I was contemplating it.

The night crept in unnoticed. We all were utterly exhausted from the hard day's work. We depleted all energy by nightfall. Even Angel had worked hard carrying the little things like cushions and pictures. When it was time for bed, no one had to rock any of us to sleep. We crashed even before our heads touched the pillows.

We awoke with the bright morning sunlight shining through the windowpanes and warming our faces. I rolled over and snuggled up to Jim. It felt so good to have him lying next to me.

"Oooh," he moaned.

"What's wrong?"

"I think someone beat the hell out of me last night. My body, I can't move it. Every single muscle I have hurts. I think I'm dying."

I laughed. "See, I told you living out here was going to help you. Living out here in the country is going to put your body in the best shape it's ever been in. You get to see that lean form – just like when I met you."

"Nooooo," he moaned. "Those muscles have retired. I feel more like living out here is going to put me in an early grave. I think I am half dead now. It's me; I'm your ghost. Now pretend you can't see me, and go away."

"Not on your life. Now get up. You need to work the soreness out," I pushed on him.

"Ouch! Don't push. That hurts. I'm not kidding. Damn," he said, rubbing his back. "I think I need to go back to work so I can rest."

"That's what I just said. You need to get up and go back to work. There's a lot more furniture to be brought out."

"No. I mean work, my job, my airline. The job I just thought made me tired. I was wrong. I will never complain again. I would rather be there working. I know that won't kill me. And if it does, at least it will be quick, not this slow, painful death that you're putting me through."

"Ahhh . . . poor baby, quit whining. You only have a couple more days before you have to leave again, so hurry and get up. We have furniture to move."

That is just what we did; we worked from sunrise to sunset. All of us, including the kids, contributed. Of course Angel played with her new toys more than she worked, but that was fine. She stayed happy and satisfied.

Gary stayed close to Jim. He missed him so much when he was gone. He and Jim talked a lot about the flights he had taken. There were questions about the kind of people he met, what the land looked like in different countries, how it feels to fly in a storm – things like that.

Gary was very interested in joining the Air Force. Everything about it intrigued him. He could not wait to become of age, but I thanked God that would be several more years to come. I hated to even to think about it.

We kept ourselves busy until Jim's last day at home. Every day our old home had something that needed to be moved, fixed, or replaced. There was never a lack of work. On Jim's departure day, we took time to enjoy our family. We decided to drive the kids to beach and have a picnic.

The weather was unseasonably warm that day. Jim played in the water with the kids. After barreling across the shore, Jim and Gary dove into the waves. Angel jumped over the little breakers in the shallow water. She had just as much fun by herself. I lay on the blanket, wiggled my toes in the sand, and just enjoyed the warm, lustrous sun. We had a full day of pleasure and relaxation together.

That night we made a campfire in the backyard, roasted marshmallows and hot dogs, and told spooky stories. We laughed and played until it was time for bed.

Jim and I were very tired, but not too tired for romance. It was short and sweet. Afterwards we snuggled in each other's arms and fell fast asleep.

I rolled over in bed and a bold ray of sunlight again burst through the window – right into my sleepy eyes. Forgetting to pull the shade the night before had resulted in my temporary blindness. I threw my hand over my eyes and staggered to the window. I felt for the string that dangled, waiting to give me relief. The new spring-loaded shade pulled down with ease, perfectly stopping at the bottom edge of the sill.

I tottered back to the bed, not wanting to believe it was morning already. I lay quietly, watching Jim sleep. He looked so peaceful; I hated to wake him up. I ran my fingers through his hair and around his face. I traced every little crevice the years had so diligently given to him. His face was strong with high cheekbones, a blessing his Indian ancestors had given him.

"Jim. Honey, it's time for you to get up."

He opened his eyes, squinted and smiled at me. "Is it morning already?"

"I'm afraid so, muscle man."

"Ohhhh," he moaned, putting his pillow over his head.

"I'm going to wake the kids so they can see you before you leave. Get up, and I'll fix you some breakfast."

"I'll be right down," he mumbled.

I walked down the hall to Gary's room and opened his door. His room was a mess. I just shook my head and called out to him to get up. "Get your sister up too, and bring her downstairs. You'll only have an hour to visit with your father before he leaves."

"Okay Mom," he faintly answered, half asleep.

I went downstairs and began breakfast. Bacon was frying in the pan, grits were simmering in the pot, and I was scrambling the eggs in a bowl when the kids came stumbling into the kitchen.

"Okay guys, I could use some help here."

"I'll help you, Mommy," Angel so sweetly offered.

"Me too, I'm about to starve," Gary replied.

"Y'all know what to do. Get started."

They helped set the table, made the toast, and squeezed the oranges to make fresh juice. Gary sat down at the table and started tapping it like a drum.

"Where's Dad?" Gary asked, never missing a beat.

"I don't know. I hope he didn't fall asleep again. He should have already been down here. Why don't you run back upstairs and make sure he got up?"

"Sure thing," he replied, getting up from the table.

He did not get to take two steps before Jim walked in. His face was drained of all color and fixed with a blank expression.

"Hey Dad, are you all right? You look like you saw a ghost."

"I … I think I did," he answered, staggering to the table and plopping into the chair.

"You did!" I exclaimed. "What did it look like? Was it a man or a woman? Did you see its face? Was it white or black?"

"Yeah Dad, what did it look like?"

"Yeah Daddy, was it that lady that talks to me?"

"Good God! I can't believe you all have seen this, this ghost! And what do you mean man, woman, black, white? How many of these damn things are here? Did it not scare any of you at all?"

"Sure Dad," Gary answered. "But all of us haven't seen it, just Mom and Angel. I haven't."

"I'm not sure if it was a ghost, I'm not even sure I really saw anything," Jim said, trying to retract his statement.

"You might not be sure, but we are," I added.

"I know I saw something," Jim said, rubbing his head. "I'm just not sure what. It was like something was there, and then it wasn't. It didn't look like a man or a woman. It just looked . . . it looked like; I don't know what it looked like. Smoke, that's really the only way to describe it. It looked like a ball of smoke or a cloud or something like that. It was just a white glow."

"Maybe it wanted to tell you goodbye. You know, pat you on the back, and tell you to have a safe trip – that kind of thing," Gary was quick to say.

"You are so funny, Son. I hope he tucks you in tonight."

"Jim! Don't tell him something like that."

"Come on, Vivian. I was kidding; I can't believe you really take this stuff seriously."

Bam! Splash! Crash!

"What was that?" We all simultaneously shouted and ran to the living room where the noise seemed to have originated.

"Oh no!" Jim shouted.

"Oh my God!" I yelled.

Gary and Angel just covered their mouths and started to laugh.

"This is not funny! Go get a pot. If we don't hurry and get these fish in some water, they'll die," I exclaimed.

Gary rushed from the room.

"How did the fish tank break, Mommy?"

"I don't know, Angel."

"Dad did it," Gary replied, re-entering the room.

"How did I do it? I was in the kitchen with you all."

"You made fun of Mommy's ghost, and it didn't like it," Angel snickered.

"You sure did, Jim."

"Will it help to say that I'm sorry?"

"It might."

"Okay, I am sorry, but that is all the time I have. I have a plane to fly. I hate to leave you with this mess, but I have to get my bags and get out of here."

"Yeah, I know you really hate leaving me with this mess."

"You know it, Babe. Now give me a kiss. I'm going to wash my hands, get my bags, and go straight out the door. You too kids, give your dad a hug. I have to go."

We all stopped for a minute to hug Jim goodbye. When he left the room, we hurried, picked up the fish, and put them into a pot of water. We stood at the door and waited for Jim to come downstairs so we could see him off.

"What's this?" Jim asked, stopping on the stairwell. "Are you all going to ambush me or something?"

"Nope, just more hugs and goodbye kisses. You know we have to watch you leave."

"Okay, one more quick hug for the air."

We all hugged Jim again and followed him out the front entrance. The kids and I watched as he disappeared out of sight. Once again, we were on our own.

CHAPTER 7

THE DIARY

I was sound asleep, dreaming peacefully, when the loud clattering from the alarm clock awoke me. I reached over to turn it off. Still half asleep, my eyes closed, I slapped the top of the clock, feeling for that snooze button. Time after time, I was fumbling for that button. My hand smacking, feeling its way across the table, I knocked over the lamp and swiped my wedding rings onto the floor.

"Ohhh . . . no; I don't need this . . . not this morning."

Brushing my hair from my eyes and turning the blaring music off, I yawned and stretched as the morning sunlight poured through my window.

"Oh my God, my rings," I said aloud.

I jumped off the bed, dropped to my knees, and inched my way around the floor. I immediately found my wedding band, but the diamond ring that was Jim's mother's was still missing. Where could it have rolled? I crawled under the bed and found nothing. I looked under the rug, under the bedside table, and under the dresser. I could not find the ring anywhere. I should have known better than to take them off. Jim had made such a fuss about that so many times before. I had to stop my search and get the kids ready for school. I would have to look for it later. I had to begin my day.

I woke the kids and headed to the kitchen. My daily routine had begun.

Gary and Angel came down for breakfast fussing and complaining as usual. I quieted them long enough to eat, then rushed them out the door. At the car, they argued about who was going to sit in the front. Back and forth, over and over, the same words I heard every single morning.

"I've got the front."

"No, I do."

"That's enough!" I shouted. "I'm so tired of hearing you two complain constantly. We're going to start taking turns weekly. Gary, you get the front one week, and Angel gets it the next week."

"I get it the first week!" Gary shouted.

"No you don't! I do."

"I called it first," Gary repeated.

They pushed and pulled each other, yelling louder and louder.

"That's it! Both of you get in the damn back seat. Now don't say another word, or you won't ever sit up front again!" I shouted.

"But Mom," Gary squealed.

"I said now! Not another word. Backseat!"

They finally got into the car – not saying a word. Both of them looked out the windows and pouted the entire way to the school. The car came to a stop; Gary opened the door and slid out, slamming it behind him. He flung his book bag over his shoulder and stomped away.

"Gary!" I called out.

He stopped and turned around. "Don't leave this car without saying goodbye."

"Goodbye," he snapped.

I looked at him for a minute, deciding whether I should say anything about his bad attitude. I did not want to embarrass him in front of his new friends, so I drove away. By the time school let out and he rode the bus home, he would be over his anger. That was plenty of time for him to think about how stupid this was.

Angel and I went back to the house and started the same old thing, the morning chores. Then I thought about my ring. Jim would kill me if I didn't find his mother's ring.

I got a flashlight and went upstairs. I shined the light around the cracks of the floor. I pulled the nightstand away from the wall. I shuffled under the bed with the light in my hand, but saw nothing. Squeezing my way around, feeling as I went, I came up empty handed. I could not give up; I knew it had to be there. Laying flat on my stomach, slithering like a snake, I noticed something against the wall under the baseboard.

My ring was wedged in a crack, and I couldn't get a grip on it. My fingers were not small enough to grasp it. The more I tried, the further it slid under the board.

I had to find something that would slide into that crack. I sat up trying to remember where I had put Jim's toolbox. I knew it was downstairs, but locating it could be a problem.

I scrambled in the kitchen drawer, finding everything but what I thought I needed. Tapping my finger on my lips, walking around in a circle, it came to me: the basement. Oh how I did not want to go back down there. The dread overcame me, leaving even my body feeling weak and vulnerable. Fingers trembling, knees knocking, I turned the cold crystal knob, which invited me into the unpredictable dungeon. I paused, holding the door tightly and scanning the kitchen for something that would prevent the door from shutting – trapping me – and leaving me at the mercy of whatever might be waiting for me down there.

"A chair, that'll work."

I wedged the chair beneath the handle and tugged on the door to make sure it was secure. Feeling confident, I entered, grasping the string for the light, which immediately came on. Cautiously, I descended the steps, inspecting every inch as I went. Jim's toolbox lay on the shelf right across from me. I took one last glance around the room. Not seeing anything, I darted over to the box. Fumbling with the latches, I was happy that two quick clicks revealed its contents: pliers, wrenches, and screwdrivers. I retrieved a tiny flat head screwdriver and scurried back up to the kitchen. Closing the door behind me, I allowed a sigh of relief to pour from my lips. I was safe.

Walking past the living room door, I called out to Angel, "Are you all right, Honey?"

"Yes, ma'am."

"You stay in there and watch television. Mommy is going to be upstairs. If you need me, come up, okay?"

"Okay Mommy," she answered.

I sprinted back up the stairs and rushed to my room. Kneeling on the floor, I slid the screwdriver along the crack below the wall and tried to pull out my ring. I was trying to be careful not to break the old six-inch cypress baseboard.

"Oh my goodness," I said aloud.

A small section of wood popped loose from the wall. I had barely tugged on it. After examining the piece of rough-edged timber, I realized it had been cut and pieced in place. Putting it aside, I tilted my head. There lay my ring. Putting it back on my finger where it belonged, I continued to gaze at the gap. There was a hole in the wall.

I lay down flat on my tummy and shined the light into the cavity. There was something pushed up into the dark hollow space. Cautiously, I reached in and pulled it out by the tip of two fingers. It was covered in dust and cobwebs. I took a deep breath, blew, and revealed an old metal box, a cigar box. It was silver in color, and on the top, there were colorful, delicately etched pictures of people in carriages. It was completely intact, with only a little rust on the edges. Removing the lid, I unveiled its secret. It was a small bluish book that was labeled "My Diary."

I shouted, "A diary!"

I scurried from beneath the bed and gently flipped it open. The pages were yellow and brittle. They were so fragile, I was scared they would crumble with each turn of the page. The first page read: *This diary belongs to Mary Beth Simmons, Jan 17, 1851.* I could not believe what I had found. I sat on the floor and started reading.

Dear Diary:

I am 16 today. Poppa sent me this diary for my birthday. So I reckon I need to write a little about myself and my family. I miss Poppa. He's gone so much of the time. I wish my Momma was still alive. Momma died when I was little. She was taken by the plague. I don't remember her much. Mammie says Poppa is out looking for me a new Momma, but I don't think I need a new Momma. Mammie takes good care of me. She's our colored maid. She's a little old short colored lady, gray hair, toothless, very quiet and very soft spoken. She makes me laugh a lot and she cooks really well. She calls me Miss Mary Boss. Mammie baked me a chocolate cake for my birthday today. They even sang Happy Birthday to me. Mammie was raped by her old white master. She had a boy named Israel.

She was sold to my Poppa real cheap when Israel was five cause Israel looked too light skinned, he had too much white blood in him. People talk you know. Israel is nice. He's my friend, and so is his sister Hester. We play games together. I taught them how to read a little bit. I taught them how to talk proper too. As proper as I know, that is. Poppa had a teacher come to my house, and she taught me how to read when I was 5. It is not allowed for colored people to do much learning, so I sneak and teach them a little. Israel doesn't pay too much attention, but Hester likes it. Hester plays with me, she is my friend. She is a slave and we are not supposed to be friends, but I don't care. The colored folk around here are hard to understand. All their words go right together. Sometimes Mammie gets to going and I can't understand a word she says. She has an older son too. His name is Jesse. He doesn't talk too much either. I don't have a lot of schooling, but I have a lot of books. I like to read. Poppa doesn't allow them to stay in the house, just Mammie. Mammie says she don't mind cause that's the way it is. I told her when I grow up, I'm going to build her, Israel, and Hester a big house on the hill. That way, she'll always be looking over me. She just laughed.

I continued to turn the pages and read.

Feb. 01, 1851
Dear Diary:

Poppa has been gone for 3 weeks. I miss him. I wish he weren't in politics. He's always gone. His trips get longer and longer. I don't ever get to go anywhere. I don't know how I will ever marry. I'm always alone with only the slaves. Thank God I have them. I never get to meet anyone, except Poppa's old friends that he brings home. I'll probably be an old maid and no one will want me. I wish I wasn't too scared to run away, cause I would.

Feb. 17, 1851
Dear Diary:

Mammie took me to Charles Towne today. We have to take a ferry boat across the river to get there. I love the boat, but Mammie is always frightened, none of them can swim. We went to the market to get fresh vegetables and we had to go the post office to see if we had any telegrams. We didn't. I strolled 'round and tried to look pretty, saw several nice gentlemen, but no one spoke to me. I twirled my dress back and forth trying to get noticed. I smiled and they nodded. That's all they ever do. I'm not sure how to catch a man. Mammie says not to worry, the right one will come along. I wonder how she knows that, but she usually is right. I still enjoyed myself very much.

I held the book in my hands, reveling in astonishment. I was so captivated – mesmerized, transfixed. I could not believe I had found a diary. I kept reading. Every page seemed to be like the last. It saddened me to read how very lonely and unhappy this young girl was.

I hated to stop reading, but I had to check on Angel. I carried it with me. Excited, I pranced down the stairs like a teenager. Turning the corner to the living room, I noticed Angel was still sitting quietly, watching television and playing with some toys. I could not wait to call Tina and tell her what I had found.

First, I had to finish doing the chores that I had started. I frolicked through the house making all the beds. Then I began scraping, scouring, and scrubbing the old wooden floors – finally waxing, polishing, and buffing them to a mirror finish. I washed, rinsed, and hung clothes on the line that was stretched from pole to pole in our backyard. I was finally finished. I poured a glass of iced tea, sat down at the kitchen table, and called Tina.

"Hello."

"Hey Tina, you'll never guess what I found."

"A body," she was quick to blurt out.

"Noooo, I . . . "

"The skeletal remains of the Simmons family."

"No, I found a . . . "

"Another secret passage, that's what it is, right? Oh that is so exciting."

I paused.

"Hey Vivian, are you there?"

"I'm here, Tina."

"Well, tell me what you found."

"I've been trying to. I found a diary."

"Damn woman, I thought you found a secret passage where all the skeletons were. So whose diary is it?"

"I thought you would never ask. It belongs to none other than Miss Mary Beth Simmons."

"No way, that is so groovy. Have you read any of it? Of course you have. I don't know what I was thinking. What did it say? Can I come over?"

I laughed. "Yeah, if you want any of those questions answered, I think you'll have to."

"I'm sorry Dear; you know I just get carried away sometimes. Let me slip on my shoes, and I'll be right there."

I sat at the kitchen table sipping my tea, getting lost in a forgotten time. I read page after page about a lonely girl who had no one – no one but her slaves, with whom friendships were forbidden. I read on.

Poppa was so angry about my friendship with Hester. He says if I don't keep her in the yard working where she belongs he will sell her. So I must hide the only friend I have. We meet in the woods and play hide and seek. We run and play like little children. Israel watches us. He never speaks. He's too shy. I tease him. What's wrong, the cat got your tongue? He just smiles with his big white teeth and downs his head.

"Mommy, what are you reading?" Angel asked, getting a cookie from the jar.

"I'm reading stories that were written a long time ago before you and I were even born."

"Well, what's it about?"

"It's about the people that used to live here."

"In our house?" she asked with a dubious look.

"Yes. It's about the people who built this place."

"Will you read to me, Mommy? I don't have anyone to play with." I looked into her lonely eyes and thought about what I had just read. I did not want my child to feel that emptiness that Mary Beth must have felt.

"Come here Angel. Jump up on Mommy's lap. How would you like to go to back to school and play with little girls your own age?"

"But Mommy, I thought you said you didn't like that school," she replied.

"I know I did Honey, but I just miss you so much when you're gone. Would you like to try going back again?"

"You mean that real school that I went to before? I can go back to school like Gary?" she asked with excitement.

"Yes, just like Gary. As soon as Miss Tina gets here, we'll take you. Come on, let's go find you a pretty dress. I'll let you pick it out."

"Okay."

I fumbled through Angel's dresser drawers for a pair of socks and panties while she looked in the closet for her dress. She happily hummed a little tune, pushing hanger after hanger aside.

"This one, I want to wear this one."

I turned to look. It was a short-sleeved flowered hip hugger dress.

"Angel Honey, I think it's a little too cold for that one. Let Mommy help you find another one."

"No, you said I could pick it out. I want to wear this one," she whined, poking out her lips and hugging it tightly.

"Okay, okay, you win, but you are going to have to wear a sweater."

"Yes ma'am, I will."

"Halloo . . . knock, knock. Where are you?" Tina called out from the front door.

"We're upstairs; come on up."

"Wow, the place looks great," she said entering Angel's room.

"I can't believe how neat and clean everything is. Are you some kind of clean freak? You're not O.C.D. are you?"

"Thanks, and no I'm not. I was just telling Angel she could go to school. Do you want to ride with us? It's only a few miles down the road. She really enjoyed it before, but I haven't taken her back because I wanted to keep her to myself."

"Sure, that sounds good to me."

"Me too," Angel shouted.

"Well, let's go. I'll drive you," Tina said, shaking her car keys.

"All righty, let's go," I said.

Angel grabbed my hand and almost pulled me down the stairs. She was so excited, her eyes were glued to the car window all the way to school. Her smile went from ear to ear.

"Look Mommy," she shouted. "A bunch of little kids are playing outside. Can I play with them? Is that my school?" Angel asked, as we pulled into the parking lot.

"I hope so. Let's go inside and make sure they still have an available spot for you."

We went inside and sure enough, they had an opening. I filled out the necessary papers again, with Angel tugging on me the whole time. She could not be still. The teachers were glad to take Angel to the playground. She was jumping up and down with excitement.

She kissed me goodbye and off she went. I was a little uneasy about leaving her, but Tina and I could not wait to get back to the house. I believe Tina was just as anxious as I was to go through all the stuff we had found.

"I can't wait to see the rest of the furniture in the attic. The things you've already brought down are gorgeous. You did say there are more things up there, didn't you?"

"There's not too much, but enough for us to look through. I can't wait to really search this place. There is no telling what else I might find. Now that Angel is in daycare again, it will give me a lot more time."

"Do you think there may be more hidden rooms?" Tina asked.

"Who knows? I have plenty of hours to spare. How about you, do you have hours to spare?" I asked, looking at Tina as I waited for my answer.

"Sure, I don't have anything else to do. But I want to see that diary first," Tina said as we pulled back into the driveway.

"Well, come on in. It's in the kitchen. Why don't you go sit in the living room? I'll bring us a glass of tea and get the diary. You can read while I finish going through the trunk we found. There are so many different pictures and papers in there."

"That sounds good to me."

I headed to the kitchen as Tina made her way to the living room. I poured another glass of ice tea for Tina and retrieved mine. With the diary under my arm, I returned. When I wobbled in, Tina was already going through the trunk. She had a handful of pictures and was looking at them one by one. She leaped to her feet to give me some assistance.

"I thought you may need a hand."

"Thanks. Did you find anything interesting?"

"Did I ever!"

"Look at this," she said, holding up a picture. "This has to be Mr. Simmons with the wooden leg. And look, this is probably his daughter, Mary Beth, beside him. But who do you think this man is beside her?"

I walked over and sat beside Tina, looking at the picture. There was a tall slender man wearing a hat that was half-cocked and covering one eye. The two men wore suspenders. The younger man was standing next to the girl we presumed to be Mary Beth.

"I don't know. I haven't read anything about another man. Maybe it's Mary Beth's husband."

"No way, she's way too young. Maybe there are some more pictures of him in here that will tell us," Tina said, digging for the bottom of the trunk.

"We think she was too young, but she didn't. Her diary depicts her as depressed at sixteen worried about being an old maid if she wasn't married."

"Wow! Thank God for change. Let's look some more."

We dug deep into the stale stuffy trunk, viewing picture after picture. There were ample amounts of Mr. Simmons with all kinds of people, probably prominent in their day. There were a few pictures of the girl we had tentatively identified as Mary Beth and one more of the mysterious man.

The man stood at attention, arms stiff at his pant legs, clearly honoring the Army uniform he displayed. His face was rough, worn, and unhappy. But still, the identity was uncertain.

I began reading letters while Tina read the diary. The letters were just as brittle as everything else; we had to handle them very carefully. We sat reading page after page. Every time we found something interesting, we would suspend the search and discuss it.

Then, buried deep in the bottom of the trunk, I found a stack of letters with a string tied around them. I gently removed them from their secret domain.

"Look at these," I said to Tina, "Letters that have not been opened."

"Who are they to?"

"Mary Beth."

I fumbled through the bunch and discovered they were all addressed to Mary Beth. None of them had been read. They were tightly sealed, secured by a thin white string. I carefully untied them, opened the first one, and began reading.

My Dearest Mary Beth,

I hope this letter finds you and Poppa doing well. I myself am fine. The army is tough, but I really like it. I really am proud to be fighting for our country. One day maybe I will be a general or someone important. Maybe then Poppa will accept my dreams.

I hope Poppa has found a way to forgive me for leaving. I am a grown man now, with my own dreams. The world is much different out here. I do not want to stay and run the plantation, please make him understand. The plantation is your dream, yours and Poppa's. You can have it all, you belong there, and I don't, no matter what Poppa might say. I don't want to be a planter.

I will be back again one day, but only to visit. I will always be Poppa's son and I will always be your brother, no matter what. I love you,

Forever your brother,

Johnny

"Wow, that's deep," Tina said sitting back on the sofa and looking at the picture of the former mystery man. "It's her brother; he must have been named after his father. I wonder what he did for his father to kick him out."

"It didn't really say he kicked him out. I think Johnny must have wanted to be on his own. In the olden days, sons were most always named after their fathers and followed in their footsteps. Johnny evidently was not a follower. He wrote he didn't want to be a planter; I guess that was the term they used for farmer."

"I wonder what happened to him," Tina said, reaching for another letter.

"Hey Tina, do you think your friend Mr. Jesse would know anything about who Johnny was?"

"He may."

"Since you know him, maybe you could talk to him?"

"I . . . don't know. He sure seemed to be real mad the last time we were there. I've seen him several times walking this way. One time I saw him standing at the edge of the woods. I called out to him, but when he recognized me, he just turned and walked away. Have you seen him out here?"

"No, I haven't. Do you think maybe he misses taking care of this place?"

"I doubt that, would you? You saw how old he is. It's probably a relief. I think he always had to stay on his children and grandchildren to work over here."

"Maybe so, but he has been taking care of this place most of his life; he might miss doing it. Would you mind trying to talk to him again for me?"

"I don't mind, but I think it's a waste of time. He sure didn't want to tell us anything before."

Tina gathered the letters, gently laid them on the sofa, and jumped to her feet. "Let's go look around in the attic. Maybe we can find some more secrets hiding in the walls."

I laughed as her chubby little fingers grabbed my arm and pulled me toward the stairwell.

Tina and I walked up the narrow steps. I took her through each of the hidden rooms we had found. Then we walked down the long hall-way that led to the living room where the secret door was.

"Why do you think they would put a hidden room onto the living room? It seems strange, don't it?" Tina asked, looking at the door that slid into the wall.

"Not really, if you think about it. This house was built, I think, during the Revolutionary War. If intruders came up unexpectedly, the family could get away quickly if they were downstairs. They probably had everything they needed stashed away in here."

"I guess that's true, but what if they were upstairs? Maybe there's another secret door," Tina said, raising her eyebrows.

"You really get into this kind of stuff, huh?"

"Yeah, I find it very exciting. Believe me, living out here, you have to grab all the excitement you can, Honey, whenever you can."

"When I first met you, you were scared of this place. You don't seem that way now."

"Well, look how long you've been here, and nothing has happened to you. And anyway, you have my curiosity up. I would like to know what happened to everyone. What secrets is this place hiding? Where and why did everyone disappear?"

"You're beginning to sound just like me, Tina. Come on, let's go look around."

We turned and walked about fifteen feet. All of a sudden, the slid-ing door slammed shut. We looked at one another, then ran to it. We tried pushing and pulling, but it would not move.

"So, how did that happen?" Tina asked.

"Who knows? Things like that happen around here all the time. We'll just have to turn around and go back the way we came in."

We zigzagged, weaved, crisscrossed, swayed and turned up the long grueling hallway, finally reaching the other end. To our dismay, that door too was immovable.

"Now what?" Tina asked.

"Maybe we should try beating on the hinges. Jim had trouble get-ting them to open at first. He just beat on these rusty hinges a little, and it opened."

"Just beat on the hinges, huh?" Tina said sarcastically.

"It could be worse," I said, "The lights could go out."

As the words rolled from my dry lips, we found ourselves in total darkness.

"Oh shit," Tina whispered, grabbing my arm. "I don't like this. What happened to the lights? What the hell are we going to do now?"

Whispering back, I replied, "I don't know. I don't think there is anything we can do."

"We have to do something. We can't just stand here and let this thing get us."

"What thing?"

"Your friendly ghost," she mumbled.

"We don't know if it's a ghost."

"No, we don't, but we don't know that it's not, either."

"Sometimes the lights do this. Maybe they'll be back on in a minute," I said, trying to reassure her as she squeezed my arm a little too tightly.

"Vivian, listen," Tina whispered.

"What? Listen to what?"

"I hear someone."

I listened intently. We heard something that sounded vaguely like a softly whispering voice. It was inconceivably creepy, a low whine, a shallow whimper. We stood silent, huddled together, not moving, not blinking, with no air escaping our lungs. We just listened to the faint buoyancy of the voice that echoed through the air, growing louder and louder until the gloomy darkness stood still.

We waited in the black silence. My palms were clammy, feet slippery in my shoes as I sweated preposterously with the growing nervous tension. It was ludicrous to be so scared, but impossible not to be.

"Is it gone?" Tina whispered.

"I don't know."

"How are we going to get out of here?"

"I don't know. Let's feel for the door and try it again."

"All right, but I'm not turning you loose."

We quietly inched along the wall, reaching blindly for the door. Grasping the knob, I tugged, but it was still jammed. Angered by fear and driven by persistence, I yanked the cold metal knob, breaking it free from its frame and thrusting us onto the grimy surface.

"*Help.*"

I chuckled as I lay on top of Tina with the rusty old knob still in my hand.

"I can't help you; I can't help myself."

"I didn't say that," Tina mumbled.

I moved slightly to a sitting position, holding onto Tina's hand. "It must be back."

"Yeah," she whimpered.

"Help," it cried again. "Please, let me out, I can't breathe. It's so hot in here. Help me, please."

Tina scrambled behind me and wrapped herself around my arm. "Who is that?" she asked.

"I don't know. Shhhh, be quiet. Where are you?" I called out, but there was no answer. The cave black hallway got icy cold, Arctic cold. I shivered as the air moved through my body. My long hair lifted and streamed into the air as the breeze swiftly passed.

"I don't like this Vivian," Tina said. "I want out of here, I want to go home."

"Me too."

Instantaneously the lights came on, and the door opened. It seemed the spirit was listening. It regarded our request and set us free.

"Let's get the hell out of here," Tina exclaimed jumping to her feet, and pulling me toward the door.

She did not have to ask me twice. I was terrified too. It was very eerie to have heard that voice again.

"I wonder who that was."

"Who what was?" Tina asked.

"That voice, the lady. You did hear it, right?"

"I heard something. I'm not sure it's a *who*. I think more like a *what*. How could you not be scared living in this place with all the weird things that go on here? Voices in the dark – come on, you have to be scared – especially staying by yourself."

"I admit, I am a little scared, but I don't think whatever is here will hurt me. I just have to find out what it wants. And I am not alone; I do have the kids."

"Me . . . I wouldn't really give a damn what it wants. I would just leave it alone and get the hell out here. I think I need a drink.

"Do you have anything?" Tina asked, walking down to the first level.

"Yeah, I just made another pitcher of tea."

"Tea, the hell with tea, I mean a drink! You know, a real drink like vodka, whiskey, rum – liquor, that kind of drink. Something strong, something good, something that makes you not give a shit."

"Oh," I said laughing. "Jim put all that in the basement. Come on, we can go see what you have to choose from."

"Basement, noooo, I think I'll pass. I was in the dark long enough, thank you very much. I don't think my heart can handle it twice."

"What happened to grabbing the excitement while you can?"

"Honey, I just grabbed enough excitement to last me a lifetime. I think I might be just a little too old for this much excitement. My heart is still fluttering. I think I lost a couple of beats back there. I probably aged a little too."

I laughed, "I think your hair did turn a little grayer."

"I don't doubt that," Tina said, patting her spiked little ponytail.

"And what do you mean, a little more? Baby Doll, this head gets a bottle of blond every five weeks whether it needs it or not."

I snickered at her silliness. "It's almost time for Gary to come home from school, and I need to go pick up Angel. Would you like to ride with me?"

"No, I better get on home."

"How about I drop you off?"

"I have my car outside, remember?"

"Oh yeah, I must have lost some of my memory in the dark."

"Memory, I think you've lost your whole damn brain! No offense Honey, but, anyone who could stay here by themselves can't be all there."

"You are probably right. Then again, at our age we need all the excitement we can get!"

"You're not going to forget that statement, huh?"

"Nope, I sure ain't."

We laughed walking to our cars. Tina got into her 1966 "Arcadian Blue" Mustang, and I drove away in my faithful station wagon. I headed into Angel's school to sign her out. She was all excited and had a lot to tell about her new friends. She talked the entire way home.

When we arrived at the house, Gary was sitting on the front steps waiting for me. I wasn't surprised he had beaten us there, but I was surprised to see that he was soaking wet. He had mud all over his school clothes and shoes.

"What in the world have you been doing?" I snapped.

"I wasn't doing anything. You weren't home, so I went for a walk around the pond looking for some bull frogs. I slipped at the edge and fell in. Mom, it was like a suction cup had me, and I couldn't get out. It was pulling me in the water, I thought I was in quicksand."

"What was pulling you in the water?"

"The water was; it was weird. It felt like the water had hands. It had a hold of me; I was screaming for help, I was so scared. I thought for sure I was going to drown. I thought I saw a little boy standing at the front door. I called out to him, but he disappeared."

"What do you mean he disappeared? Where did he go?"

"I don't know, he just disappeared. If it wasn't for that old black man, I probably would have drowned."

"What old black man?"

"I don't know his name. The one that hangs out in the woods, he pulled me out, and then he screamed at me. He yelled right up in my face."

"What did he say? And when does he hang out in the woods?"

"He's always in the woods. He just stands there and stares at the house."

"Why haven't you told me about him?"

"I don't know. I just didn't. He didn't seem like he was hurting anything. I just figured he was lonely or something. When he pulled me out, he started yelling at me, and I got scared. He yelled, 'Stay away from the pond,' but not that clearly. Then he mumbled something I couldn't understand. He acted like a crazy man, and he talked funny too."

"Thank God he was here. Did you thank him?"

"No, I ran. He was really mad, and I was really scared. He acted like I had no business being there, like this was his property. I didn't know what he might do to me, so I ran to the house."

"Come on in. You need to get yourself cleaned up. I'll fix some dinner while you're washing up. Would y'all like anything special tonight?"

"Hamburgers," Angel shouted.

"It's Gary's night to decide, Angel. Tomorrow night is your night."

"Hamburgers are fine, Mom," Gary answered.

"Hamburgers it is. I'll cook them on the grill. That way there won't be any mess in the kitchen. Now you two go wash up."

Preparing the hamburgers on the grill, I started thinking about what had happened to Gary. Who was the man that had pulled him out of the pond, and who was the little boy? Did Gary imagine him? No one had seen a little boy before. I wondered if he had fallen in the same place that I had. I never told the kids about my incident, as I did not want to scare them. However, I was having second thoughts. I felt I should tell them for their own safety.

The place was getting more and more mysterious. I wondered if other people had fallen into the pond and drowned. I wondered who the man and the little girl in the boat were. I had a house of many secrets with no answers. Who pulled Gary out of the water? I really thought Mr. Jesse would be too old; someone had helped both of us, but who?

After dinner, we sat outside enjoying the countryside. Angel was running around trying to catch the lightning bugs that joined us at dusk. She was going to put them in a jar and take them to school to show her friends.

Gary and I talked about his school and new friends. He seemed to be fond of most of his teachers, except his math teacher, Mrs. Thompson. It was a shame; he did not do too well in that subject and needed all the guidance he could get.

"Mom, I have a friend at school named Isaac. I was wondering if maybe he could spend the night here Friday or Saturday."

"Sure Gary, I don't see why not."

"He's a black boy. Does that matter?"

"No, it really doesn't matter to me, although you know that people may make fun of you for having a colored friend."

"I know Mom. They already do. When we lived in the city, no one said anything. We all played in the streets together, but here, a lot of the kids tease him. I feel sorry for him because he's a real groovy kid."

"Well Honey, living in the country, things are a little different, especially in the South. If you don't care what people say, I don't either. He's more than welcome here if he is your friend."

"Great! Most of the kids at school think this place is haunted. They think we're crazy for living here."

"What about Isaac? He's not scared to stay here?"

"No. He said he's a descendant of the slaves that lived here. He used to help his grandfather cut the grass before we moved in."

"Oh yeah," I excitedly said. "Would his grandfather be Mr. Jesse?"

"He didn't say his name, Mom, just Granddad. He did mention his grandfather would have a fit if he knew he was even thinking about staying here. Isaac said he's been forbidden to come back to this place."

"Why is that?" I asked curiously.

"He didn't say why."

"You tell him we would love to have him stay with us. Just make sure his mother doesn't mind. I would like to talk with her first. See if you can get their phone number for me."

"I don't know if they have a phone, Mom."

"If he doesn't, find out where he lives, and we'll go by his house. It's getting late, and the bugs are getting bad. We should go in."

After everyone had gone to bed, I sat alone going through the old wooden trunk, retreating in time almost two hundred years . . . looking at pictures, reading about the war, the plague, and the hard times they had to endure. The hot summer nights were without the comfort of electricity; there was no television, no radios, no fans or air conditioners – just the sounds that echoed through the wind. All God's creatures, like crickets, frogs, maybe dogs, or an occasional song from a whipoorwill. My window to that life was the old diary that depicted the loneliness of a 16-year-old child who was lost in a world where her only friends were forbidden because of the color of their skin. She was a white girl who was raised by slaves, who were thought of more as the enemy – uncivilized beings. Ironically, our ancestors trusted these so-called uncultured people to care for their children.

Slaves took care of Mary Beth almost her entire life, but were not worthy enough to be called friends. I thought about how times had changed. Then again, there were those who never changed with the times. Racism still exists throughout the States, and there are whites who still do not condone friendship between races. There are also colored people who hold the white people responsible for things their ancestors did years before they were even born.

It's sad to think about the technological feats that we have accomplished, the freedom we have, the choices we can make … yet, we still point fingers because of our color. If the world were blind, maybe that would be a blessing. How would you know? Would there be a difference? There is so much to think of and so much more to accomplish in our world today. It is a shame so much of our focus is wasted on the color of someone's skin and not placed on the person inside. The South will never change; it is what it is.

Sitting there thinking about my ancestors and thinking about Gary's new friend, who also had ancestors here, was exciting. The odds of Gary's meeting a relative who used to live there had to be astronomical. It never entered my mind that there might be someone in the school with ties to our house. Favor must have been with us, especially for Gary to become his friend.

"Is this a coincidence?" I wondered. "Maybe someone had a hand in it. Maybe the spirits of this place led Gary to this boy. Maybe they want me to find out the secrets hidden here. I have to search everything I can find. I cannot take anything for granted. I must fulfill the destiny that led me here and finish the legacy that my family forgot." Contrary to what the townspeople thought, I was a survivor and my family was too.

After school on Thursday, Gary finally brought home Isaac's phone number, and I could not wait to give his mother a call. The anticipation of learning what she may have known about the mystery of the house was overwhelming. I was hoping she was not going to be like Mr. Jesse. I wondered if she knew him or if they were related. I sat in the kitchen and dialed the number, hoping the right words would come to me.

A soft voice answered on the other end.

"Hi, this is Vivian, Gary's Mom, is this Isaac?"

"Yes ma' am," the timid voice answered.

"Is your mother home Isaac? I'd like to talk with her if she's not busy."

"Yes ma'am. She's not busy. Could you hold on, please?"

"Sure Isaac," I answered.

He was very polite. I liked that already.

"Hello," a docile voice came across the phone.

"Is this Mrs. Labore?" I asked.

"Yes it is," she answered.

"This is Vivian Godfree. How are you?"

"I'm doing jest fine, thank you for asking."

"It seems that my son Gary and your son Isaac have become good friends at school. Gary would like Isaac to come spend Friday night at our home. If you don't mind, we'd love to have him over."

"Yes, I have heard all about Gary."

I was thinking to myself, "Oh God, here it comes." She is going to unload her frustrations . . . tell me how crazy we are for living here.

"I'm glad you called me. I was going to call you later. Gary sounds like a nice young boy, or as Isaac says, 'He's real groovy,'" she said, laughing. "I really don't mind him staying as long as my father-in-law doesn't find out."

"You don't mind him staying here?" I said surprised. "Do you know where we live?"

"Sure I do. You live at the old Simmons Plantation. That's why I said as long as my father-in-law doesn't find out. He'd have a fit. I could bring Isaac over Friday right after school; I would love to meet you."

"Yes, that'll be great, I would love to meet you too, Mrs. Labore. It is very rare that I hear those words, someone wanting to come over here."

"Please, call me Edna. So the people around here are giving you a hard time, huh?"

"Yes they are. You wouldn't believe half the things they say."

"Sure I would, that's what makes this small town tick. The more gossip they can stir, the happier they are. Listen, I hate to cut you short, but Pop is coming in. I'll see you Friday, okay?"

"Yes, that sounds great."

I hung the phone up with a sigh of relief. I could not believe she said "yes." I was anxious to meet her, and I was hoping she could tell me why Mr. Jesse was so rude to me. If she did not know why, maybe she could find out. Maybe I was closer to finding the divine truth about the place. Perhaps I could help the spirits find peace.

I gave a little skip and headed to the living room. I could not wait to tell Gary the news. To my dismay, he and Angel were not there. I called out to them, but they did not answer. I started meandering up the stairs to Gary's room, then to Angel's. Everything was quiet. I called out again, but still, they did not answer. I heard a shallow voice, a whisper coming from down the hall.

"What are you guys up to?" I asked, sneaking down the hallway.

I tiptoed toward the sound; it was coming from my bedroom. I stood outside the bedroom door and listened. I could hear the sounds, however, I could not understand it. I quietly turned the doorknob, and rapidly, I pushed the door opened and jumped inside.

"What are you two doing in here?" I shouted in a playful tone.

To my surprise, it was not the kids. A ghostly glow was kneeling beside my bed; it turned and faced me. It was too beautiful to be real, a bright radiant light, a woman – or a figure of a woman. It was an unnatural, lustrous, pallid light. The supernatural figure had long wavy hair. She stood and faced me.

I did not know what to do. I stood silent, my loose lips quivered, my knees shook. I desperately wanted to speak, but still, there were no words departing my open mouth. The blood vessels in my neck were taut, but I could not produce a sound. There were so many things that I wanted to say. Where were the words? I thought, "Here's my chance, and my vocabulary has forsaken me. My brain hears my voice from within. The words are there, just stuck in the passage, waiting to exhale."

"Please, help me," she said. She reached her hands out to me.

"I . . . I . . . " finally a hoarse stuttering whisper emerged.

No words, just a stuttering, simple sound. As quickly as I muttered, a loud noise echoed from the hallway.

"Mom," it was Gary running up the stairs. "Mom," Gary called out from the hall.

The woman spun around, a startled expression passed across her face, and she disappeared. A cold blast of air circulated the room. It swooped down and vanished out the door, blowing my hair into my face and following her path.

"Wow!" Gary said excited.

"Did you see it?" I asked, running out of the room.

"See what? I didn't see anything."

"You didn't see anything?" I shouted. "Why did you yell out? You scared it away."

"I scared what away? I didn't see anything, but it sure was cold. What's wrong Mom? What was it, what was I suppose to have seen?" Gary asked.

"Nothing," I said discouraged. "Where's your sister?"

"She's downstairs. We were in the attic looking through some of that old stuff, and then we went back downstairs to watch TV. I was wondering if you called Isaac's mom yet?"

"Yes I did, but what were you doing in the attic?" I asked. "I called out for you and no one answered."

"I just told you. We were looking through some more of those old pictures and stuff. You know you can't hear anything in there, Mom. I can't wait to show Isaac some of this ancient stuff. Come look, it's great. What did his mom say?"

"I'm glad you found some good things, but from now on, let me know where you are. I don't think it's a good idea for you two to be wandering around here by yourselves. You know how those doors close and get stuck sometimes. And you need to be real careful with those old things up there too. They're irreplaceable."

"We will. Why do you want me to tell you where we are, Mom? Do you think the ghost might get us?" Gary asked, joking.

"Like I said, those doors get stuck sometimes. I just don't think it is a good idea for me not to know where you are. And the answer to your first question, Isaac's mother said he could come and stay tomorrow night."

"Groovy!" Gary exclaimed.

He jumped on the handrail and slid down to the bottom. I was glad to see him so excited. It would be nice to have some different faces around here.

A smile stayed on my face as I thought about Isaac coming over. I believe I may have been just as excited as Gary.

Then I thought about the ghostly lady. I wondered if that was Mary Beth I had seen. Could she have been the one crying and whispering in the dark? She appeared to be a very lonely person in her diary. It would be awful to spend eternity just as lonely in the afterlife.

I walked back to my room, took a deep breath, and slowly entered. The room was empty. I looked in the closet and under the bed, but there was nothing. "Could I have imagined it? No, I know I didn't. She was here," I thought.

"Mary Beth," I called softly. "Mary Beth," I called again. No one answered. "I must be going crazy," I expressed my feelings out loud and exited the room.

I went downstairs to join Gary and Angel. They were still in the living room, continuing to go through the trunk and watching television at the same time.

"Mom, look at these pictures we found," Angel said, holding some pictures up.

"Yes, I've seen them, Baby. Those are the people that used to live here."

"Some of these pictures are colored people, Mom. Do you think they were the slaves that lived here?" Gary asked.

"I'm sure they probably were," I answered.

"I bet Isaac will be really surprised to see these," Gary said, going through the pictures. "They may be some of his relatives."

"What are slaves, Mommy?" Angel asked.

"Well, if you sit down, I will tell you the story about slaves." Angel slid over, and I sat down beside her on the sofa.

"A long time ago, the white people used colored people to work for them. They had found some of the black people in the woods of Africa. Some were captured by other black tribes during different wars, and instead of killing them, they were sold to white people. Some slaves were treated really badly by the white people."

"Where's Africa, Mommy?"

"It's a long, long way from here, Honey."

"It's all the way across the ocean," Gary added.

I continued with my story, "The white men wanted the strongest ones. When the black tribes captured their prisoners, they let the white people choose which ones they wanted."

"What happened to the ones that they didn't want?" Angel asked.

"Most of them were killed, although some were made to be slaves over there. They had to work really hard, and they were fed very small portions of food — only enough to keep them alive."

"Those that were brought to the United States were chained on the ships and brought back across the seas. They stole them from their families, whipped them, and hung them up like animals. They were bought and sold like horses; the white people did not think they were civilized like us."

"What does ci . . . vi . . . lize mean?" Angel asked.

"Civilized is when you live like normal everyday people, get an education, and use manners. When you are uncivilized, you live wild and crazy, like animals in the jungle."

"Did slaves live in the jungle?" Angel asked.

"Yes they did, however they had their own beliefs and their own kind of towns. They did not have cows and pigs in pens. They hunted for their food in the deep forest. They spoke another language too. That also was taken from them. They had to learn to speak English like us."

"Well, the jungle doesn't seem like a bad place to me. Why didn't the white people just leave them alone?"

"Sometimes people make wrong decisions, and this was one of those. Many of the colored people now believe the white people should still be responsible for the past. Although this happened over a hundred years ago, it's hard for people to quit blaming. I feel sorry for those that were captured and taken from their homes, although there is nothing we can do about what happened years ago. And there are still white people who do not want the colored people to be equal to us. So we still have a long road to travel before we can all get along."

"Where have we got to go to, Mommy?"

"What do you mean?"

"She's talking about the long road you mentioned," Gary replied.

Gary and I both laughed at her. "I didn't mean we actually had to go somewhere. That was just an expression. What I meant was that it may take years before we all can get along without blaming each other."

"Oh, I bet I could get along with them. I feel sorry for them too, Mommy. Do you think Mr. Issy was a slave?"

I looked down at Angel. I wanted to discourage her from her imaginary friend, but she really believed he was real.

"I don't know Honey. Maybe you should ask him the next time you see him. For now, it's getting late. Bedtime," I said, tickling Angel to the floor.

Angel and Gary kissed me goodnight and headed to their rooms.

"May I play with you and Isaac when he comes over?" Angel asked Gary.

"No way kiddo. You're a girl. You have your own friends," Gary answered.

"Well, do you think Isaac might have a sister who will want to play with me?"

"Maybe, I'll ask him. Just promise not to bug us when he gets here."

"I promise. Thanks Gary."

I listened as the kids said their goodnights and disappeared into the safety of their rooms. I, of course, had to go through more old papers. I was confident I would find the answers to all the mysteries the house held. Someone had to have written something about what happened here.

CHAPTER 8

THE TELEGRAM

Jim had been gone for about two weeks. That was the longest time he had been away since we moved there. It was very lonely without him, although I did have a lot to keep me busy, and that took my mind off my loneliness.

I thought about Isaac coming to spend the night. I had so many questions I wanted to ask. I wondered if he knew anything about my family or the slaves that used to live here. I was hoping he did. I also wanted to ask his mother some questions without making her mad. I could not wait. I felt like a kid waiting for a surprise.

I picked up Mary Beth's diary and lay across my bed. I opened it to the bookmark and continued to read. Every page was as interesting as the one before. It drew me deeper and deeper into her world. I could not turn the pages fast enough. I wanted to absorb more.

As I continued to read, my body relaxed and my eyes grew heavy. I kept nodding, dropping my head, and resting it on my arm. Laying still, fighting sleep, I felt something cold touch my hand. My eyes popped open. Not moving my body, my eyes followed my arm slowly down to my hand. Eyebrows raised, eyelids stretched, eyes fixed without motion, I saw a ghostly hand patting the top of mine. Paralyzed with fear, I blinked several times; it was still there. I rolled my eyes upward and stared into a beautiful face. I was almost certain it was Mary Beth. She laid one hand on mine and pointed to the diary with the other. She never emitted a sound, just pointed to the book.

I turned the page, and she tightened her grip. I watched as she disappeared into the pages and seized me willfully to her side. I felt her emotions – the excitement and the displeasures she had divulged to me.

I travelled back to her generation, into a way of life that was implausible and astonishing. She invited me to see, touch, and smell everything that I read, and I took nothing for granted. I began to recognize much of place and the people. She invisibly introduced me to her world, their world, and my forgotten ancestors.

I listened intently to every word that they had to say. I was no longer reading her diary. They were telling the story, and I was the bystander. I observed their lifestyle and the hardships of everyday life. I was elated to have the chance to witness such personal affairs. I was not sure why, but it did not matter.

Mary Beth wrote briefly of her brother Johnny. He was the only one I had no certainty of. She was always saying how she missed him and would love to see him. She never wrote where he might be or gave any information on why he had abandoned the plantation.

Her friendship with Hester grew stronger and stronger. She wrote several times about the slaves who felt more like her family. They were her life. They were all she really knew. Her feelings for them were sentiments she would always have to hide. The people who raised her, took care of her, and nursed her when she was sick: this was her illicit treasure.

Every page that turned took me deeper into it. Every event that took place, I experienced firsthand. Looking over shoulders, peeping in windows, I was always in the shadow of darkness, but given approval to view every aspect of the story that was unfolding. Watching, listening, feeling their happiness and sadness, I was there, maybe on the outside looking in, nevertheless, I was there.

May 10, 1851
Dear Diary:

Mammie and I went to Charles Towne today. There was a poster in front of the trading store that made me very excited. There's going to be a dance. I sent Poppa a telegram to see if I can have permission to go to the town dance. July 4th is the annual event. Now that I am 16, it's time for me to start looking for a husband. I've never been to a dance. I don't know anyone, but I'm sure I'll have fun. Mammie says I'll meet a lot of new friends there. I hope he sends his permission back real soon.

May 17, 1851
Dear Diary:

It's been a week, and I still haven't heard from Poppa. I hope he writes soon. I'm so excited I can hardly sleep. Hester says she can help make me real pretty. She's going to fix my hair for me.

May 30, 1851
Dear Diary:

It's been so hot today. Hester and I went to the pond for a swim. We had a lot of fun. She can't swim; but I can swim like a fish. I taught her how to hold her breath and swim under the water. She didn't like it. She said she didn't like the water in her ears. When we got back, Mammie had a surprise for me. She made me a dancing dress. It's very pretty, and it is a perfect fit. Hester says she wishes she was white so she could go with me. I wish so too, because I don't know anybody . . . Israel says I looked beautiful. Of course he downed his head when he said it. I am surprised he said anything at all, he's so shy. I can't wait to go to the dance.

June 7, 1851
Dear Diary:

Hester fixed my hair today. We made it look a lot of different ways. I think I am going to wear it up on top of my head with ringlets coming down the back. I like it that way and Mammie says it looks best that way. I think it makes me look more grown up. I like it like that. I have to look my best for all the gentlemen. That's where most young girls find their husbands. I'm surely going to get mine too.

June 14, 1851
Dear Diary:

Mammie is going to Charles Towne tomorrow. I'm sure to have a telegram from Poppa. I'm so excited, I can't wait. I told Mammie to go early. The dance is in three weeks. I know Poppa will say yes.

June 19, 1851
Dear Diary:

I still have no reply from my Poppa. If I don't hear from him, I'll go anyway, even if I have to sneak. I know I really can't, but I might try. I've never been on the ferry boat by myself. I'm sure I will be scared. But if I'm going to find me a husband, I need to go. The ferry boat is not too scary in the day time, but at night, I'm sure it will be.

June 28, 1851
Dear Diary:

Mammie brought back a telegram from Poppa today. I was wrong. He won't let me go. Poppa will not allow me to go to the dance. I have cried a river of tears today. I am so disappointed in him. I do not understand why I have to live my life alone. Poppa says he is going to bring me home a husband. He has a man in mind for me to marry. I don't want him to choose my husband. I want to choose my own husband. I wish I could find Johnny, I would run away. I don't want to live here anymore. I hate it here. Johnny was right, this place is boring. If I had some money, I would leave.

I continued reading, I felt so sorry for Mary Beth. Most of the pages of her secret thoughts were solely on the dance. It was a place to find romance, a companion, a friend, a dream that had been forbidden. She had retreated into her bedroom, bolting the door behind her. Refusing all food, her desire was to die. She felt abandoned and deserted by the only family she really had, her father. With no positive outlook on the future, she lay alone in the intense heat of the day, while the silent frightening night came in unnoticed.

Times were so different then. I could not believe at sixteen, she was so anxious to marry. Worst of all, her father was choosing her husband. How awful! I continued to read, focusing on her life of long ago. I was falling profoundly deeper, getting lost in a time that only books had to offer, but no book had ever really captivated me like this one. Her diary truly gave me a realization of that era and its long-lasting effects. There were no words that could make someone feel the intensity of their reality and all that they endured. Witnessing it with my own eyes gave me a new perspective of their life.

I was living it. I was there – understanding, experiencing. Somehow, some way, I had entered a dimension of the past. Each time I read Mary Beth's diary, I was swallowed, consumed, and transported by every page it had to offer. I became confused and delusional about where I belonged – in the present or the past. The diary was electrifying, hypnotizing, and paralyzing. I had no jurisdiction over it. I gave myself to realm of the past.

Dear Diary:

It has been 2 days, and I haven't eaten anything. I don't want to live like this anymore. I have no friends or family here, just Mammie and her kids. I told Mammie I should have been black, I think I would have been happier. Mammie says that ain't true. She said I am lucky to have a father like Poppa. She says he's doing the best he knows how, but I don't think so. If Momma would have not died, I don't think she would have left me alone all the time. I wish I would have died with her.

Dear Diary:

I have unlocked the door. I did not want to die alone. I have not eaten now for 6 days. I am so hungry. I feel so weak and not in my right mind. The hot sun seems like a fire burning through my window. My body is soaked with perspiration, but I can't live like this, in this lonely world.

Mammie sat with me yesterday, and Israel sat by me today. He kept a cold washcloth on my head. He brought me a piece of homemade apple pie, my favorite. It smelled delicious. I wanted it so badly, but I can't give in. I must die. I have no desire to go on.

Mary Beth's handwriting was getting very hard to read, as the letters were running together. I wanted to help her as I watched how she lay so helplessly in bed, growing extremely weak and giving up on life. I yearned to shake her and let her know life was not supposed to be like that. A tear ran down my cheek thinking about this teenage child being so miserable.

My desperation had allowed me to become a spirit from the present and invisible to the past. I watched and listened carefully. This was no longer my life. I listened as Mary Beth took over again.

July 4, 1851
Dear Diary:

I think it has been 8 days since I ate anything. Today is the day of the dance, my dance. This was my last chance for happiness which I have been denied. What better time to leave this land? I think it's my time to let go. I can hardly lift my head. Israel has been right here with me. He slept in the chair at the foot of my bed last night. He seems to be the only one who cares - him, Mammie, and Hester. They have taken turns by my side, but what does that matter?

Dear Diary:

Day 9. Israel has stayed again by my side. He held on to my hand all night. "Please Miss Mary Beth," he said. "You have to eat. You can't just lie here and die, I won't let you. If you eat, I'll help find you a man to marry, if you will let me. I hope you can hear me, Miss Mary Beth. We love you."

Israel was never much for words. But these words seem to be from his heart, the right words, and meaningful words. I listened as he spoke softly. No one had ever told me they loved me, except Mammie. I never thought anyone else did, but maybe my Poppa, least not Israel, and his English, why it was better than mine. Some of his words he was using, I ain't never heard of. I thought I must have been dreaming.

"You're so young and beautiful, you can't give up," Israel whispered. "You have too much to live for. You have many more dances to go to. Why, the men will be fighting, merely to get a dance with you. You can't disappoint this town and this plantation, you're gonna have to run it. We can't do it without you. Please don't give up on us."

147

CHAPTER 9

JEST A MAN

Mary Beth had taken over my mind and body. My thoughts were no longer my own. She had taken over telling the story. I was only a visitor, a witness to her perception of the past. Here is her story:

Mary Beth moved slightly, absorbing all that Israel had to say. She tried to lick her lips. They were dry and cracked. She tasted dried blood as she ran her tongue around her teeth. She opened her eyes and looked up at Israel. She squinted trying to see his face. She felt weak and useless. Her body was drenched in perspiration. The unsteadiness of her head was apparent as she shook from weakness when she tried to lift it. She could barely focus on anything. Her vision was blurred, but she somehow managed to find Israel's face, and she stared into it. He looked like an angel; She saw something she had never seen before.

She lay there lifeless, helpless, and stared at him. For the first time in her life, she saw Israel as a man – and not just any man. She looked at him and saw a wonderful, caring, strong, beautiful man. She no longer saw a slave, a colored man, or a nigger, just an ordinary man. He was human, like her.

She stared at his muscular body, his big brown eyes, his black wavy hair, and his deep brown tan.

He appeared to her as a very quiet, shy, gentle, loving man – neither black nor white. She saw no color – "jest" a man – as they say. He was a man full of love, and without color, he was a man who had stayed by her side – one who had never given up, and had never left her alone. He was someone who would not let her die, the only one that seemed to care.

"Water," she said faintly. "I would like some water."

He jumped to his feet and quickly poured a cup of water from the pitcher that lay waiting on the old wooden table. He ran back to the bed and stood beside her.

"Please, lift my head. Help me Israel."

"Yes ma'am," he answered.

He was so scared to touch her now that she was fully awake. Colored folks were not allowed to touch white folk, but of course, he had to do what he was told.

She drank the water to loosen her throat. It burned slithering down as she tried to swallow. She struggled, swallowing hard to make it go down. Not saying another word, Israel helped her with each sip. Her voice was very hoarse when she spoke.

"I would like some soup, please. I need the warm broth to help my throat."

"Yes ma'am," he smiled and quickly bolted from the room.

About a half hour had gone by when Mammie came into her room carrying a tray with hot chicken soup.

"I'z so glad ta hears youes be betta child, we'z been so worried. When Israel tells me youes wake up an' ax fo' some soup, I'z drop ta da flo an' thank our God up above. I jes' so thankful," Mammie said.

"Where's Israel?" Mary Beth asked.

"Oh Israel gots chores ta do, child. He been up heah wid ya fo days and his bruddah been carryin' 'ems load. Now since ya be all betta, he gotta go back ta work."

"No," she whispered.

"Whatcha mean no? No what? What's wrong child?"

She held her throat as she spoke. The pain was unbearable as her vocal cords began to break free.

"I want Israel in here with me. He talked to me, and made me want to live. Now I want him here until I get better. If it wasn't for him, I would have died."

"But, whatta 'bout 'ems chores?"

"Ask Jesse to get someone to help him. I don't care, jest ask Israel to come back."

Mammie looked at her strangely, but she did as she was told.

A little while later, Mary Beth heard a gentle tap on the door.

"Come in," she hoarsely whispered.

Israel opened the door and stuck his head in. Grinning from ear to ear, as he always did and dropping his head down, he spoke in a soft tone.

"Did ya needs me ta do som'en' fo' ya Miss Mary Bess?"

"Yes Israel I do. I would like you to help me with my soup. I am much too weak to sit up by myself, and the soup is very hot. I am scared I might spill it. You don't mind, do you Israel?"

"Ah . . . ah . . . , no ma' am, but Momma be glad ta help ya," he answered still standing at the door.

"I know that, but I wanted you to help me, and you have to come over here, close to me, Israel. Pull that chair over here and sit down."

"Yes ma'am," he answered still grinning.

Sitting down beside her, he picked the tray up, and put it on his lap. The spoon clattered against the bowl as he nervously sat down.

He dipped the spoon and slowly eased it to her mouth. His hand shook like he was a scared mouse in a cat house. She reached up with her hand and held it to his. He blew each mouthful of the hot soup very softly before he gave it to her. Although the warm broth soothed her raw throat, she could eat very little. Each mouthful was a chore to swallow.

She laid her head back against the pillow and told Israel she needed to rest for a minute. He nodded and smiled. She stared at him, and he stared at the floor, a grin spreading across his lips. She watched as he squirmed uncomfortably in the chair. His face glowed with embarrassment, as he knew she was staring, but she could not help herself.

She slowly sat back up and asked for more soup. Israel stayed with her all day and spoon-fed her anything that she would eat. She watched his every movement and listened to each word he had to say. He had very seldom spoken before, and she did not want to miss anything he had to say. The more she looked at him, the more confused she became.

"I thought I knew this man. I have known him all of my life, but suddenly, he is so different. This is a different man who stands before me. I don't know him at all."

As she continued to stare, she felt things she had never felt before and knew she should not be feeling them.

"How could I have known him all my life, but never really have known him at all? Why did I not ever see this man before? How could I feel these things in one instant? And what exactly was it that I'm feeling?" she wondered. "Was it the closeness of death that opened my eyes, the weakness of my mind, or the pounding of my heart? Was it the beautiful words he spoke to me, or could it be the love in his voice, the love in his heart? Did it even matter why, or how this could have happened? Should I be thankful that it jest happened and has happened?"

She thought she might have been dreaming, but she hoped she would not wake up anytime soon. She thought how perfect this would be if only she were black or he were white. What was she to do?

She knew the thoughts she had were wrong, but she couldn't help herself. She had finally found a perfect man. He was someone she had grown up with and she knew everything about, but then again that was a boy she had known. She knew so little about him as a man. She never even thought of him as a man, as she only knew him as a slave. She didn't ever think of him as being a human being like her. Colored people were different. They weren't . . . white. She never considered them thinking like white folks do. So what did all this mean? What was she to do with all these things that were running through her mind and cluttering her thoughts?

Mary Beth knew what she was feeling would not be accepted, but how could she just let it go? She had found love for the very first time in her life. Her mind raced . . . "I think it is love, but how do I know? Could I love a black man? How could I – how do I love a man who is forbidden to speak to me, touch me, or even come near me unless he is told? Though it is so nice knowing someone truly loves me. Now what do I do? Did he mean the things he said to me?"

"Thank ya, Jesus," Mammie said coming into her room.

"I be so happy ta see ya sittin' up. Did ya git 'nough ta eat child? Of course ya didn't, I knows ya didn't. Whatcha like me ta fix ya? Youes names it, I'z fix it right up."

"Nothing Mammie, I'm fine. Thank you for the soup. My throat does feel better, and I don't believe I could eat another bite. I think I might need to rest a while. I still feel so weak."

"Youes right, ya needs youes rest. C'mon heah, Israel, ya hears Miss Mary Bess. We'z gonna gib'er anyting she be wantin'. An' ya gots chores ta do. Yo' bruddah hab been carryin' yo' load fo' days now."

"No, Mammie. I want Israel to stay," she said grabbing hold of his arm. "He brought me back from my death bed. I already told you if it wasn't for him begging me to eat I probably wouldn't have. I surely would have died. I want him here with me. I would like him to fan me for a while. It's very hot in here, that is, if he doesn't mind."

"Whatcha mean if he ain't mind? He do's wha' youes tell'em ta do."

"I know he will, Mammie. Jest leave him here. I also might need him to fetch some more soup or something else later."

"Yez'em," Mammie said, leaving the room with a bewildered look on her face.

She clutched her throat and turned to Israel. "Israel, please watch over me while I rest. Don't leave my side. Please promise you will be here when I wake up."

"Yez'em," Israel answered.

With that promise, she felt at ease as she closed her eyes. She could feel herself drifting into a forthcoming dream world, thinking how wonderful and happy everything was.

Her body lay heavy and limp, slipping into a deep tranquilizing sleep. She could totally relax because Israel was watching over her. Knowing that, she was at peace.

CHAPTER 10

THE QUESTION

A couple of days had passed. She drifted in and out, trying to regain her strength. She was troubled by nightmares, which continued for days, but Israel was right by her side every time she awoke, just as he had promised. Her strength was slowly coming back. She was able to sit up by herself and take short walks. She made sure Israel was there for each and every step she took.

"Israel," Mary Beth said. "I want you to move in the house with Mammie and me. I don't want you to leave my side. I need you to take care of me."

"I don't think Master Simmons would like that," he said.

"Oh Poppa will be so grateful to you. He would want you here because you saved my life. I can't wait to tell him how you nursed me back to health. He is going to be so happy. Now give me your hand," Mary Beth said, reaching out to him. "I want to hold onto you while I sleep."

Israel sat still, not moving an inch.

"Give me your hand Israel, don't act shy. You held on to my hand every day that I was dying. Now you don't want to hold it while I am awake?"

"I . . . I . . . "

"Spit it out Israel, you what?"

Israel downed his head.

"Don't act shy now. Never mind, I will finish your sentence for you. You did not know I was awake enough to feel you." Mary Beth smiled, "I felt and heard everything you said." She giggled and held out her hand.

Israel's face could have illuminated a darkened room. Smiling from ear to ear, but never lifting up his head, he obeyed and held Mary Beth's hand as she drifted to sleep. He continued to rinse a cold washcloth and put it on her head. His eyes twinkled as he marveled at her beauty while she slept.

When she woke up and saw Israel still holding onto her, her lips slightly parted and gave a partial grin.

"I thought it was a dream."

"What be a dream?" Israel asked.

"You, I thought you were a dream."

She squeezed his hand tightly and was content and warm all over, feeling so special and so loved. These were feelings she had never felt before – feelings that at first had been confusing, but had become well defined in her heart, mind, and soul.

She knew she was in love, but how would she get away with it? How could this have happened?

She thought a lot about how it could work out. There was so much sorrow throughout her life: losing her mother at a young age and never knowing her; having a father that was never around; and now being in love with a colored man. She turned away from Israel and a tear ran down her cheek.

"Miss Mary Beth, what's wrong?" Israel asked.

"Everything," she answered. "Everything is wrong. Look at you, and now look at me. We are so different, but yet so alike. Israel, for the first time, I have felt love. No one has ever loved me – not really, not real love. You have stayed by my side for weeks without leaving me. Why?"

"Ah . . . ah," Israel hesitated. "Cause I didn't want ya ta die. You were getting weak. I was scared I would lose you. Master Simmons would have killed all of us, if you had died."

"Is that the only reason? Did you stay here to save yourself?"

Israel downed his head. He did not want to answer.

"Answer me, Israel."

There was silence.

"Israel, I asked you a question."

"No, I didn't do it to save myself. Miss Mary Beth, I, I . . . "

"You what?"

Israel sat quietly not answering. He nervously started fidgeting with his hands. Mary Beth sat up and pulled him to her. She stared into his eyes. Israel was fretful; he could barely hold still. She pulled him closer to her and gently kissed his lips.

"Is that why?" she asked. "Are you in love with me?"

Israel jumped to his feet, knocking over the chair that he had been sitting in. He spun around and faced the wall. He paced back and forth.

"I'm sorry, Miss Mary Beth, I tink I needs to go."

"You didn't answer my question. Do you love me? Tell me, does your heart pound furiously in your chest when you hold my hand? Does your stomach flutter like a thousand butterflies swarming inside? Do you smile when you think of me for no known reason, jest because I'm a thought in your mind? And does your body ache and hurt like someone has whipped you, knowing this is wrong – knowing we are in two different worlds. Now tell me, is this the way you feel?"

Israel pondered the question. "Now you knows, Miss Mary Beth, I can't love you. You be white and white men would kill me fo' tinking such a thing. I tink you were sick way too long, and it messed up yo head. Maybe the lack of food has 'fected yo brain. You jest not tinking straight at all."

"I'm thinking very straight. And I don't care what white men think. I'm asking you what you think. Are you in love with me?" she asked again.

Israel said nothing. He picked up the chair and leaned it against the wall. His head hanging down, his hands cupped together, Israel's forehead was covered in beads of sweat.

"May I leave?" he asked softly.

"No Israel, you can't go any where until you answer me. Now answer me," she crackled in her weakened, hoarse voice.

He sat back down in his chair and started squirming restlessly, shaking his head, not wanting to answer.

"Israel, you have to tell me, please jest answer me."

Israel looked up and then jumped from his chair and shouted, "Yes I love you. I've always loved you. You all I can think about, dream about. When I thought you would die, I wanted to die too. I love everything about you: your eyes; your hair; your smile. I have watched you as you walk, as you talk, as you laugh, as you eat. There is nothing that I don't know about you. I have watched you all my life, from a boy to a man, from a girl to a woman, from sunrise to sunset. I have watched your gentleness with animals and people, with white folks and black folks. You were always so kind, no matter who it was. You're so beautiful, but you are white. I would be whipped and hanged from the highest tree if anyone heard me say that. I am your slave, your nigger, your colored boy – and that's all it will ever be. I learned to speak proper English from one of the slaves that was brought here from a place called Jamaica. I met him secretly in the woods. He is over at the Jenkins Plantation. I was hoping one day I could run away, go up north, and pass myself off as a white man . . . get my own business somewhere. I always dreamed of taking you with me, but I knew that would never be possible. I am forbidden to even have the thoughts that I have. So tell me again, how can I love you?"

"But you are white too," Mary Beth said softly.

"No, I am not white, nor am I black. I am neither, yet I am both. What am I? I don't even know what I am. Should I want to marry a colored woman? I am confused about what to do. Colored women don't like me 'cause I'm too white. White women don't want me 'cause I'm black, and it's forbidden. I have a black momma and a white daddy. I am a freak of human nature, a half-breed. I'm not sure who to talk to and who not to. I have always been afraid to talk to anyone. I'm a product of different forces. I'm not even sure if you call that human, Mary Beth. That's why I pretend to be shy when I'm really not at all. I am confused about which color I belong with."

"It doesn't matter what color you are. I want you Israel," Mary Beth said softly. "I don't think of you as a half-breed. I think you are a beautiful person."

"You've been sick, Miss Mary Beth. You will feel differently when you get your strength back. You should not say such things. I can't ever have you. You know this."

She pulled him to her and kissed him again. That time, he kissed her back very softly and passionately. He held her in his arms, and they both cried tears of happiness and of sadness. For they knew their love would be prohibited by both blacks and whites. There was no one they could tell, and there was nowhere they could go, for both races would be against it.

"We must find a way to be together," Mary Beth said.

"I don't think so," Israel said, holding his head down. "I don't think we can ever be together, not in this life time anyway."

"But why not? Poppa is seldom home. He has been taking longer and longer trips. We can be together while he's away. We can find a way. Please Israel, let's jest try it. I have been so lonely for so long. Both of us are different from most people. Like you said, you don't really belong anywhere, and I feel the same way. I don't belong anywhere either. Mammie knows I spend a lot of time with you and Hester. She won't think nothing about it."

Israel looked into her beautiful face and could not refuse her beauty. "I don't know, Mary Beth. Are you sure?" he asked with uncertainty.

"I've never been more sure of anything in my life. Look at you, Israel. You are more white than you are black. If we ran away together, people would think you were white."

"White," Israel laughed. "You think I look white? I always wanted to look white and even thought I could pass myself off as being white, but that was just me daydreaming."

"No it's not. I do think you look white. Israel, isn't it so strange to think … how you think you know someone really very well, only to find you don't know them at all? Why is it possible for people to judge other people by the color of their skin? Why are we raised this way? If we could walk in a black man's shoes for one day, would we change our minds? Could a white person survive being told – day in and day out – where to go, when to go and how to go? If a black person could change places with a white person, would he make things different? I have never thought about these things until now. Things I'd taken for granted have taken a whole new perspective."

"Why would a white man want to walk in a black man's shoes?"

"I didn't say a white man would want to. I said if one did, would he change things?"

"No disrespect Miss Mary Beth, but ain't no white man going to even try to walk in a black man's shoes. They wouldn't even think about it. Anyway, most black men don't own any shoes."

"Okay, what about a black man?"

"What about a black man?"

"What would a black man change if he could be white for one day? Do you think he would make a difference?"

Israel looked down at the floor without answering the question.

"Well, Israel, would he?"

"I ain't rightly ever thought about it, ma' am."

"Well, now that you are thinking about it, what would you change? You said you wanted to run away and go up north. Would you make a difference?"

"I don't think I should answer that question."

"Why not?"

"You might not like what I would say, ma'am."

"I want you to say what you think. This is not about what I like or dislike. It is what you think. What changes could be made to make everyone happy?"

"Well, we ain't got it that bad 'round here. I hear other slaves have it real bad. I don't know nothing, other than being a slave, but it ain't right owning someone like a dog. We get beat if we even look at white folk the wrong way. We get spit on, kicked, chained up and whipped. We work in rain, sleet, and snow. It makes no difference if we be sick or dying, we still gotta work. We get no Thanksgiving or Christmas. If we be lucky, there be leftovers from the master's plate."

Israel turned and looked at Mary Beth, "What would I change? I would like folks to treat us like we are human beings instead of animals. Why animals get taken better care of than we do. They get fed and groomed everyday." Israel continued, getting caught up in his speech. "No one should own us. We should be free to live and to come and go as we please. Have our own schools, and teach our children how to read and write."

"Free," Mary Beth interrupted. "Why you know that won't ever happen."

Israel turned away with embarrassment. He downed his head and stood silent.

Mary Beth leaned over to him and reached for his hand.

"Maybe we can start here," she said softly.

"What do you mean?"

"There is no way I can free the slaves, but what if we try and make things better? I have taught you and Hester how to read. Now y'all can teach the children. If someone is sick, you let me know. When Thanksgiving and Christmas come, we shall all rejoice. I will give you five acres of land for the slaves. Y'all are to plant it and use it to feed the slaves. I will help y'all if y'all help me."

"Master Simmons won't let that be."

"Poppa is not here, and like you said, this will be my place. I am going to start right now making changes."

The two laughed and talked for hours. Then hours led to days, and days led to weeks. Mammie was concerned and began watching them closer. She did not like what she believed was going on. She questioned Israel. He had to lie; there was no way he could tell her the truth.

"No Momma, Miss Mary Beth jest needs someone to be friends wid."

"Wells it ain't lookin' good, youes bein' black an all. If Master Simmons node bout dis he'd hab ya whipped an' hanged. He'd be kill us all, an' ya know he's be back in dis week."

"I know. Don't worry Momma, it'll be all right," Israel reassured her and left the room.

Mary Beth and Israel were inseparable. They swam in the pond, rowed the boat across the still waters of the pond, went for long walks in the woods, read books together, and Israel pushed her on the rope swing. Every spare minute of the day, they were together.

A romance was born to an unforgiving era. Despite all the sorrows that were sure to follow, they were willing to give this new love all that they had to give.

Sitting outside on the veranda, enjoying the warmth of the sun, they noticed a horse and buggy coming up the path to the house. They stood and stared down dusty road, recognizing the black carriage that belonged to Mr. Simmons. Mary Beth rushed down the stairs and flung open the front door. She was so excited to see her father. She had missed him so. The thought of the consequences that were about to take place never entered her mind, but Israel knew very well what lay ahead. He knew their love would never be condoned by the master.

Mary Beth frolicked outside, pacing back and forth on the front porch with anticipation. As the horses came to a halt, she noticed her father had brought someone with him. She observed the man as he stepped from the carriage. Not recognizing the man, she stood at attention and waited for her father's introduction.

CHAPTER 11

THE STRANGER

"Poppa," she said, throwing her arms around him as he approached her.

"You sho' have grown there little girl. Let your poppa look at you. Oooo . . . weee, well, you sho' ain't my little girl at all. I think you are a real woman now."

"Ah Poppa, you know I will always be your little girl."

"That's right, but that's why I brought Ben here with me. He has travelled a long way to meet you."

"To meet me, why is that?"

"He's going to take your hand in marriage. This is going to be your husband."

Mary Beth leaned over and looked behind her father at the unfamiliar visitor. Lost for words, she could feel a lump swell in her throat. Swallowing hard, she curtsied to the newcomer.

"Nice to meet you, ma'am," the stranger said, tipping his hat.

Mary Beth looked at the strange man and whispered, "But Poppa, I don't know this man. He's a stranger to me. I can't marry him."

"That won't take long. He's gonna stay here with us. It will be a couple of weeks before I have to head out again. By that time, we all will be real acquainted, everything will be set and you will have yourself a husband. Ben here is of good blood. He is what you call an Italian man. He is a very fine man, and he's a sergeant in the U.S. Army. He is fighting for our country."

Mary Beth looked at the tall dark man. He was very handsome, but he was not who she wanted to marry.

"It's very nice to meet you, sir," she said reaching to shake his hand.

"I do think you are probably a very nice man, and I don't mean you any disrespect, but I don't want to marry you."

"Mary Beth," Mr. Simmons snapped. "How dare you question your father's decision. You will marry at the end of the month, and that is final. I have to be gone for a long time on my next journey, and I can't keep worrying about you. You need someone to take care of you."

"But Poppa, Mammie and Israel can take care of me."

"No, I won't hear no more. My mind is made up. Now where is Israel? I want him to shine our boots."

Mary Beth did not answer; she burst into tears and ran toward the house.

"Don't worry about her, Ben. She'll come 'round," her father said.

At that time, Israel entered the room.

"Israel, this is Ben. He has come to marry Mary Beth. I want you to show him 'round the plantation. After you have finished that, you take his boots and get them shined."

"Yez Sir, Master Simmons," Israel answered, nodding his head.

Mr. Simmons walked up to Israel and put his arm on his shoulder.

"Ben, this here is one of the best niggers you could ever own. He don't give anyone any trouble at all. He's quiet and obedient. They don't come any better. Now you two go ahead. I need to talk to Mammie."

Israel did as he was told, leading Mary Beth's husband-to-be around the property. He explained how everyone had his or her own special area to work. He showed the man where each of his family members lived. Israel and Hester's cottage and his brother, Jesse, and his wife's cottage, were the only ones close to the house. The other slaves lived on the far side of the plantation.

"So, Mr. Simmons is very nice to you niggers, huh?"

Israel looked away to keep Ben from seeing the rage in his eyes.

"Yez sir," he answered.

"You know after I marry Mary Beth, I might make some changes around here."

"Yez sir."

"I might jest have to sell your brother."

"Sell my brother, but sir . . ."

"What, do you not like that idea, boy?"

"No sir, I don't."

"Well, I think whoever works the hardest will get to stay . . . and who listens best."

"Yez sir," Israel said hanging his head.

"You sure are real light skinned to be black. Why's that?"

"My momma was raped by her old master, sir. She got pregnant with me, so he got rid of her."

"You're a real lucky nigger, cause if she'd belonged to me, I'd have shot her. You never would have been born, boy."

Israel raised his eyebrows but didn't say a word.

"You got anything to say about that, boy?"

"No sir."

"I didn't think you did. Come on now, let's get back to the house. I need you to shine up my boots, boy."

Israel walked solemnly behind Ben. He was furious, but he could not show it. He could not believe Mr. Simmons had brought back such a monstrous man for Mary Beth to marry. Although Israel was black and Mary Beth was white, he knew he was a much better man than the person his master had chosen. If only there were some way he could prove it. That thought crossed through his mind, but it kept right on going. He knew that would never be possible.

As he entered the house, Ben struggled with each knee-high leather boot until they finally slipped free. He emptied a handful of sand from each one and tossed them onto the floor.

"Come pick these boots up, and get your mammie to clean up this mess."

"Yez sir."

"You make sure they shine real pretty, boy. I don't want to see not a speck of dust left on them, not even a little speck."

"Yez sir," Israel said, lowering his head as he moped out of sight. He quickened his step to find Mammie. He barged into the kitchen where she was preparing dinner.

"Momma, that man is a monster. I have never met such a despicable person before in my life, and he is going to marry my Mary Beth."

Mammie slapped Israel's face.

"I'z don't wanna ever hears youes say dat agin. Ya node dat she's ain't yourn, an' she ain't nebber goin' ta be yourn."

"But Momma, he said he was going to sell me or Jesse when Master Simmons left again. What are we going to do?"

"Master Simmons won't let dat be. Ya has ta tell 'em."

"No ma'am, I can't. If I did, I wud surely be the one that is sold. I can't do that, Momma."

"Don't fret none Israel, we'z tink of some'em, but youés gotta stay 'way from Miss Mary Bess."

About that time, the back door opened; it was Mary Beth. Her eyes were swollen, the tip of her nose was red, and her face was flushed from the river of tears she had cried. She sniffled as she talked, her voice cracking with every word.

"Mammie," she cried. "I don't want to marry that man. What will I do? I can't marry him, I can't and I won't."

"Now, now, my's purty one, don't youes worry none, yo' Mammie's goin' ta tink of some'em."

"I would rather die than to let him ever touch me, and I will kill myself before I marry him."

"Mary Beth don't you say such a thing," Israel said, grabbing hold of her hand. "Even if you do have to marry him, you will still be alive. You'd still be where we could see you. I couldn't bear it if anything happened to you."

Mammie stared at the two as they talked.

"Wha' be hap'ning in heah?" she asked in a stern voice.

Mary Beth looked up at Mammie.

"I love Israel, Mammie, and he loves me. I want to be his wife."

"Oh my Lawd," Mammie threw her hands in the air, shook her head, and trotted around in a circle. "Hush yo mout', child. Whatcha two done went an' do? Ya know dat can't happen."

"Sure it can, Mammie. If we ran away, no one would know Israel is black. He could pass for white."

"Youes talkin' crazy child, I ain't goin' ta hears no mo'. Youes playin' wid death, boff ya. Now youes boff go bout youes bidness. I don't wanna sees ya two no mo'. I ain't wannin' ta hears no mo' neter.'

Israel stood there staring at Mary Beth. They searched each other's faces for an answer but there wasn't one.

"Momma is right you know," he said, as he made an awkward and hasty departure.

"What do I do?" Mary Beth cried. She knew her heart belonged to Israel.

"I ain't know, Miss Mary Bess. I ain't know, but dis can't be."

Israel had returned to the language of the African Gullah just as he was supposed to do. He could not make the mistake of talking in proper English. He had to resume the life of a slave, the life to which he was born. His short time of happiness was over.

CHAPTER 12

LOSS OF INNOCENCE

Days had passed. The wedding day was getting closer and closer. Mary Beth and Israel had decided to have secret meetings under the dogwood tree on the hill. They snuck out in the middle of the night after everyone was fast asleep. Their love had grown deeper and deeper. Their passion for each other grew stronger, but knowing the end was getting closer was becoming unbearable.

It was a bittersweet love that could sign their fate. A quiet invisible force drew them together, but an explosion of hatred could tear them apart.

Their love had grown strong, but was it strong enough to withstand Mary Beth's union with another man? How could Israel endure the pain in his heart, watching his beloved Mary Beth in the arms of this stranger, a man who was cold-hearted and full of hatred?

One week before the wedding date, they just had to see each other. Mary Beth slipped out to the balcony and looked for the flicker of Israel's candle; this was the signal for them to meet. Quietly she left the house, hiked up the hillside, and leaped into Israel's arms. They laughed and cried as they reminisced about their years together. Then they lay in each other's arms, staring up at the stars and the moon.

"Israel," Mary Beth said softly. "I want to give myself to you. Will you take me? I want my first time to be with someone I love. Please love me."

"Mary Beth I can't do that. It ain't right."

"You're wrong Israel. It's not right to give myself to a man I despise. It's also wrong to marry a man I'd rather kill. And it's wrong that I can't marry you because you are black. That's what's wrong. It could never be wrong for you to make love to me. God knows our love. He knows we should be together. I want to give myself to you tonight. I don't want to wait anymore."

"Mary Beth, I can't do that. I want to more than anything in this whole world, but I can't. If Mr. Ben were to find out, he would kill us both. Then we would never be together."

"I would rather die than not have you. If I can't marry you, I can at least still have you. I've never been more sure of anything in my life. I love you and I want you to have me. I want to at least to have my first time with love in my heart – not animosity in my soul. Please, please make love to me, Israel."

Israel rolled over and brushed her hair from her face. She felt the incredible power of the passion that lay in his dark brown eyes. She put her lips to his ear and gently sucked the lobe. His neck vein bulged as the blood jetted through his body. His body was electrified – jittery and quivering with fervid desire. He was extremely nervous; although he had the muscles of a man, he was as inexperienced as an awkward little boy.

"I will always love you with all of my heart – no matter where you live or where I live. No matter who you live with, I will always love you. You are right. We should be able to make love with someone we love."

His soft lips covered her mouth, and she returned his kiss. Their lips were locked, arms clutched firmly, when Israel suddenly paused. Pulling her a few inches away, he ran his fingers tenderly down her face. He smiled; he was naïve and innocent, but his virtue was righteous and admirable.

"This will be my first time too. So tonight, we shall barter our hearts, and our lives and souls will be in each other's hands forever."

"Forever," she said as he lay across her.

He was uncertain of what to do, but instinct led his way. He remained true to his humble manner, but his modesty dissipated as their passion grew. He kissed her intimately and passionately on her lips and cascaded down her neck. He slid his hand up her dress to her soft, delicate flesh. The intensity of her desire seeped through the pores of her skin as her rage of passion took control. She trembled with fear but quivered with alliance. The magnitude of the energy of her innocence was bestowed forever.

Slowly and lovingly, he removed her dress. She stared deeply without blinking. His hunger of lust and the intense motion of desire became swift and uncontrollable. His overpowering, disobedient appetite collided with the craving of her youthful body.

Mary Beth wrapped her arms tightly around his strong shoulders. She wanted him desperately, but because of her innocence, she was scared. Her body was stiff and tense as she felt his tremble with desire. He was eager, but nervous. Their breathing grew heavy and rapid. He wanted her first time, his first time, to be right. The passion needed to last, for it might be their only time together. He slowed the pace, restricted his movement, and hoped that moment of ecstasy would last forever.

The moon slid behind some drifting clouds, leaving a soft dim light. The summer breeze blew across their sweltering bodies, giving temporary relief to their bittersweet union. The crickets and frogs sang in harmony, synchronizing with the sexual moans that soared in the dark. The dogwood tree covered their nakedness with its long sturdy branches. They heard nothing and saw nothing but their love and desire. Nevertheless, none of this would have mattered if they had, for at that time, they were the only two people on earth. The whole world could have been watching and they would not have known. Their bodies were drenched, inundated with perspiration from their heated passion. The love was all consuming. Suddenly Israel stopped and sat up.

"What's wrong?" Mary Beth asked. "Do you not want me? Did I do something wrong?"

"You could never do anything wrong. I want you more than life itself, Mary Beth, but what about tomorrow and the next day? What will happen when you marry Ben? Is it fair to take your innocence for just one night? I don't want you to regret this. This should be something special."

"But this is special. If I only have one night with you, it is worth more to me than a lifetime with anyone else. We don't need to worry about tomorrow. Let's jest live for tonight, like there is no tomorrow. Love me, Israel, love me like it is your last night to live. Love me again and again. For one night, this night, will last me a lifetime, as long as I can share it with you. If I should die tomorrow, I would die content from a fulfilled life, just because of you."

"I feel that way, too. Nothing could ever be more special than to have you. If one time is all that I may ever have, that is better than not ever having you at all."

Israel laid her back on his shirt and slowly mounted her naked young body. He kissed her neck, her face, her lips, fulfilling her uncontrollable, raging passion. As he re-entered her virtuous body, she clutched her fingers tightly to his back, burying her nails deep into his flesh. She screamed with pain and moaned with passion. He slowly and fervently took her purity.

She had received a lifetime of love in a matter of hours. With the anxiety subsiding, she relaxed and began enjoying what Israel was doing. In conjunction with the other, their bodies jerked and trembled with pleasure.

Transformed by the night, in just a few hours, a little girl became a beautiful young woman. In the darkness under a tree, a young woman swallowed by love, was completely fulfilled for the first time. Her body belonged to him, again and again until the night was gone and the sun was creeping through the trees. It would crest the hilly horizon, and the darkness would be gone.

Their bodies lay quiet under the beauty of the dogwood tree. The hours of the night had riveted, captivated, and absorbed every ounce of their being. Not one second had been taken for granted. They lay quietly, taking pleasure in each other's arms.

Mary Beth reached for her dress and slowly slipped it over her head. She stood up exhausted, but radiant. Her faced glowed with satisfaction. She gave a smile to Israel, kissed his lips, and whispered, "I will always be with you and you with me. No man shall ever take your place in my heart. It will always belong to you. Even though our skin color is different, our hearts are the same, and no one can change that. Now I have to return to the house before I am missed." She slowly turned and strolled down the hill.

Israel did not say a word. He smiled and watched the woman that he had once thought would only be a fantasy disappear into the morning mist. He sat alone on the hill reliving the one and only night he would never forget, the one night he spent with the woman of his dreams.

After Mary Beth disappeared, Israel got dressed and strutted down the hill. Although he had not slept, adrenaline was still rushing through his veins. He had plenty of energy to spare for his daily chores. He whistled a little tune as he went about his morning duties. He had never been more satisfied in his whole life, but everyone knows nothing lasts forever. His mood was about to take a drastic turn.

"Since when did milking a cow become so pleasurable?"

Israel smiled and turned to see who was behind him. His smile quickly left his face when he saw who it was: Ben.

"If you find milking a cow to be so pleasurable, maybe we should find someone else to do it. We surely do not want any niggers around here to enjoy their work, boy."

"Yez sir," Israel answered.

"And why should he not enjoy what he does?"

Ben turned around. It was Mary Beth.

"You know how it is Mary Beth," Ben said.

"No, I don't. Why don't you tell me?"

"If you start letting them there niggers enjoy their work, pretty soon they'll be wanting to take over. They'll think they own this damn place."

"Sorta like you? It seems to me, you are thinking the same thing. You act as if this place is yours. You are only marrying me. Poppa is not giving you our plantation. I may have to grant Poppa's wishes and marry you, but I don't have to give you my land."

Ben laughed, "Little do you know my dear, I already own this plantation – and you. I won it all in a poker game. Your Poppa," he said, shaking his finger as he talked. "Your Poppa bet it all and lost."

He grabbed Mary Beth by the chin and pulled her face up to his, "You, my dear, are already mine. I only promised to marry you cause I felt sorry for the old bastard. Although, you are right pretty and you do have a nice set of bosoms there," he said pinching her breast.

Mary Beth jerked her face from his clutches, drew her hand back and slapped his face.

"How dare you talk to me like that! I know you are lying. My father would never bet on our plantation. You should apologize for your rude behavior."

He grabbed her arm.

"I would apologize if I thought there was a need to, but you are living in a dream world, Missy. If you keep talking, I might not marry you at all. I might just have my way with you and be done with it."

Israel stood up and walked toward Ben.

"I don't tink that be proper. It ain't any way ta talk ta da lady, sir."

"You don't think that's proper, who the hell gave you permission to think? When did niggers worry on how white people talk to anybody? Well nigger, maybe you want to do something about it." Ben shoved Mary Beth to the ground.

Israel reached his hand out to pull her up. He knew he could not say another word. Ben grabbed Israel's hand and hit him across the face with the back side of his other hand. Israel fell to the ground.

"Don't you ever make the mistake and tell me how to talk to anyone again. And to put your hand on my woman, why I would kill you before you could blink your eye, boy. If you ever step out of line again, boy, I'll have you lynched on the first limb I see. You got that . . . boy?"

Israel dropped his head, "Yez sir," he answered.

Mary Beth jumped up and wiped the dirt from her dress. Tears rolled from her eyes and dropped to her cheeks. She looked at Israel sitting on the ground, then up to Ben. Her eyes were cold and hard. She could not believe in a matter of minutes, she had lost the warmth of the tranquility that she held all night.

"I'll never marry you, I would rather die first."

"If you don't watch your mouth, woman, I might just arrange to do that for you," Ben said.

Mary Beth lifted her dress and ran to the house. Running up the old wooden steps, she fled into the house. She cried out, "Poppa, Poppa. Where are you, Poppa?"

"I'm here Mary Beth, I'm in the library. What's wrong?"

She ran to his side, "Tell me it isn't true. Tell me, Poppa. Tell me it isn't true."

"What are you talking about?"

"Ben – the plantation. Tell me he was lying. Tell me you didn't lose the plantation, our home. Tell me I don't have to marry that cruel man. Tell me Poppa," she cried.

Mr. Simmons turned his back and walked across to the fireplace. He retrieved a pipe from his pocket and struck a match on the hearth. Puffing abundantly, he ignored her urgency for answers.

"Poppa, did you not hear me?"

"Yes, I heard you. I jest don't know what to say."

"Say it's not true. Tell me it's a lie."

He closed his eyes and gripped his lip. He sauntered over and lifted her hand. Patting it tenderly and sympathetically, he began to speak.

"He wasn't supposed to tell you. I'm so sorry, but it is true. I lost it all."

"How could you? How could you have done such a thing? How could you give me to such an awful man? I won't do it. I won't marry him. I won't."

"But you have to. It is the only way to hang on to our land. If you marry him, it will still be ours. When he dies, it will be yours again. Please my child, you must marry him."

Mary Beth stared into her father's desperate eyes. She felt his shame and saw the guilt on his face, but it was not enough. Nothing was enough to mask the hatred she had for Ben.

"Johnny was right. All you have ever cared about is this land. What about me? What about how I feel? That doesn't matter to you, does it? Well, let me tell you something, Poppa, I would rather die."

"You will not disobey me. I am your father."

"My father, what kind of father are you? What kind of father would give his daughter to such an animal? If you are my father, where have you been all my life? I have only seen you when it has been convenient for you to come home. You are more like a guest in my house. In *my* house," she repeated sternly. "This house was not yours to gamble away. You do not live here. You merely come and go as you please. I certainly do not know who you are. And if I thought I did, I was mistaken, because my father, my Poppa, was a man with integrity. My poppa is a man that is noble and has a heritage of strength. Not some weak, insensitive, self-seeking, greedy man, who stands before me."

Mr. Simmons slapped Mary Beth across her face. She stumbled

slightly and then stood straight and tall.

"And my father would never strike his daughter for speaking the truth." She sniffled, her voice quivering as she spoke.

"So if you are claiming to be my father, my poppa, I am disobeying you. I will never marry that monster. He will never have the pleasure of me by his side."

She turned and bolted up the stairs to her room. She locked the door once again, imprisoning herself from the world.

The time dwindled by, Israel paced across the plantation in front of the big house searching for a sign from Mary Beth. He was deeply worried about her well being. He could not waste another second. He snuck into the kitchen to ask Mammie to ensure Mary Beth was all right.

Mammie was hesitant at first; she too was scared of Ben. After overcoming her worries about Israel's doing something irrational, she agreed.

She eased the kitchen door open and searched the corridor for Ben. Everything seemed to be clear, so she tiptoed up the long stairwell vigilantly. She crept close to the wall, glancing over her shoulder occasionally until she reached Mary Beth's room.

Lightly she tapped on the bedroom door and whispered, "Mary Bess, kin ya hears me? Please Mary Bess, come downstairs."

There was no response. She tapped again, just a little harder and begged Mary Beth to answer.

"Is ya ahright in dare? Child, please answers me."

"What are you doing up here?" A raspy familiar voice snapped from behind.

She jumped and immediately turned around. It was Ben.

Quickly she blurted, "I is checkin' ta see if Miss Mary Bess feelin' bad. She ain't been downstairs fo' a whiles now."

"You don't worry about her. When she gets hungry she'll come down. Now you get your black ass back in the kitchen where you belong."

"Yez sir," she answered. She stumbled trying to rush away, knowing all the while, Ben was wrong. Mary Beth would not come down when she was hungry. She would die first.

"Mammie, that's your name, right?"

Mammie stopped dead in her tracks, scared stiff, not turning around.

She answered, "Yez sir."

"Well Mammie, I think it is time for you to move out of here. You need to go back to the slave quarters where you belong. I don't want no niggers living here with me. After all your chores are finished, say around 9 p.m., you need to be out of here."

"Yez sir," Mammie said with a hint of dejection in her voice as she walked away.

"Oh Mammie," he called out again.

"Yez sir," she answered once more.

"That half-breed boy out there is yours, right?"

"Yez sir, he be mine," she answered with a worried voice.

"You need to keep him out of trouble if you want him to stay here. And make no mistake, if I should want to take you one night, and you have something like that to disgrace me, you'll never see the sun rise again. I'll kill you both. And also, prepare your young daughter. I'm sure I will want some of that young stuff."

"But Master Simmons says . . . "

"Master Simmons is no more . . . "

He interrupted, "I am your owner now and I say what goes on."

Mammie did not answer. She just kept walking. Rage swept over her body. She could see how Mary Beth would want to die instead of being married that man. She was having some of the same feelings. If he were to touch Hester, she would surely kill him.

Mammie worked hard all day trying to keep Ben satisfied. She wiped, cleaned, and polished everything to a mirror finish: the furniture, floors, knickknacks – anything that she thought would give Ben reason to find fault with her if it didn't shine. His clothes were hand washed, twisted, wrung out, and hung on the clothesline to dry. His shirts had buttons sewed on and socks had holes darned. His bed sheet was pulled tight with the corners of the handmade quilt tucked neatly around the mattress. She prepared a fresh pitcher of water by his bedside.

All this was done with a smile – no complaints, and never a break. By sunset, she was dog tired and ready to go to bed. But because her new master was still awake, she had to hide her exhaustion and keep herself busy.

She quietly watched Ben through the half cracked door from the kitchen. She waited patiently for him to consume his nightly bottle of booze. Drunk, repulsive, and staggering, he finally retired to his room. Her long-suffering day, in spite of everything she had done, was far from being over. Complying with her new master, she moved each and every one of her belongings to the little shack on the hill.

Fumbling her way to Hester's room, her little old body, weak, fragile, and exhausted, she collapsed and plummeted onto Hester's cot.

"Oh my, is ya aright, Momma? Do ya needs a docta? Do's ya want me ta fetch Master Simmons?"

"No, ya stay 'way, far way as ya kin from dat house. I'z jes' tired. Dat man in da big house be crazy, Hester. I scared he may come fo' ya. Youes gotta watch out fo' 'em. If ya sees 'em com'n', youes hide."

"Why would he come fo' me, ain't he marrin' Miss Mary Bess?"

"Yez child, but dat ain't no nebber mind ta 'em. Youes jes' be careful. I'z gotta gets me some rest. I'z gotta be back up at sunrise. I'z so tired child, so dead t . . . ired."

Profoundly exhausted, she had fallen asleep before she could even finish her sentence. Hester covered her with a ragged sheet, blew out the small wax candle that flickered in the breeze of the window, and lay on the floor at her mother's side.

CHAPTER 13

THE REQUEST

Three days had passed, and Mary Beth was still isolated in her room. Ben would not allow anyone to go near her. He assured everyone, if anyone even glanced at her room, he or she would regret it. "Make no mistake," he said, "I will kill you."

Her father was ashamed, mortified actually, by what he had done. He was humiliated when he thought of the life-altering decision that he had made for his only child. He didn't want to admit it, but he had come to agree with every word Mary Beth had said.

Each night, Mary Beth sat alone on the balcony. She was seen by the silent majority of the plantation, but they didn't acknowledge her. They hesitated, and with barely a glance, one by one, they imperceptibly went about their business. On the third night, Mary Beth walked out on the balcony. She sat under the light of the full moon and asked God to help her with her troubles. The stars seemed particularly vibrant as they helped the moon illuminate the sky that night.

As her prayer passed her lips, a ray of light emanated from the hill. Her eyes strained to determine what was there. She could see someone in the shadow of the tree. Squinting, she knew it was Israel in the glowing light. He was waving, signaling her to come to the hill. Her impulse was to run without hesitation, but she knew Ben might hear her.

She slightly eased her door open. It creaked as an inch of light seeped through the crack. Discreetly, she peered through the gap that exposed the hallway. Searching, finding no evidence of him, she gradually stepped out. She pulled the knob behind her and tiptoed silently past Ben's bedroom. Taking a momentary peek behind her, she drew in a deep gulp of air and quickly pressed on. One foot at a time, she backed down the stairwell, keeping a keen eye on his room. An agonizing fear swept across her body.

Each time she heard a noise, she froze as if she were lifeless. Most of the terrifying sounds were the wooden floor creaking beneath her feet. The old worn steps had revealed her identity; she panicked, but a quiet force, an invisible power, helped her descend to the bottom. Across the foyer and through the front door, she fled into the perils of darkness.

Tears streaming from her eyes, blurring her vision, she stumbled time after time, but nothing and no one was going to stop her from her quest. Each painful step seemed like an eternity; her legs felt heavy and unable to move. She was weak from not eating, but her heart yearned for the one she loved, the one who patiently waited. With each stride, she got closer to the love she so desperately wanted.

Israel stood in the light, watching Mary Beth's fragile body struggle. The persistent power gave her strength to continue. When she reached the top, he stretched his arms out to help her. She leaped into them and held on tight. She cried hysterically, as her lips touched every inch of his face. She held him in her arms, pleading with him to run away with her.

"Please don't ever let me go, please Israel. Please just hold me tight. Take me away, Israel. Take me far away," she begged.

"There is nothing that I want more, but you know I cannot. I wish so much that I could. God, I wish so much that I could!" he whispered in her ear.

He pushed her back from him, still holding onto her arms. He stared into her blue, watery eyes, and then he softly spoke.

"I'm so glad you came. I was worried you wouldn't want to see me anymore. I thought you looked at me as a coward. I'm sorry Mary Beth."

"Sorry, sorry for what? Why would you even think such a thing?" Mary Beth asked.

"Because, I did not stand up to Ben the other day. I let him shove you to the ground and did nothing to stop him."

She regained her composure and wiped the tears from her eyes. "But you tried. He would have killed you if you had said anything else."

"I wish he would have killed me. I can't stand hearing the things that he says to you. He shows no respect for you. He only thinks about himself. It doesn't matter what rules you have made here. He is here to change them."

"I know. That is why I cannot marry him."

"Momma says you will die if you don't come out and eat. Mary Beth, please come out of your room tomorrow. You have to marry Ben. It is the only way."

Mary Beth turned away. "The only way for what?" she asked in a disgusted tone.

"It's the only way for everything, the only way for me to see you, the only way for me to live without having you."

"But Israel, I will be married to Ben. How can I face you while I'm with him?"

"It will be hard for me to see you with him, but it would be unbearable for me to live without being able to see you at all. If you die, then I will know it is because of me. Had I not revealed my feelings to you, you probably would have welcomed Ben to be your husband."

"I cannot believe you would think that I would want to marry that awful man. I disliked him at the first sight of his face. Yes, he is a nice looking man, but his attitude makes him very ugly."

"Maybe so, but if you marry him, we could still see one another. Jest like tonight. We could meet secretly, and you would still own this place. If you die, so shall all of us. If Ben does not kill us, he will surely sell us. Please Mary Beth, think about this."

"Are you saying . . . " she sobbed. Then she turned to him. "Are you saying you don't mind me being with him? Jest to have a moment then and there would be enough for you?"

"Mary Beth, I have watched you my whole life and never thought it would be possible for me to touch you. I used to beg God to make me more white so you could see me as a man, not a slave. I have listened to you fantasize about others. I have watched your eyes light up when you have seen some handsome man in town look at you. I have watched you laugh and cry. I have seen you happy and sad. I have seen you angry and tender. There is nothing I took for granted. I know everything about you. Your love for this land, your strength, your weakness – I know you. Your love for me and your desire to be with me is more than I have ever even dreamed of. Knowing that I, nothing more than a half-breed slave, have the love of such a beautiful, loving woman, that alone is enough. That means so much to me, I cannot be so stupid as to let my pride stand in front of my heart. As long as I know you love me, no man can take that away. Ben could whip me, beat me, and hang me from the highest tree — and my love would still overcome it all."

"I love you so much, Israel. I never looked at you as a slave, jest as a friend. You and Hester have been my only friends, my family. I ain't never been 'round white folks. I don't know if I would even be accepted in my own culture. But please, don't ever think of yourself as a half-breed. Whether you are black, white, Indian or whatever, you are more of a man than that Ben could ever imagine. I can't marry him. I jest can't."

"Mary Beth, you have ta do this for me, for Mammie, your poppa and for Johnny."

"Johnny! Johnny would never allow me to marry this scandalous man. He would surely kill Ben if he came home."

"I agree, but what if Johnny returns and there is no home? Everyone will be gone and Johnny will never know what happened. If you do this, maybe he will return soon . . . and kill Ben."

"Do you think this could work, Israel?"

"I wouldn't ask you to if I didn't."

"If you think this could work, tomorrow I'll tell him I intend to marry him. I must make him promise that everything here will remain the same. If I can get him to do that, I shall accept him as my husband, but totally against my will. I think this will be the hardest thing that I'll ever have to do. But, for you and your family, I shall."

"Mary Beth, there's one more thing you must do."

"What is that Israel?"

"You have to forgive your father. He was wrong, but it was a mistake. You cannot let him keep this burden on his shoulders. Something could happen to him on his journey, and you would never forgive yourself."

"I know I should, but Israel, how could he have done this? I jest can't understand it."

"I don't know, Mary Beth. Maybe he had too much to drink, I'm sure that had to be it. You know how he gets when he has been drinking."

"You are probably right. I must tell him first thing in the morning."

Mary Beth walked to the dogwood tree and leaned on it. She looked at the bright moon and slid down to the ground.

"Israel," she said, "make love to me. Love me again, like you did before."

Israel dropped to his knees and smiled. He crawled across the ground until he made his way to her feet. He removed her shoes and started kissing her toes and making his way up her thighs.

She gave a childish giggle, "That tickles."

He smiled and continued.

She twitched as a small spasm tantalized her spine, inched along her neck, and seemed to release at the end of each strand of her long, shimmering blonde hair. She arched her back beneath him, tense, but aching for the sensation she was receiving.

He slid her dress up. He caressed her soft white skin, kissing every inch of the way and stopping at her sumptuous lips. In the shadow of the night, they gave themselves completely for the second time – no guilt, no remorse, no shame. Once again, it was triumph, the defeat of deception.

When the sun rose and peeped from behind the trees, they shared a long passionate kiss and went their separate ways.

Mary Beth followed the beaten path that ended at the edge of the willow tree. She eased open the front door, slipped in, and quietly closed it behind her.

"Hmm," the horrifying sound of someone clearing their throat echoed from the room.

Terrified, she stood stationary. When she gathered the nerve to turn her head, she caught a glimpse of what she feared. Someone was there.

With a sigh of relief, she realized the sound had come from Mammie, who was standing at the foot of the stairs, waiting.

Mary Beth meandered toward her. As she got closer, all she could think was, "She knows. She knows." Mammie's expression was one of worry and despair. She was happy to see Mary Beth out of her room and alive, but troubled by what she suspected. She reached for Mary Beth's arm and escorted her to the kitchen.

"Child ya node betta dan ta do dis. Ya node youes jes' axin' fo trouble. Why Mr. Ben wud hang Israel from one dose trees, an' tink nuttin'bout it. He'd whip 'em till 'ems dead. Ya twos has ta stop dis. Yo' father, whatcha ya tink dis do ta 'em. He ain't like Mr. Ben a bit, but he ain't gonna let youes be wid Israel neider. Israel is black, child, he be black, an' dat's alls dare is ta it."

"But I love Israel, Mammie," Mary Beth whispered.

"Shhhh . . . shut yo mout. Youes ain't in love wid 'em. Youes jes' needs 'em. Youes need someone's ta love youes an' show youes love, Israel kin an' will. But it ain't be right, an' it ain't be love. An' ya boff be playin' wid youes life's, all are life's."

"I don't know, Mammie, I think it's love. If it's not love, it's everything that I need. He makes me feel so good, I think of him all day long. My stomach gets butterflies when I jest think about him. Some days, I jest sit and stare out of my window and watch him work. I believe he is perfect for me."

"Who's perfect?" Ben asked, entering the room.

Mammie jumped from her chair and trotted over to get Ben a cup of coffee. Mary Beth looked at him with murderous eyes.

"My father, I think he is wonderful. I know you had to trick him into betting our home. He would have never bet you unless he was sure he would win. You probably cheated. You're a despicable person. Cheating is the only way you could win."

"It doesn't matter how I won. What matters is that I won. It is not how the game is played, but how you play the game and who comes out on top. Remember that Mary Beth. You might need those words one day."

"Yes, you are right, Ben. It is how you play the game, and I think I am ready to play your game. I will marry you on Sunday before Poppa leaves. I want him to give me a way."

Ben laughed, "Give you away? I thought he already had."

Mary Beth reached out to slap him; he caught her hand in midflight.

He stood up and bent her hand backward, forcing her to assume a sitting position. "Don't you ever raise your hand to me again. If you do,

I'll whip you like a slave. I'll break your hand from your arm so you won't worry about slapping anyone. Understand little lady?"

She jerked away from him and stomped through the doorway.

"Mary Beth," he called, "Sunday will be fine. Mammie, you can throw together a nice little ceremony, can't you?"

"Yez sir. Be'z happy ta, sir."

CHAPTER 14

THE WEDDING

Mary Beth hurried up the stairs and stood outside her father's bedroom door. How could she apologize for the remarks she so angrily said when she had meant every word? It was all true. She swallowed deeply, restrained her pride, and tapped on her father's door.

"Poppa, are you awake?" she asked.

"Yes Mary Beth," he quickly answered. "Come on in, I am glad to see you are up and well. I was very worried about you. Please, come sit beside me," he patted the edge of his bed.

Mary Beth walked over to her father and sat down close to him.

"I must apologize to you, my daughter. I thought a lot about what you said to me, and you were right. I have not been a good father to you, and I did leave you alone way too much."

"Poppa, I'm sorry too. I got so mad at you, I jest said what came to my mind. I didn't mean all those cruel things."

Mr. Simmons laughed, "You are just like your mother. She was stubborn and head strong too. If the thought entered her mind, it rolled out her mouth before her brain had time to think about it."

Mary Beth smiled, "I know you were tricked into giving up our land. I know you had to be, but it is done, and we can't change that. I am going to marry Ben on Sunday, so we can keep this plantation."

"No child, you were right. I thought a lot about what a stupid thing I have done. I regret it dearly. I don't want you to marry Ben. He is an animal, and I was wrong to bring him here. I didn't realize what a monster he was until now. You, my dear child, can travel with me. We'll make another home somewhere else."

"No Poppa, this is our home. It's yours, mine, and Johnny's, and it will always be our home. You said Ben travels a lot, so maybe he won't be here that much. I can tolerate him. I have to. I cannot give up our home."

"Mary Beth, my sweet Mary Beth, your happiness is not worth sacrificing jest to hold on to some land. I have made a huge mistake, and I cannot let you suffer for that. We will honor my loss, as I swallow my pride and move on. This is my decision."

"No Poppa, you are wrong. It is my decision. This is my life. I don't mean any disrespect, but I am the one that has to live here. You have worked for too many years to keep this plantation, and I intend to keep it too – no matter what sacrifice I have to make. It is not just some land. This is our home, and no one man is going to come in here and take it all away."

"Mary Beth, I admire you and your decision, but you must be positive this is what you want."

"I am sure, Poppa. It has to be this way. I am sure."

"I will get Israel to hitch a wagon and take me to town. I must go fetch a preacher, but you must be absolutely sure."

"Yes, absolutely," Mary Beth answered, bowing her head.

Mr. Simmons kissed the top of her head and exited his room.

Mary Beth closed her eyes. A tear trickled down her cheek and dropped off her chin. She shivered with anguish.

She couldn't bear to think about it, yet she couldn't think about anything else. Mary Beth wore the color off the hardwood floor as she relentlessly paced back and forth. She searched for a solution, a resolution for the fate that awaited her. Every thought was traumatic, and every potential answer was improbable. The days were filled with antipathy; the nights, anxiety.

Lying in her bed half awake, she heard the rooster crow. Her eyes popped open. She sat up in bed and looked around the room. There in a corner, draped across a chair, something sparkled in the sunlight. She rubbed her eyes. An image of her mother's wedding gown emerged, a beautiful white wedding dress.

It had dazzling crystal stones across the breast. Lace rolled down the sleeves and followed down the back. The hemline flowed to the floor and had small flowers encircling it. On the floor lay an open box with a blue silk ribbon that had been swathed around it. There was a note neatly tucked inside.

Mary Beth bent over and retrieved the small piece of paper. She read the inscription aloud, "To my darling daughter on her special day."

The dress had been neatly put away just for this day, her special day, the day Mary Beth had prayed for so many times, the day she thought she would never have. Her prayers were answered, but she wanted to take them back. She wished over and over that it would have been one of those unanswered prayers.

She dropped the note and burst into tears.

"Please, please God, let this be a dream. Please wake me up."

But it wasn't just a dream. It was a nightmare, a traumatic, dreadful, horrific nightmare.

Sunday had arrived, and she was miserable. Mary Beth collapsed on the bed and wept. Mammie rapped on the door and moseyed in. Mary Beth sat up and wailed louder.

"Now now, lil' one, dis ain't no way fo' youes ta be lookin' on yourn weddin' day. Lookey at ya, yo eyes be all swollen. C'mon an' lets git ya dressed."

"Mammie, I don't think I can do this."

"I knows it baby, ev'ryt'ing will work its way out. Ya jes' ho' dat dare head up high an' tink of da goods tings. Forget bout da bad tings, tink happy thoughts. Let Mammie wipe dose tears from yourn eyes an' help ya get dress."

Mary Beth stood up, and with legs quivering, hands shaking, tears rolling down her cheeks, she raised her arms. Mammie slipped Mary Beth's night gown off and slid her mother's dress over her head. It was a perfect fit.

"Owey child, if yo Momma could sees ya now, she be so proud of ya."

"If my mother could see me now, she'd be bawling too. I'm glad she can't see me. I am ashamed."

"Ain't no need fo ya ta be shame of nuttin'. Youes beautful inside an out, don'ts ya forgit dat."

Mary Beth sniffled and tried to dry up her tears.

Hester came in and styled her hair with little white flowers. She was ready to take the dreaded walk to her waiting groom. Her father waited for her at the top of the steps. When she emerged from her room, she could see a tear running down his cheek.

"You look jest as beautiful as your mother did on her wedding day. The only difference was that she was happy when she wore this dress. I hope you will be able to find some kind of happiness in all this mess. I can't tell you how sorry I am. I have really made a mess out of things this time. I wish you would jest forget all this, and let's move on."

"No Poppa, I can't. If I did that, it would mean he wins. He might have beaten you in the poker game, but I will beat him in my house, our house. Don't worry no more. I will be fine Poppa," Mary Beth said with tears running down her cheeks.

They stood silently for a moment, staring into one another's eyes. Then, arm in arm, they solemnly sauntered down the long set of stairs to the front door. The remainder of the wedding party, Ben and the preacher, stood on the front lawn in the shade of the willow tree. They watched as the beautiful sixteen-year-old bride stepped into the sunlight. There were no invited guests at the ceremony. Mary Beth was too embarrassed for any of her father's friends to see what kind of animal she was marrying. When she turned to take Ben's arm, she saw Israel watching from the side of the house. She lowered her head in shame. Her neck arched down, she sniveled, and her voice blubbered, making a muffled whispering sound as she started to recite her vows. She never once acknowledged Ben as she repeated the words of the preacher. Ben, on the other hand, lifted her head, held her chin in his hand, and slowly enunciated each and every word. Her eyes filled with hatred, and the murderous stare froze on her face as she jerked free from his stringent clutch. When the preacher announced that they were man and wife and told Ben he could kiss his bride, Mary Beth turned her cheek to him.

Ben smiled from ear to ear and surveyed the plantation. "Well, everything is legally mine," he said boastfully. "Anytime you want to leave my premises, you may go, Simmons. I now own your life."

"You are a sorry bastard, Ben. I hate the mistake I made, but God will punish you for your evil ways one day," Mr. Simmons said.

"Yeah, you are probably right, but until he does, I am going to enjoy every damn minute I have here. I am going to start with my beautiful bride," he grabbed Mary Beth and pulled her toward the house.

She wanted to resist him, but she was legally his. She could not refuse. She began to realize how Israel felt, because now she was owned, and she had to obey her demented, nauseating husband. The tears flowed from her eyes and streamed down her dress. She struggled behind him, stumbling as he pulled her up the stairs. He tossed her onto the bed, grasped the shoulders of her wedding gown, and ripped it from her body. Never speaking, he shredded her mother's beautiful dress, exposing her naked youthful bust.

He mounted her like a wild animal. She screamed and begged for mercy. She pushed, clawed, and kicked him, but he would not stop. He savagely attacked and overpowered.

"Ahhh . . . ahhhh, stop, please, stop."

"Not on your life," he chuckled. "You are mine!"

He continued the assault, smothering her with his sweaty body and torturing her until she felt the coldness at the core of his soul. He pushed and prodded, hard and harsh, battering, shoving every inch of his manhood inside her.

She screamed and begged for him to finish and let it to be over, but Ben never even heard her cries. He got pleasure from her squirming and squealing, which only fueled his excitement.

Outside, her father looked up at her bedroom window with dismay. Tears trickled down his face as he listened to his only child scream in agony. Mammie dropped to the ground and started to pray. She pleaded with God to stop this terrible thing from happening. Israel and Hester stood silently with their heads bowed. Both of them were wiping tears from their cheeks. Every living thing seemed to stop in silence as they listened to the frantic shrieking sounds of a terrified woman.

Her shrill ear-piercing voice reverberated across the reverent land. She pleaded for the vicious assault to end, but it continued for hours. No one could shelter himself from her agony. There was no escape from her pain. They all had a hand in her decision, and they all had to suffer the consequences. The echoes of her suffering pierced them all.

Her father could not bear to listen to her cries any longer. "Hitch the wagon and drive me to the ferry, Israel," he demanded. "I have to leave. I cannot bear to stay here any longer. I will go to Charles Towne and get a room for a couple of days."

Israel was grateful Mr. Simmons had asked him to chauffeur him to the ferry, and he wasted no time in getting the horse and wagon ready. He too could not tolerate hearing the screams that bellowed from his true love.

Driving away in the wagon, they could hear her screams echoing down the long dirt driveway. The sounds followed until the house disappeared from sight. Mr. Simmons put his face into his hands and cried as he told Israel of his regrets.

"My only daughter, the one that means the most in my life, I have betrayed. I'll never forgive myself for letting this happen."

Israel was feeling the same way, for he was the one that talked Mary Beth into marrying this monster. He also was having a hard time finding forgiveness within himself. "Maybe I was thinking too much about myself," he thought. "But we can still see each other," he tried to justify his thoughts. He mumbled out loud.

"What was that Israel?"

"Nuttin' sir, I was jes' clearing my throat."

"You know Israel, it is a shame you are black. You seem to be such a fine young boy. You always have been very obedient and I am grateful for that. I hope Ben will treat you well, and I hope he will keep you on the plantation. I know you will help keep Mary Beth safe. I can trust you to do that, can't I?"

"Yez sir. I will do ev'ryting I can fo' her."

"Thank ya Israel, I don't know how Mary Beth would have ever gotten along if it weren't for you and your momma. You tell Mammie I said thank you too. Will you do that for me?"

"Yez sir, I will sir."

CHAPTER 15

T H E   B R O K E N   H E A R T

Back at the plantation, Mary Beth lay in a trance. She envisioned Israel in her mind … the gentleness of his touch and the passion they shared. How grateful she was to have had her first time with him. She lay motionless, keeping her thoughts focused on Israel as Ben had his way with her time after time. The pawing of his hands and the roughness of his voice disgusted her. When his self gratification was finally over, he stood up and stared at her. He jerked her from the bed, slapped her across the face and called her a whore.

"Who have you been with?" he demanded. He began shaking her ferociously.

"Oh my God," she thought to herself, "I didn't know he would be able to tell. What should I say?" She was trying to think of something quickly.

"I was raped," she blurted out.

He tossed her back on the bed and pulled up his pants. "Raped? Well you will continue to be raped. You are nothing," he shouted. He leaned down to her face, "You are nothing, do you hear me? You are no more than a whore. The only good you are for me is to relieve myself. Don't think you will get anything else. You are not worthy of it. You will get no pleasure or satisfaction from me. You will be treated like no more than a nigger in my bed."

Mary Beth stood up and spit in his face. "You could never give me anything else but pain, even on your best day. You don't even know the meaning of the word *pleasure*. You sicken me with the miserable sight of your face. You are disgusting, repulsive, and nauseating. I would rather be the biggest, blackest nigger than to be bedded by you."

Ben conveyed a blow to her head, sending her sprawling across the bed. His fist pounded her face, arms, and legs. She screamed as the blood spewed from her mouth. He kicked a chair across the floor and slammed other pieces within his reach into the wall. Glass was breaking, feet were stomping, fists beating, and voices screaming and swearing to God. The mournful screams seemed to be a replay from earlier. The shrill voice finally weakened to a whimper, and the entirety of the room got very quiet.

Mammie was scared Mary Beth was dead. She listened intently from the bottom of the stairwell. She heard nothing at first, but then, she heard the familiar creak of the bedroom door as it opened. Mammie scurried to the kitchen. If Ben caught her eavesdropping, he'd surely kill her.

He stomped down to the living room and poured a chalice of vodka. He sat in the old Victorian green armchair that Mr. Simmons had brought back from France. His feet were propped on the ottoman that Israel had made. He was admiring his belongings and giving a toast to his accomplishments. He drank one glass after another, muttering vulgarities and laughing to himself.

Mammie was watching from the open crack of the kitchen door. When Ben's glass dropped to the floor, her anticipation of his wrath subsided. She deftly slipped passed him and hurried to the second level to check on Mary Beth. Mammie was worried she may not had lived through the grueling beating that lasted for hours.

She lightly knocked and whispered to Mary Beth. There was silence. She diligently watched down the hall and continued to call out softly, but there was still no answer.

Gripping the crystal knob, Mammie tried to steady it, but the hinges creaked mercilessly. She clutched the edge of the door and slowly poked her head into the room, but she saw no one.

"Mary Bess, is ya in heah?"

Still, there was no answer. She pushed the door further.

"Mary Bess," she called slightly louder.

Mary Beth jumped from the floor and scrambled to the head of the bed. She screamed. She was scared to death.

"No child, no, shhhhh . . . it be me, Mammie. Ya mus' be quiet. Oh my po' child," Mammie said running to the bed. "Wha' dat mad man dones ta ya."

"Oh Mammie, look at me."

Mary Beth laid her head on Mammie's lap and sobbed.

"Look at me. Look what he did to me, Mammie. I hate him! I hate him! The first chance I get, I will kill him. I will kill him dead. He will never lay another hand on me – never!"

"Oh my Mary Bess, my sweet lil' Mary Bess, we'z gonna find a ways through dis. Don't youes go crazy on us, we'z fi gures som'em out."

"Mammie, if Israel sees what Ben did to me, I'm scared he might kill Ben himself. You can't let him see me. You can't tell him."

"Don't youes go worryin' 'bout Israel, I'z take care of 'em. Let me go fetch some water. We'z got ta git youes clean up. We'z can't let yourn purty face look like dis. Dis be yo weddin' day, no matters whoes ya be marries ta, dis still be yo day."

Mammie stood up and took a look around the room. Everything was in shambles, with furniture and pictures broken. Glass was strewn about, and clothes were torn and shredded. She shook her head as she carefully stepped over the mess.

Mammie returned to the kitchen and tried to be discreet while filling a container at the rusty old water pump. She fetched some clean cloths and returned to Mary Beth's side. Gently, she dabbed, patted and washed the injuries, clearing away the dried blood and soothing the wounds until Mary Beth drifted off to sleep.

Mammie left the house and went back to her quarters. Israel was worried about Mary Beth. He had patrolled back and forth, waiting for his mother. Finally, he saw Mammie coming across the shadowy yard through the mist, and he rushed from their tiny cabin to meet her. "How is Mary Beth? Is she all right? Did Ben hurt her badly? Tell me Momma, is she all right? Tell me," he shouted.

"Yez, Mary Bess be ahright. She'd be shaken up a bit, but she be fine."

"I have to see for myself. I heard her scream and beg him to stop. I know he hurt her. I heard all kinds of things breaking. I should kill him."

"No youes can't goes an' sees her. Mary Bess don't wanna sees ya. She tells me ta ax youes ta stay 'way fo' a whiles. She be shame of what hap'n. She begs me ta keep youes 'ways from da house.'"

Israel walked to their quarters close to Mammie's side. "I don't know if I could stand hearing that again, Momma. That man is like a wild animal. No one should be treated that way. What am I going to do?"

"Ev'ryting will works it way out, come in da house. We has ta git somes rest. Tomorrow Master Ben wants breakfast at 5 a.m., an' I'z tired. We'z figure som'em out."

She patted Israel's back and lay down to sleep.

Israel could not sleep. He began to pace the floor again. He walked to the door and looked out across the field to the big house, hoping to catch a glimpse of Mary Beth.

Filled with the burden of his guilt, he sought tranquility at the only place he knew, the hill. His eyes were as keen as a hawk's, watching for signs of movement in the candlelit window of Mary Beth's room. He sat, with legs drawn, arms wrapped around them, and his head resting on his knees. He waited helplessly in the shadow of the night in hopes she would come to him.

Hours slid away. Cradled by the despair of darkness, he slept upon the damp ground. His mental exhaustion released his body and his heart to the temporary solace of his dreams.

Little did he know, Mary Beth was watching him from her window. Her craving for his love was unbearable. She needed him to hold her, to feel his tenderness, to heal the pain hidden by the veil of her secrecy. Yet it was a secret she could not share with him, a secret hidden to keep him out of harm's way. She attentively guarded his strong placid body, just as he had watched her, silently in the dark.

With swollen eyes and distended lips, she sat there nursing the pain of a broken heart in the pitch-black night. The agony of her heart surpassed the bruises Ben had given her. Her chest throbbed with the rhythmic pulse of the blood that pumped through her veins. The soothing, contented, serene love she shared with Israel seemed to be lost — beaten and ripped from her by her demented and hated husband. Their love was hiding deep inside a secret refuge, a safe place. Somewhere she could protect it, hold it and keep it forever.

How could she face Israel again? What was she going to say to him? She imagined the disappointment that Israel would have in her. She sat on the balcony until the moon faded and the sun brought forth daylight. The wind carried a secret kiss through the air to her forbidden lover, and she lay down to sleep.

CHAPTER 16

BACK IN THE FUTURE

"Mom," a voice called from the hall, "Mom."

I shook my head. Disoriented, I stood up, wondering what in the world had happened to me. I looked at the diary and back at the hallway.

"What's going on?" I rubbed my head. I felt so weird. Was I asleep? Had I dreamed everything? Did all that happen or not? The same questions seemed to be repeating themselves. I was dazed and confused. I sat back on my bed and put my head on my hands, thinking, trying to put all my thoughts together. My bedroom door opened, and Gary marched in.

"Mom, are you all right? Were you sleeping?"

"No Gary, I was just reading."

"How were you reading in the dark? Your light was off."

"The light wasn't off."

"Yes it was. I turned it on when I opened the door."

"Well, I must have fallen asleep while I was reading. Anyway, what's the problem? I thought you were sleeping. What are you doing up? It's getting late and you have school tomorrow."

"I couldn't sleep. I was thinking about Isaac coming over tomorrow. I was wondering what we could do for fun. You think maybe we could go fishing in the pond?" I sat up trying to focus on Gary. I was trying to answer him, but struggling to make sense of what had happened at the same time.

"No, I don't think so. That pond seems to have a mind of its own. It already has pulled you in one time. I'm sure you will think of something, but for now young man, you need to get to bed. You have school tomorrow, which means rising early. Give me a kiss and get to it."

"Mom," Gary said, wiping his face. "Please don't do that in front of Isaac tomorrow."

"Yes Dear, I would not dare embarrass you in front of Isaac. That is why I'm getting my kisses tonight." I pulled him to me and began kissing all over his face.

"Mom, yuck," he said, pulling away from me. "I'm going to bed."

"Goodnight my sweet boy," I said laughing.

"Goodnight Mother," he said, closing the door behind him.

I scooted off my bed and walked out onto the balcony. I stared at the dogwood tree on the hill. After reading the diary, I felt I had been there so many times. I could picture Israel and Mary Beth secretly meeting on that beautiful knoll. I felt the love, the passion they shared so many years ago.

That had to be the reason I felt peaceful and why I could feel their passion, because it never left there. "What role do I play here? Am I the one who can put the spirits to rest? Is that my purpose? Is that what the whispering in the dark is about? Is she trying to tell me what to do?" There were so many questions for which I had no answers. It was like putting together a puzzle – one with a lot of missing pieces. I sat on the balcony for hours, hoping for a whisper, a glimmer, a spirit to call upon me, but the night was quiet. There was nothing stirring but the critters of the night. I was exhausted; finally, I gave up and went to bed.

At 5:30 a.m., the alarm went off right on time. I had slept all night with no disturbances. It felt good to get a full night's sleep, but it was disappointing at the same time. I staggered from my bed and turned the shower knob to hot, hoping the old water heater would not forsake me. I headed to my closet and chose my attire for the day. When I returned to the bathroom, it was full of steam, which was relaxing and soothing. It had warmed up the cool morning air.

Half asleep, eyes squinted, I stumbled over a shoe and hurt my toe. Cursing and hopping on one foot to the toilet, I sat down to examine my injury. When I lifted my head, I was lost for words. Written in the mist of the shower were the words, "I'm lost." I looked around the small room. There was only one way in and one way out, so I knew someone was with me. I rubbed my toe not knowing what to say, if anything. I stood up, solemnly walked through the cloudy mist and turned the copper knob to the off position.

The uneasy feeling of someone or something standing with me, beside me, but invisible, was overwhelming. I slowly looked around, and in a trembling voice I asked, "Is anyone there?"

No one answered. I no longer felt comfortable taking a shower or getting dressed, so I laid my clothes on the bed and went downstairs to the kitchen. As I passed by the kitchen window, I could see the dogwood tree on the hill. The fading moonlight and the rising sun glistened on the branches. I stood and gazed at the beautiful sight. The decades of the passion the tree held, never lost – just disguised – was remarkable. I understood why this tree had to survive.

I woke the kids and got them off to school. Gary was excited about Isaac coming over, so he was in a hurry to get dressed and get out the door. Angel was still excited just to be going to school, so both kids were trouble free that day, no arguments.

Gary had made a list of things he wanted to do and a list of things that he wanted me to pick up. So I stopped at the grocery store on the way home. My shopping cart was full. I had sodas, chips, dips, cookies, pizzas and ice cream. As I unloaded the cart onto the counter, I felt the cashier staring at me. I stopped and looked up at her.

"Don't you live on Dogwood Plantation?" she asked.

Here we go. "Yes I do," I answered in a sarcastic tone. I was ready for the smartass remarks. Surprisingly, I didn't get any.

"I think that place is so groovy, man. I am so glad someone finally moved in and is fixing it up. It is such a beautiful place."

I stood in disbelief. I think I just got a compliment about my house. "I'm sorry, did you say you think my house is groovy?"

"Yes ma'am. I haven't ever been inside, you know, with all the rumors and all, but I always wanted to. I think it's awesome."

"Awesome, huh? Well, I tell you what . . . ahh," I looked over at her nametag, "Paula, anytime you want to stop in, do so. I would love to show you around the old place."

"Really, you mean it?"

"I sure do. My son is having a friend over tonight. We're going to watch some movies and eat a lot of junk food. If you don't have plans, drop by."

"Hey, I might do that," she answered. "Then again, I don't think tonight will be a very good night. Haven't you heard? There's a terrible storm headed our way."

"Oh, no, I haven't."

"Yeah. They're calling for lightning, heavy rain, maybe even tornados."

"Thanks for telling me. I haven't heard a thing. By the way, my name is Vivian. Stop by when you can. I gotta run. I have a lot of things to prepare for tonight."

"Nice to meet you, Vivian. Make sure you have plenty of candles and batteries for tonight," Paula called out while I was rushing out the door.

I left the store feeling good for a change. Finally, I was beginning to fit in, and I could go to town and no one would stare or point at me. If people would visit, maybe they would see how lovely my home was. But what if my spirits decided to show up? Then what would I do? Does it really matter that everyone already believes my house is haunted? It would just give the town more to talk about.

It's funny how things seemed to have been imagined, but many of them were actually true. The people on the island were right: My plantation is haunted.

When I got back home, I started separating some of the old pictures in the trunk. I wanted to show Isaac's mother what we had found. My excitement was overwhelming. I had so many questions I was sure she would know the answers to.

Then Tina entered my mind. I knew she would love to hear what I had read about in the diary. I had to call her. I grabbed the phone and dialed her number.

"Hello, Tina. You will never guess what I found out," I said in a childish manner.

"Ahhhh . . . you found out who your ghost is."

"Maybe, I was reading Mary Beth's diary . . ."

"And?"

"And, she was in love with a slave whose name was Israel."

"You are kidding. A slave? You have to be wrong."

"No, really, she had an affair with him, then her father brought a husband home for her. He made her marry some Italian man. Her father bet Mary Beth and the whole plantation in a card game and lost it."

"You're telling me she married a man she didn't even know?"

"Yes, and that's not the half of it. She hated this man; he beat her and raped her."

"Get out of here. You're kidding. Did he beat her because she was having an affair with the slave?"

"No. He didn't even know about that. He was just very hateful."

"Sounds like it."

"I have some more good news too."

"Well, do tell."

"Believe it or not, Mr. Jesse's grandson is Gary's friend at school. Gary has asked him to spend the night tonight, and his mother is bringing him over later. She's picking all the kids up after school and bringing them here. She sounds real nice. She's Mr. Jesse's daughter-in-law."

"You're kidding?"

"Is that all you can say?"

"Yeah, especially while I'm in shock. You done knocked my socks off, girl. I think I'm dreaming. Let me get this straight. Mr. Jesse, a man that despises you and your whole family, his daughter-in-law is bringing her son over to spend the night with Gary in your house, and he doesn't mind?"

"Now, I never said he didn't mind. Edna, that's Isaac's mother, she said she had to keep this hush-hush because Mr. Jesse would have a fit if he knew."

"Yeah, I bet he would have more than a fit."

"You know it. I hate to cut you short, but I have a thousand things to do. I just had to tell you about the diary. I can't wait to read more."

"I'm surprised you even put it down. Look here, you better have candles and flashlights close by tonight. There's supposed to be a bad storm coming through."

"Yeah, I heard. I'll call you later."

"Sounds good. See ya."

I sat at the kitchen table sipping on a glass of tea and staring at the mesmerizing dogwood tree. I finally had figured out why that tree was so special. It too was haunted by a secret. It had watched over a forbidden love, one that never even had a chance to bloom. I wondered if it was Israel or Mary Beth's spirit that was at the tree. I know I felt someone there, and I was sure it was one of them.

Standing at the back door, I stared up at the hilltop. Surely if I go up there and say their names out loud, I should get some kind of response. I turned to check the time. I still had a couple of hours before the kids would be home. I slipped my shoes on, and to the hilltop I went.

The clouds were already moving in. The wind alternately hissed and howled, sucking the warmth from the air. It blew swiftly, rocking the trees back and forth. The blue sky had disappeared behind the dark gray clouds. The thick masses quickly swallowed the sun's arms as they tried to converge through the dense cluster. Mother Nature was beginning to take control and to transport a storm throughout our land. The air was heavy and moist. I was determined to go to the hill. I had to try to contact the spirit that was there, if there was a spirit.

I was somewhat scared of going around the pond. I surely wasn't getting close to the edge. As I neared the beautiful tree, I could understand why this would be such a perfect place. It was remarkable. Its long slender branches extended out like a huge umbrella, a perfect refuge, camouflaging everything below it.

As soon as I walked under the tree, I could feel a cool breeze surrounding me. I sat on the ground and leaned against the trunk.

"Mary Beth, are you here?" I asked aloud. I waited for a response, but there wasn't any. "Israel, is it you? Are you here?" Again, there was nothing. I silently and patiently waited. There were no strange or unusual feelings, just a steady breeze from a brewing storm.

"I found Mary Beth's diary," I said aloud. "I know you and Israel were in love. I would like to help you if I can." I looked all around. There were no signs of anyone being there, just me.

I waited, enjoying nature, watching the birds flutter against the strong wind as they sought shelter from the storm. I listened to the calling of all the wildlife resonating across my land. But time was running out. The kids would be home soon, and I had so many things to do. I stood up, brushed away the sand from my jeans and headed back to the house. As I started to walk away, I felt that cool breeze blow again, and I heard a noise, a shuffle. I stopped and listened. It sounded like leaves crinkling as if someone were walking on them. I stood very still and noticed something falling all around me. I looked up; there were white petals falling from the tree. They all fell together, as if a magnet were binding them. I watched with astonishment.

"Oh my God," I yelled out.

Right before my eyes, a man appeared. He sat in the bed of flowers and looked up to me. I was stunned. I did not know what to do, but I did not move. Then he reached his hand out toward mine. Scared stiff, I could not scream, run or move. All I could do was stare at him. I was drawn into his big brown eyes. I could feel myself slowly moving toward him. I extended my arm and offered my hand. There was a calmness about him that seemed to be contagious. It seemed I had done this so many times before. He gently pulled me to the ground beside him. I gazed at his muscular body. How beautiful it was!

He was one of the most spectacular men I had seen in a very long time. He was spellbinding, so perfect, everything balanced, completely proportioned. I could not speak a word; all I could do was stare. I was enthralled.

He was wearing a loosely fitted white shirt, which was unbuttoned, showing his ever so muscular chest. Only one, maybe two buttons were fastened. He had on a pair of black slacks that were cropped below the knees, and his feet were bare.

He leaned toward me and kissed me. It was soft and gentle, in spite of everything, I was in a trance. He put his arm around my shoulder and guided me onto the bed of flowers that he evidently had made. He slowly climbed on top of me, lifted himself up slightly, and stared into my eyes. He took one hand and pushed my hair from my face, staring into my eyes. He held my face in his hands and passionately kissed me again. There was no resisting him, nor did I want to. I was totally in his control. Kissing my face, and then making his way down the side of my neck, he put his fingers through mine and raised my hands over my head. He let go with one of his hands and moved it slowly down my body. My breathing was rapid and heavy; my body, heated. I wanted to kiss him, hold him, and devour his love, but I could not move. All I could do was lay there and enjoy his passion. I was totally under his spell. I was not scared at all though. It seemed so right, as if I had been there so many times before. I loved everything he was doing. I wanted to feel every touch. I wanted more . . .

Beep . . . Beep . . . Beep . . . "Mom," a voice blew faintly through the air. "Mom," I heard again from a distance. I still could not move. "Mom!" the voice screamed.

Suddenly I woke up and leaped to my feet. I broke free from this force that I was being held under and looked down at myself. I was a mess. My hair was full of leaves and flower petals. My clothes were all twisted and half off. My mind was cluttered and chaotic. I was unsure of what had happened to me. Had I been asleep? Was I dreaming?

Confused, I stood under the tree and tried to compose myself. I heard several voices, and I looked to the house.

"Oh my God," I mumbled.

The children and Edna were standing at the bottom of the hill staring up at me. I wondered what they had seen. What had I been doing? I was not sure. I brushed off and descended the hill.

Gary had a disgusted look on his face. Angel went straight to her sand pile, while Edna and Isaac stood smiling as I reached the bottom of the hill.

"You must be Edna," I said holding out my hand.

"That's me," she said pulling her hair back from her face. "This wind is really starting to get up, huh?"

"It sure is. I think I must have fallen asleep under the tree up there," I said pointing to the top of the hill. "I didn't hear you drive up. I hope I didn't keep you waiting.

Edna did not say a word. She turned and looked around the yard for a brief moment, then added, "What a magnificent place to sleep."

I just smiled back and looked down at Isaac. "So you're Gary's friend. I'm glad to finally put a face with your name. I hope you boys have fun tonight."

"Yes ma'am," he answered.

"Come on, let's go in and get out of this wind. I believe this storm is starting to move in pretty quickly."

"I have to agree with you," Edna replied. "I just have to tell you, this place really looks wonderful. You guys have been busy."

"Yeah, Mom's working us to death," Gary quickly blurted out.

"Come on in, Edna. I'm sure the boys can find a lot of fun things to do. If not, I can find some more work."

"Out of here," Gary said, pulling Isaac away.

"I am so glad you came over, Edna. Have a seat."

"Wow! I just can't get over how different this place is. It really looks great," she said looking around.

"Thanks. May I get you something to drink?"

"I can't stay long," she replied.

Earlier, I had made some cookies that had filled the house with their fresh-baked aroma. There is nothing more inviting than home-made baked goods, and I surely wanted to make Edna feel welcome.

"Can you stay long enough for some freshly baked cookies?" I asked, holding the tray out to her.

"You got me there. These are great," she said, taking a bite out of one.

"Thanks again. I wanted to show you some of the things we found in the attic."

"Found in the attic? I wasn't aware anything was left here. I would be very interested in seeing them. Did you find out what deep secret this plantation is hiding?"

"What do you mean?" I quickly asked.

"I mean what happened here so many years ago."

"To tell you the truth, I was hoping you could tell me."

"Me? I don't know a thing. Oh, I get it – You thought because I am married to Henry, I should know. No Girl, sorry. Shoot, they won't even talk about this place. Mr. Jesse has always forbidden it. If he knew I let Isaac stay here, why he probably would never speak to me again."

"But why? I don't understand. What happened here that was so terrible? He could have never lived here. It's been vacant for almost a hundred years I think."

"I'm not sure how long it's been empty, you know how old people are. You can't tell them anything."

I looked away for a minute and then back at Edna. "You know, I wish there was some way I could sit down and talk to him. I found a diary written about one hundred and twenty five years ago. A woman named Mary Beth wrote it. I'd like to read him some of the things she wrote about his family. She really thought very highly of them."

"Mary Beth. That's a catchy name. If you want, I'll mention it to him."

"Would you really? I would love for you to. Would you ask him to talk with me? I have a lot of pictures here too," I said, reaching into the old trunk.

"I can't do it while Isaac is here, but maybe sometime soon. Look, I really would like to stay and look through them, but I'll have to make it some other time. I need to go home and get ready for this storm. If Isaac gets to be too much trouble, just call me," she said, walking toward the door. "Make sure you have your flashlights on hand. You don't want this storm to leave you in the dark."

"You're right, I don't. I already have everything laid out. And don't worry, Isaac will be fine. They'll find plenty of things to get into."

"That's what I am afraid of," she said laughing. "Isaac, I'm leaving," she yelled to the top of the stairs.

"Bye, Mom."

"Stay out of trouble."

"You know it, Mom. I'll see ya tomorrow."

Edna smiled and shook her head. "Good luck, Vivian – with the boys and your mystery house."

"Thanks."

I was disappointed as I watched Edna get into her car and drive away. I was certain this time I was going to have some answers, but it was a dead end once again. Maybe she would be able to convince Mr. Jesse to come see me. Perhaps he would be interested in the pictures.

"He is my only hope for deciphering the mystery in this place," I said aloud, looking down at the old pictures.

"Mom," Angel called out.

"Yes Honey, I'm coming." I returned the pictures to the old trunk and made my way to Angel.

"Angel, where are you?"

"Right here Mommy," she said, walking up behind me.

I squatted beside her. "What do you want, Baby?"

"I want someone to play with me. Gary has a friend, and I want one too," she dropped her head down with a very sad look on her face, her lips pooched out, pouting.

"You have friends at school, don't you?"

"Yes, but I want to bring them home like Gary did."

I couldn't help but to laugh at her. I took her hands in mine, "I'm sure you will bring someone home with you after you get to know them better."

"But kids laugh at me and call me names. They say you're a witch and I belong to the devil. They say our house has ghosts in it."

"Honey, don't you worry about the things those kids say. I bet they're just jealous because they don't live in this big old house. You know we don't have ghosts."

"Yes we do Mommy. Mr. Issy is a ghost, and he only lets me see him. So, I don't care if the other kids know we have ghosts. I just don't want them calling you a witch or me a devil's child. You're not a witch, are you Mommy?"

"Of course not, and you're not the devil's child. That is nonsense. But why do you think Mr. Issy is a ghost?"

"Because he told me so. That's how he can do all kinds of magic. He's funny. He makes me laugh, and I have a lot of fun with him. You know what Mommy?"

"What?" I asked.

"I guess I do have a friend like Gary. I had forgotten about Mr. Issy. He's always here. He plays with me, and he makes me laugh, just like Gary's friend. He's not imaginary Mommy; he's real. He told me that you knew he was here. He said you just really didn't want to see him."

"Why would I not want to see him? Of course I would love to see him."

"I don't know. He just said it. He said that you really love him and you go up to the hill so you can talk to him. If you talk to him, why do you say he is not real, Mommy?"

"That is not why I go to the hill," I snapped. "I go up there to be alone. It's peaceful up there. I don't talk to anyone."

"If you go up there to be alone, why were you up there when we came home from school? No one was here then. Were they Mommy?"

I stared at Angel, not knowing how to answer her. I was not sure why I had gone to the hill. I thought I had fallen asleep and dreamed all the things I felt and saw. I felt like someone else took over my body, willing it to go there. Now I was beginning to wonder.

"No Angel, no one was here today. Maybe I was hoping to meet your Mr. Issy. You know what?"

"What?"

"The next time I go up there, I will ask to be able to see him too. But for now young lady, how about let's go fix some pizzas for supper?"

"Okay, can I help you?"

"You sure can. You're a big girl now, and the next time you see Mr. Issy, tell him that I am ready to see him."

"Okay Mommy, I will."

Convinced it was probably him that I had seen earlier, I determined that Mr. Issy must be Israel.

Angel and I prepared a simple pizza dinner. We all sat at the table getting acquainted with Isaac, whom I liked immediately. He was very polite and well mannered.

It was bizarre to think about the past between our two families – to know, over one hundred years ago, our great grandparents may have sat at this same table and ate their meals. They probably were not together, but they all gathered here at one time or another.

I caught myself staring at Isaac several times. I just could not help myself. I wondered whose descendant he was. Was it Hester, Jesse, or maybe even Israel's? He was very fair skinned with large dark eyes and a slender build. He could have belonged to Israel. He fit the description in Mary Beth's diary.

"Mom, do you have a problem?" Gary shouted.

"No, I don't have a problem. Why?" I said, not realizing, but continuing to stare.

"Because, you're staring and smiling at Isaac, and you're not saying anything. You look really weird."

I shook my head. "I am sooo, sorry. I didn't realize I was staring."

It was apparent that Isaac was very uncomfortable.

"I was just thinking about all of our ancestors that used to live here, Isaac – yours and ours. Do you know . . . ?"

"Here we go. No, he doesn't, and he doesn't care," Gary interrupted. "Come on Isaac, let's go upstairs. Mom is obsessed with this house and its so-called secrets."

"I'm sorry," I shouted as they vacated the room.

"May I go watch TV, Mom?" Angel asked.

"Sure Baby, you go ahead."

I felt bad for staring at Gary's friend. Certainly he could not be too mad at me. I hope I did not make Isaac feel too uncomfortable. I looked forward to his coming back. If he was uncomfortable, I may not ever get a chance to talk to Mr. Jesse, and he is the only one that seems to know what happened here. "I believe he is the final link to our plantation," I thought.

"Or . . . *is* Mr. Jesse the only way for me to find out what really happened here?" I said aloud, picking up the diary. Mary Beth had taken me inside before. Maybe she would do it again.

Heading into the living room, I sat with Angel for a few minutes and watched television. She was content with a Charlie Brown special. I could hear the boys upstairs playing, and from the sound of things, they too were having a good time.

I decided to retreat into the yard for a breath of fresh air. The speed of the wind was revitalizing. I got a vigorous, refreshing, robust rush from sitting in its breeze. I situated myself on the lawn furniture. Mary Beth's diary in hand, I began to read. I could feel myself again drifting back in time. As I proceeded to read, I seemed to fall into each page of the book, to be granted access to every sight, smell, and feeling. I would say I felt like I was watching a movie, but it was more like I had been cast in one. I had a part, but I wasn't sure what it was.

As I read each word, I began to hear it. I felt like I was the ghost trapped between worlds. I was lingering in mid-air, absorbing each word as they spoke, seeing each movement made. I had become a part of their lives. I was traveling back and forth in time, becoming a ghost of the future, walking into the past. I was never visible to the apparitions that I viewed, but it seemed they knew I was standing silently in a corner. I observed as Mary Beth began to write in the diary that I had been reading. I had been reading everything about her: her happiness; the grief; the pain and the pleasure. There were no secrets that she could hide from me.

Dear Diary:

I am so ashamed. I don't know what to do. It has been 3 days since I married Ben. He has not touched me since that dreadful first night. I think if he does, I will kill him. My face still aches from the bruises he put on me. My lips are busted in several places, I can barely open my mouth, and it hurts so badly. The only thing that keeps me alive is Israel. I love him so much. I close my eyes and see his beautiful face and feel his gentle touch. I want to be with him so badly. If only he could be married to me. I am so sad without him; my tears are like an endless river.

I lingered, reading all about her lonely life and watching her write every word. I would close my eyes with her and feel her pain. I had nothing but empathy for her. For days, she stayed hidden in her room with her heart full of agony and sorrow. The sensation of betrayal, the loneliness, and the emptiness inside her were overwhelming. I read on and experienced each and every word.

Late one night, sitting on the balcony, she noticed Israel. Silently watching him in the dark, she picked up her diary and began to write everything she felt.

Dear Diary:

Through the thick fog, I can see Israel. He's standing up on the hill. He stares up at my bedroom, I watch him as I stay hidden in the shadows of the night.

He stands there all alone. I know he is waiting for me; and I have to go to him. I have to hold him, touch him, and feel him against my body, my heart, and my soul. I have to feel that love we shared. He and he alone can take away this pain. I can't stand it any longer.

She lay her diary down, turned and dropped her head in shame. "But what if he does not want me? What should I do? I am so scared. Will he hate me for what Ben has done to me? Am I a whore? Will he think of me in that way? I have to find out. I can't keep wondering what he must think of me; I must know."

Mary Beth snuck out of her room, walked down the long hallway and tiptoed past her father's room, where Ben slept. The steps creaked as she descended. Pulling the front door open, she heard Ben call out. Quickly, she closed the door and hid behind the drapes.

She trembled and waited, terrified that he was coming for her again, but she heard nothing. Quietly stepping from behind the curtains, she crept back up the stairs. Reaching for the doorknob of Ben's room, she slowly turned it, closed her eyes and slightly pushed it open. Easing her head through the crack and cautiously peering inside, a tear ran from her swollen eyes and dripped down her face. The fear inside tormented her mind, making her nauseous, not able to see into the darkness of his room. She pushed the door a little wider, and with clenched fists, she silently said a prayer and inched into the room.

She moved around the room quiet as a mouse to the edge of his bedside. In the dark, lying in the stench of his booze, was her husband. She glared down at him and felt intense hostility take control of her body. She thought of how much she wanted to kill him. Out of the corner of her eye, she saw a glimmer on the nightstand. There was Ben's ivory handled, steel blade hunting knife. Easing her way across the room, she picked it up and felt the sharpness of the blade across her hand.

She closed her eyes, and the memory of the assault replayed in her head. Tears streamed down her face. She was holding the knife with both hands, and slowly, she lifted it above her head. Taking a step toward Ben, she stared into the shadow of his face, her body quivering as she wielded the knife. She leaned over his body, brought the knife down to his throat and accidentally touched him with its sharp point. He responded with a jolt and a mumble. Startled, she dropped the knife and bolted from the house.

Mary Beth rapidly ascended the hilltop through the black, wretched night. Her long beautiful hair blew in the wind, shadowing the fading bruises on her face. The grassy knoll was slippery and wet from the fallen dew of the night air. Her white nightgown dragged through the mud behind her as she fled. Visibility in the dense fog was minimal. It swallowed her body completely. However, she did not need to see. She had climbed the hill so many times before, she could do it blind. Nothing mattered but what awaited her on top of the hill.

The fog separated as the moon escaped from behind the clouds, and Mary Beth could finally see Israel. His body was slumped into a sitting position leaning against the tree, while his head rested on his knees. She stopped and pulled her hair down to conceal her bruises.

"Israel," she said softly.

"Mary Beth!" he shouted. He jumped to his feet and pulled her to him. Israel started kissing her face with no concept of the severity of the injuries that Ben had inflicted upon her. She jerked away in pain.

"What's wrong, Mary Beth?"

She turned her back and the tears jetted down her cheeks. She began sobbing uncontrollably.

"Mary Beth, what's wrong?" he asked again.

She turned to Israel and pushed her hair back, revealing her wounds. "You must kiss me gently."

He saw the bruises and shouted, "Oh my God, how could he have done this to you? I will kill that bastard. I will kill him for beating you this way."

"No Israel, you cannot. It is all my fault. He knows I have been with someone. He could tell. He said I was nothing but trash, a whore. I told him I was raped. I didn't know what else to say. I don't know if he believed me."

"What did he say to that?"

She turned away again. "He said that . . . " she sobbed. "That will be the only way he will ever touch me too. He said I was only worthy of being raped." Sobbing louder she continued, "I . . . I think that may be true, but he won't ever put his hands on me again. If he tries to touch me, I will kill him myself. I can barely sleep at night. I'm so scared he is going to come into my room. I went into his room before I came up here. I wanted to kill him. I was going to kill him, but he woke up."

"What do you mean, he woke up?"

"He didn't really wake up. He just moved. He's too drunk to be awakened. I was holding his knife, and I was going to stab him. I accidentally touched him, then I dropped the knife and ran. I hate him Israel, I hate him," she cried.

Israel turned toward her. She tried to look at him, but blinded by the tears, she could not see anything.

"I won't let him hurt you again, I promise. I'm so sorry I could not protect you. I will never let him touch you again. I will die first. Come sit under the tree in my arms. Sleep, while I watch over you. Let me protect you tonight. I am here by your side. Lay your head down and sleep."

And she did.

.

CHAPTER 17

THE SHINY REVOLVER

Early one morning right about dawn, a scream echoed across the farm. It was so shrill, it awoke Mary Beth from a dead sleep. She sat straight up in her bed and listened, but heard nothing. Leaping to her feet, out to the balcony she ran. Chickens were scattering across the yard, a dog scurried under the porch tucking his tail between his legs as he went, and the horses huddled together in a circle with their ears perked, staring, snorting at the woods. Searching the yard, she noticed nothing unusual. In her heart, she knew something was not right. She retrieved her robe from the end of the bedpost and ran downstairs. Mammie was preparing breakfast. She too had heard the scream.

"Who was screaming, Mammie?" Mary Beth asked.

"I aint' know, child. I hears it, but I ain't sees nuttin'."

Mary Beth ran to the back door, but before she could fully get it open, Hester fell onto the porch crying hysterically.

Mary Beth knelt down beside Hester. "Hester, what is wrong?" she asked.

Hester tried to catch her breath. She was sobbing and sniveling with every breath, her hands clenching her dress tightly. Her lips quivered as she began to talk.

"I didn't know. I swears it. I ain't know."

"You didn't know what, Hester?"

"Talk up child. What ain't you knows?"

"I . . . I still be a sleeping. I hears a noise an' I wake up. It still be dark in da house. I thought it be Israel making all dat noise, but it ain't. It . . . It be Master Ben. He . . . "she sobbed louder. "He . . . "

"He what child?" Mammie angrily asked, grabbing her by the arms. "Did he be touchin' ya child?"

She shook her head. "He came in da house. It be dark, I couldn't see who it be, I thought it be Israel. He sat on da end of da bed an' I kick'em. I thought it be Israel." She looked up at Mary Beth. "I ain't know it be your Master Ben. I ain't know."

"It's all right, Hester. Did he hurt you?"

"He jes' slap me 'cross my face. But den he . . . he . . . ," she cried again. "He start pullin' at ma clothes. I beg 'em ta stop, but he ain't listen. He tears me clothes off, I tried ta fight 'em. I screamed. When I'z screamed, Israel came in. He pulls Master Ben off me an' hits 'em. Master Ben, well, he gots up an' knock Israel ta da flo'. Den he . . . " she cried some more.

"He what Hester, what did Ben do?" Mary Beth grabbed hold of Hester and shook her. "Where is Israel?"

"He's bein' whip. Master Ben, be whippin' my bruddah," she dropped down on the porch and sobbed.

Mary Beth ran across the yard to the other side of the hill where the slave quarters were, but she saw no one. She rushed into the cabin, but no one was there. Turning to the fields, she saw Jesse, Israel's brother.

"Jesse!" she screamed. "Jesse," she doubled over, huffing and puffing. She gasped, "Have you seen Israel?"

"No ma'am. I ain't see 'em dis mornin'."

Jesse came closer to her.

"Jesse, listen to me, you have to help me find him, Ben has him. He might be in big trouble. Ben might kill him. Think, where would he take him?"

"Oh no! Not my bruddah. He can't kill my bruddah. Israel be a real good boy."

"Come on, Jesse, help me look. We must find him."

Mary Beth and Jesse ran through the woods calling for Israel. They crept all around the pond yelling his name. Mammie and Hester joined in the search. They looked in the barn, the woods, and the main house. There were no signs of Ben or Israel. They searched for two hours without a trace. The sun was in full light. No longer would darkness obscure their search.

The heat brought out mosquitoes and gnats. They swatted and scratched at the endless supply of insects that swarmed and ambushed them at every turn.

Sweat ran down their faces as they desperately searched the land. The pursuit was hopeless; there was no sign of Ben or Israel.

"Let's go back to the main house," Mary Beth said exhaustedly.

"Maybe now they'll be there."

"Miss Mary Bess, I needs ta get back ta my chores. If Master Ben comes back an' my chores ain't done, well, he jes' might sale, or kill me an' my fam'ly."

"You go ahead, Jesse. Don't you worry about anyone else being hurt. It won't happen again, I promise. I jest hope we are not too late to help Israel."

"Now Miss Mary Bess, don'ts worry none 'bout Israel," Mammie said. "He be's a big boy, he be ahright. We needs ta get youes back an' change out yourn bed clothes. If Master Ben sees youes lookin' like dat, he might jes tink ," she paused. "He jes' not like it none, dat's all. He still be yourn husband, whet'er we be likin' 'em or not."

"Mammie, I don't give a damn what Ben does or does not like. He's not my husband neither. I will never claim to be married to him again." She turned and looked at Hester. "Don't ever call that bastard, my Ben, he ain't nothing of mine. He will never be considered mine," she angrily shouted, entering into the house.

"Yez' em," Hester answered.

Everyone returned to their chores. Mary Beth changed her clothes and started pacing the floors. Constantly patrolling from the living room to the porch, from the porch around to the back door, through the kitchen and back again, she finally returned to her room and rushed out to the balcony in hopes of seeing Israel. She stared at the tree under which they had shared their love.

"God, please let Israel be all right. Please don't let that monster of a man hurt him."

She leaned on the railing and searched the grounds slowly and carefully. Nothing, she saw nothing. She began to weep. Her eyes flooded with tears. The more she cried, the madder she got. Leaping to her feet, she stormed from her room and stomped down the hall to her father's room. She swung the door open and trudged over to the nightstand, jerked out a drawer and emptied it onto the bed. Her Poppa's cold black, shiny revolver fell out and tumbled to the floor.

Without blinking an eye, she quickly picked it up. She closed her eyes, clenching the stone cold metal, and holding it close to her chest. Hands shaking and knees knocking, she drew the gun under her chin. As she inched her finger to the trigger, tears spilled down her cheeks and dripped to the floor. Her eyes closed tightly. She squeezed the trigger slowly . . . snap! The gun clicked. She pulled the trigger over and over, and it snapped again and again. She opened her eyes and looked down at the bed. The bullets were never loaded. She knew the gun was never loaded, but in all the confusion, she had forgotten. Thank God it wasn't.

"What am I thinking?" she said aloud.

Taking a deep breath and standing quietly for a moment, she reached down and picked up one of the cartridges. She fumbled it around in her fingers for several minutes, and then she began loading the bullets one by one until the chamber was completely full. As she turned to leave the room, she saw Ben's belongings draped over a chair. The rage built. Her heart began to race like wild horses, her palms began to sweat, and she could feel perspiration beading on her forehead. Her hand began to shake once again. She fired a shot – then another and another. She fired until the revolver just clicked as the chamber turned round and round. When she realized the gun was empty, she walked over and picked up Ben's fancy clothes. She smiled when she saw they were full of holes. Then, she tossed them to the floor and spit on them.

She turned back to the bed, picked up another handful of bullets and reloaded. She raced out of the bedroom door and hurried to the stairwell. Mammie met her halfway up the stairs.

"Miss Mary Bess, is youes ok? I'z thoughts I'z hears some shots."

She spotted the gun in Mary Beth's hand. "What youes goin' ta do wid dat dare gun, Miss Mary Bess?"

"I am going to kill that bastard when he comes through the door. I hate him, I hate him, I hate him. I can't bear to think what he might have done with Israel. If Israel is still alive and I pray he is, I won't let Ben ever get the chance to hurt him again. And if he did kill Israel, he'll never get the chance to hurt any of us again. I'm going to kill him, Mammie. I'm going to kill him dead as hell."

"Child, youes need ta tink whatcha be sayin' heah. Youes not yourn self, c'mon let's go talk 'bout dis."

"I don't want to talk. I just want to kill him."

"I knows ya do, but lets jes' talk a minute, heah?"

Mammie put her arm around Mary Beth and walked her to the living room. She talked her into putting the gun on the table by the front door. Mary Beth's body started to tremble. She dropped down on the sofa and began to cry.

"Mammie, what will I do if Ben has killed Israel?"

"Don't youes worry none, child, Israel be a real strong boy. He be ahright, jes' put yo' head in Mammie's lap an' rest."

Mary Beth cried. She laid her head in Mammie's lap as she tried to console her. She wiped the tears from Mary Beth's face and sang a comforting hymn. Mary Beth lips quivered as the tears subsided.

Suddenly the front door swung open.

"Get your hands off my wife, you filthy black ass nigger!" shouted Ben. "And get your black ass back into the kitchen where you belong and off of my furniture."

Mammie was terrified. She jumped to her feet, rolling Mary Beth to the floor. She bowed her head and trotted away, repeating over and over, "Yez sir, yez sir."

"Don't you go any where, Mammie," shouted Mary Beth. "She is not a filthy nigger, you bastard."

Ben walked over to Mary Beth. Mammie stopped and waited.

"How dare you contradict me bitch," he slapped Mary Beth across the face. She fell to the sofa. He whipped back around to Mammie and struck her too. Her frail body plummeted to the wooden floor. "I said get the hell out of here, now!"

Mammie struggled to her feet. Leaving the room, she saw the gun. She started toward it, turned slightly, peered over her shoulder, and looked at Ben. He was still staring at her. Hesitantly, she continued on and removed herself from his presence. She mumbled to herself as she went. Closing the kitchen door behind her, she heard Mary Beth ask about Israel. She was screaming, cursing at Ben, using words Mammie didn't even know she knew.

Mary Beth struggled time after time to get up, but before she could get her legs straight, Ben would backhand her again. He grabbed her long blond hair and yanked her through the house. He went into room after room as if he was searching for something. Mammie stepped to the door and watched. She wanted desperately to help, but she knew better than to intervene.

Mary Beth clutched at his hand and begged him to let her go. He stared at her, his face blood red and filled with rage. "You're going to die, you nigger loving bitch."

He continued hauling her through the house like an animal until he reached the kitchen. Mammie heard him coming and snuck out the back door. He pulled out drawer after drawer, slinging them through the air, until he found what he evidently was looking for: a knife.

"You see this?" he shoved the knife to her face. Then slowly, he pulled it down her cheek. "I'm not going to kill you. I'll just make it so no one else will want you. I am going to cut that pretty face up in pieces."

"No Ben, please stop," Mary Beth cried. "Please don't do this."

Mammie peeped in through the screen door. She covered her mouth to keep from crying out. She shook in horror, but was unable to do a thing.

"What did you do with Israel? Where is he? Did you kill him? Answer me, please," Mary Beth pleaded.

She knew if Israel were dead, it would not matter whether Ben killed her or not.

Ben finally replied, "You're still worried about that damn nigger, huh? What is it with you and them? Although it shouldn't be any never mind to you. No, I just made him wish he was dead, just as you will when I finish with you. You care way too much for these black thieving bastards. I think it is time for some trading to take place. After I'm finished putting you in your place, I will go to Charles Towne to the slave market. I'm going to get me some new niggers and get rid of these ones here. I need to teach you where your loyalty belongs, where it is supposed to be. That's with me, not some filthy black ass nigger."

"You might think of them as filthy niggers, but they are better than you'll ever be."

Then Mammie heard Mary Beth scream again. "Noooooo! Please

don't touch me, I'm begging you."

Ben heaved her back into the living room.

Mammie snuck back inside and ran to the kitchen door, easing it slightly open so she could see what was happening. She peered through the crack and saw Mary Beth crawling to her knees, pushing herself from the floor, and staring directly into Ben's face.

"No, I'm not begging anymore, I'd rather you kill me than beg you for anything. I'm done begging."

Mammie knew there was going to be trouble. She eased the door shut and paced around the kitchen table.

"Oh Lawdy," she whispered. "He gonna kill 'er, he gonna kill 'er. What ta do? Oh my dear Lawd, help me."

Then all of a sudden, she heard a loud popping noise. Mary Beth screamed again and again.

Ben yelled, "I will kill you!"

Mary Beth cried out, and with a loud thump, her lifeless body fell to the floor.

BANG! BANG! BANG! BANG! Everything was silent.

Mammie stood very still and listened for movement, but there was no sound. She scurried to the door and looked into the living room, but she was unable to see anything that explained what she had heard. She pushed the door a little wider, then she screamed at the unforgettable sight.

Mary Beth was draped half on the sofa and half off. Her arm hung to the floor, and blood was dripping from her fingertips. Thick strands of her long hair had turned red, saturated by her blood – and Ben's. Mammie scampered across the room to her body.

"Oh my Lawd, oh dear child!"

Then she noticed Israel. He was standing at the front door holding the gun with both hands.

"Oh dear Jesus, whatcha gone and done boy?" Mammie asked.

"Ya shoot Miss Mary Bess, Israel?"

Israel stood paralyzed, not moving or saying a word. Mammie hurried to the sofa to aid Mary Beth, and she saw Ben. Covering her mouth with her hands, she shrieked,

"Oh Lawdy, Jesus. Oh my Lawd."

Ben too lay lifeless in a pool of blood on the floor. Israel had also shot Ben. Mammie twisted around and stared at Israel. Ben had really beaten him badly. One eye was swollen, bruised and shut, and blood was still pouring from his nose and mouth. His shirt had been ripped off him, and his entire body was striped and swollen. He wore the bloody marks of a braided whip across his chest and back. Ben had surely whipped Israel half to death.

Israel was still standing in the same spot shaking and holding the gun that Mary Beth had laid on the table. His good eye was wild with rage, staring blankly down at Ben. Mammie walked over to him, pried the gun from his fingers and threw it to the floor.

"It be ahright son, it be ahright."

"Did I kill her Momma? Is she dead? Oh my God, oh my God! What have I done?" He covered his face with his hands and dropped to his knees.

"Israel, lookey heah at me," Mammie said, stooping down to him. "Youes gots ta git a hold of youesself. Ya needs ta sit down right heah an' lets me check on her.

Mammie prudently went back over to Mary Beth. Her body trembled as she stepped over Ben. She wondered if he were still alive and was frightened that he may grab hold of her.

Squatting down beside Mary Beth, she lifted her head back onto the sofa and began to examine her bloody body. Her face was badly beaten, and new bruises were already forming on the surface. Mammie brushed Mary Beth's hair from her face; she noticed a trickle of blood from the side of her head. Using the bottom of her own dress, she gently wiped the open wound.

"Oh God!" Israel shouted. "I killed her, didn't I? I shot her! I was shooting at Ben, Momma; I ain't mean to shoot her. Oh my God, what have I done?"

"Israel, go fetch yo' bruddah. Ya hears what I say? Goes an' fetch yo' bruddah. We'z need 'em ta help us. Hurry, Israel!" Mammie yelled.

"Help us? Nutt'in don't matter. No one kin help us."

"Youes jes' do as I tells youes ta. Now go, hurry."

Israel moaned as the pain jetted through his body. He struggled to his feet. His weak body limped away in misery.

Mammie whispered, "Mary Bess, don'ts youes leave us, Israel be jes' fine. Youes gotta come back."

She looked down at Ben. Lying at her feet, he too was covered in blood. She spat in his face and said to Mary Beth, "Ben ain't heah no mo', he ain't never gonna hurt us agin. Jes' like ya say, he be gone, gone for good."

Israel re-entered the house with Jesse. Mammie was sobbing and holding Mary Beth in her arms. Both of them were covered in blood. Mary Beth was lifeless. Her arm swung limp in the air as Mammie rocked back and forth and cried.

"Oh God! Oh my dear God! Is she dead, Momma? Did I kill her?" Israel asked again.

"No Israel, ya ain't do dis. Ben do dis. She ain't been shot, she been beat. She be beat, bad. Ben beat her wid dat," Mammie pointed to the floor where Ben lay. Mr. Simmons's blood stained cane was beside him. Ben had beaten her with her father's cane.

"She ain't be dead yet. She still be living, but barely. If ya ain't come in whens youes did, she surely be dead. We'z gotta get a docta."

"A docta," Jesse snapped. "And what we gonna say? Oh, Israel here shot Mr. Ben cause he be married ta da woman he be in love wid? Or we kin say, Mr. Ben beatin' Miss Mary Bess, cause she be in love wid Israel, dis heah nigger slave? Or, maybe we jes' say we didn't like 'em so we kill 'em. Ya know dey will hang Israel from da highest tree dey kin."

"How ya know 'bout Israel and Miss Mary Bess?"

"Whatcha mean how I know? I ain't blind, an' I ain't be born yestaday."

"Who else know dis?" Mammie asked.

"I don't care how he knows or who else knows. Nutt'in ain't matter but her," Israel blurted out. "I ain't lettin' her die. If I have to die to save her, then so be it."

Mammie glared down at Ben, then at Israel. "Ain't nobody else dyin' heah. I gots a plan." She gently laid Mary Beth back down and moved toward Ben. "Ya two pick up Ben an' lay 'em on dat rug."

"I ain't touchin' dat man," Jesse said, backing away.

"He be dead, Jesse. He ain't gonna hurt ya. Now ya do as I say."

"Dead or not, I ain't touchin 'em."

"C'mon Jesse, ya gotta help me."

Jesse stood there for a few seconds. Realizing how desperate Israel was, like it or not, he knew he had to help. Together the two boys moved vigilantly toward Ben. Jesse pushed at him with his foot. A dreadful moan sputtered from his mouth, as the last breath of air gushed from his lungs.

Jesse and Israel vaulted backwards. Jesse fell over a chair and then quickly sprang to his feet.

"He ain't dead," he exclaimed. "He ain't dead."

"He is dead, Jesse," Israel replied, trying to convince himself of that fact.

"Ya ain't hear 'em breathe? I heared 'em. Da man ain't dead, I tells ya dat right now."

Israel gave the body a swift hard kick. Ben didn't move. He turned Ben over, and again, a moaned escaped his lungs.

Jesse jumped and yelled out, "See, he ain't dead."

"It don't matter, Jesse, whether he is dead or not, we're buryin 'em."

"Ya be crazy bruddah. I ain't buryin' dis man if he ain't dead."

Israel stared at Jesse for a minute. Then, he bolted up the stairs. They could hear him scrambling around up there, but they didn't have a clue what he was doing. A few minutes later, he returned.

He leaped from the step toward the front door.

"Whatcha doing Israel?" Mammie asked.

Bang, bang, bang. Both Jesse and Mammie jumped with fear.

"He damn sho dead now," Israel said after shooting Ben in the head.

"Ya sho he's dead?" Jesse asked. "Ain't nebber saw no dead man."

"I'm sure Jesse," Israel said, marching his way to Ben.

There was no remorse, guilt, or pity felt from anyone for what Israel had done. They all were just scared about what would happen next.

Rage and hatred built up inside Israel as he looked down at Ben. He snarled, spit on the body, and kicked it as hard as his pain stricken leg would allow. Ben moaned again when his body slightly rolled.

"He's dead," Israel said, poking out his lip and shaking his head up and down.

Jesse was still not convinced, but cautiously, he helped anyway.

"I'll get 'ems feet, but I ain't touchin' 'ems head."

"C'mon Jesse, jest pick the man up."

They bent over, straining to lift the dead weight. Israel's stinging body cringed with the slightest movement. His muscles contracted, causing spasms throughout, but he did not quit. He was determined to do whatever possible to get rid of that monster.

Finally, they managed to pick Ben up and lay him on the rug.

"Now roll'em up," Mammie said.

"Roll 'em up!" Jesse angrily shouted. "What'cha mean, roll 'em up?"

"I ain't need no back talk boy. Youes hear me. I says, roll 'em up an' I means jes' what I say. Roll 'em up," she repeated, clenching her lips tightly.

"An' what we gonna do wid' em whens we roll 'em up? Jesse asked.

"Youes gonna tie some rope roun 'em an' som'em heavy, den trow 'em in dat dare pond."

Jesse shouted, "Trow'em in da pond! Trow'em in da pond! We'z can't trow dis man in da pond. We'z all be hung. I ain't trowin 'em in no pond, I tells y'all dat right now. I ain't gonna do it!"

Israel stared down at Ben, then over at Mary Beth. He leaned down, picked up the corner of the rug and began to roll it up.

"C'mon Jesse, if deys ain't got no body, deys can't hang us. Dey got ta find da body first. Now help yo' bruddah."

"I ain't like it, I ain't like it a tall." Jesse leaned down to help Israel. Then he stood back up and shouted again, "Youes crazy! Youes boff be crazy!"

"Crazy we'z may be, but we'z still livin', an' Ben dare ain't. Not dat Ben," Mammie said looking at Israel.

"Not that Ben. What'cha talkin' bout Momma?" Israel asked.

"I'z talkin' bout youes bein' da new Ben."

"Da new Ben!" Jesse shouted. "What! I knows youes crazy now,"

Jesse said, walking around in a circle and shaking his head. "Master Ben mus'of be hit youes in da head too. Israel ain't no Ben."

"How am I the new Ben? What'cha talking 'bout?"

"Ain't no one sees Master Ben 'fo. No ones but da preacher man. We'z gets Hester ta fix yourn hair an' youes kin put on Ben's fancy clothes. Youes kin be Ben," Mammie said, walking around Israel, looking him up and down as she spoke. "Youes know how ta talk dat dare proper words an ah."

"Momma, ya forget what color he be. Dis boy be a colored boy, a nigger. He ain't white, he be a slave. How ya gonna make 'em white?" Jesse asked.

"Youes look down dare at Master Ben's face. It ain't be too much lighter den Israel's. He be an Italian an all dat. Israel be real smart. He talk like white folk do. He wantin' ta be wid Mary Bess, now he kin," she said, nodding her head.

Israel tried to smile with his swollen lip. She could see his face lighting up despite the bruises. His body seemed to come alive. Then he sternly said, "Let's get this animal into the pond. I need to fetch a doctor for my wife."

"Yo wife!" Once again, Jesse raved. "Yo wife! Jesus, ya boff be crazy. I ain't sure what been hap'en' in dis heah house ya two been livin' in, but som'em ain't right. Ya boff be talkin' crazy. I tink da docta might needs ta look at y'all first. "

Jesse looked up at Mammie. Then, he looked at Israel's battered body. He stood there staring at the two, and the they stared back at him. He mumbled a couple of times as he bent over to help Israel move Ben's body.

"I mus' be crazy, too, but I reckon we'z gotta die sometime. Da way it looks, death pro'bly be real soon, we'z ain't got much ta choose from, huh? Let's hurry up an' get rid of dis pig," he mumbled as they wobbled across the floor carrying Ben.

"Yo wife, Mr. Ben, we'z all done los' our minds," he said, staring at the motionless body.

"We'z gotta hab a story 'fo youes go fetchin' da doc." Mammie covered her mouth with her fingers and begin tapping her lips. She walked back and forth, putting together a plan that she hoped would work.

"We'z kin say Miss Mary Bess went ridin' on hers horse, and one of da workers finds hers on da ground not movin'. We'z say she mus'of fall off da horse."

"That ain't going to work Momma. Look at me. I'm bruised from head to toe. What are we going to say happened to me?"

"Youes right. Youes tell 'em youes an' yo's wife gots robbed. Tell 'em, two men jump ya in da woods. Yeah, yeah, dat's it, dat pro'bly work."

The two boys listened carefully to the plan and nodded in agreement. Mammie crept out the front door to ensure there was no one in yard. Once confirmed, Israel and Jesse struggled to lift Ben's dead weight.

They began to carry him toward the pond. As they moved stealthily across the yard, they cautiously studied their surroundings, hoping no one was watching.

They laid Ben close to the pond and searched for something to help weigh the body down. A watered down log found at the edge of the bank was exactly what they needed. It was extremely heavy, evidently submerged for some time.

Jesse ran and got some heavy duty rope from the barn. They secured the rope tightly around the rug and the tree that became the burial chamber for Ben's body.

They were exhausted, but there was no time to rest. They lifted Ben one last time. Resting him on their shoulders, they waded out chest deep and tossed Ben as far as they could.

The body hit the water with a splash. It trundled repeatedly, and then, it bobbed up and down like a fishing cork. Finally, it began to sink, feet first, sending ripples across the water. It slowly disappeared from sight. The two brothers stood watching and waiting, not uttering a word. Neither Jesse nor Israel moved a muscle until it had completely vanished, leaving not a trace of evidence. They looked at each other, and still not saying a word, they turned and began to leave the scene.

"Oh no!" Jesse bellowed out. "Oh dear Jesus!"

"What's wrong?" Israel asked.

"Look at me. I be covered in 'ems blood. Look, it be all over me." Jesse stood holding out his arms. "Get it off me! Help me!" he screamed.

"Calm down, be quiet, jest wash it off. It'll wash off. Splash some more water on ya. You're okay, ya hear me? It's okay. It's off of ya."

Jesse looked down and examined himself. "Okay, okay, youes right, it be off of me now. I ain't want no part of dat dare man on me. Let's get out of heah. Let's go," Jesse said, looking at his body to reassure himself.

"We gotta hurry. I gotta change my clothes and go fetch the doctor."

"I tink youes crazy, Israel."

"Yep, I sure am."

Then, not saying another word, they quickly rushed from the pond and went their separate ways.

Jesse returned to the slave quarters to pass the word to his family. He had to get Hester and send her to the main house to help Israel get ready.

Israel galloped up the steps and entered the house. He had to change his clothes, his hair, and his life. He walked into the house a slave, a nigger, a poor boy, but he would exit as a prominent, well-established plantation owner. This would be a rebirth he had imagined, one for which he had waited a lifetime, but never thought possible. He was on the walk to freedom.

Although he wished over and over he could be white, he never imagined he would become someone he despised and wished death upon time after time . . . someone he knew very little about. However, the important thing was that Ben was the husband of the woman he loved. Before then, he didn't care to know anything about Ben, but at that point, he searched his mind for Ben's mannerisms and speech patterns. He knew he had to convince the doctor and everyone else that he indeed was Ben.

"Momma, do you think Mary Beth will be all right?" Israel asked, re-entering the living room.

"I don'ts know son, ya mus' hurry."

Israel knelt down beside Mary Beth, grasped her hand, and kissed her battered forehead.

"I will be right back, my love. You hold on."

With urgency, he climbed the stairs to the second level of the house. He paused for a minute outside Ben's bedroom door. Still a little uncomfortable, he eased the door open, poked his head around the corner and inched his body forward. Slipping against the wall, he turned the flame on the kerosene lantern to high. Inhaling deeply and exhaling slowly, he retrieved a pair of Ben's trousers and a shirt from behind the door. He stared down at his wet raggedy clothes and ripped them from his body.

Ben's clothes were fancy, very expensive, and unlike anything Israel had ever touched before. The silk shirt slid smoothly over his muscular body. The pants were made from wool called tweed; they were very heavy and rough. Israel proceeded and put them on . . . they fit perfectly. It seemed destiny had already been written.

He took a few moments to stare at himself in the full-length mirror and could not believe the transformation. He was taken aback by the revelation that a light skinned slave could become a dark skinned white man. He lifted his hand, wiggling his fingers, rubbing the fine clothing and taking in the fine things he had never had. "It's really me."

"Yep, it be you. Oooowee, youes look good," Hester said.

"Whatcha think, Sis?"

"I tink ya looks good, bruddah."

"Do you think I can do this?"

"Yeah, sho' do. Lookey at ya. If I ain't node who youes was, I'd tink youes be white. Ooowee bruddah, youes look soooo good. When Jesse tells me what hap'n, I'z tink youes an Momma done los' yo mind, but dis might work. Come over heah an' lets me get yo' hair right. Ya know ain't nobody really node Master Ben. Ain't no reason youes can't do's dis."

"I hope you're right, Mary Beth's life may depend on it," Israel replied as he walked over to Hester.

"It ain't jes' Mary Bess life, it be our life too. We'z all 'pendin' on ya."

"I know, Sister."

Standing in front of the full-length mirror, Israel slipped on Ben's shoes. Turning sideways, he examined himself one more time. Conquering his fear, he walked over to the bed, claimed a black hat from the top of the bedpost, positioned it on his head and tipped it to Hester.

"Hey little nigger girl, go get your brother Jesse to fetch my horse."

"Yez sir, right away Master Ben," Hester snickered.

"No. That is not my name."

"Whatcha mean, dat ain't yo name?"

"I would like to introduce myself to you. My name is Israel . . . Israel what? What's gonna be my last name?"

"Whatcha mean, yo las' name? Yo name pose ta be Ben, som'em.

"No. I ain't gonna be called Ben. Ain't no one in town knows him. Dey don't know what his name was, I jest need a last name."

"I ain't know what Master Ben's las' name be."

"I ain't sure, neither. I think som'em like Ricco or Riccio. I know, my name is, Israel Riccardo."

"Israel Ricardo, what kinds of name dat be?"

"I hope Italian, little sister. Ya pray for me while I be gone. I hope dis plan will work."

"Don'ts ya worry none Israel, ya kin do it. Ya has ta do it, fo' Miss Mary Bess."

"I has to do it fo' us all," he said, exiting the room.

He made his entrance into the living room where Mammie was talking softly and placing a cold cloth on Mary Beth's head.

"How's she doin' Momma?" Israel asked.

"She ain't be doin' no good, Son," Mammie said, turning to Israel. "Ahhhh, but lookey dare at you. Youes sho 'nough looks real good. I knows youes be a fine lookin' man. Youes be so han'som'," she exclaimed, walking around him. "Now youes betta hurry, or it be ta late fo Miss Mary Bess. She ain't move, she jes' lay dare."

"I'm scared Momma, what if somebody recognizes me? I might say the wrong thing and get us killed. What if I can't do this? I don't know if I can act like he did. I ain't hardly ever talked to no white folk. Jes' the folk round here."

"Youes be ahright, I knows youes kin do it. Youes jes' keep sayin' yo' name is Ben and youes married to Mary Bess Simmons."

"No Momma, I ain't going to be Ben. My name be Israel. Israel . . . "

"Riccardo," Hester shouted.

"Yeah, Riccardo. I ain't gonna be called, Ben. Like you said afore, da only person be knowing Ben's name was the preacher man. He don't come 'round here."

"Okay boy, ya be careful, holds yo head up high, an' go gets on dat horse an' ride. Youes kin do it, youes gotta. Jes' 'member, Mary Bess' life 'pends on ya."

Israel walked over to Mary Beth and kissed her cheek. He stood over her, holding her hand, and staring at her body. Then, without saying another word, he turned and rushed out the door. He mounted Ben's prize black stallion and rode away, determined to succeed.

Mammie and Hester remained at the entryway until he was out of sight. Then they hurried to clean up the blood-splattered room. The floors and walls had to be scrubbed. Things were broken and knocked over, and pieces of glass fixtures were shattered during the course of the brawl. Mammie, Hester and Jesse worked hard to tidy the mansion and return it to its spotless condition. When all was cleaned, Jesse returned to his small cabin.

A few hours had passed, and Mary Beth's condition had not improved. If anything, she was getting worse.

Mammie and Hester took turns comforting her, praying for her to regain consciousness. They sang sweet gospel songs in soft harmony to soothe her soul. A tin pan full of cool water and two white cloths were used to keep the swelling under control.

Mammie lifted Mary Beth's head and slid her body beneath it. She ran her long ebony fingers through Mary Beth's blond silky hair. Tears trickled from her eyes, as she feared the girl's death might be near. There was no response from Mary Beth, no matter how hard they prayed. Mammie and Hester sat in the dimly lit room and sobbed together. They knew the outcome looked bleak for them all.

CHAPTER 18

D A B E T ' R E E R I D E R S

Hours had passed, and Israel had not returned with the doctor. Everyone was worried, scared of what might have gone wrong. Mammie stood at the window, holding back the curtain and peering down the long dirt road.

"Som 'en be wrong. Israel shoulda been back long time 'go." She walked back to Mary Beth and stared down at her unconscious body.

"Miss Mary Bess, I wish youes wake up an' tells us what ta do. We'z be in a real mess heah." Mammie clasped her hands together and dropped her head.

"Hester, run an' fetch yo bruddah. We'z needin' ta be's tinking what we'z gonna do if Israel be caught."

"Ain't nuttin' we'z kin do but hope and pray, Momma. Ya know Israel be real smart. He be jes' fine."

"Sometime smart ain't be anough. Ben was 'pose ta be smart. Lookey where dat got 'em."

"Yeah, but he be a drunk too. Israel don't drink. He be jes' fine, don't worry, Momma."

"He ain't back yet, an' I'z is worried. Go fetch yo bruddah like I tells ya ta."

"Okay, Momma," Hester replied.

Mammie changed the cool cloth on Mary Beth's head. "Can't ya hears me in da child? Youes gotta wake up. I be real scared. We'z be ins big trouble. I'z don'ts know what ta do. Please, wake up." "Momma, look," Hester shouted, returning with Jesse. "There's someone coming up da road dare."

Mammie ran to the window and stared down the long dirt driveway. They were unable to tell who it was. Jesse and Hester stood on the front porch watching the dust billow from beneath the galloping horses. Leaning from side to side, they tried desperately to identify the passengers.

The sun had faded behind the trees, leaving just enough light to cast shadows on the narrow road. Jesse walked down to the bottom step, hoping to get a better view, but still, he was unable to see who rode closer to the house.

"It looks like t'ree of dem. Yeah, dare be t'ree riders," Jesse exclaimed.

"T'ree," Hester blurted. "Dare should be only two. Oh Momma, he be caught, Israel be caught."

"C'mon, ya churren gets in da house. Youes need ta sneak out da back an' hide."

"What 'bout ya Momma? We'z can't jes' leave ya."

"Don't youes worry none bout me. Now get. Hurry fo' dey gets heah," Mammie whispered.

Jesse and Hester reluctantly left Mammie behind. Obeying their mother, they scurried out the back door and hid. Mammie dimmed the lantern as low as it would go. She crept over to a darkened corner and waited for her fate.

A few minutes later, the front door slowly opened and in walked three men. Mammie sat quietly and watched as each one entered into the house. The kerosene lantern flickered as the door slammed behind them. The wind waltzed across the room, blowing the curtain from the window.

Trying to recognize each man, Mammie observed through the darkness. As they stepped into the light, she was hoping one of them was Israel. A tall, overweight white man with a beard was first. A slightly shorter man, wearing glasses and a tall black hat, stepped up next. The last man stood at the door in the dark. Mammie stared into the shadowy foyer, frustrated and anxious to know if it was Israel. She waited patiently, not moving a muscle, barely breathing, as she peered through the darkness, praying it was her son. The mysterious man stayed in the dark hallway.

The tall man made his way over to Mary Beth. He picked up her limp hand and held onto her wrist for a couple of minutes. He squatted and leaned close to her, evaluating her badly swollen black and blue face.

"Jesus!" he shouted. "I thought you said she had fallen from her horse."

The man in the dark emerged: It was Israel.

"Yes, she had fallen from her horse, but I also told you, we had been beaten and robbed. The two men had beaten me to the ground, grabbed my wife and fled with her. They had taken Mary Beth and dumped her body a mile or so further down the road. One of the workers found her lying in the woods."

"How about bring me a lantern over here? I need more light."

Israel looked around the room and saw no one. He was concerned for his mother and sister. He lifted the lantern from the table and carried it close to the doctor.

The doctor lifted Mary Beth's eyelids and examined her eyes. He turned her head to the side and uncovered some dried blood matted in her hair. The other man peered over his shoulder. He too leaned down and studied it a little closer.

"I can tell you this didn't happened jest from a fall."

"I told you, she was beaten by some men. She fell limp and has not moved since," Israel replied nervously.

The doctor looked up at Israel. Israel stood silent, lost for words, sweat beading across his face. He was almost certain the doctors realized he was desperately trying to cover something up. His face lined with fear, his legs trembled.

"Master Israel did everything he could fo' Miss Mary Bess," Mammie replied from the dark.

The doctors stood at attention, startled by her presence, but Israel was relieved. He smiled and nodded.

"Are you the one that found her?" The tall doctor asked again.

"No sir, I'z didn't find her," Mammie answered with her voice cracking, still not moving from the corner.

"Well, she can thank God someone did, cause she probably would be dead by now. Whoever did this really did it good. If you look close on her head here, there's a huge gash. She must have been hit with something."

Mammie stared at Israel and sighed with relief. She cupped her hands together, shaking them in a silent prayer, thanking God for bringing Israel home safely.

The shorter man took off his hat and set it on the table next to where Mary Beth lay. He squatted down to hear what the doctor was saying.

"What do you think is wrong with her?"

"I'm not quite sure. She seems to be breathing fine. Her heart rate is good, and her color is good too. She just ain't responding. Would you like to take a closer look?" the doctor asked the short man as he moved aside.

"Yes I would, but I need better lighting than this. Do you have some more lanterns you can bring in here?" the short doctor asked, turning toward Israel.

Israel stood firmly, staring blankly at the doctor.

"Well, do you?" the man asked again.

Again, Israel did not respond. Mammie stretched her eyes wide and tilted her head to Israel, trying to get him to answer. The men stood side by side, also waiting for an answer, but Israel just stared back, dumbfounded. He was unaware anyone had asked him for something. He was always just told to get it.

Mammie cleared her throat and started coughing, trying to get Israel's attention. He turned toward her and realized she was trying to tell him something. He looked at the doctor and finally caught on.

"Yes, of course. I'm sorry, I jest seem to be in shock over all this. There are many more lanterns. I'll get them for you," Israel started walking from the room.

Mammie started coughing again, loudly that time. Israel stopped and turned to her. She was shaking her head back and forth. The tall one asked if she was choking. She answered, "No," then, she looked at Israel and at the lantern, and he again caught on.

"Go fetch some lanterns," he demanded.

The tall doctor looked at him and replied, "I was beginning to wonder if you were going to let that nigger just stand here and let you do her work. I know you might be new to the South, but you'll catch on. This plantation will help show you what them niggers are good for."

The two doctors laughed as they squatted back down to Mary Beth.

Israel was furious, but he tried to laugh with them. Then he stated, "Yeah, you're right, I got a lot to learn. Now what about my wife, is she going to be all right?"

"Yes, I believe she will," the shorter man answered, taking the lantern from Mammie. He again looked into Mary Beth's eyes. "Her pupils are fixed and dilated," he said as he studied them. "I think she has a concussion, and most likely she is in a coma. With this kind of head trauma, it's not uncommon."

"Will she die from this?"

"Could, but not usually."

"So, what do we do for her?" Israel asked.

"Well son, you need to keep her as comfortable as you can. Try to keep her cool, and keep a cold cloth on her head. These things normally don't last very long."

"Define very long," Israel said with grave concern in his voice.

"Sometimes a couple of hours, a couple of days, maybe a week or two. It's just hard to determine."

The tall doctor smiled. "You learned that in New York? You could tell that by looking into her eyes, huh?"

"Yes. Look here," the short doctor said, pulling her eyelids back up. See how her eyes don't seem to change from the light?" he asked, holding the lantern close to her.

"Oh yeah," the other doctor said, shaking his head.

Israel interrupted, "You mean that's it? That's all you can do? You don't have any medicine or anything to give her? You're telling me I'm supposed to . . ." he turned his head away for a second. "I'm supposed to let her just lie there? How will I know if she is getting better or worse? How will I know if I need to get you back here again?"

The older doctor frowned and knitted his eyebrows.

"Look here boy," he snapped, "I told you before, this is Dr. Murray. He came all the way from New York City. He is one of the best. I think you need to have a little more respect here."

"Oh that's all right," the short doctor said. "People who have loved ones like this get upset easy. If he wasn't upset — or should I say considerably concerned — I might wonder about him. This is his wife."

Israel looked at the two men staring at him. He started to feel awkward and got fidgety, especially since the doctor had called him "boy." He thought maybe they knew.

Mammie noticed his nervousness. She quickly spoke up, getting the attention off Israel.

"Do youes want me ta fetch youes some mo' cold cloths, Master Israel?"

Israel cocked his head to the side and smiled. It was very clear that he enjoyed the sound of "Master Israel."

"Yes Mammie, a pan of cold water and a cloth will be fine." He turned to the doctors, "If that is all you can do for my wife, I will walk you to the door." He picked up the black hat and handed it to Dr. Murray.

The doctors were stunned by Israel's boldness. He had an arrogant air that seemed to come from nowhere. Israel opened the front door.

Dr. Murray put on his hat and stopped in front of him. "If there is not any change in about a week or so, you can find me in town."

"Thank you both for coming. I will be happy to tell Mr. Simmons about the diagnosis of his daughter when he returns. I'm sure he will want to thank you personally."

Both men nodded as they passed Israel. They mounted their horses and rode away.

"Ohhhh Israel," Mammie laughed. "Youes showed dem real good. Youes sho' put dem, high an' mighty white men, right in dem dares place."

She laughed and stooped over, holding her hands between her knees.

"Ain't no ones even tink youes not Ben. I'z told ya, youes could do it, now we'z all goin' ta be ahright. Youes hab a plantation ta run, wid all deze heah nigger slaves. Youes a white man now, youes be our master." She laughed and laughed with joy. "An' dose big words youes be sayin', I ain't ever heard dem 'fore. Ya be's som'em else."

Israel smiled, picked up Mary Beth's hand and held it against his face.

"Ain't no plantation worth losing Mary Beth. If she don't make it, Momma . . . " his eyes were glassy and full of tears. "If she don't make it . . . " he looked back down at Mary Beth. "Without her, I can't do this."

"What'cha talkin' bout child, youes can't do what?"

"I can't pretend I am Ben. I don't want to be that man. He's responsible for this. If she dies, I'll die with her."

"Boy, don't be talkin' nonsense. Ain't nobody dyin', she gonna be fine. Ya keep prayin', don't youes give up."

"I ain't going to give up, Momma. I'll never give up as long as she is breathing."

CHAPTER 19

DA NEW BEN

Ten days had come and gone, and there had been no change. Everyone was worried that Mary Beth would not come out of the coma. Israel and Mammie took turns caring for her around the clock. Every night, he slept in a chair close by her side.

On the eleventh morning, the wind blew strongly; a storm was brewing in the air. Mammie pulled the curtains back and noticed Hester out by the pond.

"Whatcha doin', Child?" she shouted.

"Dere be a storm comin', Momma. I needs ta scatter deese heah 'erbs an' roots roun' da pond. We'z gotta keep Ben at res' in dare, an' deese tings will help."

Mammie watched from the back porch. She shielded her eyes from the flying debris. Hester continued to jabber strange words and throw her mixture to the wind. The rain came, and Mammie scurried for indoors. Hester persistently chanted as the cold water began to pour over her body. It dripped off the ends of her hair and sent shivers down her spine, but she continued. The ritual lasted for hours. Exhausted, she dropped to her knees, said a prayer, and hurried inside to change her wet clothes.

"Look at ya, child, youes soak an' wet. Youes goin' ta catch da deaf of youself. Com' up da stairs an' let's get youes dried off."

The night was black and wicked. A candle flickered in the drafty old house. The storm was getting worse. Israel sat on the floor nestled close to Mary Beth, holding her hand tightly. The thunder was so loud it shook the house, and lightning lit up the sky like fire works. The old windows rattled as the wind blew swiftly against the brittle glass. The tin roof rumbled with the pounding rain. The vibrations sounded like a herd of wild horses. Israel watched the willow branches scratching against the windows.

"Mary Beth," he said, "why don't you wake up so I can hold you? I know you are scared of storms. Can you hear this one, Baby? Listen, it's calling out to you. It's begging you to wake up, Baby, I'm begging you to wake up. Listen to the thunder, Mary Beth. If you would open your eyes, you could see the fireworks. The wind is calling for you like wild wolves. It's howling around the house, our house, begging you to wake up. Can't you hear it, Baby? I wish you could because I know you would wake up if you could just hear it. Listen to it, Baby, listen."

He stared down at her, waiting for movement, but nothing happened. He watched her lifeless body just lying in limbo, not moving a muscle. He patted her face with the cold washcloth, and then he rested his head on her chest, closed his eyes, and sobbed.

"You can't leave me now. This is what we been waitin' for. It's all good now. We kin be together. I know you gots to hear me."

A voice whispered in the darkness, "Yes, I hear you."

Israel quickly sat up, "Mary Beth!" he shouted. "Oh Mary Beth, you've come back to me. I was so scared I was going to lose you."

"Why would you be scared?" she asked softly. "Why would you lose me?"

"The doctors said you might not ever wake up."

"What doctors? What are you talking about?" she said, rubbing her head. "I can't recall anything. What happened to me, Israel?"

"You don't remember?"

"No, I don't remember a thing."

"Mary Beth, Ben tried to kill you. He was beating you with your father's cane."

She sat up, her eyes wild with fright. She whispered, "Where's Ben? If he catches you here . . . " she searched the room, "he will kill you. You must leave."

The lightning lit up his face. The bruises were still visible. "Oh my God, did he do that to you? You need to go. I'll be all right. I don't want him to catch you."

She put her hand on top of her head and felt the bumps that the thick wooden cane had left. A frightened look shrouded her face as she touched the open wounds.

"Ben's not here any more. You need to lie real still."

"My head hurts terribly," she said, rubbing the side. "I remember Ben . . . he came in screaming, and he was like a crazy man."

She rubbed her head some more. "I think ... yes, we were arguing about you. I . . . I can't remember anything else. Everything else is a blur. What happened?"

"Mary Beth," Israel dropped his head. "Ben can't hurt you any more; he is not going to hurt anyone again."

"What do you mean Israel? Where is Ben?"

"He be sittin' right next ta ya, child. Dis be da new Ben," Mammie said, putting her arm around Israel as she entered the room.

"The new Ben? What are you talking about, Mammie?" Mary Beth looked at Israel. "Why are you dressed in Ben's clothes? Tell me what happened," Mary Beth asked again, confused about the whole scenario.

"Dey be an accident, Miss Mary Bess. Ya 'member we'z can't fine Israel, nowhere? We'z look every wheres, but we ain't fine 'em."

"Yes Mammie, we all were looking for him."

"Wells, den Ben came home. He be real mad. He start beatin' on ya an' start ackin' likes a wild man. He slapped me down ta da flo'."

"Yes, I remember that too."

"Do's youes 'member dat gun youes put over dare?"

"Yes," Mary Beth answered, looking at Israel.

"Ben started beatin' ya real bad. He gets youes poppa's cane over dare an' hits ya over and over again. Israel walked in da house 'bout dat time. He ain't be tinking bout nuttin' but you. He ain't rightly tink at all. He jes' pick up dat dare gun ya laid over yonda and shoots 'em. He ain't even know what he do. He jes' shoots 'em. I be in da kitchen when I hears da noise. Den I come runnin' in heah, but it be ta late by da time I'z get in heah. Youes and Ben boff be covered in blood. Israel thought he be kilt ya boff. He ain't nebber node nuttin' 'bout no gun. He sees it, he sees what Ben be doin' ta ya an' he jes' picked it up an' shoots. Ya boff must be falled at da same time, so Israel tinks he kill ya boff, but Israel only kilt dat ole Ben. If he hadn't, youes boff pro'bly be dead. He's didn't means to, it jes' hap'n dat way."

Mary Beth, disoriented and woozy, tried to sit up. "What do you mean you shot and killed Ben? What did you do with him? What did you tell the doctors when they came out? Do they know what happened?"

Mammie and Israel told Mary Beth the whole story. They told how Israel was now her husband, how he had gone to town and fooled everyone. No one had ever met Ben, no one but the preacher, so they didn't know who Ben was.

After hearing all the details, Mary Beth smiled at Israel. "You mean now you are really my husband? Now we can be together? Ben is really dead?"

"You're not mad at me?"

"Mad at you? I should thank you. I jest want us to be together. Isn't that what you want?"

"Yes Mary Beth. If that is what you truly want, I would love to continue to be your husband. It is a dream any man would be blessed to have. I am honored to be your servant."

"You are not my servant; you are my husband. I couldn't want more than that in this whole wide world. We'll have to figure out what to do about the preacher. We sure don't want him to let everyone know what Ben looked like. As soon as I get better, I will have to go to Charles Towne and see what preacher knows."

"Dat be a good idea," Mammie blurted. "We'z don't needs no one snoopin' 'round lookin' fo' trouble."

"Don't worry Mammie, no one ever comes out here. You know that. Everyone can thank my dear father for that. You know the town thinks that he is jest an old bitter gambling drunk."

Mammie looked away and then back again. She sat down by Mary Beth and lifted her hand. "I didn't knows, ya node 'bout dat child. Ya knows it ain't be true, yo father loves ya very much, an' he been real good ta all us. He be a very good man. Sometime he jes' wants people ta tink dat he be mean."

"Oh, I know Mammie, it's all right. I know who my father really is. Let's not even worry about any of this right now. My head really is hurting. I think I would like to go to my room."

"Yez'em, ya goes on an' git some res', I fix ya up som'em good ta eat.

I tink dat storm done gone, ain't not'ing ta be scared of no mo'."

Mary Beth lay across her bed trying to remember what had happened. In her mind, she was beginning to piece together that horrible night. She continued to have short flashes all evening.

She picked up her diary and began to write.

Dear Diary:

Poppa should be coming home soon. I've missed him so. I hope things will be all right when he gets here. Mammie is cooking in the kitchen and it smells wonderful. The aroma is drifting throughout the house and all across the farm. She is cooking a special dinner just for me.

I am so excited. I can't wait to tell Poppa about Israel and how he saved my life once again. I am hoping he will approve of our marriage. I have so much I want to tell him. I'm sure he will be pleased that Ben is dead and the plantation is ours again. I am so glad I can relieve him of his guilt. We are going to make this plantation one to be proud of.

I held a mirror up to my face and cried when I saw what that awful man did to me. I could barely recognize myself. Both of my eyes are swollen and black and blue. My lips are also swollen and busted open in several places. My head has a bald spot on the side where Ben ripped my hair from my head. I am so ashamed for letting that monster take control of my life for the 3 months that he was here. I hope God will forgive me for wishing him dead and now being happy that he is.

I am very tired now. I think I need to rest for a while.

The night came in unnoticed, and the storm quickly blew away, leaving only dark clouds as remnants of its existence. The house became black, and with the moonless night, Mary Beth had lost all vision. Everything was a shadow.

Mary Beth was running through the darkness, screaming for Mammie and Israel, but no one answered.

She ran into room after room, hands held in front of her, feeling her way in the dark until she bumped into someone. Unable to see, she became terrified. Before she could ask who it was, he jerked her up and pulled her close. There was an unfamiliar odor about him, and he was wet and cold.

"Poppa is that you? I cannot see, Poppa."

There was silence.

"Israel," she cried out.

Again, there was no response.

"Why don't you answer me? Poppa, are you trying to surprise me?" She asked, laughing a little to dissuade her fear, but he still did not say a word.

She began running her hands around his shoulders and face, searching for something recognizable. He was too slender to be her poppa.

"Israel," she shouted. "This is not funny. Please let me go. You're cold and wet, and you're scaring me." He did not say a word.

She pushed on his chest, trying to free herself. Leaning back, she tried to look at his face, but without light, she was unable to get a glimpse of the person. All that was visible were teeth; he was smiling.

She turned her head from side to side. A soft glimmer of light came from a nearby window. She peered back and stared into the eyes of the silent face. Her body began to tremble. Terrified, she soiled her nightgown. She opened her mouth to scream, but could release only a faint whimper. She searched deep inside for some kind of sound. She struggled to push her voice through the opening of her lips. Finally, the voice box that had defied her broke free and screamed.

She kicked, pounded, and beat on the chest of her hated husband. Ben had reappeared. He held onto her arms and laughed loudly. It echoed throughout the house as if it were empty, bouncing from wall to wall.

She put her hands over her ears to drown out his laughter. She was screaming to the top of her lungs and thrashing around wildly to get free, but he was too strong.

Her arms were swinging through the air when she heard Israel's voice. Staring intensely through the darkness, she could not pinpoint where the sound was coming from. He repeated her name several times, but the sound was muffled and far away.

Her body shook frantically. She opened her eyes and the percep-
tible view of Israel's face became clear. He was shaking her, awakening
her from a bad dream. It all was all just a nightmare.

She rose up into Israel's arms and cried. Hysterical, she began to tell
him about her dream. He continued to reassure her that Ben was dead
and that there was no way he could ever hurt her again. With a tight
grip around his arms, she wept on his shoulder.

Mammie bolted into the room. She stood in the doorway and stared
in distress.

"I thoughts I heared ya screamin' Miss Mary Bess," she said with a
bewildered look on her face.

Israel quickly jumped to his feet.

"She was screaming, Momma. She had a real bad dream. She thought
Ben had come back."

"Don't ya worries no mo' 'bout dat ole man, he be gone fo' good,"
she said as she moseyed over to the bed. She grasped hold of Mary
Beth's hand and continued to glance up at Israel as she talked to her.

"Mammie, it was jest a bad dream, I'm sorry for screaming. I'm jest
so tired. I'm scared to fall asleep. I'm scared of Ben. I want Israel to stay
and protect me. I know you said Ben is dead, but it is just too soon for
all of this to sink into my brain. I'm scared, and I jest don't want to be
alone."

Mammie never said another word. She turned, gave Israel a concerned look, then exited the room.

Mary Beth smiled at Israel, "Jest hold me tight." She closed her
eyes, snuggled in his arms, and fell fast asleep.

Mary Beth soon made a complete recovery. She and Israel started
living as husband and wife. They continued to rendezvous under their
special dogwood tree. They made changes for the better throughout
the plantation. It was more prosperous than it had ever been. The fields
were full of many different kinds of crops and fruit trees. The vegetables and fruits flourished, filling many baskets. The pigs and cows
had mated and given birth to several new babies. The market was giving top dollar for everything they brought in. Everything was finally
falling into place, and all was well.

The orange ball of fire slid from sight, allowing the moon to rise day after day. The plantation became a farm full of happy people. Mary Beth and Israel made sure the slaves were given good care. They worked harder to bring in more money. Then they bought more slaves and cleared the fields for larger gardens. They erected new fences to house the new cattle. The plantation had become a great achievement in everyone's eyes.

Although very few people had the pleasure of meeting Israel, his name was well known throughout the South as a successful planter. He was very knowledgeable about how to manage a plantation. Little did they know, it was how the slaves were treated that made the real difference. They were given twenty five acres of land to share and plant their own crops for harvest. Every family had a different section of the farm. The more they produced, the more they got back in return.

Mammie and Hester moved into the big house and took care of Mary Beth and the new Israel. They were given their own rooms in the quarters of the east side.

Mary Beth continued to write in her diary daily, filling it with many pleasant events.

April 23, 1854

Dear Diary:

Although we very rarely go to town and very rarely have guests, there is always plenty of warmth, laughter and love throughout our land. The bad memories of Ben have disappeared. His name is very seldom spoken.

Sometimes Mammie and the others would slip and call Israel by his first name, but it was quickly corrected. A slip of the tongue like that could have gotten everyone killed. Everyone has to remember he is Master Israel.

Israel has to withdraw from his family in a lot of ways, but he always tries to remember who he really is. He helps the slaves in the fields, milks the cows and even slops the pigs. He is proud of it all, and I am proud to have him as my husband. This has been one of the best years of my life. I only wish I could share this with Poppa and Johnny. I miss them so much.

Israel walked in and plopped onto the bed. Mary Beth put her diary on the bedside table and bounced over to him. Situating herself on the edge of the bed, she appeared to be glowing, and her smile was as wide as the sea.

"Whatcha grinning so for?" Israel asked.

"Well, you know we have been living together as man and wife for some time now."

"Yes. So?"

"So . . . no one has asked any questions about you."

"Sooo," he said again.

"Soooo, I don't think anything will be said about our new baby." Israel's mouth dropped open. Then, he whispered softly, "A baby."

"Yes, we are going to have a baby."

Then he shouted, "Baby! You mean we're going to have a baby?"

"Ummmm, yeah," Mary Beth laughed.

"Oh my God, a baby! Are you all right? Should I get you something? Here, put your feet up," he said, pushing a pillow under her legs. "Oh my God, I'm going to be a daddy, but how? I mean, I know how, but . . . what should I do? Do you need me to get you anything?"

"I'm fine Israel," she laughed. "I'm only about three months along. We still have six months to go."

"Oh my God, six months, a baby!" he shouted again. "Do Momma and Hester know?"

"No, I thought I should tell you first."

"Well, come on," he pulled her from the bed. "Let's go tell 'em – right now, let's go tell 'em."

"Israel," Mary Beth laughed as he pulled her down the hallway.

"Israel, it is late. Mammie will be asleep."

"We'll wake her up. She will be wide awake when she hears the news."

"Momma!" he shouted, "Momma!"

Mammie came running into the hall.

"What be wrong! Why ya shout fo'? Is ya sick Miss Mary Bess?"

"No Momma, she is not sick, nuttin' is wrong."

"Well den, why ya holler like dat. I'z be sleepin' an' ya be scared me ta death. What be wrong wid ya boy?"

"Momma, we're going to have a baby," Israel said with a grin from ear to ear.

Mammie stood motionless without blinking an eye. There was only a paralyzing stare.

"Did ya hear me, Momma?"

"I heared ya."

"Well, aren't you going to say something? Isn't that great? I'm going to be a daddy, and you, you are going to be a grandmother."

"Dat ain't so. I ain't goin' ta be yourn child's grandmamma. Do youes forget who youes are? Ya be Master Israel, 'member? I'z happy fo' ya boff, but don't forgets who ya be. Come, let's go down ta da kitchen. We'z need ta talk."

Israel and Mary Beth followed Mammie, playing and picking at each other like schoolchildren walking behind her. They pulled out chairs and had a seat around the table. Mammie put on a pot of water for coffee and sat down with them.

"I ain't wanna spoil dis moment, but dare be a few tings youes ain't tink 'bout. I knew dis day would come, I jes' ain't tink it be dis fast. Youes ain't white, Israel. Ev'rybody tink youes be white, but youes ain't. No madder how much ya be dressin' in dem fancy clothes, ya still ain't white. Youes can't change what be under dem."

"Israel knows that Mammie. It don't matter to us. You know that."

"It do madder. What hap'ns when yourn baby be born black?"

"Black!" Israel pushed back the chair and rose to his feet. "It ain't going to be black. Why would it be black? I ain't black, Mary Beth ain't black."

"I'z be black," Mammie interrupted. "I'z be ya momma. Wedder youes want me ta or not. Ya ain't wanna tink 'bout it no mo', but I is yo momma, and I is black. So youes could be havin' a black baby. Ya ain't white."

"I know you are my momma. You'll always be my momma, and I am proud of who you are. It don't matter to me what color you are. I never wanted to be your master. This was your idea, but it has worked out for the best for all of us. I never knew who I was, whether I was black or white. I never belonged anywhere, but now look at me. It don't matter anymore what color I am. I don't have to say I'm black anymore. So see, Momma, it don't matter what color you are or I am. My baby will be an Italian like I'm supposed to be now. He or she may be a little dark, but it should be . . . "

"Should or shouldn't, it may be's black, too," Mammie interrupted again. "Dat baby still could be jes' as black as me, den whatcha goin' ta do? Ain't goin' ta be no Italian, dat's jes som'em ya made up. It ain't real. Ya be black, Israel."

Israel stood staring at Mammie and Mammie at him, both became very agitated. Mary Beth spoke up.

"Well, I think we shouldn't worry about anything like that until this baby is born. No matter what color it is, we will love it no less. This child was conceived in love, and it will be born and raised with love. This baby will be raised color blind. It will see people for who they are. We will teach it to love everyone and to treat everyone as an equal."

"Huh, we sees 'bout dat. It won't be, it won't ever be," Mammie said, returning to her room.

"Don't worry Israel, it'll be all right," Mary Beth reassured him.

"I hope so, Mary Beth. I hope it won't matter what color it is. All I know is I will love it just the same. I don't think I've ever heard Momma talk so bitter toward us."

"She's jest worried. It'll all be all right."

"I can't understand Momma being so upset. I thought she would be happy too."

"Don't worry, Israel, I'm sure Mammie will come around. Like I said, she's just worried about you. Everything will be just fine, you'll see."

Israel rested his head in his hands on the table.

"What will we tell the baby if it is black, Mary Beth? We won't be able say we are its momma and poppa. It will think that we own it, like it's one of the slaves. What will we do then?" Israel asked.

"Don't worry about it Israel. Let's pray we won't have to cross that bridge. Let's ask God for it to be born white."

"Oh, so it does matter to you if it is black. You won't want a black baby," Israel said sternly.

"Israel, how could you say such a thing? I will want this baby even if it is purple. I can't believe you said that. You know how much I love you and how much you and your family mean to me. How could you even think that I would not want our baby? I just never thought about it not being white. I never thought that our baby might be a slave one day. That's a scary thing to think about."

"Tell me about it. I was a slave the day I was born."

"When Mammie was pregnant with you, she knew you would be a slave. She knew all her children would be slaves, but even though they were slaves, they still knew she was their mother. She was still able to raise each and every one of you. I don't know what I'll do if I can't raise my baby. That thought has never entered my mind. How could I allow my own child to call me 'Miss Mary Beth'?"

Israel scooted his chair over to Mary Beth and put his arms around her.

"Don't worry Mary Beth, our child will be fine. You are all white and I am half white. Our baby will be white too. Come on, we should go to bed."

In the heat of a summer night, beneath the moon and stars, on a hill under a tree, a child was conceived by two people deeply consumed by a forbidden love. The birth of this infant may bring death to its father and shame to its mother. Both parents knew their beloved child might one day have to carry its own haunted secrets.

Arm in arm, they headed up the stairs. Mary Beth stopped suddenly and looked up at Israel.

"Do you think I should go into town tomorrow and see the doctor?"

"Is something wrong? Are you hurting? Should I go get him now?"

"No, calm down, there is nothing wrong with me."

"Then why do you need to go to the doctor?"

"The preacher is right next door to him. I should get checked out by the doctor to make sure everything is all right, and I could stop in and see the preacher too. I think we need to see what he recalls about you. He is the only one that could identify you with any certainty."

"Mary Beth, it has been well over a year, and no one has said a word. You know I have been in and out of town."

"Yes, I know, but you haven't run into the preacher man. What happens if I should need the doctor when I go to give birth? We have to know that you will be able to fetch him and not be found by the preacher. He may not let you return if he recognizes you."

"That is so true, Mary Beth. It never crossed my mind that I might run into him. I should go with you."

"Okay, we should do it early."

CHAPTER 20

THE TRIP TO CHARLES TOWNE

Lying in bed, back to back, neither Israel nor Mary Beth spoke a word. Their minds were bottled up with concern; their bodies, full of anxiety. Their world was turning upside down, and they could not to stop it.

The thought of their baby being born black weighed heavily on them. How could Mary Beth give her child away to the world of slavery? There was no way that would be possible, but how could she hide it if it were born black? The thought had never crossed their minds, and having children had never crossed their minds. The only thing they had focused on was their happiness. If any two people deserved to be happy, they were Mary Beth and Israel.

Israel had many of the same thoughts running through his head. He was raised in slavery with firsthand experience of being whipped, kicked, and spit on. He knew what would be in store for his child if it were born black. He pondered over the question of whether they had committed a wrong deed by making a baby and whether they were being punished by God. All the anguish that he had buried deep inside had resurfaced. He also was worried about the preacher in town. If he recognized him, would he be whipped to death for pretending to be white? Of course he would. There would be no question. His baby would never get to know him. He wondered if Mary Beth would tell the baby he was its father, and if she did, what would she say? He knew the next day was going to unveil the answer. He would know his identity. He would either remain Israel, the plantation owner, or he would again be Israel the nigger slave. Terrifying as it was, the answer had to be revealed.

The darkness felt lonely and isolating to both of them. They lay in the shadow of the night together, but they felt alone. Their bodies were slightly touching, but neither felt the warmth they normally shared. There was a wall; it was invisible, but it was there. It had to be there that night. Without it, their inevitable speculation about what might happen would be too much to endure.

Israel was up before dawn. He sat at the window and gazed at a rooster that was sleeping on his perch in a tree limb. It was 5 a.m., an hour before dawn. He could not sleep, so there was no reason to lie in bed and let his mind run wild. He slipped on his clothes and quietly exited the house.

Solemnly, he walked to the barn. He brought out two horses, tied them to a hitching post, and began to groom each one from head to toe. When he was finished, he slowly hitched them to the wagon, one harness, one buckle, one strap at a time. Then, with the reins in his hand, he somberly led them to the front lawn and waited.

Mary Beth awoke to find that Israel was not in bed and was concerned for his state of mind. She slid on her best dress, sat in front of the mirror, and brushed her long, silky blond hair. She secured it neatly on top of her head and walked out of the serenity of her home.

Mary Beth wanted to comfort Israel, but could not find the words. She walked over to the wagon, and her eyes never met his as he offered his hand to help her. Then with a little leap, he joined her.

"Giddy up," he said with a click and a slap from the reins.

The horses trotted off, and they headed into town. Both were extremely nervous, but they tried to pretend they were not. They gave little smiles to one another in lieu of words. Every time they tried to make small talk, the conversation would stop abruptly.

Mary Beth watched the horses' hooves pounding against the dry loose dirt. With every stride, a ball of dust barreled from beneath, and the powdered dirt swirled through the air. She covered her face with a handkerchief as she silently observed their pace. The journey to the ferry boat seemed to be endless. In all actuality, it took two hours.

The ferry was the only way to get off John's Island and go into the city. Some people had small boats, but Mary Beth had never needed one. The ferry was fun, and had always been like an adventure.

Normally it was a ride she eagerly anticipated. Drifting slowly across the water was a tranquil experience. She loved to survey the water in hopes of getting a glimpse of the dolphins that often swam nearby. She viewed the alligators, which lay in the sun on the muddy banks, warming their thick tough hides, but there were none that time. That day, she was anxious to get it over with. She needed to know what their destiny would be.

Israel was very fidgety. Mary Beth watched as he seemed to revert to that shy little boy she had grown up with. He no longer was sure of himself. He had abandoned the persona of being intelligent and white. His face glowed with embarrassment when he was spoken to. He was questioning who he really was and how he should talk and act. He began to pace back and forth across the ferry. Mary Beth knew she had to do something.

She slowly walked up behind him and wrapped her arms around his waist. She kissed him on his neck and spoke softly, "Quit worrying. It will be fine."

He turned to her, nodded his head, and replied, "I know. I know it will."

Stepping from the boat, they quietly walked through the busy town, nodding occasionally at those who passed their way. Mary Beth decided to go see the preacher alone. She wanted to find out what the talk of the town was. Everyone talked if there was any news – bad or good, true or false – they all knew, and they all shared it.

Israel was going to go to the stables to see what stock was for sale. He would go to the store for some needed supplies, just to keep busy while they were apart.

They both stopped on the wooden platform that stretched across the town in front of the shops. Quietly, hand in hand, they nodded to the townspeople, observing their reactions and making sure no one noticed Israel was not white. The smiles were natural and inviting, so Mary Beth gently pulled away and disappeared into the doctor's office.

Concerned this could be the last time he would get to touch his beloved wife, he had held on tightly. Israel hated to let go, but he had no choice. She was right; they had to find out what the preacher might recall. He stayed out of sight for hours, but frequently, he would peek down the street searching for Mary Beth. Frustrated and afraid, seized by anxiety, he could not take it anymore. He rushed from the shelter of the store and hurried down the street.

Curious about what was taking so long, he glanced through the window of the doctor's office. Mary Beth was not there. He spotted the back door of the church, slid around the corner, and squinted as he peered into that window. There she sat, but something was wrong; she was weeping.

Israel did not know what to do and became petrified. He did not know whether to run, hide, or just go ahead and kill himself. He was frozen against the church, paralyzed with fear. What was he to do? He couldn't leave Mary Beth, but how could he help her?

He began to pace back and forth as he always did when he became upset. He removed his hat and ran his fingers through his hair, searching for the proper words to explain what had happened to Ben.

Mary Beth caught a glimpse of Israel at the window.

"Israel," she called out.

Israel plastered himself against the rough exterior.

"Israel," she called out again.

Israel slowly walked around to the front of the church.

"I could see you from the window. Is anything wrong?"

Israel stammered before uttering a few incomprehensible words. An unfamiliar man standing next to Mary Beth stared blatantly.

Mary Beth realized Israel did not recognize this man.

"I'm sorry Israel, this is Preacher Matthew. Preacher Matthew, this is my husband, Israel."

"Preacher Matthew," he blurted out. "What happened, I mean, where's the umm . . . the umm . . . "

Mary Beth knew Israel was very agitated, so she spoke up.

"The preacher that married us was transferred. He requested to move on to North Carolina. It was crucial for him to go, as he had family that needed him."

"That's great! I mean, it is great that the town was able to replace him. I noticed you crying. Are you all right?"

"Ohhh, I was looking at the records of when we got married, and I found the paper my poppa and momma signed when they were married. It was a little emotional for me, that's all."

"If you don't mind my saying so, sir, it is probably because she is with child," Preacher Matthew said. "Women go through a lot of different emotions when they are with child."

"Yes sir, I've noticed that," Israel replied.

"I guess you are both right. I am emotional. I am also tired. Are you ready to get back to the plantation?"

"Very much ready. I am anxious to get those crops harvested."

"Israel . . . now I know who you are," the preacher replied. Israel and Mary Beth stared at one another. The anticipation of that second lingered. What did he know, and how did he know?

"You are that man who owns the Simmons plantation, right?"

"Yes, that is right."

"Well sir, it is my honor to meet you. The whole town has been talking about you."

"Why is that, sir?"

"Please, drop the sir. Since I have been here, people say you are the best crop grower in the South, and your cattle and hogs are the best at the market. I was wondering how you could be that knowledgable at both. What is your secret?"

With a sigh of relief, Israel answered. "Well sir, I mean, Preacher Matthew, I had a good teacher, my momma. She taught me everything I know."

"Your momma? I sure would love to meet her. I thought you would say your dad or granddad. How is it that your momma knew so much?"

"She has always been a very hard worker, and she always tried to get the best out of everything. So . . . she tried different things, and when they worked, she made sure I knew about them."

"I hope I may get an invite out to your plantation and get a first-hand look at what you do."

"Well of course you can," Mary Beth answered. "Anytime you want, you are welcome, but for now, we must leave."

"Oh, I'm sorry for keeping you so long. It has been my pleasure to meet you both, and I will take you up on the invite."

"Please do," Israel shook his hand and smiled.

Israel and Mary Beth walked all around town. They went through the market and all around the stable yard together. Being seen together for the first time as man and wife, as terrifying as it was, was exhilarating. They had to overcome their fear and see the reaction of the towns-people.

Mary Beth loved introducing Israel as her husband and was proud of the confidence he exuded in public. She made sure they knew that he was responsible for the plantation's success. There were people who even asked Israel for pointers. Israel just replied, "It is just luck." Of course, he could not reveal that his insight had come from being a slave – when his life depended on making sure the crops and animals produced well. As soon as he was able to walk, he was in the fields.

Mary Beth loved conversing with the other women too. The only white folk she had been around were her father and Ben. All she had ever known were slaves.

She witnessed a white man kicking a young colored boy in the street. The man spit on the boy, belittled, and criticized him freely. He reminded him again and again that he was worthless, and said if he did not sell at the market, he would be hanged, because he wasn't worth feeding.

People snickered as they walked past. It seemed many of them thought the abuse was amusing. Mary Beth was mortified. She lifted her dress and stomped into the street.

Israel reached for her arm, but was unsuccessful in grasping it.

"Excuse me, sir."

The man turned, stood sternly and inspected her from head to toe, then answered.

"Yes ma'am, what kin I do fo' ya?"

"Did I hear you correctly? Are you selling this young boy?"

"Well, I was thinking on it. Why?"

"How much for him?"

"Why?"

"I would like to buy him."

The man rubbed his chin and stared down at the colored boy.

"Well now, this young nigger has a good back ya know, and he don't eat much neither. He's got a heapin' mo' years left."

"How much?" Mary Beth sternly asked again.

"I'll take a dollar fo' him."

"I'll give you fifty cents." She opened her small change purse and retrieved some coins.

Eyebrows raised and head cocked, she stared and waited.

"Okay, you kin have 'em fo' fifty cents. Ya better watch 'em. He's trouble."

Israel walked over and offered his hand to the child. Terrified, the boy leaped to his feet and brushed the dirt from his clothes.

Mary Beth gave a nurturing smile, and together the three boarded the ferry.

"What is your name?" Israel asked.

"Leroy."

"Nice to meet you Leroy, my name is Mr. Israel, and this is Miss Mary Beth."

The boy nodded.

"Do you have family here, Leroy?"

"No ma'am."

"Well don't you worry about that none. We have lots of families that will treat you well, but you do have to work. We all work."

"Yez 'em, I a very hard worka, I sho' ya."

Israel laughed, "You remind me of myself when I was your age."

"How dat be . . . " the boy paused, "youes white."

"Israel means he used to work very hard to please his poppa when he was your age."

"Yeah, that's what I meant."

The young child studied Israel for a few minutes, but he never asked another question. He offered no details of his life. He answered what was asked of him and no more.

Mary Beth stared at Leroy and agreed with Israel. He did remind her of Israel when he was young. The unsure, shy little boy was very light skinned, probably was a product of a white father, whom he did not know and never would.

Israel leaned over and whispered in Mary Beth's ear, "You can't save them all."

"No, but I jest saved him."

She smiled again at the child and snuggled against Israel's arm.

They left the town feeling more complete, more grateful and more at ease with their relationship. They had accomplished a task that others would not dare attempt or even consider. They had successfully kept a true secret that only few knew, and they dared not tell. If it were to be revealed that a black man and a white woman had married and were with child, their fate would be death. However, they had just pulled it off in plain view, and everyone in town welcomed them.

They exited the ferry and traveled down the long dusty road back home. Observing every detail, Leroy pulled his legs tightly to his chest and trembled like a whipped pup. His new masters seemed nice, but he had been through many, and looks, he learned, were deceiving most of the time.

"Leroy, you don't have to worry about us hurting you. We have rules jest like the others, but we will not whip you. If you don't work and pull your own weight, you will be sold. That is our main rule. If you need something, you ask – never steal anything. We will house you with a family that may have some boys your age and that is where you will live. Jest keep your chores up, and we will all get along jest fine."

"Yez 'em."

"They will teach you everything you need to know. If you have any questions regarding anything, you may come to the main house and ask us. Is that understood?" Israel asked.

"Yez, sir."

Leroy settled in with a family and became a very hard worker. He studied the chores that he was unfamiliar with. Intrigued and hungry for knowledge, he watched, listened, and learned. He asked very few questions at first, as he calculated each task the other slaves completed and tried to learn their trades without being bothersome.

As the months passed, Leroy began to emerge from his shell and mingle with the other boys – though he always stayed cautious, occasionally looking over his shoulder, waiting for that kick to his back or slap in the head. He periodically let loose a giggle, exposing the empty gap between his two front teeth.

Mary Beth often watched him from her balcony. She wondered how people could be so cruel. This was a child, not an animal. She decided it was time to make him feel more welcome on the plantation. She asked one of the yard slaves to fetch him and bring him to the main house. She was not sure how she was going to accomplish that task, but she knew it was something that needed to be done. She was sure Israel would be able to help, so down the stairs she went in search of him.

"Israel," she called out.

"I'm here, in the kitchen."

"I have a problem," she said.

"What kind of problem?"

"I have asked Leroy to the house. I want to make him more comfortable here. I've been watching him, and he still doesn't act like he belongs here."

"And, where's the problem?"

"I was hoping you could do that for me."

"I thought you said you wanted to make him feel more comfortable."

"Well, me, us, you, what's the difference?"

"Evidently nothing, you know I can't refuse you. I think I may have jest the job for him."

"I didn't mean work, Israel. That's all that child has ever known."

"Don't worry, it's not real work, and I'll be right by his side."

"SSShhh, here he comes."

The innocent little boy timidly approached the back door and knocked. His head drooped halfway down, but his eyes were bulging wide in a frightened state, surely wondering if he had done something wrong.

"Come in, Leroy," Mary Beth said smiling.

"Yez 'em," he said, slowly opening the door and stepping inside. He looked at the floor and began scuffing his feet back and forth.

"Don't be scared. We have a special job we would like you to do for us. Israel and you are going to work on it together."

He gave Mary Beth a bewildered look. He must have wondered why his Master Israel was willing to help him do anything. Masters were not supposed to work, and if they did, surely not side by side with slaves, but he did not question it. He just nodded.

"So Israel, what kind of task do you have in mind?" Mary Beth asked.

"Don't you worry none about what us men are going to do. It's a secret. You kin keep a secret, can't you Leroy?"

"Ain't nebber had a sekit, sir."

"Sure you have, everyone has had some kind of a secret," Mary Beth replied.

Israel laughed, "Think about something you might have done and you didn't want anybody to know, so you kept it all to yourself. You've done that before, haven't ya?"

"I fo'git, maybe, ain't rightly sure."

"It's all right. I trust you," Israel said, patting the little boy's back. "Let's go to the barn. I'll show you."

The two exited, and Israel turned and smiled at Mary Beth as he strutted down the steps.

After that, they paired up daily, meeting in the old barn and working on their secret project for several hours at a time. Sometimes Israel would sit in the yard for a couple of extra hours at a time with Leroy, just talking. Mary Beth smiled as she watched them from the window, thinking how wonderful he was with the young boy. She knew he was going to make a great father.

She would pass the barn now and then and try to peek inside, but Leroy had a keen eye and always caught her. He would run to the barn doors and push them together tightly until she walked away.

"I was jest trying to see what you boys were up to," Mary Beth said sarcastically.

Leroy replied, "It's a sekit."

"I know, I know, I was jest lonely, I thought maybe I could help y'all."

Leroy looked over to Israel. Israel shook his head, then whispered to Leroy.

"Go take her for a walk."

"Huh?" Leroy whispered back.

"Take Miss Mary Beth for a walk," he said a little louder.

Leroy shyly slipped through the crack of the door. Holding his head down and kicking at the dirt, he asked Mary Beth if she would like him to walk with her.

"That would be a wonderful idea, Leroy. Where would you like to go?"

"Wid ya, ma'am."

Mary Beth laughed, "I know with me, but is there anywhere special you would like to walk?"

"No ma'am."

"How about up to the hill? Israel and I used to go up there all the time. I usually go by myself now and write in my diary."

"What's a diwey?"

"It's a small book that I write in about our daily life."

"Wha' fo'?"

"I think it would be a good thing to have when I'm old and can't remember the wonderful things that happened around here anymore. Also, one day my child may want to read it jest to understand how life was for us. Do you know how to read, Leroy?"

"No ma'am."

"How old are you?"

"Don't rightly know. I tink seven."

"Seven, that's a good age to learn. Would you like me to teach you?"

"Don't know ma'am. Don't wanna get'n trouble. Master Israel ain't like me learnin' dat stuff ?"

"Sure he will. He used to sneak and learn when he was young. He won't mind."

"Why he sneak ta learn? His poppa not want 'em ta have no learnin'?"

Mary Beth had forgotten Leroy did not know who Israel really was. She avoided the question and picked up the conversation as if it had never been mentioned.

"What if I meet with you in the evening, right before dark and teach you how to read? Do you think you would like that?"

"I s'pose I would, ain't rightly know what I need ta read fo'."

"Oh Leroy, you jest really don't know how magical books can be. They can take you to places far, far away – to other countries, cultures, fantasies."

"I ain't even know whatcha be talkin' bout, cult'ers an' ah dat. I ain't tink I needs ta know."

"What about your life? Wouldn't you like people to know how you have lived ... things you have seen and done in your life?"

"My life ain't been what people like ta hears 'bout. Ain't been notten ta talk 'bout."

"One day it will, trust me."

"If Master Israel ain't mine none, I reckon I kin."

"That will be great. I think I'll have a bench brought up and put under that gigantic oak tree in front of the house. We'll do our learning there, okay?"

"Yez 'em, no ma'am," he began to cry.

"What's wrong, Leroy?"

Leroy sniffed and wiped his tears away, but he didn't answer her.

"Did I say something wrong? Please tell me. We can't fix it if I don't know what's wrong."

Leroy began to cry a little harder. "I ... I ain't wantin' ta be whip, Miss Mary Bess. I scared of learnin', ain't spose ta know tings like dat."

"Who says?"

"Ev'rybody node it, ev'rybody buts you. Slaves ain't spose'n ta do no readin'. We's spose ta work, not be readin'. And da utter slaves be gittin' mad at me an' all."

"Why would they be mad at you?"

"Cause dey say y'all treat me dif'rent. Dey say, youes ac' like I be special."

"Well, you are special, and I own this plantation, and I say what you can and cannot do. And there ain't going to be any whipping around here. Has anyone here been hurting you?"

Leroy sniffed a little before answering, "No ma'am."

"Well, if anyone has anything to say to you, come to me and we'll fix the problem. Jest think, if you learn to read and write, you can teach the others. You can become their teacher."

Leroy seemed to like that idea. His face glowed as a toothless smile came across his face.

"Kin we'z keep dis a ... whatcha call dat ... seekit," he blurted. "Kin we'z keep dis a seekit?"

"It's a secret, and if that's what you want, we can keep it that way."

"Yez 'em, fo' 'while anyways."

"Okay Leroy, I'll meet you under the oak tree tomorrow at sunset."

"Yez 'em," he answered.

Mary Beth was very excited, but little Leroy was less than enthused.

He meandered back to the barn to help Israel, but he did not mention a word about Mary Beth's offer to teach him. Still unaware of how Israel would accept it, he had a second secret to keep. He had grown very fond of Israel, and he did not want to upset him.

Every day, Leroy snuck to the barn to help Israel with their secret project. Sometimes Israel would let Leroy work alone, which made Leroy very happy. He finally had a home.

Mary Beth continued to teach Leroy how to read and write. He wanted to learn more and more. He studied every night and he tried to memorize everything he was taught. In turn, he started teaching the slaves in the fields as they worked. He would pick a word that he had learned and teach them how to spell it. At night, for those that wanted to know more, he started teaching the letters of the alphabet. He had earned a nickname, "the teacher," and he stood proudly as they called him by it. He would smile, knowing he was of some importance.

CHAPTER 21

THE BIRTH

Months passed by, the summer brought in the fall, and the fall, the impending birth at Dogwood Plantation. Mary Beth was glad to see the passing of her first trimester, but morning sickness had become a daily part of her routine well into her second. When her eyes opened from a good night's sleep, she automatically reached for the bedpan. Every morning when Mammie prepared breakfast, the aroma of fresh frying bacon made Mary Beth sick, but then again, there was not much that didn't. The sight of the slop that was prepared to feed the pigs, the sweaty odor of the horses she adored, walking pass the chicken yard — everything turned her stomach.

The trimester of sickness had passed with the seasons. She was entering her eighth month. Mammie fulfilled her cravings for apple pie, which abundantly transformed into weight gain. She made sure Mary Beth stayed happy and satisfied. She ate good hearty meals and took long walks for exercise.

Mammie walked into the kitchen of the big house and called out, "Miss Mary Bess." There was no answer, so she called louder, "Miss Mary Bess, I'z gots som'em fores ya. Me an' Hester been doin' some sewin' fo' da lil' one. Do's ya hears me?"

Everything was silent; Mammie walked into the living room. No one was there. She crept up the stairs to Mary Beth's bedroom. Quietly, she eased open the door and peeped in.

"Mary Bess, is ya in heah?"

"Yes Mammie, I'm out on the balcony."

"I'z startin' ta worry. I'z calls out a couple of times an' youes not answer. I'z 'ginnin' ta tink som'em might be wrongs wid ya."

"I'm sorry Mammie, I didn't hear you. I was watching Israel and Jesse out there in the field. I was thinking about calling Israel in, but I was scared to."

"Scared of wha', child? Wha' ya gots ta be scared of?"

"The baby . . . I think it's trying to come early."

"Da baby!" Mammie shouted. "It be try'n' ta come now, it ain't be time, yet."

"I know that, but I don't think it does. I jest been having little pains here and there. They're not too bad."

"Why ain't ya come an' gets me? Nebber mind, ya jes' come lie down. If it ain't hurtin' bad, yet, we'z still gots some time. Ya jes' lays down on dat soft bed an' let me goes an' fetch Israel an' Hester. We'z might need dem heah ta help."

"Mammie, don't tell Israel, yet. If you still think we have some time, don't bother him."

"I'z tink, youes got time, dat don't means dat youes do."

"Well, let's jest wait awhile and see. Why were you calling for me? Did you want something?"

"Me an' Hester sewed up some clothes fo' da lil' one. We make quilts from some ole blankets an' some of Israel's ole clothes. We'z didn't know if youes would want dims or not. I'z put dems in a box an' took 'em ta da ole shack. We'z didn't wants ya ta find dem, ta dey be finish."

"Well, of course I want them. I know how much work it takes to make a quilt, and I can't wait to see it. Why don't you go and get them, I'll be jest fine. I'll jest lay right here and wait for you to get back."

Mammie smiled and rubbed Mary Beth's stomach.

"Yo momma be a very good lady, an' I'z knows ya gonna be jes' like her."

"Thanks Mammie, I think you better hurry up and go. This little one is starting to push again."

"Oh, it'll do dat fo' hours, but I'z hurry anyways. I'z be right back, don't youes worry none."

Mammie hurried down the stairs and walked quickly across the field to the old wooden cottage. She observed Israel and Jesse standing in the back of the plowed up cornfield. She hesitated, thought about calling out to Israel, but changed her mind. Mary Beth was right; there was no need to worry Israel if the baby wasn't close to entering the world. The two boys watched their mother as she accelerated. She threw her hand in the air, gave a slight wave, and rushed ahead.

The plantation was starting to feel the effects of the early winter air. All crops were harvested, and the fields had been cut and plowed. The slaves that lived on the plantation had to make sure they had their own food and that they could provide warmth for their quarters. Mary Beth and Israel gave them plenty of seedlings to grow their own crops. The vegetables that were grown were canned and stacked neatly onto shelves in their cupboards. There were beans, okra, tomatoes, corn, and squash to last the winter, and there was enough wood cut and stacked high against the sides of their tiny wooden shacks. Wood was an important resource for them. It was their means of staying warm in the winter and cooking throughout the year. Everyone had a certain amount to cut per household, so it was used wisely. Nothing was ever wasted. The smoky scent of wood-burning stoves filled the air year round.

The wooden shutters on the little houses were pulled taut against the windows to help keep cold drafts from blowing through. There were no glass windowpanes – nothing but empty holes. In the summer, the shutters were propped open to welcome the breezes that cooled the small cottages. Of course, the mosquitoes, flies, and other insects came in too, but the slaves on Dogwood Plantation were still luckier than most.

Mammie pushed open the slatted door of the small shack and shuffled inside. The cold wind wisped through her frail body and made her shiver. Hesitating for a moment, remembering the many years of her life she had spent there, she stepped forward and gathered the baby's clothes, along with the quilt that lay neatly folded in the corner.

"I'z so glad I'z don't live in heres no mo'. I ain't miss'n' dis place a tall. I'z hope I ain't ever gots ta come back."

After retrieving the gifts that she and Hester had worked so diligently on, she trotted out the door and headed back across the farm.

Israel and Jesse remained in the cornfield talking about the next year's planting. The two were trying to make a decision about what crops would be best for sale at the market when a shrill squeal echoed across the field.

"What was that?" Israel asked looking about.

"I ain't gots a clue," Jesse replied.

"Issssrael!" a voice screamed through the yard. "Issssssrael!" The shrill sound carried over the trees, scattering the birds across the fields.

Israel heard the squeal and watched the birds flutter in the dried up cornfield. He then noticed that Mary Beth was standing on the porch, doubled over and holding her stomach.

"Oh Lord," he shouted, galloping across the mounds of dirt and hurdling over the corn stalks. He stumbled, but recovered in mid-air as he rushed to Mary Beth's side. Jesse followed close behind.

"What's wrong, Mary Beth? Is it the baby?" Mary Beth nodded.

"It's not time. You still have another month. It can't be the baby!"

"Well Israel, I don't think your baby cares. It's coming now!"

"Now!" he shouted. "Oh my God! Momma!" he screamed to the top of his lungs. "Momma!"

"AHHHHH," Mary Beth squealed again.

Israel tossed his head to the side and screamed with her, "Mooooomma!"

Mammie, gasping for air, came running from the hill. Her feeble body trembled as she tried to muster enough energy to get there.

"I'z hurry'n', get 'er in da house," she panted, searching deep within her body for some much needed oxygen. "Lays her down on da bed an' put a pot of water on, I'z comin'."

"Hurry, Momma, hurry!"

"I'z hurry'n' boy, jes' as quick as I kin."

Jesse helped Israel get Mary Beth to the bed. He fetched a pitcher of water and rushed to put it on the stove, as Mammie requested. The old hand pump was slow, but Jesse pumped ferociously, quickly filling the pot. Mammie stood at the foot of the bed and prepared Mary Beth.

"Now we'z talked 'bout all dis, now all da talkin' be over. Dis be da real ting."

"But it's too early, Mammie," Mary Beth cried.

"Ahhh it ain't ta early. Lookey how big youes belly is. It be jes' da right size. Now I'z gots ta spread yo legs ta see where youes baby head is. Dis may hurt lil' bit, but I'z try ta do bess dat I kin. Israel, youes hold on ta hers hand. Mary Bess ya needs ta squeeze Israel hand when youes gets a pain. If youes feel dat baby be tryin' ta push out, den youes push wid ah yo might. It gonna hurt, but youes do it anyway. And youes don't stop ta I tells ya ta."

Mammie examined Mary Beth; the baby was searching for its exit. Mary Beth screamed in pain. She squeezed Israel's hand as Mammie had instructed. She squeezed so hard, the color dwindled away, causing his fingertips to turn white. She grabbed his shirt and pulled him to her, then pushed him away. Her legs drawn up tightly to her chest, she dropped with exhaustion. She begged for water. Her throat was parched, and her lips were dry, crusty and cracking. Israel continuously kept a wet cloth on her head and laid a second one to her lips.

Hours had passed. She gripped the sheet and drew up her knees again. Her bottom lifted off the bed, then lay back down. She begged Mammie to do something. Her lips began to bleed from the dryness. She tossed back and forth. The tears rolled down her cheeks. She huffed and puffed, blowing and sucking at the air. Her hair was drenched with perspiration; her body trembled and shook as she tried to push out her baby.

"I can't do this," she screamed. "You have to get it out of me," she pleaded.

"Yeah, youes kin," Mammie reassured her. "It ain't gonna be long now, we be real close ta havin' us a baby. Ya jes' keep pushin'. Sit her up Israel, sit her up."

"What's taking so long, Momma? Is something wrong?"

"No boy, ain't nuttin' wrong. Dis be yo baby, he jes' a lil' stubborn, jes' like you is.

"Ohhhhhhhhhh! Ohhhhhhhh!" Mary Beth sat up and screamed. "Ohhhhhhhhhh! Ohhhhhhhhhhhh! Help me God! Please help me dear Jesus."

"Dat's right child, youes ax fo' God's help." Then Mammie shouted. "I see da head, I see da head, we'z almost dare. Youes kin do it, Miss Mary Bess. Da nex' pain ya be havin', push'em out. Ya hears me, child, push 'em out, push 'em hard."

Mary Beth tossed her head from side to side and screamed. She squeezed her eyes shut tightly; her face blew up like a balloon and turned blood red. She squeezed Israel's hand so tightly, Mammie could hear his knuckles cracking. Then she collapsed in the bed.

"Wah, Wahhh," the little one cried. The first breath of life was piercing and brilliant.

"Lookey heah, it be a girl, a beaut'ful lil' girl."

"Look, Mary Beth, we have a girl. We have a little baby girl,"
Israel smiled and brushed Mary Beth's hair from her face.

"I want to hold her. Please, give her to me."

"Wait jes' a minute child, I'z got ta wash her up."

Mammie washed the little baby, wrapped her in the patchwork quilt, and laid her in Mary Beth's arms.

Tears of joy ran down Mary Beth's face.

"She is beautiful, she is so beautiful. Look at her. She's perfect. I think we should call her Caroline after my mother."

"Caroline be a beaut'ful name. Yo' momma be proud of dis lil' one. She look jes' like her too," Mammie said, holding onto the baby's finger.

"Well Momma, you were right about taking after her grandmomma. She did take after her grandmomma. It jest happened to be Mary Beth's mother."

"Thank ya Jesus," Mammie looked up and grinned. "C'mon Israel, let's take Lil' Miss Caroline out of heah. Miss Mary Bess needs to gets some rest. She been workin' real hard da pass few hours. She gonna needs all da rest she kin gets."

"Please, bring me my diary. I want to write everything I feel right now."

"Ain't ya wanna ta res' first?"

"No Mammie, I want to write everything down before I forget what it was like. I want to remember every little detail."

"Beleese me child, ya ain't need ta write dat down. Youes ain't gonna ev'r forgit dat," Mammie laughed, handing Mary Beth her diary.

"Thank you, Mammie."

"Youes welcome child, thank ya, fo' dis beaut'ful lil' baby."

Mammie and Israel left her room, carrying the brand new addition to the household.

A few minutes later, Israel re-entered the room. "Mary Beth, don't go ta sleep. I have a surprise for you. I'll be right back."

"What is it Israel?"

"You'll see, it's a surprise."

Israel chuckled and frolicked away. Mary Beth, filled with total contentment, lay back to rest. She envisioned every second of the birth in her mind. Her face glowed with joy as she picked up her diary and started to write. Before she could get the first word written, Israel had returned.

He and Leroy came into the room carrying something large covered by a quilt. They were grinning from ear to ear.

Mary Beth sat up in the bed. "What is that?"

"Leroy, I'll give you this honor."

"Huh, whatcha mean?"

Israel laughed, "I want you to uncover our gift to Mary Beth. Show her what we made for the baby. Show her the secret that we have been keeping from her."

Leroy smiled a sheepish grin and pulled off the quilt to reveal a beautiful crib made from cypress wood they had cut from the swamps. Hand carved, sanded, and etched, it was a beautiful piece of furniture that anyone would have been proud to have.

"Oh my goodness, it is beautiful," Mary Beth exclaimed. "I can't believe you two made this."

"We'z did make it, Miss Mary Bess, I pomise. Mr. Israel ain't be tellin' no story. We'z really make it."

Mary Beth laughed, "I didn't mean it like that, Leroy. I meant, it is so lovely, it's jest hard to believe you two could have done all this by yourselves."

"But we'z did. We work real hard. Mr. Israel said it had to be perfec'."

"And it is," Mary Beth replied.

"C'mon Leroy, Mary Beth needs her rest. Let's go see my baby. You would like to meet her, wouldn't you?"

"Yez, sir."

Israel walked over and kissed Mary Beth on the head. "I'm so proud of you. You really did good. Now get some rest."

Mary Beth smiled and watched as they departed. She picked up her diary again and began to write.

Oct. 8, 1854

Dear Diary:

I gave birth to a beautiful little girl today. She is perfect in every way. She is so tiny, it is hard to believe it hurt so much. The pain that I endured over the past several hours was indescribable. I wanted to give up so many times. I felt like I had touched death — only to be born again. I was given a miracle. I was given a choice to die or to live. I decided to live. Not only shall I live in my body, but I shall live in my baby's heart, body and soul. I believe only a mother shall ever get to experience such a miracle. I thank you, God, for letting me have this experience, for allowing me to give birth to such a beautiful being.

I have checked her out from top to bottom, and she seems perfect in every way, from her ten little fingers to her ten little toes. My little Caroline has blonde peach fuzz on top of her little apple head, and she has big dark eyes. She looks just like the pictures that I have seen of my mother. I wish she could be here; I'm sure in spirit she is. I also want to thank you, God, for letting her be born white. It is not that it matters about her color. If she had been born black, I could love her no less. But being white, she will have every opportunity to succeed in whatever choices she would like to make. She has been born free.

I promise to raise her in the most loving family life she could ever have. I want to teach her to be polite and gentle to all mankind. Although she will never know that the black heritage is her own, she will learn all about their culture, and she will never look down on them. She will accept them and enjoy what she will learn about them. I want to teach her about everything I possibly can. She is my Angel. I want to teach her to stand up for what she believes in, to make a difference in this world. I feel the darkness and despair that have lingered here for so many years have finally been lifted. I am so happy.

CHAPTER 22

THE UNEXPECTED GUEST

As seasons swiftly passed, so did the years. The plantation had been made complete with little Caroline. She had brought nothing but pure joy to everyone she talked to. Her angelic face seemed to touch all mankind, especially Israel. She was the apple of her daddy's eye. She was extremely smart for a five-year-old. Mary Beth read several books a day to her, and she enjoyed every one.

"Push me, Daddy. I want to swing high up to the sky."

"All the way to the sky?"

"Uh, huh."

"But how will you get down?"

"I don't know, maybe you can come and get me."

"That's a long, long, way, and what will Mommy and Mammie say? They would miss us."

"Yeah, well, maybe you can push me up to the treetop."

"But what if you get stuck in the tree? Mommy would be really mad at me."

"Yeah. Maybe . . . maybe you can . . . ahhhh."

"Maybe I can jest tickle you to the ground and forget about the tree," Israel said tickling Caroline.

Mary Beth watched from the window and smiled at the two playing under the gigantic oak tree. After playing a little game of chase, Israel fell to the ground exhausted and little Caroline followed his lead. She lay her head on Israel's shoulder, and the two, huffing and puffing, stared up through the enormous limbs, watching the sun slide out of sight as the day came to an end.

Mary Beth was not the only one watching them play. Jesse was staring, watching them as they relaxed in the shade. He was angry, watching his brother doing nothing. Jesse was working hard in the fields. The sun scorched his black skin, causing blisters to erupt across his back. The idea of his younger brother having such a leisurely life was overwhelming. The aggression was exploding inside him.

Jesse came in from the fields; he was furious. He walked over to the well and drew up some water. He took a small sip from the cup, then poured the rest over his body.

"Jesse, what are you doing up to this house and why are you drinking from our well? You know this well is forbidden to the slaves."

"Don't ya drink from it? Ya tink ya be betta den me?"

"C'mon Jesse, you know it ain't like that."

"It ain't like what, Israel? If ya drink from dis heah well, how comes I can't?"

"Cause you know why."

"Why Daddy, how come Jesse can't have some water?"

"Yeah Daddy," Jesse mocked. "Why come I can't drink from dis well?"

Israel stared at his brother. Not knowing what to say, he looked down at Caroline and told her to go to the house.

Little Caroline ran to the house as she was told. Mary Beth stood at the window watching, but unable to hear what was said.

"What's wrong with you, Jesse?" Israel shouted. "Have you lost your mind? You know you can't come up to the house like this."

"Why'z dat bruddah, I mean, Master Israel? Ya be bedder dan me, dat's whatcha tink, right? Youes walk roun' like youes somebody. Youes ain't nuttin', youes a nigger, ya jes' like me. Youes forget dat didn't ya. Ya wears dem dare, fancy clothes, an' nice shoes. Ya forget whose ya is, ya tink ya is white, but ya ain't."

"I haven't forgotten who I am. And you're wrong. I am white. I am jest as much white as I am black. I have been where you are, and I will never forget that. I have climbed the mountain of shame, and I fell into the arms of heaven. We have risen to glory, thanks to who I am, but mostly because of who Mary Beth is, for I am only just a man, a man a beautiful white woman saw and loved. She was blind to my color, as I am to hers. So forgive me, if I don't act like who you think I should."

"Ack … ack … dat be all ya do, is ack. Youes ack like youes, youes Mr. Big Stuff, walkin' 'round point'n fingers. Whens da las' time youes been dirty? Whens da las' time youes work?"

"Haven't I made it better for you and your wife? Why you got it better than any of the other slaves around here. I've looked out for you, Hester, and Mammie. I made sure you were taken care of."

"Mammie," Jesse shouted. "Mammie, be yo momma, boy. Ya forget dat too, didn't ya?"

"I know she is my momma, I could never forget that. I thought everybody was happy for me, for us. I can't pretend to be the master part time. I might mess up. I could treat y'all like you're spose to be treated, but I don't. I try to treat y'all better than that. Tell me what I'm doing wrong."

"Ya ain't work. Ya jes' always tell us what ta do. Always givin' orders like some big man now. Po' Momma still work her tired body ev'ry day."

"Boy, the sun done gone to your brain. If I was working out there in those fields and someone came up, what you think they would say?"

"Come heah! Ain't nobody ever come out heah. Whens da las' time we'z hab somebody heah?"

"I know it's been a long time, and you are right, not too many people do."

Israel turned away; he heard the stamping sound of a horse's hooves. He turned to the long dirt driveway.

"See Jesse, if you look up the road there, somebody is coming now." The two men stared up the narrow road to see the unexpected guest.

"Who ya tink dat is, Israel?"

"I ain't got a clue, Jesse."

The fast pace of the horse stirred up too much dust for them to identify the rider. Israel and Jesse witnessed the rider beating the horse from side to side with the reins, kicking and screaming to hurry it along.

Jesse turned to walk away, but Israel grabbed his arm and asked him to stay.

"Something must be wrong with him. That man is riding like a maniac."

"I ain't want'in ta be 'round, if some'em be wrong," Jesse replied.

"He may need our help, jest wait a minute."

They stood side by side, glaring, trying to see who the visitor was. The horseman headed in a straight line directly toward Israel and Jesse.

"If dat crazy man don't slow down, he gonna runs us over," Jesse exclaimed with concern.

Israel waved his arms in the air, "Slow down," he yelled.

Disregarding Israel's request, the man continued.

Approaching from a few feet away, he jerked a whip from his saddle. The two brothers' eyes filled with fear, but they didn't have time to flee. They jumped to the side, and Israel pushed Jesse to the ground out of harm's way. The man cracked his whip across Israel's back, knocking him off his feet. He quickly snapped it back and popped Jesse across the face.

Mary Beth screamed and ran from the house. Mammie heard the cries and followed.

Mary Beth ran yelling, begging for the horseman to stop. He did not acknowledge her voice and snapped the whip several more times.

She leaped to the man's leg and began pounding on him. She begged and screamed for him to stop.

Mammie scurried to Israel and knelt down to assist him. The man snapped the whip back, whirled it through the air, and cracked it across Mammie's back. Mammie yelled in pain.

The lathered horse danced, stomping its hooves high in the air and landing hard on Mammie's body. The man turned his horse toward Jesse, who was trying desperately to get on his feet. The agitated horse snorted, reared up, and trampled across Jesse's chest. He screamed as the horse pummeled him over and over, until his lifeless body moved no more.

Mary Beth ran to Mammie and Israel and threw herself over them both, trying to shield them from the mad man.

She screamed at the stranger to stop as she buried her face between their bodies.

"Get off them niggers, Daughter."

Mary Beth looked up; it was her father. "How dare you shame me this way," he screamed.

"Shame on you, shame on you!" she shouted. "How do I shame

you? You are the one who brought that animal here for me to marry and left me alone with him. I was raped, beaten, nearly killed, and I shame you? Israel saved my life. If he had not killed Ben, Ben would have killed me. I owe him everything. You owe him everything."

"Ya owe this filthy nigger nuttin'g. That was his job. He was supposed to take care of you. He promised me."

"No Poppa, you're wrong. That was your job. And talk about promises – you got a promise from a nigger, Poppa. If you didn't trust him you would never have asked him to promise you anything. You knew he was good, you said it yourself many times. You're the person that shames me," she screamed to her father. "Your so-called filthy niggers are my family. They're the family you gave me to, the only family that I have ever had, and I love and adore them. Where have you been all my life? You gave me to Mammie. She has been my mother. She raised me."

Mr. Simmons drew back his whip again. A little voice echoed across the yard. In mid-air, he stopped and turned. Caroline was running with all her might, screaming for him not to hurt her momma and daddy. Mr. Simmons was stunned; he did not know there was a child.

Caroline tried to scurry around the horse, but it was excited and could not be still. The frightened horse jumped and knocked her to the ground. The child screamed as it stomped her tiny leg.

Mr. Simmons tried to control his horse, but with all the screaming and whipping, he was unable to direct it. Mr. Simmons got off the horse's back and went to the aid of the girl.

Mary Beth rose up and saw her father going for her baby and was alarmed he might hurt her. Hysterical and scared to death, she jumped up and ran with everything she had. She rammed him like an angry goat. His body flew in the air and slid across the ground.

"Have you lost your mind child?" he screamed.

Using the head of the whip, which was still in his hand, he pushed himself up. "Take yourself and that child to the house, now!" he shouted. "I will deal with you later."

Mary Beth was scared and didn't know what to do. Disobeying could cause him hurt Caroline. She looked over at Mammie and Israel still lying on the ground. They were crying, hurt, and scared.

She glanced to where Jesse lay. He had not moved at all; the light had dwindled from his eyes and was replaced by a glazed stare. She presumed he was dead. All three were covered in blood.

Israel looked up and muttered, "Do as your father has told you, Mary Beth."

"I don't want to leave you and Mammie," she sobbed.

"It'll be all right. I don't want Caroline to see any of this. Just remember, I love you both with all my heart."

Tears streamed down her face. She knelt down and kissed his forehead. Slowly, she stood up and lifted Caroline in her arms.

Little Caroline screamed to her daddy. She did not understand why her mother was leaving her father with this mad man. Mary Beth kept reassuring her that he would be fine. She held her head tightly against her shoulder, trying to shield her from the hatred that Mr. Simmons held for the slaves.

They could hear Mammie begging, trying to explain, and screaming for Master Simmons to stop. But her pleas were ignored.

Mary Beth hurried to the safety of their home. She could not bear to witness what her father was doing. She carried Caroline upstairs where the voices were imperceptible.

The innocent little girl cried herself asleep. Mary Beth peered from the window in search of her family, but darkness had covered the plantation. Screams echoed throughout the fields; gunshots rumbled and flashed in the night. A huge fire was burning across the field. Mary Beth was anxious to know where Israel and Mammie were, but apprehensive about leaving the house. Caroline's safety was her main concern.

Hours had passed when she finally heard the front door screech open. She huddled in the bedroom corner beside Caroline. She knew the sound of her father's wooden leg as he relentlessly plodded up the massive stairwell. Louder and louder, step by step, the thud grew nearer. Within minutes, the bedroom door swung open. Mr. Simmons hesitated in the doorway. His eyes were brimming with rage, and blood saturated his clothing. His expression was empty, blank, devoid of humanity. His face was that of a man gone mad. Mary Beth had never seen her father like that. She trembled and cringed in the corner. Caroline awoke and screamed with fright when she saw the strange man standing in their room.

"Get over here," he screamed.

Mary Beth sat Caroline in the corner and told her to stay.

"No Momma, please don't leave me," she begged.

"It'll be all right, Caroline. Poppa, let me explain."

"Explain, explain what? I don't want your explanation. I heard enough in town."

"In town," she said surprised.

"Yeah, in town. The whole damn town was talking about how great you were doing," he shouted. "I thought that was wonderful. I even got excited a little bit. I even laughed with them when they told me my new son-in-law was a better farmer than I was. I told them I didn't know Ben knew anything about farming. Then they asked who Ben was. They said your husband was Israel, and he was a big success. I thought it was a mistake, a slip of the tongue; I even made a joke about it. Then someone described him. I was in shock, humiliated. I got angry and hit the man in the saloon. He didn't know why, and I didn't explain. I jumped on my horse and rode hard to get here."

"But Poppa, they don't know that Israel is black. They think he is Ben. They think he is an Italian."

"Yeah, I know what they think. It doesn't matter what they think, girl, I know. Don't you understand?" he shouted, "I know."

CHAPTER 23

THE BATTLE OF SPIRITS

Back in the Present

I opened my eyes; on my left side stood a lady shaking my shoulder. I thought I was in a trance or maybe dreaming. Slowly I stood up and turned to the ghostly figure. That time, the spirit did not disappear.

"Mary Beth," I said softly.

There was a slight pause. Then, the sweetest sound flowed from the spirit's mouth.

"No, I am Caroline. I wanted you to see what I remember, so I took you there."

"Caroline, all this time I thought you were Mary Beth. Why did you take me there, Caroline?"

"My mother, you have to find her. I can't rest until she is found."

"Where do I look?"

"I have no idea. You have seen all that I know. That was the last night I have any memory of my mother. Please find her."

Then as quickly as she had appeared, she faded away. Never answering my question, she just vanished.

The storm was getting worse. The lights blinked on and off until all power was lost. The telephone lines and trees were blown down, and the exterior shutters beat a rhythm upon the house with each gust of the ferocious wind. It howled and screamed like a wild dog's frenzy. The faint light flickered from the candles and kerosene lanterns as the wind swept through the darkness. The branches of the willow tree scratched, clawing on the side of the house like tiny fingers begging unmercifully to come inside. Lightning streaked the sky, dancing, lashing throughout the night. The house wavered as the thunder roared in fury.

In my empty living room, I sat alone and huddled in Jim's favorite chair. The children were playing quietly upstairs when I heard a knock at the door. At first, I thought it was the storm, but the tapping continued, so I went to check it out.

Taking a kerosene lantern with me, I was reminded of the visions of the past that I had been allowed to witness. I carefully walked to the entryway. Peeping out the windows, I saw something that almost caused me to drop my lantern. I could not believe the man who darkened my doorway was Mr. Jesse. Quickly I opened the door and invited him to take shelter from the violent weather.

"What are you doing out in this storm? Come on in, is anything wrong?"

"My grandson, where he be?" he asked in a worried voice.

"He's upstairs playing with Gary. Is anything wrong? Why are you here in the middle of this terrible storm?"

"Please get 'em. You and yo fam'ly should leave dis house tonight. It ain't safe ta be heah."

"What are you talking about? We are not going anywhere in this storm, and I am not letting you or Isaac go back out in this weather, either. Now come on in, tell me what's going on. What did I do to you? Why do you dislike me so?"

"No!" he shouted. "I ain't wantin' to come in. I come ta get Isaac, He ain't staying here."

"I am not getting him unless you tell me what's going on. Then maybe I'll get him, but it will have to be a very good reason."

Mr. Jesse stood there with the rain running down the brim of his hat, dripping to his shoulders. His face was cold and drawn from worry. The lines pulled deep from his forehead down into his cheekbones. The rain sat in the folds of his wrinkled skin with no way to discharge until he expunged it with the palm of his hand.

Taking off his hat, he wiped the mud from his shoes and stepped inside. He nervously marched over to the stairwell and looked to the top. He seated himself on the bottom step with his back to the wall.

"Over a hundred years ta dis very day dere be a terrible storm, jest like tonight. The story was the rain and lightning came all week, ev'ry where be flooding. No one had ever seen such a storm. They didn't even know it was coming."

"Master Simmons had come home from his long journey. He had not been home for years. When he gets here, he be some kinda upset when he found out da secret."

"What secret?" I asked.

"Miss Mary Beth be in love with a colored slave name Israel. She node it be wrong, but she go and do it anyway, she jest do it anyway. Master Simmons went crazy when he finds dis out. He got da whip and beat Mammie, so dey say; she falls ta da ground and she ain't breathe no mo'. He whip her to death cause he tinks dis be hers fault. Mammie, that be Israel's momma," he said looking up at me.

"Any hows, he den goes after Israel. When he finds him, he hanged Israel right up there, on dat dere hill. He didn't hang 'em in da air doe, he let hims toes still be touchin'. He jest put da rope roun' hims neck and let him hang. Da thunder shook de eart, da lightning popped da ground and lit up da sky round'em. Israel be scared, but Israel still hold 'ems head up high. For some reason Master Simmons got lil' Miss Caroline, dat be Israel and Miss Mary Beth's child, he took her out into dat terrible storm. He put her in da boat wid him, no body know why he did dat. Israel could see him from da tree where he be danglin' from. He be beggin' Mr. Simmons not to put da little girl in dare, but Mr. Simmons ain't listen. Da wind be a blowing awful. It blow so strong it tipped da boat right over. Dey boff falls out into da water. Master Simmons hab dat ole wooden leg ya know, and he jest went straight to da bottom of da pond."

"Israel be screaming for his baby girl, he struggled ta get free. Da rain came down harder and harder. Israel can't hardly see anymore, but he still struggled ta help his baby girl. The rain came down and settled right under his feet. He done dug a hole from struggling. The rain beat hard against da dirt, till it washed the groun' right out from under Israel's feet. He kept struggling to get free, but it be no use. Hims feet jest dangeld in da air. Da rope gots tighter and tighter till he could no longer breathe. When hims head dropped down, Momma say the story was, you could hear Miss Mary Beth scream for miles. She say her voice echoed cross da land like a pack of wolves. She say you could hear pounding and screaming for hours. She say den, it jest got quiet. The storm blew away and Mary Beth was not heard from agin. She be a coward and let all deese peoples die, even hers own little girl."

"My God, that is terrible. I knew Mary Beth was in love with Israel, I read it in her diary, but it just ended. I never knew what happened. I couldn't understand why the diary just ended. I can't believe Mr. Simmons was so vicious. No wonder you hate my family. Believe me, I'm not at all like that. You should not hate me for something I didn't have anything to do with. Finish telling the story. Who was your mother? And what happened to Caroline? Did she drown?"

"Hester be my grandmother," he answered.

"Hester, Israel's sister?"

"Yez'em, dat be right. My father was her son. We were named after her brother that your grandfather killed."

"I am so sorry about the things my grandfather did, but please don't blame me. Please tell me what happened to Caroline."

Before he could answer, Gary ran to the top of the steps. "Mom, I can't find Isaac. Have you seen him?"

"No I haven't. I thought he was upstairs with you."

"He was thirsty so he came down to get something to drink, but he didn't come back up."

"Oh my God," Mr. Jesse shouted. "We has ta find him quick."

"Let's go check in the kitchen," I said leading the way. "I'm sure he's probably getting something to snack on."

The back door was open when we entered the room. The floor was drenched from the blowing rain. The screen door slapped against the old cypress wood. I struggled against the force of the treacherous wind to close the door. Gary ran to the window and looked out.

"Mom, look!" he yelled.

The lightening struck and lit up the back yard like the sun at the peak of day. Blinded by the light, I shuffled to Gary's side. Isaac was walking up the hill as if he were in a daze. I ran out of the back door and walked onto to porch. I shielded my eyes from the stinging rain and called out to Isaac.

He never acknowledged that he heard me. His body leaned forward, feet digging into the mud, seemingly oblivious to the storm. He maintained his pursuit.

"Oh no," Mr. Jesse shouted. "I told ya dis place be dangerus."

"I'll get him. You stay here with my kids," I said running back inside the house. I grabbed my rain slicker and forged my way into the storm. I knew Mr. Jesse was too old to be in the violent weather, and Isaac was left in my care. He was my responsibility. I ran across the porch and slipped on the wet boards, crippling my knee. Gary came to my aid. The pain was excruciating. The warm blood flowed down my leg, mixing with the cold water.

"Go back in," I shouted. "I'm all right. You help watch Angel."

He gave me his hand and helped me to my feet. I painstakingly hobbled down the steps to the back yard. I could no longer see Isaac through the opaque curtain of the falling rain. I called for him, but he did not answer. The cold ferocious water scourged my body like lashing whips. The wind whirled debris through the air like a hurricane. Cupping my hand over my eyes, I searched for Isaac, but my task was impossible until the lightning struck and danced up the hill, exposing the boy near the hilltop. He never noticed any danger as he continued toward his fate.

I called out to him again, but there was no response. I desperately tried to run after him, but the squall of the southeaster was extremely strong. Against the strength of this brewing monster, I could barely stand. Halfway up the hill, the lightning struck again. Isaac was under the dogwood tree. The branches had wrapped tightly around his throat. He thrashed wildly in the air, as if he were wrestling with someone.

I started running with everything I had. The storm was brutal. I slipped again and again, tumbling to the bottom of the hill with each blunder. It seemed to be a hopeless battle against the wicked storm, but steadfast, I planted my feet into the wet soil. Intently pushing forward, burying my feet into the mud, I began to climb the unforgiving hill. I clenched an unyielding clump of grass and tugged with all my might, committed to pulling myself up the muddy mound. The wind was atrocious, demanding to take me down, but I was tenacious, and I proceeded to crawl my way to the top. I was bombarded by the wind gusts, which forbade me to stand. Finally, exhausted, I reached the top. Lightning struck the ground, sending vibrations throughout my body and urging me to heed the warning to go back.

"I won't give up! Do you hear me?" I screamed.

The thunder shook the earth below my feet. The lightning lit up the tree where Isaac was hanging. I reached for the limbs. Isaac's eyes were bulging. Unable to speak, he quivered in fear.

"Hang on," I yelled, trying to pull him free from the tree branches.

Lightning pounded the ground around us. I again ignored the threat and continued my task. A second explosion caused the earth to erupt; the water was knee deep. The more I tried to get Isaac free, the tighter the branches got. For every one that came loose, another one appeared and cinched tighter around his throat. Then all of a sudden, lightning struck again and knocked me off my feet. It struck the tree limb where Isaac was hanging and dropped him to the ground. He lay still.

I crawled over to him and lifted his head, removing a tiny branch that clung to his neck. He still did not move. I began to shake him and yell his name. The howling wind was deafening as it soared around us.

All of sudden, I heard a shrill high-pitched scream that drowned out the deafening squall. There were horrible noises coming from the house. I stood up and braced myself against the horrific storm. I squinted through the pouring rain, trying to discern all the commotion.

A whisper in the dark softly conveyed to me, "Help her."

I looked down the muddy hill and saw Angel walking across the yard; she was coming straight toward the pond. I screamed for her to go back, but she kept coming. There were many unfamiliar voices calling Angel through the blackness.

Isaac lay limp and lifeless on the ground. I pulled him from the rainwater and supported him against the tree. Lightning popped and lit up the earth again and again. Mr. Jesse's feeble body wobbled, trying to catch up with Angel. The torrential rain fell from the sky, and the water gushed down the hill. I tumbled and slid my way to the bottom. I watched in horror as Angel began to sink into the dark murky pond. The water swirled around her tiny waist. Mr. Jesse had a tight grip on her hand. He was pulling with all his might, but something stronger had the other side, drawing her in.

The wind continued to howl like wild animals, and the lightning persisted. The earth rumbled and shook each time the sky displayed its power. The noises from the house were pounding out of control. The shutters slapped hard against the old wooden frame. The windows were exploding, and the screams that the wind carried were piercing.

I was frantically trying to make my way around the pond to my baby. The flashing beam continued to blink on and off like a signaling flashlight. Mr. Jesse was exhausted, but still trying to rescue Angel from the depths of the unforgiving pond.

Unexpectedly and from nowhere, an invisible force picked Mr. Jesse up, hurled, and launched him across the top of the water like a skipping stone. Then, inexplicably, he disappeared. Gary screamed from inside the house, but I could not see him.

I looked at Angel; she was vanishing into the clutches of the unseen spirit. Gary screamed once again.

"Look out," he yelled.

Jetting across the yard, Gary went straight for Angel.

I screamed. Adrenaline rushed through my body, pushing me through the heavy storm. I ran, begging the spirit not to take my little girl. The entity squealed a high-pitched scream. A streak of light hit the ground and opened the earth. Two more spirits were released and rose from the depths of the murky water. Angel was tossed to safety on the bank.

I watched in disbelief as the ghostly apparition fought for my child. There were no shapes or sizes – just ghostly lights, whipping, whirling, and fighting in mid-air.

I succeeded in reaching Angel and pulled her tightly to my chest. She was shaken, but unscathed by the event. I picked her up and ran with her, praying to the reach the porch where Gary was waiting.

"Take her inside," I yelled out as I got within his range. Without hesitation, I turned and struggled my way back up the hill. I had to rescue Isaac.

The storm was atrocious. My body was exhausted, but somehow I searched deep inside myself and summoned enough energy to reach Isaac.

Conscious, sitting in a daze, he muttered, "What happened? Why am I outside?"

"I'll explain later. Are you all right?"

"Yes ma'am, I think so."

"Can you walk?"

"Yes ma'am."

I grabbed his hand and started pulling him down the hill. The spirits from the pond whirled in front of us.

"Ahhhh!" Isaac screamed.

The entity was pulling, trying to take him back.

"Help me," he cried.

"You can't have him," I screamed out. I wrapped both my arms and legs around him and cradled him on the ground. A voice screeched through the storm.

"Poppa, no, it's not Israel. Look Poppa, I'm here, I'm here," the voice whispered in the dark.

Isaac and I were scared to death.

It was Mary Beth and Mr. Simmons. They stood in mid-air facing each other, hovering above the pond.

I noticed a white glow lingering beneath the murky water. I jumped to my feet as it savagely spun from the black water and became visible. Without a doubt, it was Ben.

"Mary Beth, I've come for you," he said sadistically.

"You'll never get my daughter again. I made that mistake one time, but not again," Mr. Simmons shouted.

Mr. Simmons turned and prepared to fight. They tumbled across the top of the water, squalling, battling through the storm. Their voices deepened to devilish tones and distorted as their haunted secrets exploded.

Intertwined in combat, the ghostly figures plunged into the depths of the black water.

Mary Beth smiled down at Isaac, and then swiftly, she disappeared into the house.

The howling wind grew calm. The rain had been reduced to a drizzle, and the horrendous storm was moving on.

With Isaac safe beside me, we quickly ran to the house. Gary and Angel were frantic.

"What happened, Mommy?" Angel asked.

"I don't know Baby," I answered.

"Mom, there's something you have to see," Gary exclaimed, pulling me up the stairs. "Come on."

We all followed him.

"Look," he said, pointing to a hole in the wall. "She was in there."

"Who?" I asked.

"The whispering lady – She's the one who saved Angel. She kept beating on the wall and screaming over and over again. I was scared, but I didn't know what else to do. So, I got a ladder and a hammer, and I pulled those boards off the wall. I let her out."

I was very surprised to learn what Gary had uncovered on the attic stairwell: another room. Boards had been removed and a small, quaint room had been revealed.

I climbed the ladder, entered the hidden attic cubby and observed my surroundings. Across the tiny room, under that small round, unique window, lay a blanket. I lifted the blanket, and a skull rolled from beneath it.

"Oh my God! That's a person's skeleton," Isaac said, walking up behind me.

"Yes, I think it is."

We noticed some papers lying about the floor, and I started to read them aloud.

My father has gone mad. He has locked me in this room away from everyone. He knows that Israel and I are in love. He knows we have a child. I think he has killed Mammie. I haven't seen or heard from her at all. He has been whipping Israel every day. I see him from the window. I beg him to stop. I beg him not to kill him, but I'm scared he is going to anyway. He has hanged him on our tree. I don't know what he has done with Caroline. I haven't seen her. I'm so scared and helpless. I have tried desperately to get out of here, but there is no way. He has removed the door and boarded up the entrance. I watch the man I love day after day hanging in the hot sun. I don't know how much he can handle. I don't know how much I can

"Where's the rest of the story? Come on, don't leave me like this. Gary, help me look."

We all searched around the room for more papers. I could not understand why that page had ended right in the middle of a sentence.

Angel and Isaac joined in and helped with the search. The room was very small. There was barely enough room for all of us to move around.

"Do any of you see any more papers?" I asked.

Angel shouted out and pointed. "There's a piece."

I looked around, and sure enough, tucked under the edge of the skeleton was another handwritten note. I slowly pulled it free and began to read.

The storm is terrible. Israel is still hanging. The lightning is striking all around him. I keep beating on the wall for Poppa to help him. He says he wants me to watch him die. He says he will die slowly so he can think about what we have done. I think he might have killed my baby. I want to die too.

"So this is what happened to her," a voice came from across the room. I quickly turned around. Mr. Jesse was standing on the ladder and looking into the room.

"No one ever knew," he said.

"Thank God, you are all right. I was so worried about you, Mr. Jesse."

"Yes ma'am, I be fine. My little bruddah saved me. He finally know da truff. He be at peace now. All da spirits came alive tonight. Dey all were reunited fo' one last time. Now dey can rest, cause dey all be at peace now."

I smiled and walked over to him.

"Our families have been through a lot together. Now that Mary Beth has been found and her spirit set free, we can all get along."

"Yes ma'am, I tink so. Whatcha goin' ta do wid her remains? Ya not goin' ta call da town people out heah ta git her, are you?"

"What would you like me to do?"

"I think she should be buried beside Israel. That's where she would wanna be."

"I agree. Do you know where he is buried?"

"Yes ma'am, I do. I'm going to take Isaac home, and I'll be right back. I have something you may want."

"What's that?"

"I'll be right back."

"Mr. Jesse, you are pronouncing words correctly."

"Yes ma'am," that was all he said.

The kids and I walked with Mr. Jesse and Isaac back downstairs. Mr. Jesse left the house. He had come to realize I would be the last to condone the actions of my great grandfather. He knew I was not a bad person at all.

CHAPTER 24

THE LEGACY

It wasn't long before Mr. Jesse returned.

"Hello, Mr. Jesse," I said opening the door. "Please, come on in."

Mr. Jesse did not acknowledge. He entered the half open door and went straight to the living room. His head lowered, solemnly walking past me, I heard him mutter something that was not understandable.

Mr. Jesse was carrying a box. He moseyed over to the fireplace, holding onto the box for a moment and seemingly not wanting to let it go. He eased it onto the mantle.

The expression on his face was that of one who was losing his best friend. I could see him debating whether to release the mysterious box or not. He retrieved it and turned around. He removed the lid and exposed some handwritten letters.

"These are my mother's letters. They were given to her, and she gave them to me."

"I promise to take care of them if you will let me read them."

"I'm not sure if I'm doing the right thing. Isaac is supposed to get these. I promised my momma I would make sure they were passed down to the family."

"I give you my word, I'll take good care of them, and I will give them back after I read them."

"After you read them, you will know who I really am."

Jesse spoke in perfect English, not one syllable mispronounced.

"Who you really are, what is that supposed to mean?"

Mr. Jesse never spoke another word, and never looked up at me. He walked over to me, put the box in my hands, turned, and walked away.

He stopped at the front door, and with his hand on the doorknob and his back to me, he said, "You're going to be surprised."

I, of course, immediately walked to the sofa and started to read. The first page was not addressed to anyone; it just started with a simple sentence:

To whomever is reading this:
This is what I heard; this is the legacy of our family:

As I read that first line, I could feel myself drifting away again.

Months had passed. Johnny had written home several times and had never gotten any response. He decided to return to Dogwood Plantation and confront his father. It was time to bury the past. Too many years had been lost over stupidity. He wanted to make amends.

He traveled the long hot journey alone. His first stop was in Charles Towne. He thought it would be best to get a room there, because he was scared his father still might not allow him to come home. The townspeople were very surprised to see him.

He went to the market to see some familiar faces he once traded with. Several folks asked him what had happened to his family. No one had seen them in months. Johnny knew something was wrong. He mounted his horse and rushed to see.

When he arrived, he was shocked by what he found. The plantation stood quiet and vacant. No one was stirring about, no one to be seen. The grass had grown high, the flowers had quit blooming and the dogwood trees had all died – all except the one on the hill, the one that Israel and Mary Beth had found love at. The tree stood on the big hill like a protector, a guardian angel. It seemed to be the only thing left with any life.

Johnny walked around and called for his father, but there was no answer. He called for Mary Beth, but silence filled the air. He ran to the slave quarters, only to find the old wooden huts empty. He dropped to his knees and cried. His family was gone. He was all alone in a place that he always despised.

"What happened here?" he said aloud. "Where could everyone have gone?"

He decided to move back into the house until he could find some answers. He searched every room for clues, but found nothing. Days had passed without any signs of his family. He was ready to give up and go back to the city. Then, late one night, he caught a glimpse of someone running across the front lawn. He ran out to see who it was. The person had a long coat and a wide brimmed hat on.

Johnny called out for the person to stop, but they did not.

The figure ran through the woods, and he ran after it. He chased it in and out of trees through the darkness of the night until he got close enough to leap on and bring them down to the dirt. He rolled on the ground until he pinned the person down.

"Who are you?" he shouted. "Where is my family? What have you've done with them?"

"Get off me," the voice shouted. "Please get off me."

To his astonishment, he had not tackled a man, but a woman. He rolled quickly off of her and helped her up. He held onto her arm and stared into her face. She was black. Her eyes were open wide with fright and her body trembled as she tried to talk.

"Please don't kill me, please," she begged.

"Who are you and what are you doing here? Are you a runaway slave?"

"No sir," she answered. "I live heah," she said, her voice cracking with every word.

"What do you mean, you live here? Where are my father and my sister?"

She moved closer to him. "Johnny, dat be you? Oh thank Jesus."

"Who are you? How do you know me?" he shouted.

"I am Hester, Mammie's daughter."

"Hester," he said.

"Where is Mammie and your brothers? What happened to everyone?" he asked.

"Gone, dey all be gone. No one left but me and ..." she paused.

"And who?" he asked.

"My little girl," she answered and began to tell the grueling story.

"We stay hidden in da basement. My little girl won't talk. After da ac'dent she jes' quit talkin'. She sees ev'ryting dat hap'ned. I reckon it be too much fo' her lil' mind ta handle."

"What accident?"

"It be a terrible storm dat night. Da worst I ever sees. The wind blew trees over, da tunder shook da ground like an earthquake. Da lightin' lit up da sky like daytime. I hears screams an I came out runnin' ta see. Da rain came down so hard it be stinging my eyes. I heared Mamma tellin' me ta run. I didn't knows what fo'. Den I see what fo'. It be Master Simmons, he gone crazy. He whip my momma til she be dead, he hanged Israel on da dogwood tree on da hill, an' he, Miss Caroline ... it be terrible. I tried ta help, but I be ta scared. I ain't know what ta do or who ta tell. So I jes' hid."

"Why would he go crazy like that? What happened? Where is Mary Beth?" Johnny demanded to know what had happened to his family.

Hester walked into the house and asked Johnny to follow her. She walked to the fireplace and opened the secret door.

I listened closely to every word as I heard the voices come down the long hall. I was scared. I had not heard anyone in a long time, anyone besides Hester. I hid in the corner of the basement. When Hester came in, she called for me. At first I was scared, but she promised it was all right to come out, so I did. That is the first time I had ever met Uncle Johnny.

"Uncle Johnny!" I shouted out loud.

The writer of the letter - whose identity I was still questioning - went on to say . . .

To the reader of this account, again I will say that I hope this satisfies any questions you might have about our family.

Although my grandfather made a terrible mistake that night and almost ended our generation, I survived, thanks to Aunt Hester and Uncle Johnny.

That horrible night when the boat tipped over, Hester, who could not swim, risked her life to save mine. She pulled me from the black murky water and ran with me. We hid in the woods for weeks. Hester would sneak up to the big house and get us food.

I was in shock for many years; I made no sounds at all. I did not speak, cry, or even whimper at anything. I was just there.

After weeks of staying in those dark, frightening woods, Hester and I snuck back into the big house. We stayed hidden in the basement, only coming out for food, until Uncle Johnny came home.

Uncle Johnny stayed with us until I was old enough to marry. Eventually, I did start talking again. Uncle Johnny was so funny. His sense of humor made me bury that tragic night and come out of my shell. He was a very gentle and kind man. He did everything he could to make me laugh, and one day it finally worked. I was given his last name and he raised me as his daughter.

Uncle Johnny never married and had no children of his own. He was a very private man. He worried about people finding out about my mother's secret.

He stayed on the plantation and rebuilt the home he despised. He bought more slaves and made the plantation bountiful again.

Uncle Johnny had come home to make amends with Grandfather Simmons because he had tuberculosis. He did not want to die without making up with his father.

303

Although that was not possible, Johnny made peace by simply being there. His life was shortened by his terrible disease.

We buried him down the path by a big rock in the woods away from the house. The path was not far from the road that led into town. We thought maybe his spirit might catch a ride with one of those passersby that may have been going to one of the big cities. We believed he might be happier there.

After Johnny's death, the plantation was not the same. I hated the big house. It was cold and lonely. I had inherited everything and wanted nothing, nothing but someone to love me.

And like my mother before me, I found love. I found it with a slave. His name was Leroy, and I learned my mother had saved him many years earlier. Although he too was a half-breed, we could not marry because he was too dark. So we kept our life together a secret. We had one lovely son, who we named Johnny, after my uncle.

Little Johnny, like his uncle before him, hated the plantation. He hated the fact that he was half black, even though he didn't look it. At the age of 16, he left home. I have not seen or heard from him since.

Hester married and had 5 children; her next to the youngest son, Jesse, is my favorite. He loves the plantation and says he will never leave. I don't believe that he will.

He likes the simple life. He still talks in Gullah. He knows how to talk like we do, but he prefers not to. He says he wants to keep his mother's language, even if it is not correct.

He built him a small house not far from the big one. He keeps the old place up, but he says the spirits don't rest there, so he doesn't come in.

Jesse tries to keep the colored heritage alive, but blames the white folk with too much hatred. Grandfather Simmons was very good to his slaves, better than most. But he could not accept what he believed to be his daughters' shame. Jesse never could excuse the fact that Mr. Simmons killed his grandmother and most of his relatives. Its a day I'll never forget and wish

I couldn't remember. Even though in that era, it was how it was.

Israel, who was my father, was found hanged on the very tree where he had found love. Hester, by herself, cut the rope and laid her brother to rest. She buried him under the tree. That is the only tree that survived that terrible storm. It blooms beautifully every year. I always say it's a present from my dad to my mom.

Mammie and Jesse were buried somewhere close to the pond. Hester could not carry them, so she dug two holes close to where they lay and rolled them into their graves.

None of the graves have ever been marked with real markers, but a little flower bed is replanted every year where we believe the graves are.

We never knew what happened to my mother. All those weeks we stayed in the woods, we never saw or heard from her again. Hester thinks she might have drowned looking for me, but we do not know.

We always heard her spirit in the big house, but never could find her. I wish we could have found her body to put her to rest with my father.

I hope maybe one day Little Johnny will return like his uncle did. I hope he has found himself a wife and that they have beautiful children. I hope his children will understand the decisions that we made and accept our choices.

I am writing all this so maybe one day, one of my great grandchildren can learn the importance of love — no matter who you are — or who you think you are. I hope the person or people reading this are somehow related to me. Maybe you have come here to make this place your home. Teach your children that life is what you make of it, not what you find out about it.

Should we be a mirror of our ancestors' actions? Absolutely not. We make choices in our own lives that do not reflect — nor should they reflect anything a family member has done. We can learn from their mistakes, thereby changing the future and saving the next generation from the consequences of their beliefs. No one should be held responsible for someone else's actions.

One bad seed can ruin the whole tree, but sometimes it just makes something very beautiful. When you start searching and digging for your roots, the tree might not branch in the direction that you are hoping for. You might find the a bad apple, one with a spot on it. The color might not be the same, but in the end, it really doesn't matter. It just gives you ... another choice, and your choices will make you the unique person that you are.

With all My Love,

Caroline

I felt like I was waking up from a dream. I stood in my living room and looked around. I was back in the present without any warning.

I held the letters close to my chest in disbelief. I finally understood the haunted secrets of my family, generation after generation. I cannot imagine being in love with a man that both my family and all humanity forbade me to love. The idea of being in love with a man that my family had to purchase like cattle is heartbreaking.

It is great to know how the years have passed and how the times have changed. Freedom is a gift to everyone. We all can make our own choices.

"Well Grandpa, I think you would be proud of me. I have found all the family secrets, and now it's time to put them to rest. I think we will have a burial for Mary Beth's remains tomorrow. We will put her next to Israel, the man she loved. Finally, the two can be together. Everything will become normal around here and all spirits – including those of the living – will be at peace."

"No, you have jest begun," a hoarse voice whispered behind me.

I spun around only to get a glimpse of Mr. Simmons fading in and out of a smoky haze.

"What do you mean? I have found Mary Beth, and now I know the truth."

"There's still more to learn, my child, a lot more."

Then, just like that, he was gone.

There have not been any more secrets uncovered, and at my age, I doubt that I will be hunting diligently. Maybe my children or grandchildren can become the next spirit chasers, but I think I have done my job. Most of the time, our house has been quiet, but on those stormy nights, when the wind howls like a pack of dogs, we still feel a presence as though we have uninvited guests.

The elderly Vivian slipped the pen in its slot, closed her journal and whispered, "In my mind's eye, that is what I remember."

The end, for now!

ABOUT THE AUTHOR

Excitement, mysteries, and the unknown are captivating to me. Solving a mystery, makes my blood boil, I love it.

As a child, I grew up in a rural area in South Carolina. Reminiscing of my childhood made me want to become a writer. My cousin and I made up many stories to act out as children. We would pretend to be whatever or whomever we wanted to be. As an adult life is not that simple, we are who we are, but as a writer, I can become that child again and create my own fantasy.

Some people read a story to escape our everyday lives and some people write to break free from the captivity of realism. I break free and go all over the world in just a matter of days.

I have been with my husband for thirty-three years; we have two wonderful sons, four great stepchildren and twenty-three grandchildren. I have a wonderful mother and four siblings. I love and enjoy all my family very much.

I love all animals, horseback riding, boating, the beach; if I am outdoors, I am happy.

Life is too short to take for granted and not enjoy. I am not a person to let it slip away; I am carefree and loving every minute.